Lord of the White Hell

Book One

Ginn Hale

Blind Eye Books
blindeyebooks.com

Lord of the White Hell
Book One
by Ginn Hale
Published by :
Blind Eye Books
1141 Grant Street
Bellingham WA 98225
blindeyebooks.com

Edited by Nicole Kimberling
Cover and interior art by Dawn Kimberling

First Edition August 2010

Printed in the United States of America

ISBN: 978-0-978986162

This book is dedicated to Angus, who was a better friend than he could have ever known.

Cadeleon & Neighboring Kingdoms

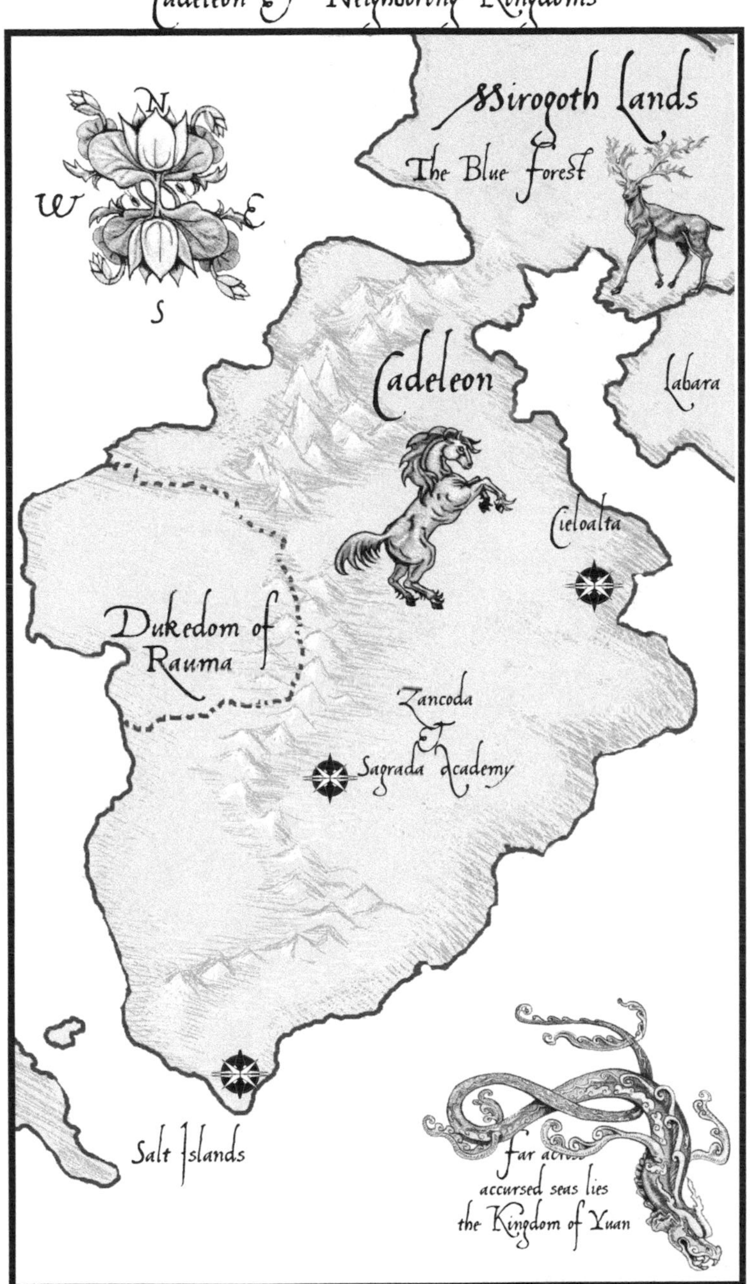

Chapter One

Kiram woke as the carriage jolted against the rough cobblestones of the country road.

After six days of sleepless travel he couldn't believe that he had dozed off today of all days. He frowned at the creased front of his white linen shirt and tucked a loose edge back into his dark pants. His curly blonde hair was always a wild mess after he had slept on it. He tried to smooth it with his hand, feeling the tight spirals spring back as his fingers brushed over them.

His book, *Modern Mechanism*, lay on the carriage floor. Dozens of strips of paper protruded from between the pages, displaying Kiram's notes and diagrams. He retrieved the book, straightened his notes, and carefully wrapped the book in the remains of his parchment and tucked it into the wide pocket of his new Cadeleonian wool coat.

Kiram had packed very little clothing and only a few of his favorite books. Tools and crated machine parts filled most of the space in the carriage. Many heavier crates groaned against the ropes securing them to the roof of the carriage. The driver had charged Kiram's mother twice the normal fare because of the weight, but she had been proud to pay it. Those heavy, oily pieces of metal had won Kiram the right to attend Academy Sagrada.

No full-blooded Haldiim had ever before been accepted into the school, and a century had passed since the half-blood Yassin Lif-Harun studied there.

Lif-Harun's formulas had altered the very heavens. A statue of the man stood in the Royal Park. Kiram's father had already pointed out the spot where he thought Kiram's own statue would one day stand. If his parents had been allowed to, they would have sent another half-dozen carriages filled with praise dancers and red-dyed doves to announce their youngest son's arrival. Fortunately the school permitted only one carriage per student.

The carriage struck another bump and Kiram shoved the stack of rocking crates back against the carriage wall. Sunlight streamed in through the red carriage curtains, filling the space with a warm glow. The dark wood radiated a late afternoon heat. The brown coat he'd worn for the trip over the mountains felt sweltering hot now and smelled of his sweat. Kiram stripped it off and stretched his long legs as best he could in the cramped confines.

He couldn't be far from the Academy Sagrada now. Maybe an hour, possibly less.

He pulled the curtains aside and gazed out at the walls of wild, green forest that arched over the road. There was a flash of brilliant blue wings as a flock of jays took flight from the overhanging branches. He thought he caught a glimpse of something white moving fast between the trunks of trees but he lost sight of it as the road turned away.

As he rode further, the dense brambles and towering oak trees gave way to groomed hedges and open fields divided by low stone walls. A flock of white ducks waddled along the roadside, tended by a young, bored-looking boy.

Far across a fallow field, Kiram spied a horse and rider. The horse was brilliant white in the bright sun and rider's skin seemed almost as pale as the horse's hide. His black hair stood out in sharp contrast, as did his deep blue Academy Sagrada uniform.

Kiram doubted that his own uniform, well made as it was, would look so good on him. He wondered if the rider was an upperclassman or even an instructor. Kiram stared in amazement as the lean man urged his horse ahead and the two of them seemed to fly over the stone wall then raced across the road and through the opposite field.

He didn't spare a glance for Kiram's carriage, the herder boy, or even the flock of now startled ducks. A few moments later both the horse and rider were little more than a distant haze. Kiram tried to keep track of the rider's blue jacket, but eventually he lost sight of it amongst the fields of blooming sunflowers.

Kiram felt his pulse surging through his body. This was exactly what the academy promised for his future, such fearless prowess, such determination and beauty. Perhaps even adventure.

Kiram had been patient for days but suddenly he felt as though this slow, creaking carriage would never reach its destination and he needed to be at the academy now. Desire and excitement coursed through him like a physical pang.

As the carriage rolled up to the heavy stone walls that surrounded the academy, Kiram gripped the latch of the carriage door. He hardly took in the fortress-like towers of the main building or the chapel's brilliant blue spire. He stared at cobblestone paths and green lawn of the grounds, searching for his fellow classmates. Several boys dressed in academy blue strolled toward the chapel, but none of them captured Kiram's attention the way that single rider had.

The carriage jerked to a halt, and Kiram slipped slightly forward, his hand pulling the door latch. Instantly the carriage door sprang open and he spilled out onto the muddy ground in front of the stable. He struggled up to his feet to see two older men in gray scholars' robes gaping at him. Just behind them, leading his brilliant white horse by its reins, stood the rider.

"I'm fine!" Kiram announced, though no one had asked. "I just…the door opened and I wasn't looking…"

Kiram could feel his face flushing bright red. Not even his dark skin could hide such an intense blush. He regained his feet quickly but to his horror the rider's expression shifted from slight concern to amusement. His handsome smile somehow made Kiram's humiliation far worse. He glared at the rider and then dove back into the cover of the carriage to retrieve his coat.

When he turned back the rider had disappeared into the stables. The two scholars hurried to Kiram's side. They were both typical Cadeleonians, pale skinned and thickly built with brown hair and eyes.

One of them was older, probably in his late forties with shots of gray scattered through his close-cropped hair. The other scholar wasn't more than a decade past Kiram's own age, perhaps twenty-seven. He wore his hair a little long and his cheeks were dappled with freckles.

"I'm Blasio Urracon," the younger scholar introduced himself, "and this is my honored brother, Scholar Donamillo Urracon."

Kiram bowed to both men. Cadeleonian names often sounded odd to him, so he made special note of their pronunciation. Many Cadeleonians found Haldiim informality rude and so Kiram was careful to use proper titles as he addressed his new teachers.

"Scholar Blasio and Scholar Donamillo, it is an honor to meet you. I'm Kiram Kir-Zaki, your humble student."

Scholar Blasio smiled at Kiram's politeness. "It's a pleasure to meet you at last. Javier was just saying that he'd seen your carriage so we came to greet you." Scholar Blasio gestured back towards the stable where the rider had been standing. He frowned at the empty spot. "I suppose he's brushing down his horse. We're short a stable hand at the moment—"

"It's no matter," the older brother, Scholar Donamillo, cut in. "Kiram will be formally introduced to staff and students at dinner tonight."

Scholar Donamillo's tone was much more reserved than Scholar Blasio's, and his expression stern. Kiram couldn't help but think that the older man had taken a quick dislike to him. Probably because he was supposed to be a gifted thinker and he'd just fallen out of a carriage onto his face.

Scholar Donamillo looked a little past Kiram to the crates stacked atop and inside the carriage. "Are all of these yours?"

"Yes, sir. They're the components I've fabricated for the Crown Challenge."

Scholar Blasio grinned. "You brought them all the way from Anacleto? What dedication. That's fabulous!"

Kiram warmed to Scholar Blasio for his enthusiasm but he also noted Scholar Donamillo's expression of disapproval.

"I'll have the groundsmen unpack these," Scholar Donamillo stated. "I suppose that one of the tack sheds can be spared to provide a workshop for the project. No doubt it will take a great deal of space."

"Thank you, sir." Kiram bowed again to the older man. "I'm sorry for the inconvenience."

"Yes, it's good that you realize that this does inconvenience us. It is not common to accept a new student directly into the second-year courses, much less accommodate his individual studies." Strangely, Scholar Donamillo's stern expression seemed to soften as he looked over the wooden crates. "I can only hope that you will prove to be the mechanist genius your teachers claim you are."

The label 'genius' brought a second flush to Kiram's cheeks and also a gnawing anxiety to the pit of his stomach. At seventeen, most of his achievements were still built upon his father's innovations. This would be the first time he would have to rise to a challenge alone.

"I will do my utmost to win the Crown Challenge in the academy's name," Kiram assured Scholar Donamillo. The older man offered him a slight smile in return. He reached out and brushed a clump of mud off Kiram's shirt.

"No doubt you will want a bath after your long journey. Scholar Blasio will take you up to your room."

"Yes, sir." Kiram snatched up his coat and his gray trunk and followed Scholar Blasio across the lush, green lawn to the three-story stone building that dominated the grounds.

"This is the dormitory. First-year students are all housed on the first floor of the west wing, in the old armory room." Scholar Blasio pointed to where the west wing jutted out from the main building. The windows were barred. "With everyone in a single room the night wardens can keep them out of trouble more easily."

Kiram was glad that he hadn't been forced to come as a first-year student. He couldn't imagine sleeping while crammed in a single room with a hundred noisy Cadeleonian boys. The smell alone would have driven him mad.

"Second and third years are housed together on the second floor. Those young men who stand to inherit titles, of course, stay on for a fourth year of Lord's Law. They each have private rooms on the third floor."

"What about the watchtowers?" Kiram gazed up at the two jutting towers that rose up from the third floor.

"The west tower is used for storage and the east one is for special cases." Scholar Blasio looked a little uncomfortable. "Let's go in, shall we?"

Inside, the building was dim and cool. Crests of Cadeleonian noble families, all woven in academy blue, decorated the walls. The royal crest of the Sagrada family was inlayed in gold over all the doors. Scholar Blasio led him past a statue of a rearing stallion, through a huge dining hall, and then up a massive staircase.

"Four of the lecture halls are located on the first floor, the rest are in the east wing," Scholar Blasio told Kiram as they walked up the stairs. "The dining hall and common library are directly below us."

"Everything seems so heavy and huge," Kiram commented. "It looks a little like a fortress."

"It used to be one. Three hundred years ago, during the first Sagrada dynasty, this was one of their great strongholds. After the Restoration the reinstated Sagrada king turned the fortress over to one of his favored vassals to train young lords in the arts of war and law. Of course, things have changed since then but we have not forgotten our history. In fact, it's right under our feet." Scholar Blasio paused on the stairs and pointed back down to a radiant, black design that spread across the stones of the floor below them.

"That is exactly the spot where one hundred years ago Calixto Tornesal opened the mouth of the white hell and defeated the Mirogoth invaders."

Kiram studied the fine web of black cracks. He didn't believe in the white hell or any of the other Cadeleonian hells but the sight of the burned, pitted stones still gave him pause. Standing in an ancient fortress, with a scholar relating the story and pointing out its exact site, it seemed almost plausible that a Cadeleonian nobleman had traded his soul for the power to drive back an invading army.

Even so, Kiram couldn't credit it. A soul could not be given up any more than joy or kindness could be bottled and sold at market. Only in death could the soul leave the flesh.

Kiram glanced to Scholar Blasio, searching his face for some sign that he was joking, but his expression was serious.

"Calixto's descendants still hold the pact of the white hell." Scholar Blasio looked meaningfully at Kiram.

Kiram wasn't sure if he should respond with reverence or revulsion. At last he decided to simply be honest. "In Haldiim tradition we don't believe that people are condemned to hells. We believe that in death all creatures pass through a shajdi and then are reborn in a new form."

Seeing Scholar Blasio's furrowed brow, Kiram continued, "Most modern Haldiim, like my family, don't give much credence to the tales of shajdis hidden in sacred forests or the Bahiim who opened them and claimed power over life and death. If shajdi ever did exist, it was in the ancient past, and they have gone now. But really, most of us understand such stories as metaphors for the balance of birth and death."

Only the very religious Bahiim took shajdis as literal gates between life and death, and the last thing Kiram wanted was to be taken for a superstitious ascetic who'd spend hours talking to trees.

"Really?" Scholar Blasio cocked his head slightly. "So, you aren't afraid of the hells?"

"No, as I said, we don't believe in hells. Shajdi make for amusing stories, though."

Scholar Blasio gazed intently at Kiram, studying his face. "So you wouldn't be afraid of a man who had been hell-branded? Who had the gate to a hell burning within him?"

Kiram simply shrugged. "I suppose not."

"It wouldn't worry you at all to, say, sleep in a room with him?" Scholar Blasio sounded almost incredulous.

"So long as he wasn't insane or sick with black pox I wouldn't be afraid to sleep in a room with any man," Kiram replied. It wasn't entirely true—certainly he wouldn't want to sleep in a room with a thief or murder or, honestly, a man who stank terribly…

"Well, that's good to know. Your room is on the third floor, in the east tower." Scholar Blasio continued up the stairs. Kiram followed him in quick strides. "It's away from the other rooms so it will be quiet enough for you to study, and unlike the other rooms, it's very spacious."

Kiram thought he knew where all of this was leading and decided to just get to the point, instead of having Scholar Blasio nervously list the amenities of his living arrangements when he'd already stated the east tower was reserved for special cases.

"You want me to room with one of these hell-branded men? A descendant of the Tornesal line?"

"You don't have much choice," Scholar Blasio admitted at last. "The other upperclassmen have refused to room with a Haldiim. They have no objection to you schooling here, but sleeping in the same room, when their souls are unprotected, is out of the question. However, since Javier's spiritual state is already…compromised, he risks nothing in sharing a room with you."

Kiram wanted to demand what exactly it was that these people imagined he was going to do to them in their sleep but then his thoughts stopped short as he registered the name Javier and remembered the dark, sardonic eyes of the rider.

"Javier? The man with the white stallion?"

"Yes, Javier Tornesal, Duke of Rauma. He will be your upperclassman."

Chapter Two

More than spacious, the room was vast and nearly empty. Two beds stood against opposite walls, one of them little more than a wood frame and mattress while the other seemed well used and only half made. A dresser and writing table stood beside it and several black, leather-bound books lay on the table along with an inkwell and a penknife.

Normally, Kiram would have found some excuse to look through the books. This once he wasn't paying so much attention to them.

Instead he stared at the maze of thin red-brown lines that curved and spiraled across the floor like a gigantic map of the heavens.

For a brief moment Kiram thought of Yassin Lif-Harun. He wondered if it was possible that the academy had left one of the famous astronomer's early drawings intact out of reverence. Almost at once Kiram noted that the lines on the floor didn't match any particular constellation and that the ink was far too fresh to have been spread across this floor a century ago.

Long shafts of light poured in from the slit windows, illuminating a series of ellipses and the scrawling, strange letters that they enclosed. The ink seemed to shift in color, rusty brown in some areas, deep red in others.

Kiram glanced to Scholar Blasio, hoping for an explanation, but the man didn't seem to take any note of the floor. He pointed the barren bed pushed up against the west wall.

"The housekeepers should have your bedding brought up before dinner, but if they don't all you need to do is pull the bell cord just outside the door and someone will come up directly." Scholar Blasio pulled the heavy, oak door back open. "You saw the bell chord, didn't you?"

"Yes." Kiram didn't bother to look at the dark blue braided cord a second time. He frowned at the arc of letters surrounding a dark red line at the foot of his new bed. The writing was Cadeleonian but Kiram didn't recognize a single word.

"The bath is through there." Scholar Blasio pointed to a narrow door just past the writing desk. "In the summer, though, many of the students prefer to wash in the orchard lake. The water is quite shallow and warm. I used go there myself when I was a student but now that I'm an instructor I don't go so often. It's best that instructors and students don't mix." Scholar Blasio kept his gaze away from the floor, and even the bed and desk against the east wall. He gripped the iron doorknob in one hand.

Kiram realized that just standing in this room disturbed the scholar.

"Fifth bell will sound for dinner. It's best to come dressed formally. You have your uniform, I assume?"

Kiram nodded.

"Good, good…" Scholar Blasio faded off, staring out one of the dozen tall, narrow windows. The knuckles of his hand went white as he continued to grip the doorknob.

"You could sleep in the stables, you know," Scholar Blasio said at last.

"With the animals?" Kiram couldn't hide his offense at the suggestion. He wasn't some stray dog that a student had taken pity on. He had been invited by the headmaster to study at the academy. His mother had already paid a full year's tuition.

"No, of course not." Scholar Blasio blanched, and the freckles on his face looked suddenly very dark. "It's a lovely room really. Lots of light and Javier says that it's quite warm in the winter. The fireplace is huge. I'm sure you'll be comfortable here."

Kiram pointed to the floor but Scholar Blasio spoke before he could get his question out.

"You probably want to unpack and wash up. I'll just go down and see about your bedding." With that he slipped out of the room and pulled the door shut behind him.

Kiram would have laughed at the scholar's awkward exit if it hadn't been so disconcerting.

For a few moments he stood in the doorway, studying the floor. He had never believed in Cadeleonian superstitions and didn't think now was a good time to start. He boldly walked across the floor and when he caught himself picking a careful path between the flowing lines of ink, he forced himself to step directly on the strange words, just to prove that they were meaningless.

He reached his bed without incident and laid his trunk on the floor. The big, white mattress looked inviting. Kiram ached to lie down and sink into it, but he and his clothes were both too filthy.

He opened his trunk and found his soap tin as well as the thin white prayer clothes that his uncle had insisted he pack. Hidden beneath them, Kiram discovered a small satchel stuffed with dried mint leaves and pieces of his favorite rosewater taffy. A gift from his mother. Doubtless she'd hidden several in his things, as was her habit.

A wave of homesickness overwhelmed him. He had only just arrived at the academy and already he felt completely out of his depth.

"To fear what you do not understand is to mistake ignorance for safety."

Traveling Haldiim scholars were constantly repeating that proverb. For the first time, Kiram thought he might understand why they would need to.

The bathroom was little more than a closet with a large iron tub and several porcelain jars of cool water. Kiram washed quickly. When he was done he pulled the stopper out of the base of the iron tub and listened as the water drained away. A moment later he heard the faint sound of the water pouring out of some rainspout just outside the building. That was a clever design, Kiram decided, and he felt a little of his delight with the academy returning.

He dressed in his prayer clothes. The thin cotton clung to his damp skin, but it was better than putting his dirty travel clothes back on.

He left the bathroom and started for his own bed. Then one of the books on the nearby writing table caught his attention. A circle of gilded script shone from the black leather cover. Like the words scrawled across the floor, each of the curling letters looked so close to common Cadeleonian writing that Kiram thought that he ought to be able to read them. If he just glanced at the words' lengths and shapes, they seemed recognizable. Only when he looked closer did they melt into gibberish.

He picked the book up and leafed through it. A deep, woody scent drifted up from the thick parchment.

The last third of the book was empty. But the pages that did contain text were crammed with blocks of tightly packed, hand-written script. Every few pages there were drawings of circles and curling lines. Some looked like ornate knives, others like tangled briars or strangely skewed constellations. The very same designs that decorated the floor.

Three that resembled blades were almost under Kiram's feet. They seemed to be pointing at the other bed in the room. Javier's bed, Kiram assumed. The dark blue blankets were slightly rumpled, revealing an expanse of clean, white sheets.

Kiram laid the book back on the table and turned to his own bed. As he did, he realized that the door to the room stood open. Javier Tornesal leaned against the doorframe, silently watching him.

He was tall even for a Cadeleonian and very well dressed. The black silk suns of the Tornesal crest adorned the sleeves of his dark blue jacket. The same silk stitching ran down the length of his fitted riding pants and the seams of his leather boots and gloves. He wore a large gold signet ring on his right hand.

And yet, for all his refined dress, there was still something about Javier's lean build, unkempt black hair and hard dark gaze that reminded Kiram of those rangy youths who haunted the smoke alleys of Anacleto and made their money with their knives. Kiram's father called them 'street snakes' and no Haldiim from any good family ever spoke to one of them.

"I would have announced myself but I didn't want to disturb your reading." Javier's voice was softer than Kiram had expected and much lower.

"I wasn't—" Kiram cut himself off. It was bad enough that he'd been caught going through Javier's book; he shouldn't also try to lie to the man about it. "I know that I shouldn't have been reading your book but I recognized the writing on the cover of the book as the same that was on the floor and I wondered what it all meant. I'm sorry."

Javier regarded him for a moment, a slight curve spread across his sharply bowed lips. "Did you figure it out?"

"No," Kiram admitted. "I couldn't read any of it."

"Don't sound so disappointed." Javier crossed the room to the bedside. As he passed, Kiram caught the scents of leather and sweat. He noticed tiny spears of golden straw caught in the laces of Javier's black boots. Javier picked up the book and for an instant his amused expression seemed to falter; then the hard arrogance returned and he tossed the book to Kiram.

"Look through it all you like." Javier sat down on the edge of his bed and began pulling off one of his boots. "Only the eyes of the damned can read it."

The soft leather cover felt hot against Kiram's palm. "That's not possible. Any script written can be learned and read."

"Of course it can be learned, but only for a price." Javier's tone was unconcerned, but when he looked up at Kiram his expression seemed so serious that Kiram found it difficult to meet his intense, dark gaze. "Relinquish your soul to me and I will reveal every mystery of the white hell to you."

Kiram didn't believe in the white hell but there was a strange appeal to the way Javier offered him the knowledge, like some exotic, dangerous proposition right out of the storybooks of his childhood. Such proposals always led the young heroes to adventure and romance.

Javier suddenly laughed and tossed his boot down on the floor.

"Are you actually considering the offer?" Javier shook his head. A lock of his black hair fell across his face and he shoved it back brusquely. "You'd sell your soul to me in exchange for a reading from my insane great-grandfather's diary? And they say all you Haldiim are clever conmen."

"I didn't agree," Kiram objected though he could feel a guilty heat flush his face. "I didn't even believe you."

"You did," Javier replied with a smile. "I could see it in your face."

"No, I didn't." Kiram sat down on his own bed. "I just didn't know what to say to you. You haven't even introduced yourself and here you are offering to buy my soul. How am I supposed to know that you aren't a madman?"

"Indeed." Javier relented so easily that it surprised Kiram. "Who's to say I'm not a madman?"

For a few moments there was silence. Kiram couldn't think of anything to say and Javier seemed intent on removing his remaining boot. At last, he placed the second boot beside the first and pushed them both to the foot of his bed and began to unbutton his jacket. "I assumed that Scholar Blasio told you who and what I am."

"He said that you were the only student here that had nothing to lose by having me in his room."

"Well, nothing except my privacy, it would appear." Javier's gaze flicked to the book in Kiram's hand.

"I explained that already." Again that intense heat flushed across Kiram's face. He prayed that the natural darkness of his skin would hide his guilty blush. "I apologized and I swear I won't do it again."

For some reason Javier laughed at this. "Do it all you like. Just remember that I may require payment of you in return."

Kiram thought Javier was joking again but he couldn't be absolutely certain.

Javier tossed his jacket onto his bed and then slid his long white fingers through the laces that held his shirt closed. He wore a gold medallion of some kind around his neck. Kiram wondered if it was another crest but his attention quickly slipped from the medallion as Javier pulled his shirt entirely off. Kiram couldn't help but notice how black the hair of Javier's chest looked against his pale skin. The sharp pattern of it was nothing like the blonde down of Kiram's own body.

Javier glanced to him and Kiram looked quickly away.

"To be honest, there's nothing of much interest in the book. Those marks around your bed are blessings to protect you in your sleep when your soul is vulnerable. This here," Javier pointed to one of the designs beside his stocking feet, "is a ward to keep the white hell that lives in me from hunting while I sleep. You should be safe."

"You really believe that there's a hell within you?" Kiram asked.

"I know there is," Javier replied and this time there was no trace of humor in his voice.

Javier loosed his belt buckle and pulled the leather belt out from the loops in his pants. Then he started working the tiny gold buttons of his pants apart. A surge of shock rushed through Kiram, though he could not quite bring himself to avert his gaze.

"Are you taking off all your clothes?"

Javier cocked his head slightly and regarded Kiram. "Why else would I be unbuttoning my pants?"

"Why are you taking them off?" Kiram ignored Javier's question.

"Well, while you might bathe fully dressed," Javier said with a smile, "I prefer to wash naked."

Kiram didn't have a reply for Javier's sarcasm. He busied himself with unpacking the belongings in his trunk. He heard Javier's pants fall to the floor.

"Did you leave any water?"

"What?" Kiram glanced back at Javier. Only the gold medallion remained on his body; otherwise he was a perfect expanse of white and black, like a figure seen at night when all the color had drained from the world. Only the faintest hint of red colored his nipples and genitals. As Kiram took in the sight he felt his face flushing once again.

"Water." Kiram belatedly remembered Javier's question. "There's enough water left for another bath."

"Excellent," Javier replied. "Saves you the work of hauling a bucket up for me."

He strode to the bathroom but didn't close the door behind him. Was that a normal Cadeleonian behavior or more hell-branded eccentricity? Almost unwillingly Kiram stole a glance at Javier's naked back.

Javier slid a ceramic tile aside to expose a cupboard in the bathroom wall. A shaving razor as well as towels, soap, and scrub brushes filled the space. Another clever design.

"Hey." Javier glanced back over his shoulder at Kiram. "Come over here and give me a hand."

"With what?" Kiram demanded. He hoped this wasn't more of Javier's strange humor.

Javier simply waved a scrub brush at him. Kiram rose and joined him in the bathroom.

There were dozens of common bathhouses back home in Anacleto but most were in the Cadeleonian section of the city. Kiram's family had two private baths and certainly would never have expected Kiram to have to scrub the back of some strange man. The idea of it both excited and unnerved him.

"What should I call you?" Javier asked as he soaped himself. Kiram watched the thick white bubbles slide along the curves of Javier's muscular shoulders and thighs. He wondered if all Cadeleonian men were so at ease in front of one another. Was it so common that the scents and sights of their naked bodies no longer affected them?

"Kiram is fine, unless students at the academy go by their family names."

"Given names, otherwise half the school would be answering to the name Grunito. There are two enrolled right now and more on the way."

"What about you," Kiram asked. "Just Javier?"

"Upperclassman Javier, if we're in public."

Kiram ran his hand over the bristles of the scrub-brush. They felt too stiff to use on skin as fine as Javier's. Though now that he was standing so close, Kiram could see that there were imperfections in Javier's body. The most noticeable was the raw, half-healed scar that ran up his left wrist.

Kiram placed the scrub brush against Javier's back and drew it gently up along the line of his spine and then over his jutting shoulder blades. Javier leaned back into Kiram's ministrations just slightly.

Other scars nicked and cut across Javier's lean body but most of those were much older and had faded to white. On Javier's right shoulder there was a circular scar that looked almost like a written word. Kiram didn't recognize it, but the shape was familiar. Kiram had no doubt that this, too, was written in that same hellscript. Scholar Blasio had called Javier hell-branded. Kiram wondered if this was the actual brand.

"Put some force into it," Javier instructed. "You're not brushing a kitten, you know."

Kiram scowled at Javier's back. He had wanted Javier to like his touch, not mock his ignorance. Kiram shoved the bristles of the scrub-brush hard against Javier's skin leaving a red track. Javier pulled back from him.

"Touchy, aren't you?"

"I'm just ensuring that you will be clean." Kiram could hear the petulance in his own voice.

"Ensuring that I won't have skin is more like it. Haven't you ever done this before?"

"No," Kiram admitted.

"Let me show you, then." Javier's voice never lost hint of mockery but it did seem to soften a little.

He turned and caught Kiram's hand in his own. Facing Javier, Kiram felt suddenly awkward and shy. His grip on the scrub brush seemed unsteady as if the heat of Javier's fingers were drawing all the strength from him.

Javier pulled Kiram's hand to his chest, guiding the scrub brush over his sharp ribs and down along his flat stomach.

"Like that, you see? Firm but gentle."

Kiram couldn't reply. He could hardly think. Javier's closeness, the heat and scent of him, the sensation of his skin against Kiram's own, it all overwhelmed his senses. Anticipation and confusion rolled through him.

If he had been standing like this with Musni, or any other Haldiim youth, he would have known what to think and what to do. He would have known that this was a seduction.

But the Cadeleonians were not like the Haldiim, and Kiram knew that their laws forbade even the thoughts that raced through Kiram's head.

Kiram's breath felt ragged. He couldn't pull his gaze away from Javier's face, his dark eyes, his sharply curved lips. Kiram almost leaned into Javier, almost laid his lips against the graceful curve of Javier's neck. But then he saw the slight quirk of Javier's mouth.

It was that terrible smile of his. He was simply toying with Kiram, making a joke of his confusion and desire.

Angry humiliation surged through him. He jerked back from Javier's grip and hurled the scrub brush. It struck Javier hard across the cheek.

"You can do it well enough yourself," Kiram growled. "Don't think that because I'm Haldiim I'll play the part of your bathhouse whore." Then he turned and left the bathing room, slamming the door closed behind him.

Kiram strode to his bed and briefly he considered just taking his trunk and returning to the carriage to be driven back home.

But his pride as both a Haldiim and a scholar rebelled at the thought. That was just what Javier and the other students at the academy wanted, wasn't it? That was most likely what all this arcane gibberish on the floor and the taunting exchange in the bathroom had been about. They didn't want a Haldiim outshining them in their own precious academy.

They could all burn in their stupid hells. He was going to stay. More that that, he was going to rub their faces in his accomplishments.

The rant running through Kiram's mind was so engaging that he almost missed the polite knock at the door. Kiram forced himself to swallow back a filthy Haldiim insult. Instead he pulled the door open.

Several serving men in gray uniforms stood in the hall. One was loaded with the bedding that Scholar Blasio had promised. The others had brought up furniture. None of them met Kiram's gaze or spoke to him. He didn't bother to greet them either.

They scurried into the room like skittish mice, awkwardly sidestepping the symbols on the floor. More than one of them made Cadeleonian prayer signs as they moved through the room. Kiram purposely stepped on several of the symbols, making his disdain as clear as he could.

In moments Kiram's bed was made with fresh sheets and blue blankets as well as two pillows. A tall dresser stood at the foot of his bed. A writing table and a chair were deposited near the dresser.

Amidst all the moving in, Javier appeared from the bathroom. He wore a towel wrapped tightly around his narrow waist. A bright red mark stood out on his left cheek. His mere presence seemed to panic the servants. One man drew back so quickly that he tripped over Kiram's trunk. He scrambled to his feet and made a quick blessing sign over his own chest. The servants fled from the room, more than taking their leave.

Kiram found it pleasing to slam the door closed behind them with unnecessary force.

Out of the corner of his eye, he glimpsed Javier taking a fresh pair of pants from his dresser. Then Kiram turned purposefully to his trunk. While Javier dressed, Kiram finished unpacking. He hid the satchel of taffy among his clothes and tucked it away in his dresser.

His books went on his table, as did his Silver Leaf medal.

"Dinner bell will be soon," Javier said from behind him. "You should get into your uniform."

Kiram gave no response. He placed his inkwells and sheaves of parchment on his writing table and then needlessly straightened them.

"Look," Javier began quietly, "you can't just—"

Kiram rounded on him.

"I have nothing to say to you and no desire to hear anything you might say to me." It pleased him to see the surprise in Javier's expression. No doubt he was used to scaring everyone around him and having his own way in everything. Well, Kiram had no intention of being bullied or toyed with. "I have to live here, but that does not mean that I want anything to do with you, do you understand me?"

Kiram had the momentary gratification of seeing something like hurt break through Javier's smug countenance. The expression instantly twisted into that smirk that Kiram already hated.

"As you please, Underclassman Kiram." Javier offered him a sarcastic bow, then departed.

As the door fell closed the dinner bell rang out, but Kiram found that he had lost his appetite for Cadeleonian food.

Chapter Three

For the first week, Kiram's anger inspired relentless study and defiant perfectionism. However, as the days passed, his energy faded. He found himself fluctuating between delighted discovery and lethargic melancholy. The classes he attended greatly affected his mood.

During Scholar Donamillo's natural science demonstrations Kiram reveled in the new world of understanding that opened up to him. Brushed amber gave off sparks and dead insects twitched their limbs when shocked by those tiny lights. Leaning close to one of the scholar's mechanisms, Kiram could feel his hair standing up on end; he wasn't sure if it was from excitement or the currents flowing through copper wires. More than once the class had become a conversation between himself and Scholar Donamillo, while the other students scribbled confused notes.

He excelled in his mathematics classes as well. While his meaty classmates slumped in their seats, counting on their fingers, Kiram would simply hand his solution to Scholar Blasio. Often, as the scholar read Kiram's work he took on a blissful expression, as if he were listening to a piece of music he loved.

After the first week, the little formality that had stood between them gave way to fellowship. Scholar Blasio delighted in Kiram's quick solutions and would often grin and address him as 'young Scholar Kiram', as if he were a colleague.

He never received such a compliment from the lanky, scarred instructor of the war arts, Master Ignacio. The first time Kiram had attempted to wield a Cadeleonian long sword he had lost his grip of the hilt and sent the blade flying towards the master.

Fortunately, Master Ignacio's reflexes were much faster than his gray hair and weathered face had led Kiram to expect.

Kiram had apologized and explained that he'd never used a sword before. The Haldiim were archers, not swordsmen. The first impression lasted, though, and now Master Ignacio only provided Kiram with a wooden blade and eyed him as if he were a reckless menace.

He pretended not to notice the snickers of his fellow classmates during the war arts demonstrations. When they overpowered him in daily practice he simply dropped his blade and stepped away, never allowing them the opportunity to gloat. This tactic frustrated Master Ignacio and prompted more than one speech on the importance of confidence and the crime of cowardice on the battlefield.

Only two other second years were as bad at swordplay as Kiram: Nestor Grunito, a plump youth who was obviously half blind, and Fedeles Quemanor, a tall, handsome, black-haired simpleton, who spent most of the class time singing the names of horses to himself. Master Ignacio often made the three of them practice together, while he focused his attention on the students with real promise.

Kiram's distaste for war arts was only exacerbated by the fact that Master Ignacio often called Javier over from the third year riding practice to demonstrate perfect battle forms. Kiram scowled at the master's obvious pride in Javier's prowess.

Though, Kiram couldn't help but stare when Javier countered one of Master Ignacio's attacks, lunged past his defense, and brought the tip of his blade to the master's chest. It wasn't just his accuracy or audacity that fascinated Kiram; it was the pure beauty of his movements. He didn't waste a single gesture or ever hesitate. He moved the way an animal would, utterly assured of his nature.

Kiram found his own awe aggravating and consciously worked at dismantling it. He decided that much of Javier's grace could be attributed to arrogance. Of course he never hesitated or second-guessed himself. The man was probably incapable of conceiving of himself making a mistake.

"He's terrifying," Nestor whispered to Kiram.

"You can hardly see him," Kiram replied.

Nestor squinted intently at Javier through the bristling mass of his sandy brown bangs. He wasn't exactly Kiram's friend but over the last two weeks they had grown comfortable with each other.

Unlike most of the other second-year students, Nestor shared Kiram's intellectual curiosity. He asked questions in natural sciences, took the highest scores in their law classes, and clearly possessed the talent and inclination to be an artist. He, like Kiram, hailed from the port city of Anacleto, though Nestor's father was an earl whereas Kiram's father was the indulged husband of a very wealthy Haldiim merchant.

Nestor retrieved his delicate spectacles from their ivory case and placed them on the bridge of his beak-like nose.

"Still terrifying," Nestor said as he watched Javier demonstrate a maneuver called the King's Cross. "How do you ever fall asleep with him in the room?"

Kiram rolled his eyes. "Look, I know that no one is actually afraid of him. You don't have to keep pretending."

Nestor peered at Kiram through the thick lenses of his spectacles. "What are you talking about?"

"If people actually thought Upperclassman Javier was some kind of demon, why would they all hang around him at dinner or even agree to allow him into the academy?"

"He's the Duke of Rauma. Who's going to tell him that he can't attend the academy?" Nestor went quiet as Master Ignacio walked past them. After the master was out of earshot, Nestor leaned a little closer to Kiram. "It's not really Javier that people fear. He's actually nice enough. My brother Elezar and he are best friends. But the white hell trapped in him is something else. You just haven't seen it, that's why you're not afraid."

"Have you ever seen it?"

"Once. When the royal courier came to confer the dukedom upon Javier, the white hell broke free. The instructors were able to contain him with muerate poison that time but last year…" A troubled expression came over Nestor's round face and he lowered his voice to a whisper. "Last year a stable hand was murdered. Torn apart. The headmaster denied that it was the white hell but everyone knew it was. Javier didn't attend classes for two weeks after it happened."

Kiram didn't have a response for that. It was the first time that anyone had explicitly told him what there was to fear in rooming with Javier—he was quite probably a murderer.

Kiram was still wrestling with the idea at lunch, when he took his usual seat between Nestor and Fedeles.

The first day he had taken breakfast at the academy he had made the mistake of seating himself next to a second-year student he didn't know. The young man had knocked Kiram's food to the floor and hissed that he could eat down there, but not with decent men.

To Kiram's relief and surprise, Nestor had intervened right away, offering Kiram a place with him at another table. The day after that Fedeles had joined them, though he had offered no reason other than singsong jumbled words.

The three of them were the only older students seated at the tightly packed first year benches. The majority of second and third-year students filled the long tables ahead of Kiram. Those tables weren't any more attractive than the stained one Kiram sat at but service from the kitchen reached the other second-year students sooner and with better portions.

The tables at the far eastern end of the huge dining hall were a different matter altogether. They were draped with cloths and the benches were beautifully carved. Fresh air and bright light poured in through the windows just behind them.

One table was reserved for scholars, the war master, and the holy father. Kiram only saw all the instructors gathered together at the table on Sacreday when Holy Father Habalan read prayers over the evening meal. Otherwise, the scholar's table was generally only half full. The remaining ornate tables belonged to students whom Nestor told him were the angels and devils of the academy—the brightest and most dangerous young men. Many were third and fourth-year students, who would one day be the lords of Cadeleon. It didn't surprise Kiram to spot Javier there, attended by his gang of loud companions.

Nestor's older brother, Elezar, always sat at Javier's right. Like Nestor, Elezar possessed a hawk-like nose and bristling brown hair, but he stood even taller than Javier and was built like one of the rippling bulls emblazoned on his gloves. Nestor, by comparison, looked more like a fresh egg.

Already, several upperclassmen had coined the term, 'stick and ball' to refer to Kiram and Nestor.

Kiram frowned at his bowl of lumpy brown stew. Nestor had already finished off his serving. It was apparently the staple of first-year students' lunches at the academy.

Kiram took a listless mouthful and swallowed. It tasted nothing like the dishes his mother's cook would have served on a hot afternoon like this one. Briefly he reminisced over the cool cucumber slices, lemon wedges, and mint leaves that had flavored his last meal with his family. At that moment he missed the flavors of lamb and figs almost as much as he missed his parents. He couldn't believe how he had taken the thick yoghurt and honey for granted.

Kiram glanced to Fedeles, who grinned at him.

Despite being quite simple, Fedeles made better company than most of the other students of the academy. He never tried to tease either Kiram or Nestor. In fact, he seemed only half aware of their presence. For the most part, Fedeles drifted in a smiling fog. Occasionally, he would look at one of Nestor's sketches and name the man or animal pictured. He was particularly fond of horses.

"Lunaluz," Fedeles whispered dreamily.

Nestor nodded absently and continued to ink in the horse's braided mane. Kiram glanced at the picture. As a rule he couldn't tell one horse from another, a fact that had deeply disturbed

Master Ignacio the first day of riding class, but even he knew this horse. It was Javier's white stallion.

Until two weeks ago, Kiram wouldn't have imagined that there could be much difference between horses. Though admittedly the only ones he'd been familiar with were the nags that hauled Cadeleonian wagons and carriages outside the Haldiim district. The huge, glossy warhorses that the academy required their students to ride seemed like an entirely different breed of creatures. Between calculating gazes, sarcastic snorts, and immovable obstinacy they seemed to possess personalities that were as individual as their riders.

Like Javier, Lunaluz was known for his pride and prowess.

Kiram scowled at Nestor's drawing. It seemed that everything around him today was set on making him think about Javier.

"Did it have to be Lunaluz?" Kiram asked Nestor.

"Lunaluz," Fedeles echoed the name.

"He's a beautiful animal. So is this big fellow." Nestor handed Kiram the inked page that lay beneath his present drawing.

"Firaj." Fedeles sighed happily.

"Really?" Kiram asked. In his mind his new horse, Firaj, was much more intimidating. His first day of riding he'd simply clung to the black beast's back and prayed that the animal wouldn't kill him. He had not made much more progress in the subsequent classes.

"He's such a handsome old man." Nestor smiled at one of the sketches of Firaj's face.

"Handsome? I have nightmares about him."

A loud burst of surprised laughter interrupted Kiram's thoughts. Across the rows of wooden tables, he saw that several upperclassmen had clustered around Javier. Nestor's brother Elezar stood among them, as did the future count of Verida, Genimo Plunado.

Javier held a water glass in one hand and a spoon in the other. He dipped the spoon into the glass and then flicked the water up into the air. A white spark flashed up from Javier's hand as the water took flight. The droplet struck the tabletop as a small chunk of ice. Another cheer went up.

Kiram wanted to believe that this was just some slight-of-hand trick that Javier preformed but he had seen enough of Javier's magic now to acknowledge that the tiny white sparks that danced from his fingers were genuine. At some point Javier must have touched a shajdi and a little of its magic remained with him. But touching a shajdi was not the same as being possessed by a demon or having a door to hell inside him. It astounded Kiram that these Cadeleonians didn't grasp that.

Elezar snatched up the piece of ice and crushed it between his teeth. He grinned at Javier and said something. Genimo Plunado shoved his thick chestnut hair back from his face and leaned closer to Javier. When Javier threw another droplet of ice into the air Genimo caught it in his mouth. Javier continued performing his trick, receiving smiles and laughter, until his glass was empty.

"If they like him so much, why don't any of them room with him?" Kiram muttered to himself.

"You might as well ask why they don't sleep in the stalls with their horses," Nestor replied. "They're afraid of getting kicked to death, you know. The horses wouldn't mean them any harm but they'd just kick in their sleep and that would be it."

"He's not a horse," Kiram replied.

Nestor shrugged. "Are you going to eat the rest of your stew?"

Kiram shoved the blue porcelain bowl to Nestor. For a moment Nestor seemed to wrestle with some indecision, then at last he slipped his drawing papers back into their leather case and helped himself to the stew.

"Anyway, they don't all like him," Nestor said quietly. "My oldest brother Timoteo hates him. I think Genimo does as well. But Javier is already the Duke of Rauma. Only one of the Sagrada princes could afford to make an enemy of him, and I don't think anyone would want to face him in a duel. He'd eat their souls."

"Feed them ice and witty conversation is more like it," Kiram muttered.

He didn't want to admit it but he was a little jealous of the clever chatter and friendly pranks Javier performed for his classmates. After only a few days of total silence he had regretted his declaration that Javier was not to speak to him. More than that, he resented Javier's respect of his absurd demand. He knew it was all petty and beneath him, but he couldn't help himself.

The evenings in their shared room were agonizingly quiet. And that was if Javier was even there. Half the time he didn't appear until the night warden shouted for lights out. The nights he was alone, Kiram tried to believe that he was happy with the emptiness of the room and the opportunity to spread his cogs and iron cylinders out across the floor without criticism or comment. But the truth was that he felt deeply lonely.

To Kiram's surprise, Fedeles leaned up against his side the way a dog might. Reflexively, Kiram petted his head. Fedeles smiled, his eyes focusing on something far away. He was a handsome youth and sweet natured. Kiram wished that there were some way to know what, if anything, Fedeles was thinking. Kiram knew Fedeles was older than himself but he seemed so childlike. The simplest things, like cheese or apples, delighted him. But he loved horses most of all. Kiram noted the irony in the fact that he, who was terrified of the beasts, was forced to ride them every day, while Master Ignacio only allowed Fedeles to watch.

"Nestor? Would you mind if I gave one of these sketches of Firaj to Fedeles?"

Nestor looked at Fedeles for a moment then shrugged. "I want to turn in the one of him running, but any of the others should be all right."

"Which one would you like, Fedeles?" Kiram leafed through the drawings watching Fedeles' eyes as they flickered down to the pages.

"Firaj," Fedeles whispered as Kiram came to the drawing of the horse's head. Kiram handed it to him and Fedeles crushed the drawing against his chest.

He sang quietly to himself. Strung through the lyrical murmurs of gibberish and horses' names, Kiram suddenly caught a strange refrain and he glanced to Fedeles.

"Help me. Please help me." Fedeles' dark eyes were wide and terrified. His constant smile looked suddenly like a terrible grimace. Alarm shot through Kiram.

"Fedeles?" Kiram asked. "Is something wrong?"

Fedeles bowed his head, his unkempt black hair falling across his face, and Kiram thought he saw a shudder pass through Fedeles' body.

"Lunaluz," Fedeles whispered dreamily. When he lifted his face to Kiram's his expression was soft, sweet, and lost.

The school bells rang out the end of the lunch hour. All around them students stood and gathered their belongings. Fedeles sprang lightly from the table, laughing, and skipped away.

Kiram turned back to Nestor, who was gulping down the last of the stew.

"Did you hear that?"

"The bell? Of course," Nestor replied.

"No. What Fedeles just said. I think he was asking for help. You don't think he's hurt or something, do you?"

"He seems fine. I mean, as fine as he's ever been since his seizure." Nestor gathered his drawings and corked his inkwell. "He picks up phrases and things. He probably heard some one praying for luck with the next math test and was just repeating that."

"Maybe," Kiram replied. Fedeles had looked so stricken; it was hard for Kiram to think it was just some kind of mimicry. What if he was ill or in some pain that he couldn't communicate? "What kind of seizure did he have?"

"I wasn't at the academy when it happened, but my brother Elezar said that the hand of the white hell reached out and grasped him."

"You mean Javier caused it?" Kiram lowered his voice to a whisper as other students strode past them.

"No, it was the white hell itself," Nestor said. "Fedeles is Javier's cousin and the white hell has a taste for their bloodline. That's what Elezar says. And he was there when it happened."

"Yes, but what exactly happened?" Kiram asked.

"It was three years ago, when they were all first years. Elezar and Fedeles were leaving Scholar Donamillo's class when black sparks suddenly burst up, dancing across Fedeles' body, burning into his flesh. Fedeles was screaming and thrashing as if he was on fire. The white hell was trying to get into him."

"What did Elezar do?" Kiram couldn't imagine what his own reaction would be such a sight.

"Elezar didn't do anything. What could he do?" Nestor straightened his spectacles. "Javier heard the screaming and came running. He grabbed Fedeles and drew the hellfire off him. If you ever see Fedeles without his shirt you'll see the scars where the hellfire burned his body. He's been…odd ever since then."

Kiram studied Nestor's face intently.

"I'm not making it up," Nestor said. "Ask anyone. That's really what happened to Fedeles."

"It doesn't mean he doesn't need some help."

"If he needs help, Javier will give it to him." Nestor waved his hand as if brushing the thought aside. "Javier doesn't let anything happen to Fedeles. Why do you think everyone puts up with Fedeles running all around the academy?"

That afternoon, Kiram tried to concentrate on his work but throughout the fine arts class his mind continued to wander back to that brief glimpse of terror contorting Fedeles' innocent face. The image found its way into each of the charcoal studies that Kiram produced.

At the end of the class the instructor raised one wiry white brow and inquired about the brain fever that had apparently burned away his sense of good taste.

Kiram apologized and promised to make the work up on his free day. In the hallway a few minutes later, Nestor simply handed him a few of his own sketches to copy.

"Thanks." Kiram was genuinely touched by the offer.

"No problem," Nestor replied. "I really liked the studies you did. They looked like those devil-haunted souls that are always carved into the underside of chapel altars."

"Is that so?" Kiram pulled one of the piteously contorted faces out from his leather satchel. It didn't strike him as anything like a holy image, but then he knew little of Cadeleonian iconography. Haldiim were not permitted in Cadeleonian chapels unless they were undergoing conversions.

"The eyes are too flat," Kiram said.

"Yeah, but that makes it all the creepier." Nestor grinned at the image. "He looks like he's been lost for a hundred years in the sorrowlands and is turning into a wraith."

"You want it?" Kiram offered.

"Of course." Nestor took the drawing happily and tucked it away with his own, far superior works.

In history class, Kiram was far too occupied to think of Fedeles. It took all of his willpower not to argue with the doughy instructor, Holy Father Habalan, while he rhapsodized over the glorious reign of King Nazario Sagrada. Among the Haldiim, King Nazario was remembered as the Crowned Impaler. His rule had been a time of mass executions and public torture. His purges were the reason that even now huge walls surrounded the Haldiim district in Anacleto and archers still stood guard atop them. Haldiim mothers might pay taxes to the Cadeleonian kings, but the memory of Nazario's atrocities ensured they would never trust Cadeleonian lords to protect them.

Kiram had no idea of how he would write an essay chronicling the king's innovations without his writing degenerating to a string of obscenities. He had to bow his head just to keep the plump holy father from seeing his revulsion.

Afterwards Nestor asked if he was sick.

"Just tired." Kiram forced a smile. It was difficult to look at Nestor and know that his ancestors were probably among those noblemen who hunted Haldiim shepherds for sport and impaled lovers for their evening's entertainment. And yet when he did meet Nestor's gaze, no such malevolence showed in his expression. Kiram felt his anger drain away. Nestor wasn't responsible for his ancestry. He couldn't help being Cadeleonian any more than Kiram could take credit for being born a Haldiim.

"I'll feel better after dinner," Kiram said.

"Maybe not," Nestor replied. "It's bean night tonight."

They shared a scowl at the thought of the flatulence-inducing stew they would soon be served. Then Kiram smirked.

"Poor Javier." Kiram smiled maliciously. "His white hell demon may well choke to death on the fury of my fart demon."

Nestor responded to that with scandalized laugh and clapped him on the back. "That's the spirit, Kiram!"

Nestor's company buoyed Kiram through their riding lessons and dinner. Though when Kiram noted Fedeles' absence from their table Nestor just replied that Fedeles did as he pleased, and more than likely, eating a sludge of beans didn't suit him.

After dinner Nestor left to attend his upperclassman and Kiram found himself alone, pacing the vast corridors of the academy library.

Kiram adored the Sagrada Academy's library.

Walls of knowledge surrounded him. Shelves abounded with rare texts, written before printing presses came into use, and displaying page after page of beautifully detailed illuminations. Filed among countless tomes lay treasures of unpublished scientific studies, penned more as letters between the scholars than as formal presentations.

Any other day Kiram would have been happy to pour over them for any details that might aid him in his project for the Crown Challenge. But this evening his mind wasn't occupied with steam pressure or cooling chambers. Instead he kept remembering Fedeles' tortured expression and Nestor's offhand explanation of his condition. He thought of the white flickers that played between Javier's fingers and his gaze fell upon the gilded spine of a book titled *On the Nature of Hells and the Damned*. What did it mean to be one of them? What kind of force was hellfire and how could it hunt a particular family? How could a script be legible only to the eyes of the damned?

Kiram took the book from the shelf and, feeling almost ashamed of his interest in Cadleonian superstition, he scurried up to the privacy of his room with the text tucked between two history books.

He cracked open the book and turned its ornate pages carefully, enjoying the leathery scent of the vellum as it wafted over him. Reading through the pompous language and gilded letters he soon discovered that many of the people described as possessed by the Cadeleonian priests would have been diagnosed with 'dancing nerves' by a Haldiim physician, like his uncle Rafie.

Again the image of Fedeles' terrified grimace came to him. It hadn't been nerves nor mimicry that Kiram had seen in his expression but terror and pain, and Kiram was now positive that Fedeles had been genuine in his appeal for help.

After considering the matter for a moment, Kiram decided that Javier would be the person to tell about Fedeles' troubling plea. After all, Javier took responsibility for Fedeles. He would want to know this and only the pettiest of men would withhold something so important.

It would be a relief to put his pride aside and just talk to the man, and he couldn't have asked for a better reason to do so.

Now if only Javier would make an appearance. Kiram glanced out one of the high windows. He knew from Nestor that several of the upperclassmen routinely went off academy grounds and rode down to Zancoda city to solicit the prostitutes at the Goldenrod Inn.

Kiram found it difficult to imagine Javier waiting in some dank tavern for his turn to dally with a worn-out barmaid. But there weren't many other places he could be spending his evenings. Kiram had wandered the grounds on many previous nights and while he refused to admit that he had been looking for Javier, he certainly hadn't stumbled upon him during any of his rambling walks.

Outside, the summer sun sank into the shadows of the surrounding orchards. Clouds glowed like beaten gold against the darkening blue of the sky. Maybe another half hour of light was left. Then the night warden would call for lights out, and the last roll would be taken to assure that all students were in their beds.

Kiram stood and paced the length of the room. Now that he wanted to talk to Javier, where was he? Probably having a big-breasted Cadeleonian woman scrub his back in just the way he liked.

"Kihvash," Kiram spat the Haldiim insult as crudely as a salt merchant. He glowered down at the stables. Then he noticed a tall figure in the shadows. His hair was black enough and his skin pale enough to be Javier. Even the man's height was close enough to have passed, but the way he moved was completely wrong. The figure shied back into the cover of ornamental hedges and then bolted wildly to a water trough. His arms flailed out, waving a piece of paper and then clutching it back to his chest.

It had to be Fedeles. He was already at the stable doors. An instant later he disappeared inside. Even Kiram knew that it would only take a few wild movements for Fedeles to spook one of the horses and get himself killed.

Kiram didn't pause to think about what he should do. His common sense would make a coward of him and he knew it. Of all Master Ignacio's lectures, it was the one Kiram hated to hear the most, and yet it fueled his sprinting legs and pounding heart as he raced out of the dormitory.

Chapter Four

The interior of the stable was dim and hot. Strong, earthy smells of horses—their feed, their bodies and their excrement—saturated the still air. Warm light streamed through the open door, casting a long shadow at Kiram's feet. All across the packed dirt floor, broken pieces of straw caught the light, glinting like flecks of gold.

From the deep, shadowed stalls, horses watched him. There seemed to be something disapproving about the way their dark eyes followed his movements, as if they knew that he was only a second-year student and not allowed in the stables unescorted. Fedeles was nowhere in sight.

He walked the long aisle between the stalls, searching for any sign of Fedeles, and at the same time too afraid of the big horses to approach any of the stalls.

"Fedeles?" Kiram couldn't bring himself to shout and risk being discovered. Instead the words came out in a forced whisper. The horses' ears pricked up at the sound.

He was rewarded with a soft, almost cooing response from farther down. Kiram hurried ahead. He saw Firaj—his own big black gelding—before Fedeles. Then, as he came closer to the stall, he realized that Fedeles stood inside the stall with his face pressed into the big horse's shoulder. With one hand, he absently stroked Firaj's neck while the other still clutched the drawing Kiram had given him at lunch.

To Kiram's relief and surprise, Firaj seemed completely at ease with Fedeles' presence. The horse lowered his head and snuffled through Fedeles' tangled black hair.

Kiram tried to sound firm while keeping his voice low. "You have to come out of there right now. You're going to get in trouble."

Fedeles lifted his grinning face from Firaj's dark coat and shook his head. Even in the dimness of the stable, Kiram could see the wet tracks of tears on Fedeles' cheeks.

"Killing him…" Fedeles' voice was soft and melodic, as if he were singing a lullaby. "Don't make me go. Don't make me. They'll hurt him…"

"Someone is hurting him?" Kiram glanced to Firaj. Had Fedeles seen someone treat Firaj poorly, or simply misinterpreted the ministrations of some groom? Either way Kiram was touched by Fedeles' concern. Perhaps this was what Fedeles had been asking Kiram to help him with earlier. And when Kiram had failed to understand him, Fedeles had gone to protect Firaj alone. "Are you guarding him?"

An expression of wonder and relief came over Fedeles' face. He nodded, and then to Kiram's surprise he released his hold on Firaj and stepped closer.

"Who is hurting him?"

Fedeles opened his mouth but only a choked groan came out. A grin jerked across his face and Fedeles clutched his hands over his mouth. He leaned heavily against the wooden slats of the wall and more tears poured down his face.

"Help me," he whispered.

"I will," Kiram assured him, though he had no idea how. He wasn't sure who, if anyone, was threatening Firaj or if that was even the real problem. In the two weeks he had been at the academy he had never seen Fedeles like this.

"Don't cry." Kiram spoke in the gentle tone he usually reserved for his nephews and nieces. He wrapped his arm around Fedeles' shoulders, offering him a loose hug, which Fedeles returned. Feverish heat radiated from his body and the smell of hay clung to him.

"It's all right, Fedeles," Kiram whispered. "Firaj is fine. Look."

The horse pulled a mouthful of hay from the small heap in his feed trough. He chewed sleepily while gazing at Fedeles. Then Firaj lifted his head, studying something farther down the aisle of stalls. Kiram looked back but couldn't see anything.

Fedeles tightened his grip and suddenly Kiram realized how very strong Fedeles was.

He whispered, "Don't make me go."

"We both have to go. We're not supposed to be in the stables right now and the night warden will be calling—" The rest of Kiram's words were drowned out by a furious shout from the far west door of the stable.

"Fedeles!"

All around, horses' heads came up, their ears pricking at the sudden intrusion of noise. Fedeles released his grip on Kiram and edged back into Firaj's stall.

"Fedeles, if you make me look through this entire fucking stable I swear I will beat you blind!"

It was Upperclassman Genimo.

Fedeles caught Kiram's hand and pulled him into the shadows of Firaj's stall. Kiram wondered just how much trouble the two of them would be in if they were caught here.

"Fedeles." Genimo's voice was much closer now. Kiram could see the black silhouette of his body moving through the gloom of the stable. "If anything happens to these horses, it will be your fault. The grooms will blame you and never let you come in again."

Kiram felt Fedeles tense. His grip on Kiram's hand almost hurt, but Kiram didn't dare to pull free for fear of drawing Genimo's attention.

"If Lunaluz were to lose an eye, even Javier would hate you then. They would have to put him down because of you, Fedeles. A blind horse is no good to anyone."

"No! Lunaluz!" Fedeles bolted out of the shadows, pulling Kiram forward with him.

Kiram wanted to run for the door but Fedeles didn't budge. He stood in the center of the aisle, grinning as Genimo closed the distance between them. Kiram didn't like the way Genimo swung his riding crop as he approached them.

"What in the three hells are you doing here?" Genimo demanded of Kiram.

"I came to find Fedeles," Kiram replied.

"And what? Hold hands?" Genimo sneered at Kiram. "Practicing your filthy Haldiim seductions on the idiot, are you?"

Kiram's outrage momentarily overpowered his fear. "I just wanted to get him out of the stable."

"I don't want to go!" Fedeles gripped Kiram's hand desperately. "I don't want to. Firaj, Lunaluz, Firaj—"

"Oh, shut up!" Genimo snarled at Fedeles.

"No!" Fedeles began a panicked chant. "No, no, no, no..."

Seeming to catch Fedeles' agitation, the horses stamped the ground, releasing short nervous snorts.

"No, no, no, no…" Fedeles seemed hardly aware of Kiram. He clenched his eyes shut as if focusing all his attention on just repeating his refusal.

"Shut the fuck up!" Genimo snapped. "Shut up!"

"Calm down," Kiram told Genimo. "You're only making him worse—"

"You never speak to me in that tone, heathen!" Genimo lashed his black riding crop across Kiram's cheek.

The shock of being struck stunned Kiram more than the explosion of pain. He barely registered the wet heat of his own blood spilling down his jaw.

Never in his life had anyone treated Kiram with such disrespect. Pain and outrage flooded him. He jerked his hand free from Fedeles' grip and slapped Genimo's face.

"Khivash," Kiram spat.

The blow resounded with less brutality than Kiram would have liked, but it took Genimo off guard. He staggered back half a step. Then he launched himself at Kiram. His first punch forced the air out of Kiram's lungs and threw him back against the wall.

Fedeles wailed, "Lunaluz! Lunaluz!"

Kiram tried to regain his balance but Genimo was already up against him, pinning him against the wall. In desperation Kiram sank his teeth into Genimo's forearm.

"Whore!" Genimo drove his knee into Kiram's groin. Blinding, nauseating pain shot through him. His knees buckled and he collapsed to the ground.

"You piece of shit," Genimo snarled. "How dare you lay your filthy, heathen hands on me?"

Genimo hauled Kiram up by his hair and punched him again, this time in the face. White flashes exploded through Kiram's vision. The sickening hot, wet sensation of blood gushed from his nose and poured over his lips. He choked as blood ran down the back of his throat. He could hardly think for the pain.

"God, you're pathetic." Genimo smirked at Kiram. "You're a worm. A piece of shit—"

Suddenly a greenish mass of horse dung smacked into the side of Genimo's head. His face flushed scarlet with rage and he released his hold on Kiram to turn back to Fedeles. Kiram slid down the wall to the ground. Beside Fedeles stood Javier, hefting a muck shovel in one hand.

"No, Genimo, what is clinging to your hair is a piece of shit." Javier's tone was light, and his expression almost friendly as he strode closer. "What you had the poor sense to toss around just now is something entirely different."

Genimo's fury seemed to dissolve into a stunned fear. He backed away.

"If you run," Javier said, "I'll bring the white hell out to hunt you. So I wouldn't if I were you."

Genimo froze. Javier glanced to Kiram and for a moment his playful smile disappeared. Then he turned his attention back to Genimo.

"You ought to ask before playing with my things." Javier wiped the back of the filthy shovel across Genimo's chest. "And if you break something of mine, you know I'm going to be annoyed, don't you?"

"Scholar Donamillo sent me to fetch Fedeles for his treatment and—" A terrified tremor ran through Genimo's voice.

"Not what I want to hear." Javier jabbed the shovel into Genimo's chest.

"I…I…" Genimo's face was bloodlessly pale. His eyes were so wide that Kiram thought that he could see white all the way around Genimo's black, gaping pupils.

Kiram suddenly remembered his uncle describing the men he had treated during the bread riots. Many had died in states of terrified shock. His uncle always said that they had rabbit eyes. Kiram thought he knew what his uncle had meant now.

"I'm sorry, Javier." Genimo swayed on his feet and then sank to his knees.

"You're sorry?" The sadistic amusement in Javier's voice disturbed Kiram, and yet there was a part of him that was deeply pleased to see Genimo on his knees and covered in excrement. "I can't imagine what you could be sorry for. Except that I caught you."

"Please…Javier, I swear I won't do it again."

"You certainly won't." Javier gave a hard laugh. "In fact you may not do anything ever again."

Javier held his left hand out over Genimo's head. White sparks flickered between his fingers.

Kiram caught the unmistakable scent of human urine and realized that Genimo had pissed himself.

"Don't kill me," Genimo sobbed.

Javier flicked his fingers across Genimo's forehead. The moment Javier touched Genimo's skin a tiny white bolt burst up from his hand and drove into Genimo's skull. Genimo jerked backwards and then collapsed to the ground.

Kiram stared at Genimo's prone body in horror. He felt suddenly sick and he wasn't sure if it was from the throbbing pain deep in his groin or from the sight of such an offhanded murder.

Javier knelt down beside Genimo and lifted his head off the floor slightly. Genimo's neck sagged against Javier's hands like a dead snake.

"You killed him," Kiram whispered.

"Killed him?" Javier glanced up to Kiram and shook his head. "How dramatic you are."

Javier bowed his head close to Genimo's. Small white sparks skipped across Javier's hands and jumped through Genimo's hair. "Sleep. Dream of rats devouring your intestines." Then he lowered Genimo's head almost gently back to the stable floor.

Javier stood and turned back to the door of Firaj's stall.

"Fedeles, come out." Javier's tone was neither as amused nor as cruel as it had been with Genimo. He sounded a little exasperated.

"No," Fedeles replied from behind the door.

"I'm not going to take you to your treatment. Kiram is hurt and you promised to look after him, didn't you?"

"Yes." Fedeles sounded sulky.

"Come on, then," Javier said. "Help us get back to our room."

Chapter Five

Fedeles rushed ahead of them, opening doors and singing the names of horses triumphantly.

When they reached their room, Fedeles lingered outside the open door and then at last scampered away.

"Is he going to be all right?" Kiram asked as Javier lowered him to his own bed.

"Fedeles? He'll be fine. He's got his room all to himself tonight and he's gotten out of his treatments for another day."

"But I think something's wrong." It hurt his entire face to speak. The gash in his cheek throbbed and his head ached. "This afternoon he asked me to help him."

"He gets that way when he misses his treatments. He hates them, but if he goes more than a month between treatments he becomes agitated and then delusional. He starts seeing things and hearing things that aren't there."

"He said something about someone hurting Firaj, I think." The earlier conversation seemed muddled and confused as he tried to recall it. Kiram sagged back into his mattress. A dizzy, whirling sensation engulfed him each time he closed his eyes.

"Here." Javier lifted his head and propped a pillow under him. His hands felt warm. "Don't fall asleep just yet, all right?"

"Why not?"

"Well, I've got you talking to me for the first time in two weeks. I'd rather it not end too quickly." Javier left briefly, then returned to Kiram's bedside with the basin of water and a washcloth. "You really don't know the first thing about fighting, do you?"

"I know that a quick fist is the first sign of a slow wit."

This elicited a laugh from Javier. Very gently, he washed the blood from Kiram's nose and mouth. Kiram hissed in pain as Javier began to clean the cut across his left cheek.

Javier leaned closer, examining the wound. "This is really deep. Did he catch you with his signet ring?"

Kiram clenched his teeth as Javier continued to clean the cut. "He used his riding crop."

"He cropped you? God, he's a shit." Javier rinsed the blood out of the washcloth. "Maybe I should have killed him after all."

"I'm glad you didn't."

"Really?" Javier pressed the damp washcloth lightly against Kiram's cheek.

"Murder is a profane act." Kiram found it distracting to have Javier so near him. His attention kept straying to the faint shadow of stubble along Javier's jaw and the woody scent of his skin. "It would have injured your soul to kill him when he begged you for mercy."

"I have no soul to injure," Javier replied easily.

"Yes you do." Kiram couldn't help his annoyance. He was so tired of way Cadeleonian beliefs stripped the soul from anyone or anything they pleased. "Every living thing has a soul. Trees, birds, dogs, cats. Even demons—and I don't believe that you are one—but even if you were, you would still have a soul. You aren't a piece of furniture or a rock, you're just an egotist and maybe a bit of a flirt—I haven't decided yet. But you definitely have a soul."

"I'm not sure if I should be offended or comforted by that pronouncement of yours."

"You should just believe me," Kiram said and he realized that the pain was making him short tempered. Still, he added, "I'm sorry, but in this matter your religion is simply wrong."

"And you say I'm an egotist." Javier's smile widened. It wasn't the same smile that Kiram had seen him give Genimo in the stable. There was nothing sharp or cruel about his countenance now. His touch was gentle, almost caressing.

"You'll have a scar from this, I think." Javier poured salve from a glass jar and worked it between his fingers.

"It won't be my first." Kiram tried to sound casual about it. His mother was going to be horrified when she saw it. "I have another scar."

"*One* other?" Carefully Javier spread the warmed salve over Kiram's wounded cheek. It smelled astringent but dulled the pain almost immediately. For an instant Kiram wondered at the lucky coincidence that Javier would have such a salve ready at hand. Then he remembered the countless nicks and grazes that had scored Javier's pale body, the raw red scar that ran up his wrist, and the huge curling crest burned into his right shoulder. Obviously the life he led required such a salve, if not something much stronger.

"I'm a scholar from a good home," Kiram responded. "How many scars could I possibly have gotten?"

"Well, one obviously." Javier glanced over Kiram's body curiously. "Somewhere."

"Here." Kiram offered his right hand for Javier's inspection. Javier gently spread Kiram's fingers apart then explored the tender expanses of his palm and wrist. The sensation made Kiram's entire body feel suddenly too warm.

"Are you talking about this little white line along the inside of your thumb?"

"Yes. I got it making candy with my mother. I cut my thumb while snipping taffy." Kiram felt a little embarrassed, but he had only been six years old.

"And that's really the only other scar you have?" Javier pushed the sleeve of Kiram's shirt up, inspecting the dark skin of his arm.

"I wouldn't have dared to get another," Kiram replied, but he was only half thinking about the conversation. "My mother made such a huge scene of just this one."

Javier seemed to come to some decision. "You should get out of this shirt. There's blood all down the front."

Kiram didn't move to stop Javier as he began unbuttoning his shirt.

"Your mother would hate to see this, I imagine." Javier paused, his hand resting over the last three buttons of Kiram's shirt, radiating warmth across Kiram's stomach. "All those letters you've been writing, they're to her, aren't they?"

Kiram nodded. Not only had the pain in his cheek faded but also he felt strangely languid. He wondered what had been in the salve that Javier had treated him with.

"And the rest of your family?" Javier looked almost troubled. "You're close with them?"

"Very. The letters are for the whole family," Kiram said, "but Mother loves to read them aloud. Whenever my brother Majdi writes she reads his letters at the evening meal and asks what people would like her to write back. Now I guess she's reading my letters, though I still haven't received a response."

As he spoke Kiram could see a kind of uneasiness come over Javier. He withdrew his hand from Kiram's stomach and straightened as if to rise from the bedside.

"What about your family?" Kiram grasped desperately for anything to say, just to keep Javier there beside him.

"Fedeles is all of the family I have left. There's Fedeles' father, but he isn't from the Tornesal bloodline."

"Just Fedeles?" Kiram couldn't imagine having only one cousin. He had over a dozen.

"We're a cursed lineage. Of course we've had our fair share of drunken idiots who rode off cliffs in the night as well. It certainly saves me the trouble of purchasing too many New Year gifts."

"I'm sorry." Kiram couldn't think of anything else to say. The thought of being so alone seemed heartbreaking to him.

Javier gave a flinty laugh.

"Be sorry for Fedeles if you must, but don't waste your pity on my account." Javier strode back to his bed and began pulling off his boots. "I control the white hell and rule Rauma. It's all worked out beautifully for me."

"Do you miss them?" Kiram asked.

"No," Javier replied but Kiram didn't believe him. The answer was too fast and too flat.

Javier set his boots aside and glanced back to Kiram. "Do you think you might be able to walk yet?"

"I don't know." The change of subject took Kiram a little off guard but he respected it.

"You should probably give it a try. See if you can make it down the hall to the toilet before the night warden gets up to our floor. It's going to hurt like hell when you first try to piss but do it anyway." Javier busied himself with the silver buttons of his jacket. "If there's blood, call me right away. I'll take you down to Scholar Donamillo and he'll treat you."

Kiram made the trip to the toilet and was relieved to discover his body still functioned properly. When he returned to the room, he found Javier had already washed and gone to bed. Only one oil lamp remained lighted. Kiram washed himself quickly and returned to his own bed.

"Good night," Kiram whispered to Javier.

"Good night," Javier replied softly. After a moment of silence he added, "Thank you for looking after Fedeles."

"It wasn't—" Kiram couldn't say that it wasn't any trouble. It had been. It had gotten him in the first fight of his life, but oddly he didn't regret it.

"It's just what friends do for each other," Kiram said at last.

"I suppose it is."

Kiram waited for him to add something more but there was only silence and the darkness of the night.

Chapter Six

The next morning Kiram felt better and most of the swelling in his nose and groin had diminished. Still, Genimo's crop had more than left a mark. Even in the crowded din of the dining hall other students gawked as Kiram passed by. Several snickered behind his back but none of the other students met Kiram's gaze directly. And only one of them kicked his leg out to trip him as he walked past.

He took his usual seat between Fedeles and Nestor.

Nestor only glanced up over the rims of his delicate glasses and then returned his attention to the inky figures on the page in front of him. "You look awful."

"I know." Kiram's entire face ached as he moved his mouth. The gash across his cheek had closed to a thick scab, while his upper lip was bruised to a dark purple and swollen.

Once bowls of morning porridge and pots of bitterly over-brewed tea were distributed, Kiram attempted to engage breakfast. It hurt to open his mouth wide and he wasn't sure that this sticky, beige mass was worth the effort but he soon discovered that hunger mitigated discomfort. He swallowed a spoonful of the bland porridge. Both Nestor and Fedeles had already finished their servings.

Fedeles flipped through the yellowed pages of a tattered book. The black-printed letters were overwritten with hundreds of scrawling notes and weird little symbols. Fedeles turned the book upside down and then right side up again. His hair was a wild tangle and his clothes looked unkempt as always, but Kiram thought he seemed more clear-eyed and aware of his surroundings than usual. He met Kiram's gaze, and for the first time he didn't seem to be looking through a dreamy haze.

"Eat up," Fedeles whispered.

Nestor sketched absentmindedly. The figures filling his sheet of parchment trailed off into loops of ink and then were engulfed in newer drawings. All around them students only half dressed in their blue linen uniforms chatted and laughed. Some of them exchanged class notes while others tossed banned dice. Their voices formed waves of noise, which crashed through the silence of Kiram's two companions.

"Is something wrong, Nestor?" Kiram asked at last.

"You shouldn't have put up such a fight," Nestor whispered. "Especially not against Upperclassman Javier. He could have really hurt you. Ladislo says that if you just close your eyes and take it, it's not so bad. Fighting won't do you any good."

"What are you talking about?" Kiram asked.

Nestor's pale face flushed deep red.

"Ladislo gets bent because he's little," Fedeles murmured. "A little pony. Pretty little pony."

"You know, they say that if your upperclassman gets bloody-minded and horny, there isn't much you can do. It's best not to put up a fight. Unless you have an older brother or something." Nestor scowled at his empty porridge bowl. "Upperclassman Atreau leaves me alone but I'm not...pretty like you."

"I'm not pretty."

"Yes, you are," Nestor cut him off. "There's no point arguing about it. Obviously you're too pretty for Javier to resist."

"Resist? Javier didn't do anything to me." Kiram suddenly realized what Nestor was implying. "He certainly didn't force his attentions upon me."

"Didn't he?" Nestor asked, his expression lifting for the first time all morning. "I thought...you know, because you're Haldiim and pretty...and who's going to say no to Javier Tornesal?"

"It was nothing like that." Kiram needed to stop the direction of Nestor's thoughts. He himself didn't want to think too much about the vulnerability of his position with Javier. It led him too quickly into confusion, remembering Javier's gentle touch and at the same time his cynical smile and those white sparks skipping between his fingers. "I got into a fight with Upperclassman Genimo last night."

"You didn't win, did you?" Nestor looked strangely hopeful.

"I wish," Kiram said. "No, Javier took care of Genimo."

Nestor's eyes went wide. "Did he kill him?"

"No, he didn't even hurt him. He just scared him. And Genimo deserved what he got." Kiram scanned the rows of students crammed in around the long wooden tables, searching for Javier. He had not seen him since last night. This morning when Kiram had first woken, he'd discovered Javier already gone. Only the faintest hint of the woody scent of his soap lingered in the washroom and the tub had been perfectly dry. Kiram guessed that Javier must have woken very early, perhaps even before sunrise.

"You haven't seen him, have you?" Kiram asked.

"Genimo?" Nestor asked. "Not this morning. He's probably hiding from Javier."

"I was thinking of Javier, actually." Kiram took another taste of his porridge. It wasn't so bad. He supposed that if he got hungry enough he might even begin to appreciate its paste-like qualities. He imagined that his mother would have sieved it to make some kind of edible glue for one of her sugar bouquets. His uncle might have used it for a medicinal plaster.

"Chapel," Fedeles announced.

Kiram looked at him, unsure of what had prompted the statement.

"Javier's taking his penance in chapel," Fedeles clarified. He looked and sounded so reasonable that it surprised Kiram. Nestor also took note, squinting at Fedeles over the rims of his glasses. Then Fedeles' sober expression melted into a wide smile. He stroked one of the heavily defaced pages of his book. "Lunaluz. Ghosts are looking for him."

"Well, ahm, actually Fedeles is probably right." Nestor sounded as if he couldn't quite believe what he was saying. "Not about ghosts, but about Javier being at chapel. If he did assault another student, then he's probably submitting himself for penance."

"What do you mean, penance?"

"We all have to submit to chapel punishments when we sin." Nestor pulled a distasteful scowl. "But Javier, being hell-branded, is much more vigilant than the rest of us. Ever since that groom was killed he's taken penance weekly. My brother Elezar says that the punishments keep the white hell from growing stronger."

"What kind punishments are they?" Kiram disliked the sound of all this.

He couldn't help but think of the filthy, bleeding Cadeleonian penitents who whipped themselves outside the churches of Anacleto during the week they called Our Savior's Misery. Once, when he had still been a child, he had witnessed two zealous penitents lashing each other's genitals with wire whips. His mother had clamped her hand over his eyes but he had already seen flesh ripping away in fatty globs. Droplets of blood and gore had spattered the sleeve of his shirt. For weeks after that Kiram had woken, shouting and thrashing from violent dreams.

"Sometimes Holy Father Habalan orders bleedings, sometimes caning," Nestor said blandly. "It all depends on the sin and the circumstances. No matter what he'll give Javier muerate poison to keep the demon in him weak throughout the physical punishments."

The porridge in Kiram's mouth suddenly felt too thick and sticky. He forced himself to swallow it, and then shoved his bowl aside.

"He shouldn't be punished for defending me from Genimo." Kiram started to his feet but Nestor caught his arm and pulled him back down to the bench.

"He could have called one of the scholars over if he had wanted to," Nestor said. "He knew what he was getting himself into. You'll only embarrass him if you go running in and make a scene like some girl. It'll make both you and Javier look... strange."

"But no one should have to suffer for doing the right thing."

At this, Nestor just rolled his eyes. "You're making too much of the penance. Javier does it all the time. We all do. Only crybabies like Ladislo make a production of it. If Javier really did protect you, then respect his decision and don't embarrass him. It'll be for your own good."

"How can his pain be for my good?"

"It's not a bad thing to have the whole academy know that your upperclassman will take his responsibility to protect you seriously. You know, before you got here, Atreau got into an outright brawl with the Helio twins on my account and he had to do a full week of penance for it. But after that everyone in the school knew that Atreau wouldn't just stand by and let certain things happen to me."

"What about your brother? Wouldn't he protect you?"

"Oh, of course." Nestor grinned. "Elezar just about killed Cocuyo Helio for spitting on me. You can tell the twins apart now because Elezar broke Cocuyo's cheekbone and it didn't heal quite straight."

Kiram involuntarily searched the dining hall for the whip-thin Helio twins. Nestor was right; Cocuyo's right cheek was slightly too flat to be a perfect match to his brother Enevir's jutting features.

"But that's not my point," Nestor went on. "I'm not rooming with my brothers, and they won't always be able to protect me, especially if the king sends me to serve in a neighbor's lands. But now everyone knows that even if I'm away from my family Atreau will defend me. And more importantly for Atreau, everyone knows that the Grunito family is allied with him now. So now he's got Elezar and Timoteo both on his side in a fight."

"Yes, but it's not going to do Javier any good to have everyone know that he's allied with the Kir-Zaki family. No one here even knows my family."

"Kir-Zaki of Kir-Zaki Candies? Everyone eats them." Nestor rolled his eyes as if Kiram were thick as a pillar. "But, yes, you're right that Javier doesn't need allies. But you do. You can bet that all the bullies and bastards in the academy—especially the twins—have been waiting for someone to do something to you to see if Javier would ignore you or if he would do his duty. Now everyone knows that suffering penance isn't going to keep Javier from protecting you."

"But wasn't rescuing me enough? Doesn't that prove that he'll defend me?" Kiram challenged.

"No." Nestor frowned at him intently. "The penance is the most important part. It shows everyone that he's serious. You know, it's almost like a kind of ceremony. It proves the strength of his conviction. It shows everyone that he doesn't care how much he may suffer, he'll still beat the crap out of anyone who threatens you."

"I guess I understand that," Kiram admitted, though he thought the entire matter sounded brutal and primitive. "But I don't like the idea of someone else being whipped on my account."

"Don't worry about that. Javier is tough. He'll probably just shrug the penance off. Father Habalan isn't all that harsh anyway." Nestor lowered his voice. "My mother hits a lot harder."

Kiram smiled at that.

He wondered if Nestor was right about the penance. Maybe he was overreacting. If all the Cadeleonians accepted penance regularly, they couldn't all be enduring hideous whippings.

"I'm more worried about you and me right now." Nestor carefully cleaned the small lenses of his spectacles and then replaced them on his nose. "I imagine we're both going to have to keep clear of Genimo from now on. He's the type to hold a grudge."

"Do you think Fedeles is in danger, then? Isn't Genimo his upperclassman?" Kiram asked.

Fedeles just gave an oddly amused snort.

"Genimo would have to be suicidal to do anything to Fedeles. Javier would flat out kill him. He's said as much." Nestor lowered his voice slightly. "Don't tell anyone I said so but Genimo is Fedeles' nanny really. He has to keep track of him, give him baths, brush his hair, and make sure he gets to Scholar Donamillo for his treatments."

"Rats chew him up if he's mean." Fedeles picked up Kiram's bowl and pushed it back to him. "Eat up, skinny."

Nestor eyed Fedeles almost suspiciously. "You're making more sense than usual, Fedeles."

"It's a curse," Fedeles muttered. He didn't look up from his book.

"Well," Nestor went on, "Fedeles is right about you needing to eat. You and I are both on Master Ignacio's double training list. Elezar posted it this morning and told me. We're going to have two extra hours of war arts starting today and going on until the autumn tournament."

"Two extra hours?" All thought of Javier and his penance suddenly dissipated. "That's insane! Not only will it kill me, but there's no point. It's not as if I'll ever have to don armor and defend my holdings."

"No, but you will have to don armor and defend your honor in the autumn tournament." Nestor's tone was deeply resigned. "Trust me, you do not want to be beaten by a bunch of first-year underclassmen from the Yillar Academy."

"But not me," Kiram protested. "Surely Master Ignacio can't expect me to compete."

"I think he does, actually," Nestor replied. "He expects everyone to compete. More is the pity for both our sorry asses."

For the third time, Fedeles grinned and told Kiram, "Eat up."

Kiram obeyed almost numbly. Who in their right mind would send him out to compete on the tourney field? There had to be some kind of mistake. And yet deep inside himself Kiram felt a terrible certainty growing. Master Ignacio wasn't going to let him get out of the tournament just because he was utterly unsuited to battle. The lanky war master simply wasn't that reasonable.

An hour later, when he and Nestor took their second tier seats in the circular lecture hall for mathematics, Kiram's fear was confirmed. Scholar Blasio beckoned them down to him and informed them that they were to report to Master Ignacio. Though he paused midway through to frown at Kiram's beaten condition.

"I got into a fight with Upperclassman Genimo," Kiram explained. He had considered lying but he wasn't practiced at deception and he doubted that both Javier and Genimo would tell the same lie that he would. "I didn't start it."

"No, of course not. Javier said that you got caught in the middle of an altercation between himself and Genimo, but I had no idea that you had been so directly involved." Scholar Blasio winced as his gaze moved over the scab on Kiram's cheek. "A little extra training in war arts might not be such a bad idea. It couldn't hurt for a young man such as yourself to learn a little self-defense."

"But I'll fall behind in mathematics," Kiram argued.

"I very much doubt that you could ever fall behind in mathematics, Kiram." Scholar Blasio offered him a sympathetic smile. "And you will only miss my class on the odd days. Even days the two of you will be excused from fine art."

At this Nestor's expression crumpled. Kiram saw a brief amusement flicker over Scholar Blasio's freckled face. "It will only be for a few months and you'll both be happy for the extra practice come the week of the autumn tournament."

"Certainly some students must be excused from participating in the tournament." Kiram lowered his voice, as three other second-year students entered the lecture room and took their seats.

"Fedeles doesn't compete, but his is a very rare case. Barring broken legs, high fevers, or black pox, I couldn't imagine Master Ignacio excusing either of you. You're both healthy young men. Though…" Scholar Blasio cocked his head just slightly and studied Kiram. "There is a possibility that Scholar Donamillo could request that you be excused, since you're already spending your free hours working on the Crown Challenge."

"What about Nestor?" Kiram asked quickly. "He's been… helping me."

"I have," Nestor agreed, though his response sounded almost as much like a question as a statement.

Scholar Blasio shook his head. “I doubt that Scholar Donamillo will believe Nestor’s assistance is that necessary to your work, but you could always ask. He should be attending the infirmary now, so why don’t the two of you ask him?”

“Yes, sir.” Kiram nodded respectfully as did Nestor. They both pretended not to hear the derisive comments of the other students as they left the lecture room.

Chapter Seven

As they walked along the vaulted hall towards the infirmary, Nestor forced a smile. "At least *you* may have a way out."

"No, it's either both of us or neither." Kiram had decided. In the past two weeks Nestor had offered him his sketches, advice, and support. He wouldn't abandon him to endure Master Ignacio's merciless tutelage alone.

"Really?" Nestor looked truly touched.

"Absolutely."

"Let's hope Scholar Donamillo excuses us both, then."

A strange, howling noise cut through Kiram's agreement. Kiram stopped in his tracks. The howl stretched out, echoing through the hall. A deep grinding sound, like the deep rumble of an eyestone crushing through wheat, rose over the cry.

"What was that?" Kiram asked Nestor.

"Probably one of Scholar Donamillo's mechanical cures." Nestor pretended to shudder. "Sounds like he's testing it on some poor dog, doesn't it?"

Kiram nodded. He had only ever seen mechanical cures as diagrams on theater flyers or in paintings outside circus tents. His uncle disparaged them utterly, but Kiram had always been curious. The sound of this one was terrible, and Kiram couldn't help but feel a pang of pity for the poor animal trapped within its iron grasp.

As they came closer to the infirmary the howling cries faded to soft little gasps. The grinding of iron gears only grew louder. When they reached the huge, double doors of the infirmary, Kiram knocked but there was no response.

"I doubt that Scholar Donamillo heard that," Nestor shouted over the grinding roar.

Kiram raised his hand to pound on the door but then suddenly the heavy mechanical noise stopped. The following silence was so complete that it startled Kiram a little. Then peals of dreamy laughter and singsong syllables drifted through the infirmary doors. Kiram recognized Fedeles' voice at once and realized that he must have been the howling creature. Doubtless it was the treatment that both Genimo and Javier had mentioned.

Kiram had to step back as one of the infirmary doors swung open. To Kiram's horror, Genimo stepped out of the infirmary and leaned against the door, propping it open. When he caught sight of Kiram he looked like he might spit on him but then seemed to think better of it.

Scholar Donamillo stepped through the open door, leading Fedeles by one arm. He frowned at the sight of Kiram and Nestor.

"You're here for your injuries?" Scholar Donamillo asked Kiram.

"No, sir. But Scholar Blasio said that we should speak to you."

"In a moment, then." Scholar Donamillo returned his attention to Genimo.

"Fedeles is still weak. You'll need to keep a close watch over him for another hour or so."

Genimo nodded. Kiram studied his cheek for any sign of their altercation, but his blow hadn't left a mark. Only the purple bruise on Genimo's forehead attested to his involvement in the previous night's fight. Though Kiram was sure that if Genimo's sleeve were rolled back there would be bite marks.

Fedeles seemed unaware of any of them. He swayed, as if listening to a melody no one else could hear, smiling serenely and gazing at the far wall as if it were a vision of encompassing beauty.

"Come, Fedeles." Genimo caught one of Fedeles' hands and led him out of Scholar Donamillo's grip as if he were taking a dance partner. He placed one of his hands against Fedeles' back, steadying him.

"I'll send word to Scholar Habalan that you should be excused from his class this afternoon," Scholar Donamillo told Genimo.

"Thank you, sir." Genimo politely bowed to Scholar Donamillo and then led Fedeles down the hall and up the stairs. Kiram watched them go, unsure of what to think. The night before Genimo had threatened and terrified Fedeles, and now he was leading Fedeles like a doting uncle tending an invalid child.

"So, Scholar Blasio sent you?" Scholar Donamillo prompted.

"Yes." Kiram quickly turned his attention back to Scholar Donamillo's severe gaze. After two weeks of classes with the scholar, Kiram no longer found his expressions daunting. From time to time he even thought he caught glimpses of affection crossing the older man's face.

Nestor, on the other hand, was not one of Scholar Donamillo's favorite students. He bowed his head and kept his distance.

"Scholar Blasio said that we should speak to you about being excused from the additional war arts training because I'm already spending most of my free time—" Kiram would have gone on but Donamillo cut him off with a shake of his head.

"Unfortunately this morning when I put the question to Master Ignacio, he would not allow the exemption. Apparently he has already made arrangements for your training. Upperclassmen have been pulled from their free hours to tutor the two of you." Scholar Donamillo studied Kiram's cheek for a moment. "Did anyone treat that?"

"Upperclassman Javier applied a salve to it last night," Kiram replied. He wished he had known what exactly the salve was. He guessed that Scholar Donamillo did because he nodded approvingly.

"It looks clean, but if it should become red or painful come to see me." For an instant an almost sly look flickered over Scholar Donamillo's hard features. "I wouldn't want all the practice of war arts to cause you to develop a fever in the injury. That could keep you from practice for quite a while."

"Ahm. Yes, sir." Kiram wasn't quite sure of how to interpret Scholar Donamillo's words. It sounded like he was telling Kiram to pretend that his injury was worse than it was. In fact, Kiram was almost positive that was Scholar Donamillo's meaning. But it would also mean lying to Master Ignacio, the prospect of which terrified Kiram.

"You had both best report to Master Ignacio now." As Scholar Donamillo stepped back into the infirmary, Kiram caught a brief glimpse of huge iron supports curving like the ribs of a globe around a sphere of milky glass. Golden lights flickered from within the mechanism, then died away. Then the door fell closed.

"They are going to wipe the floor with us," Nestor groaned.

"What are you talking about?" Kiram asked, still thinking about the majesty of the mechanism he'd glimpsed. "Who are you talking about?"

"The upperclassmen." Nestor looked at Kiram as if there could have been no other answer. "Scholar Donamillo just said that Master Ignacio had pulled them out of their free hours just to tutor us. They are going to be furious!"

"You don't think that they'd actually hurt us, though?" Even as Kiram asked the question he realized that hurting the two of them was bound to be part of their training. No doubt the more Kiram or Nestor annoyed any given upperclassman, the more often he would seize on the opportunity to train them a little too hard.

"We are bent over a barrel," Nestor said flatly.

Kiram simply nodded. The two of them made their way from the main building to the dark low structure of the sparring house like condemned prisoners.

Chapter Eight

Like the stables, the sparring house seemed suffused with the living presence of its occupants. Here, instead of horse feed and leather, the heat and sweat of men filled the air. The pungent scent saturated the gray mats of the wrestling ring as well as the sawdust-strewn floor. Even with windows all along the length of the gallery propped open, the heat and smell of men remained.

Here and there dark spatters stained the sawdust. He had always wondered if those spatters were blood and felt afraid to touch them. Now that he had some idea of how easy it was to draw blood, he realized that the sawdust was there in the first place to catch the dribbles of gore and keep the floors beneath from becoming stained.

"At least we aren't the only ones," Nestor commented.

Master Ignacio had listed three other second-year students for intensive training. They lounged beside the wrestling ring, standing in the shafts of hard light that fell through the open windows. Kiram knew all of them by sight but not well enough to have any opinion of them as individuals. They moved among the mass of second-year students who snickered at Kiram's accent and squinted at Nestor, mocking his poor vision. They were neither instigators nor protestors, just followers.

All three possessed a blandness of appearance that made them hard to tell apart. Pale, splotchy skin, lank brown hair, long faces and bodies like marionettes with all their weight built up in their jutting joints. None of them were as slender as Kiram or as big as Nestor and all three seemed pained to see that they had been classed with the two of them.

"That's Ladislo in the middle, there." Nestor squinted at the young man, then whispered, "To be honest I can't really see why Procopio bends him. He's not much to look at, is he?"

Kiram tried not to stare at the plain young man. He seemed a little more fine-boned than the other two but otherwise there was nothing exceptional about him.

"Bland," Kiram decided.

"I guess Procopio is just too broke to buy anything better in town."

As they drew closer to the wrestling ring, Ladislo seemed to notice them. He spat into the mass of wood-shavings and sawdust on the floor.

"If I were Procopio, I'd save up." Kiram couldn't keep from making the comment. Nestor gave a soft laugh but then cleared his throat as if he could play it off for a cough.

Kiram and Nestor stopped at the edge of the wrestling ring. Nestor kicked a few wood shavings across the boundary lines painted on the floor. The other three students gazed at the two of them with studied disinterest.

"Is Master Ignacio somewhere around?" Nestor's tone was amiable as always, despite the cold looks he received from all three of the other second-year students.

"He's showing the upperclassmen where the fencing gear is stored and having them bring down medical supplies in case someone puts out his eye." Ladislo looked pointedly at Nestor.

"Did you hear which upperclassmen—" The rest of Nestor's question was interrupted by another of the second-year students—Kiram thought his name was Chilla—jamming his thumb against one nostril and blowing a huge glob a snot out of the other.

"No," Chilla said flatly.

The third boy, Ollivar, glanced uncertainly between Chilla and Nestor. Then he broke from the other two and joined them at the edge of the wrestling ring.

"I think Master Ignacio decided to use our own upperclassmen to tutor us and make sure that it sticks." Ollivar glanced briefly to Kiram, mainly to eye the red scab on his cheek.

"My brother Elezar is your upperclassman, isn't he?" Nestor gave Ollivar an easy smile and Kiram felt a brief shot of annoyance at Nestor's unflagging friendliness. He'd probably smile at a dog after it bit him.

"Yeah," Ollivar replied. "You've got Atreau Vediya, right? What's that like?"

"He's a northerner." Nestor gave a shrug. "He's never cold enough. Dead of winter and he has to have the window propped open. I don't mind, though. I don't get cold easily. None of us Grunitos do."

Ollivar nodded as if this were some kind of sage wisdom. He looked down at his feet and then at Nestor, but he never looked at Kiram. Even when Kiram stepped closer to Nestor, Ollivar simply tilted his head away so that he didn't make eye contact. Kiram wondered if Ollivar, like so many Cadeleonian sailors, believed that the Haldiim cast curses with their pale eyes.

Not for the first time, Kiram wished that he could.

"So, is Elezar tough on you or not?" Nestor asked Ollivar.

"He's fair," Ollivar replied.

Nestor nodded. "He hits hard though, doesn't he?"

"He sure does," Ollivar admitted. He cocked his head to the side slightly, looking Nestor over. "Ladislo got a couple sugar cones from his mother. You want to come over and have one with us?"

Nestor's face brightened at the mention of the candies, but then he looked troubled. "Sure, so long as you've got enough for Kiram and me both."

Ollivar scowled at this.

"If you don't that's fine," Nestor said with a shrug. "Kiram and I don't want to cause a fight between all of you over a couple sugar cones."

"Nobody wants a fight," Ollivar agreed.

“That’s why we have to do this extra training, isn’t it?” Kiram couldn’t keep from making the comment.

Ollivar laughed despite himself and he even met Kiram’s gaze. He seemed to consider Kiram, as if he were an animal that he didn’t quite trust. Then he started back toward Chilla and Ladislo, beckoning them to follow. It was only a matter of crossing a few feet but Kiram knew it signified more.

Ladislo was particularly sullen about handing over his sugar cones, but he did it. Ollivar broke them apart and distributed the cracked pieces of spun sugar amongst the five of them.

As the candy melted over his tongue, Kiram closed his eyes and allowed himself to reminisce about his mother’s candy kitchen, with its smells of bubbling cane sugar and honey and his mother’s floral perfume pervading the atmosphere.

The first mechanism he had built had been for his mother’s candy kitchen. It had been a taffy pulling machine. Whenever she had felt that Kiram was exhausting himself in his studies she had claimed it needed repair and stole him away to her airy sanctum of perfume and sweetness.

Seeing Ladislo’s glum expression, Kiram couldn’t help but feel sorry for him, for having to share a gift from his mother. “Thank you for the sugar cone, Ladislo.”

At first Ladislo seemed taken aback, but then he recovered his bland demeanor. “Mother sends the same cheap candy every few weeks. I’m getting sick of it.”

“It still tastes pretty good.” Nestor sucked the last trace of sugar off of his finger. “Have you ever had one of the Kir-Zaki sugar cones?”

“My father says that the Haldiim defile the water they use for their sweets.” Ladislo stole a glance at Kiram. “He says that they make Cadeleonian men flaccid.”

Nestor laughed out loud at this. “Tell that to my dad. The only two things he can’t get enough of are Kir-Zaki candies and sex. Half the brats in our house are nicknamed for the candy that inspired their conception. All boys so far, too. Mom blames that on the candy as well.”

Kiram wondered if being given credit for Lord Grunito's virility would have pleased or annoyed his mother. Before he could decide he noticed several men coming down the stairs.

He whispered, "Master Ignacio is back."

All five of them went quiet and straightened to attention as Master Ignacio and the upperclassmen approached.

Elezar Grunito was the easiest to recognize. His neck was like a bull's, and his thick chest and bulging shoulders reminded Kiram of a fit war horse. He carried a large wooden trunk easily on one shoulder.

Behind Elezar, Kiram picked out Atreau, Nestor's upperclassman by his long, black, braided hair. He also spotted Cocuyo Helio's whip-thin body and broken cheek. He didn't know the other upperclassman by name, but Nestor quickly provided it.

"The greasy one with the scraggly black beard is Procopio."

Then Kiram realized, with embarrassing disappointment, that his own upperclassman was not present.

Kiram wondered if Master Ignacio would see to his training personally, or if he would be assigned to one of the others. He prayed that it wouldn't be Procopio. From all Nestor had told him, Kiram had no doubt that Procopio would misuse any power granted to him.

Then the far door swung open. Even with the bright sunlight burning his figure to a black silhouette, Kiram still recognized Javier instantly. To his mortification he felt his heartbeat quicken as Javier approached.

His black hair was wet from a recent bath and his shirt clung to his damp skin. His left wrist was bandaged, but it didn't appear to trouble him. He strode to Master Ignacio and bowed deeply. "Forgive my tardiness, sir. I just completed my penance at chapel."

Master Ignacio frowned at Javier. "Your tardiness is not important. However, I am surprised that after last night's behavior a single afternoon of penance would be sufficient to cleanse you of all sin."

"Holy Father Habalan felt it was enough, sir."

"Holy Father Habalan is known for his easy nature, not for his thorough pursuit of the eradication of sin. If you want to remove a stain you don't just give up after a single scrubbing. You know that."

Javier peered up at the war master, seemed to search his face with the pleading expression of an errant child.

When Kiram asked his father for forgiveness, he imagined that he wore the same face. Only he could not imagine his own father returning his gaze with such condemnation.

Finally Javier said, "I will return to chapel directly after this class if it pleases you, sir."

"It does not please me, but it will have to do. I would rather you had not made the mistake in the first place." The war master's gaze flickered to Kiram and then back to Javier. "But since it cannot be taken back it must be bled clean. Tell the Holy Father Habalan I said as much."

"Yes, sir." Javier stood.

Kiram started to open his mouth to object to Javier doing penance at all, when Nestor gripped his arm so hard that Kiram gasped. But he took the hint and kept his complaint to himself.

Javier took his place with the other upperclassmen, and Master Ignacio turned his hard glare back to Kiram and his fellow second-year students. He scowled at them as if they were vermin he had caught raiding his pantry.

"This week the five of you will master the first level of hand-to-hand combat." Master Ignacio's voice boomed through the nearly empty space as if he were addressing an entire class. "And if you do not perform to my complete satisfaction by the end of the week, I swear by God, you and your tutors will suffer. Do you understand me?"

"Yes, sir," Kiram shouted out the response along with the rest of his classmates. Nestor already looked nervous and Kiram noticed that Nestor's upperclassman, Atreau, didn't seem much more confident.

Master Ignacio spun on his heel so that he was facing the upperclassmen.

"Break them, beat them, work them till they vomit. I don't care, but have them trained in the first forms by the end of the week." As he spoke, Master Ignacio shifted his gaze to skewer each individual upperclassman. "Do not disappoint me."

"Yes, sir." The unified shout from the upperclassmen rang with a fervent intensity. Of all five of them, Kiram thought that only Javier looked perfectly assured of his success. Though Elezar's worried glances didn't fall on his own underclassman, Ollivar, but on Nestor.

Master Ignacio continued, "You have two hours before the first years will need this space. Use it wisely. And remember I will hold you responsible for your charges. If you need me I will be riding with the fourth-year students. But I would strongly advise you not to need me."

After Master Ignacio left the sparring house, uncertain silence settled over the vast gallery. The sound of distant voices filtered in through the open windows. Master Ignacio's voice drifted to them from across the courtyard as he called for his horse. The upperclassmen stared at each other in perplexed resignation.

Eventually, Javier said, "By the end of the week Master Ignacio will expect them to know how to hold a stance, drive an attack and fall back. I say we walk them through the motions today and tomorrow. On Mediday we have them fight each other to see what they've learned and what they're still missing."

"Sounds fine to me," Elezar agreed. "Any wagers on which boy will win?"

None of the upperclassmen seemed excited about the prospect. Atreau regarded Elezar as if he might be crazy.

"I think we're already wagering our skins on each of our own underclassmen," Javier replied.

"Fine." Elezar sighed. "But mine's going to beat the crap out of the rest of yours. I'd put money on that." Elezar strode towards Ollivar with such a hard, calculating look on his face that Ollivar took an involuntary step back.

"We'll see," Javier replied.

They paired off and spaced themselves throughout the gallery. Jackets and shirts came off right away. Kiram would have liked to remove his boots as well but he knew Cadeleonians didn't go barefoot unless they were too poor to do otherwise. None of them seemed able to appreciate the feel of the ground beneath their feet.

Kiram stood, waiting for instruction, while Javier gave him the once over. "You've done some kind of training before you came to the academy, haven't you?"

"Not really." Kiram tried not to stare at Javier's exposed body. The bright sunlight accentuated every curve of lean muscle and illuminated his pale skin. The deep cleft of his chest led Kiram's eyes down over his flat stomach to the fine line of hair that rose just above Javier's dark blue pants. Even standing in the light of the midday sun, something nocturnal, almost ghostly, pervaded Javier. Kiram could understand why so many of the other students were hesitant to touch Javier's bare flesh. He seemed too radiant and too dark all at once.

"Not really?" Javier cocked one black brow. "You wouldn't be willing to be a little more precise, would you?"

"I've studied with a dance instructor since I was ten," Kiram offered. He felt suddenly embarrassed of his own slim body and lanky limbs.

"Dance..."

"And I've practiced archery as well," Kiram added quickly.

"It shows in your arms and chest." Javier touched the curve of Kiram's shoulder lightly, hardly brushing his skin. His fingers were dry and unexpectedly cold. "You have an archer's stance. You're certainly not built to be a foot soldier."

"I know." Kiram lowered his head. His failure would mean punishment for Javier as well as himself, and he hated the thought of that. "This isn't going to work, is it?"

"Of course it will work." Javier touched his shoulder again but this time more firmly. "You can't fight the same way the Grunito boys do, but trust me, there are other ways to bring them to their knees." The way Javier smiled and his sensual tone almost made

Kiram flush. "Now stand straight for me. Let me see what Master Ignacio has already taught you."

Kiram squared his shoulders, standing at attention the way he did for Master Ignacio.

"Legs a little farther apart. You want to be as stable as possible. Don't lock your knees." Javier placed his hand lightly on the back of Kiram's knee. "You want to be balanced. Bend into an oncoming impact and still stay on your feet. That means keeping your knees supple and responsive."

Javier lifted his hand to Kiram's chest and pushed him. Kiram stumbled back a step and Javier shook his head.

"You're too stiff. Just relax and let your body respond naturally." Again Javier placed his hand against Kiram's chest and pushed. This time Kiram tried not to tense at the contact. He allowed his weight to drop against Javier's hand. As Javier shoved him, Kiram bent his knees slightly and felt his balance steady.

"Better." Javier pulled his hand back suddenly and Kiram stumbled forward. "But you probably shouldn't actually lean on a combatant."

"Sorry." Kiram straightened.

"Don't be. Normally I wouldn't care if you fell into my arms, but since we're in mixed company..." Javier shoved a lock of his dark hair back from his face. "I'm afraid I really can't take full advantage of the situation."

Kiram's entire face flushed red and Javier laughed. Elezar appeared amused, while Atreau just shook his head. Nestor squinted at Kiram but had obviously missed the entire exchange.

"Try not to get so easily flustered," Javier said. "The boys from the Yillar Academy are going to say a hell of a lot worse things to you during the autumn tournament."

Kiram nodded. He didn't want to tell Javier that the words themselves hadn't flustered him. It had been Javier's intense gaze and the easy way his tone slipped from jovial to sensual. Kiram was sure that the information would only serve to feed Javier's conceit and fuel more of his heartless flirtations.

Kiram resumed the square, Cadeleonian fighting stance.

"Good stance but…" Javier suddenly shoved his hand into Kiram's chest. The strike landed faster and harder than Kiram expected. He stumbled back.

"Still too stiff," Javier finished his criticism.

"Sorry."

"You don't have to apologize. Just concentrate. You need to find your center of balance and maintain it. It won't matter how many maneuvers you master if you can't stay on your feet."

Javier's words reminded Kiram of one of his dance instructor's lectures. She had told him to stay balanced at all times and to remember that the center of his body rested on the edge of his hips. Even during the supplest twist or most exhausting leap he needed to remain centered in his hips. He shifted his stance slightly, disregarding Master Ignacio's insistence on stiff shoulders and squared hips, and slipped into his familiar dancing stance. This time when Javier shoved against his chest, Kiram swiveled aside. Only Javier's fast reflexes kept him from falling forward. Kiram couldn't suppress a pleased grin.

Javier's expression changed as he considered Kiram's new stance. For the first time Javier's study of him was neither playful nor condescending but hard and calculating.

"Let's try that again."

The second time Kiram pivoted aside, Javier twisted with him and then toppled him with a quick shove. Kiram hit the floor.

"You weren't supposed to fall over." Javier frowned down at him.

"Well, what did you expect? You pushed me hard enough." He could feel wood shavings clinging to his back and working down into his pants.

"You looked like you knew what you were doing," Javier said. "You're not actually hurt, are you?"

"No," Kiram admitted.

"Good." Javier grabbed Kiram's hand in a firm grip and pulled him to his feet. "Let's keep working on your stance, then."

Kiram spent the next two hours learning to dodge Javier's rapid strikes. When he successfully evaded, Javier pressed the assaults, harder and faster. Kiram twisted out of reach only to have Javier trip his legs out from under him.

Despite the constant falls, there were moments of triumph. At least once during each exchange, Kiram moved fast enough to evade six strikes in a row. The two of them circled and spun as if they were dancing until, inevitably, Javier overtook him and brought him down.

By the end of the lesson, sweat and sawdust caked Kiram's body. His dark blue pants were strewn with wood shavings. As he wiped away the sawdust clinging to his knees, large clumps of it fell from his curling hair. Javier brushed off Kiram's back.

"You did well." Javier hardly seemed to have broken a sweat. "Better than I would have expected, to be honest."

Giddy from exhaustion, Kiram grinned at the compliment.

"Not much of a fighter's body, but you have the right spirit." Javier paused, mulling something over. "If nothing else you're tenacious. In a real fight sometimes that makes all the difference."

Even if he hadn't fully mastered a balanced stance, Kiram felt certain that he had learned something more integral to combat. It was just what Javier had said. Combat demanded dogged persistence, of both his body and spirit. More than once he had been tempted to remain on the floor after Javier knocked him down, but his pride had not allowed it and now he was glad.

As exhausted and bruised as he was, he was standing at the ready, meeting Javier's approving gaze with a tired grin. He wasn't lying on the floor gasping like Ollivar, or crouching with his hands wrapped around his ankles as Ladislo was. Nor did he feel as miserable as both Nestor and Chilla appeared. Chilla sported a large red scrape across his forehead. Beads of perspiration dripped from Nestor's hooked nose; his chest and back were red and slick with sweat.

Elezar opened up the wooden trunk he'd brought with him earlier and tossed a roll of bandages to Chilla and Ladislo. He dropped a small towel over Nestor's head.

"Wipe up," Elezar said gruffly.

Nestor wiped the sweat from his face and then flopped back onto the mats of the wrestling ring.

"At lunch this afternoon," Javier interrupted Kiram's contemplation of Nestor, "I think you and Nestor should sit with Elezar."

"What? Why?" Kiram asked.

"The two of you look too vulnerable out there with the first-year brats." Javier briefly frowned at the back of Procopio's head as the young man stood over Ladislo. "You should be sitting nearer to your upperclassmen."

"Elezar isn't my upperclassman," Kiram pointed out.

"No, but he's my friend and he'll look after you while I'm at chapel."

Kiram couldn't keep from scowling at the mention of chapel. "Why are you suddenly doing all these things for me? I mean, taking penance and this sudden interest in my wellbeing?"

Javier shrugged and offered Kiram a sharp smile.

"I might be thinking of taking Elezar up on his wager. I could make a pretty sum if I can keep you in one piece during the tournament."

Kiram gave Javier a sour glare, but his upperclassman didn't seem at all concerned. He picked up his shirt and light jacket.

"I'll see you after I'm done at chapel. Remember what I told you. Take your lunch with Elezar."

Chapter Nine

An hour later when the school bells rang out the lunch break, Kiram followed Nestor to the third table beneath the arching windows of the eastern wall of the dining hall. Nestor was overjoyed at the invitation.

"The higher tables get the better servings, you know. And every Sacreday they receive wine and sweet cherries." Nestor beamed as he seated himself across from Elezar.

Elezar acknowledged his younger brother with a quick, affectionate wink and then continued to speculate with Atreau about which of the horses were the best jumpers.

"Lunaluz has endurance. On the long course there is no way Llama can beat him. That's where I'm putting my money."

Atreau seemed about to reply but then his eyes flicked to Kiram.

Elezar looked as well and frowned. "Don't just stand there like a knee-less moron. Sit."

"What about Fedeles? Shouldn't someone sit with him?" Kiram stepped back from the table. "I think I should wait for him with the first-year students."

"Fedeles is none of your concern. He sits where he wants, with whomever he wants," Elezar stated. "You, on the other hand, will sit where you've been told to sit, Underclassman."

"I am not your—"

Nestor jerked Kiram down onto the bench beside him.

"Fedeles is eating up in his room today, and we'll get better food here anyway," Nestor said quickly. Then, to Elezar, "It's fine. Really. Kiram and I are happy to eat with you. Thanks for the invitation."

"That's good to hear." Elezar eyed Kiram suspiciously. "Because I'd hate to think to that Javier's underclassman is some kind of ungrateful runt who'd insult his generosity."

"No, no, it's nothing like that. We're both honored and thankful for the chance to dine with the older students." Nestor bumped Kiram's leg under the table.

Kiram knew he was behaving badly and a little pointlessly as well. It was Javier who he wanted to argue with, not Elezar. As it was, he was only aggravating Elezar, worrying Nestor, and living down to the Haldiim reputation for rudeness.

"I don't mean to seem ungrateful." Kiram bowed his head politely. "I had assumed that Upperclassman Javier would want me to remain with Fedeles. But since he's dining privately I would be honored to accept the invitation to your table. Thank you, Upperclassman Elezar."

"Well, that was prettily said," Atreau commented with a smile.

"Pretty indeed. I guess your friend has some manners after all, Nestor." Elezar tossed a copper coin to Nestor and gave him another conspiratorial wink. Nestor beamed as he stuffed the coin into his jacket pocket.

Kiram felt almost as if he should take a bow, like some kind of stage performer. Instead he accepted a glass of lemon water from a servant.

Elezar returned to his conversation with Atreau. Other third- and fourth-year students took their seats at the table, adding their opinions to Elezar's speculations on the upcoming tournament. Nestor watched their interaction with fascination, now and then pushing his spectacles up higher on his sharp nose.

Kiram watched them as well. He had seen all of these students before, though he knew very few of their names. They were the young men he always saw lounging around Javier, laughing at his jokes and marveling at his tricks. None of them seemed to take more than a moment's interest in either himself or Nestor. They made wagers with Elezar or chatted among themselves, grumbling about mathematics and law classes.

Nestor pressed closer to Kiram as a last upperclassman squeezed in on his left. With both Nestor and himself added to the table, the seating was tight, but Kiram noticed that no one took the space to Elezar's left, where Javier usually sat.

Kiram wondered if the place was left empty out of respect for Javier or fear of him.

"Elezar," a freckled young man called from the far end of the table. "Who's that with your brother? Is it Javier's brilliant Haldiim?"

Kiram felt his face flush but he wasn't sure if it was due to being called Javier's or brilliant.

"It is, indeed," Elezar replied. "Second-Year Underclassman Kiram Kir-Zaki."

The freckled upperclassman narrowed his gaze at Kiram. "So, are you really the genius Scholar Donamillo claims you are, or did Haldiim seduction get you into the academy?"

Kiram gripped his glass, barely suppressing the urge to hurl it at the freckled upperclassman.

"He won the Silver Leaf Challenge last year, and he's already beaten both your best scores in Scholar Blasio's class, Morisio, so I'd put my money on him being a genius," Elezar replied before Kiram could respond. "You're just going to have to accept that Master Donamillo has found a new favorite."

"Jealousy is so unbecoming in a gentleman," Atreau commented. The freckled upperclassman went scarlet but said nothing. He drank a little of his water and kept his eyes averted. Kiram was astounded. Both Elezar and Atreau had come to his defense without hesitation. He wanted to thank them but neither of them seemed to think anything of the interaction. They were already back to discussing shield designs and the newest black barrel cannons.

Javier had said that Elezar would protect him but somehow Kiram hadn't imagined that it would be from his own peers. Kiram was suddenly glad that he'd come to the third table. For the first time he had a hope that he might one day belong in the academy.

For the rest of the meal, he and Nestor quietly exchanged comments on the superior quality of the bread and stew served at the high tables. Slices of soft golden cheese were served along with fresh apples and pears. Nestor looked like he might weep from joy as he devoured the fruit.

Kiram enjoyed the food as well but he found himself glancing to the door from time to time, wondering when Javier would return from chapel.

After lunch and through his afternoon classes, the thought lingered with Kiram. Between art and history he dashed back up to their shared room, but there was no sign that Javier had been there.

How long could his penance last? Terrible images of ruined flesh rushed into his mind and Kiram's worry increased.

When he and Nestor took dinner at the third table with the upperclassmen, Genimo and Fedeles were there as well. Fedeles sang the names of his favorite horses and leaned against Kiram. Genimo sat at the opposite end of the table. The place at Elezar's left was once again left vacant.

Kiram hardly noticed his meal. Nestor pointed out that this was the first time that he could recognize the cuts of meat on his plate. The pork and apples were followed by a course of cheese and bread. Kiram chewed without really tasting anything.

He couldn't help but notice that Elezar also stole glances at the door as if he, too, worried over Javier's long absence. After dinner Elezar stepped up next to Kiram.

"If he isn't back by dark come get me," Elezar whispered. Then he strode away to join Atreau and the other upperclassmen for an evening ride.

Kiram went to his room to work on his history paper while he waited. He managed to write a string of obscenities about Nazario Sagrada, also known as Nazario the Impaler, Scourge of the Haldiim. He couldn't concentrate. He paced past the windows relentlessly. Outside the blue sky turned golden as the sun burned over the horizon. He suddenly thought that he'd been doing the same thing last night, pacing and waiting for Javier. And Javier had not come.

Kiram gave up on waiting. He headed downstairs and across the academy grounds toward the chapel.

A high wrought iron fence surrounded the ornate building. Small, flowering trees and rose bushes filled the inner courtyard. Deep gold light flashed off the glittering stained glass windows of the sanctuary building.

Kiram peered over the wall and then very cautiously swung the wrought iron gate open. He was forbidden from entering the chapel, but he tried to assure himself that the courtyard might be a different matter.

Still, his heart pounded wildly as he stepped on Cadeleonian holy ground. He crept from shadow to shadow, slowly circling the perimeter fence, searching for any sign of Javier.

Kiram found him lying under a pear tree. His white skin shone like moonlight from the shadows of the tree. His eyes were clenched closed and dark blood pooled around his outstretched arm.

Chapter Ten

Panic bolted through Kiram, scattering his thoughts in a dozen different directions. A stream of blood still trickled down from Javier's wrist. Kiram had no idea what to do.

Only the memory of his physician uncle's battlefield stories gave Kiram any direction. He whipped off his jacket and dropped down beside Javier. As he wrapped the sleeve of his jacket around Javier's arm he noticed that there were already bandages swathing his wrist. Javier's dark red blood soaked through them.

Kiram knotted the sleeve of his jacket just above Javier's elbow and twisted it tight to form a tourniquet. He should have used some kind of stick to twist the knot even tighter. Kiram was sure his uncle had mentioned using a stick, but Kiram didn't dare let go of the jacket now. He held the thin cloth in place, applying pressure to the wound.

His uncle always said to apply pressure. Kiram wracked his memory for anything else. Raise the limb above the body; slow the flow of blood from the heart to the wound. Kiram lifted Javier's limp arm up onto his lap.

This was what his uncle would have done, wasn't it? Kiram couldn't remember his uncle ever saying he'd used a jacket sleeve for a tourniquet.

Nor had he ever mentioned how hot fresh blood felt or how pungent it smelled. He had not told Kiram that a man's mouth could turn ice blue from blood loss or that his taut muscles would loosen and hang like slabs of cold meat. Javier's chest didn't rise or fall.

Kiram felt suddenly, sickeningly sure that Javier was dead. Something between a wail and a sob clenched Kiram's throat but he couldn't get the sound out. He couldn't even pull in a breath. Every muscle of his body seemed to clench and shake.

Then Javier opened his eyes. He looked at Kiram and forced a slow smile, as if his own death were a joke.

"Well, if it isn't Kiram Kir-Zaki. What are you doing here?"

"I came to find you." Kiram could barely gather his thoughts to speak. He was relieved that Javier was alive but almost unable to credit it. "You were—you looked like you were dead."

"Yes, I do that from time to time." Javier's laugh emerged as a dry rasp. He closed his eyes and, as if it took all his concentration, drew in a slow breath.

Faint color returned to Javier's lips, though his skin still felt cold. A living tension slowly spread through the muscles of Javier's body.

Blood clung to Kiram's fingers like hide-glue. He tried to wipe his hands on his pants but they wouldn't come clean. "There's so much blood."

"Muerate poison keeps wounds open. It can be a little messy…"

"You weren't moving." Kiram found the quaver in his own voice disturbing. He shouldn't have been this upset. Javier was alive and he seemed to be recovering his strength. But the thought of his death, the sensation of his limp body, and heat of his blood had been burned into Kiram's mind. Never in his life had he been so close to someone dying. It had seemed so immense and terrible and he had been so utterly helpless to stop it. Now he couldn't believe that Javier was alive, staring up at him and carrying on a conversation as if this were a trivial matter.

"I think Scholar Donamillo must have administered a little too much of the poison before Holy Father Habalan bled me." Javier sounded disinterested. "I can't feel my left hand."

"I tied a tourniquet around your elbow to slow the bleeding," Kiram said. For the first time he noticed little tremors moving beneath the blood-soaked bandages. Then he saw a tiny white spark skip over the mass of cloth.

"Take it off, will you? I don't think it's doing any good now." Javier tried to sit up but then slumped back down against Kiram's thighs, muttering, "Damn."

Kiram worked the knots loose and slowly unwrapped his jacket from around Javier's elbow. He watched Javier's wrist closely, fearing a sudden gush of blood. Instead more white sparks danced through the bandages. Javier's fingers twitched minutely.

"You're not supposed to be on chapel grounds," Javier said as if he had just realized where they were.

"No one said anything about the grounds, just the chapel." Kiram folded his jacket, to hide the bloody sleeve. His hands still trembled. He wished he could make them stop.

"I'm not certain that the holy father would be sympathetic to that argument. And honestly, as exciting as this illicit meeting in the garden is, I think it might be getting a little late." Javier frowned up through the branches of the pear tree at the darkening sky. "We should get back to the dormitory."

"You need to see a physician. Scholar Donamillo—"

Javier shook his head. "Scholar Donamillo is hardly as entertaining as you are."

"Entertaining?" The word was an utter anathema to everything that Kiram felt. "I thought you were dying."

"Really?" Javier gave Kiram one of his sensual, mocking smiles. "Were you scared for me?"

"Of course I was, you ferret-faced moron!"

"Ferret-faced? Such harsh language on holy ground, Kiram."

"How can you laugh?" Kiram hissed. "I thought you were going to die. I was terrified for you and you—you're just an utter pig."

Kiram was horrified to feel tears welling up in his eyes. His vision blurred. He stood quickly and turned his back so that Javier would not see.

"Kiram," Javier said gently, as if he were addressing a child. "I'm sorry."

"No, you aren't." Kiram wiped his face angrily. "You're amused. You think it's all just some huge joke. But it's not. You were ice cold and there was so much blood and I—I really thought—I—" Kiram hated the way his voice broke. He sucked in a deep breath of air and refused to look at Javier. He didn't think he could bear the sight of another of his satirical grins.

"Obviously you're just fine now." Kiram kept his tone as cold as he could. "So I'll be going."

"Don't," Javier said, but Kiram didn't stop. He stormed through the trees as if he didn't care who saw him. He wouldn't let Javier laugh at him creeping from shadow to shadow.

The sweet scent of night jasmine floated over Kiram as he followed the winding path through the grounds. The air felt thick, like it might rain soon. Deep shadows filled the overhanging branches of fruit trees but thin rays of light still shone through the wrought iron bars of the gate. Kiram pulled it open.

"Kiram, damn it, slow down!" Javier's voice was closer than Kiram expected and far more strained. Despite himself, Kiram turned back.

Javier stood a few feet away, leaning heavily against the thin trunk of a plum tree. His breathing came in slow deep gasps. A sheen of sweat covered his face.

"You left your coat." Javier gripped the stained blue jacket in his right hand.

"I can't believe you." Kiram returned to Javier. "You can barely walk."

"I could manage a hell of a crawl, though." Javier closed his eyes and bowed his head back against the smooth trunk of the tree. "Will you just put up with me, Kiram? I need your help."

"You're an ass," Kiram said, but he couldn't summon any real anger. Javier already had his sympathy. It embarrassed Kiram to be so easily won back. "Fine, but I'm just repaying you for what you did yesterday."

He ducked under Javier's right arm, taking half of his weight. Javier leaned against him. The scent of blood overpowered the jasmine in the air. He wrapped his arm around Javier's waist and helped him out through the gate.

"I'm taking you to the infirmary," Kiram said flatly.

"Please don't," Javier whispered, and there was nothing seductive or laughing in his tone. He sounded so desolate that it reminded Kiram of Fedeles. "I don't think I could endure Scholar Donamillo tinkering with me like I'm one of his mechanisms. Not today." He bowed his head against Kiram's neck.

"You need a physician."

"I don't, I swear. I've done this a thousand times. I just need time. The white hell will heal me." Javier straightened a little as if to prove that he was already recovering. Kiram could feel the strain trembling through Javier's muscles.

"Fine, we'll go to our room. But if you haven't recovered your strength by the time the warden calls last roll I'm going to summon Scholar Donamillo up to see you."

Through the twilight Kiram picked out the distant shapes of several students lounging in front of the dormitory. Farther across the grounds he thought he could see the shadows of riders returning to the stables. He thought he recognized Elezar among them.

At the sight of the riders, Javier changed course, so that he was facing into the deep shadows of the school orchards. "We can circle around to the back of the dormitory. There's a pulley lift near the scullery. We can use it to get up to the tower rooms without climbing the stairs."

"Why don't I just go get Elezar?" Kiram suggested.

"No." Javier shook his head. "I don't want the other students to see me like this. Not even Elezar."

Kiram studied the footpath that skirted the perimeter of the orchard and then disappeared behind the dormitory. Remnants of an old wall jutted up in places and Kiram supposed Javier could rest against one of them if he needed to.

Kiram took as much of Javier's weight as he could and they walked slowly. Kiram heard calls echoing through the trees and Javier told him it was a red owl calling for its mate.

As they moved on, Kiram felt heat returning to Javier's body. By the time they had reached the cider shed, Javier was standing straight and moving easily. He kept his arm wrapped around Kiram, and Kiram held his waist, feeling the muscles of his hips flex and relax beneath his fingers.

"So what kind of bow do you use?" Javier's tone was unconcerned and Kiram thought that the question had probably been chosen simply for the sake of conversation. It still surprised Kiram slightly, if only because it seemed like days since he had told Javier that he practiced archery.

"My favorite is a short compound bow that my uncle Rafie brought back from the Yuan kingdom."

"Yuan?" Javier's brows lifted. "That's a long way to travel for a bow."

"His partner is a Bahiim." As always Kiram felt a twinge of embarrassment at the disclosure that his uncle's partner was a religious zealot who talked to trees, but then he realized that Javier probably didn't know much, if anything, about the Bahiim. "They traveled a lot when they were both younger. Now they've settled down in Anacleto."

They passed between the shadows of overhanging tree branches and shafts of dull gold sunlight. When the warm light fell across him, Javier's white skin looked as if it had been gilded.

"What kind of business does he do? Your uncle, I mean?"

"He's a physician."

"So, he and his business partner traveled to Yuan just to practice medicine?" Javier raised a black brow; his expression was slightly teasing. "You're sure they weren't smuggling Sueno root?"

"I'm sure." Kiram smiled at the thought of his fastidious uncle Rafie keeping company with smugglers and addicts. He'd be scrubbing them down in hot baths in a matter of minutes. "My grandmother would probably have been happier if Uncle Rafie had chosen to follow a smuggler to Yuan. At least the rest of the family wouldn't have thought she raised a religious fanatic."

"So they went as missionaries?"

"Not exactly. They were invited by a merchant's family to lift a curse from the household." Kiram sighed, knowing that he would have to explain. "His partner, Alizadeh, is a Bahiim, a priest of the old church. The Bahiim battle curses and put ghosts to rest and I don't know…talk to trees and things like that. My parents think Alizadeh's a lunatic, but he's always been kind to me and he's quite charming."

Javier stared at Kiram as if he couldn't quite put all of Kiram's words together in any way that made sense.

"So, this man, Alizadeh, your uncle's…"

"Partner," Kiram provided. It was the word Haldiim always used when speaking in the company of Cadeleonians. It sounded businesslike and Cadeleonians easily accepted two men uniting their houses if it was for the sake of profit.

"His partner," Javier repeated, "is a kind of exorcist?"

Kiram shrugged. "Something like that."

"A Bahiim." Javier seemed to consider this for a few moments, then he asked, "So when he went to Yuan, did he lift the curse?" Javier's casual level of interest seemed to have risen.

"There was none," Kiram replied. "A store of grain had gone foul and mistakenly been used to make a medical poultice. My uncle figured it out, destroyed the poultice, treated the victims, and that was that."

They reached the iron gate enclosing the low beds of the kitchen garden. Javier placed his bloodstained left hand against the lock. Kiram heard a slight crackling noise then the solid clunk of a bolt sliding back.

"You don't believe in curses, do you?" Javier shrugged out of Kiram's grasp and pushed the gate open. Kiram felt strangely aware of where Javier's body had pressed against his own and the absence felt wrong.

"I believe in the possibility of curses," Kiram allowed. "But it seems like there are usually better explanations for why things go wrong."

"Fouled grain or just plain bad luck?"

Kiram nodded cautiously. Something in Javier's tone put him on edge. It was the seriousness of it, Kiram realized.

Javier closed the garden gate behind them and laid his hand up against the lock again. This time Kiram saw white sparks skip from his fingers to the metal.

"It's not as though I don't believe in powers," Kiram said quickly. The last few weeks living with Javier had led him to believe in shajdi powers more than he ever had before. But meeting Javier hadn't stopped Kiram from applying reason. "When it comes to things like curses and deviltry, people make accusations too easily. They use curses to justify their prejudices."

"Are you thinking of King Nazario?" Javier glanced over his shoulder at Kiram. "That was a long time ago."

"It was, but things haven't changed so much. Even now if a Cadeleonian is well connected he can accuse any Haldiim of cursing his fields and have the Haldiim stripped of his property and imprisoned."

The gate locked with another deep click. Javier turned to face Kiram. He looked thoughtful but not offended. "That's true, but these days, even in northern counties, there has to be a trial."

"Of course. But all the evidence is just gossip about evil glances and angry insults. If it were a trial over a robbery, the judges would at least know what theft was or how it occurred. But no one even tries to question what a curse really is. How does it function? Can one be created by pure chance or does it require will and direction? People hear the words, curse or demon or devil and they simply throw aside all their powers of logic and reason."

"And you think reason can be applied to a curse?"

"Yes." Kiram forced himself to meet Javier's dark gaze. "Without reason there is only fear and folly."

"Well spoken." To Kiram's surprise Javier's smile was genuinely warm. "That from Bishop Seferino, wasn't it?"

Kiram nodded.

Javier said, "He's an excellent source for closing quotes. I used him for a speech last week, in fact."

He strolled between the beds of summer vegetables and Kiram followed alongside him. Yellow light glowed from the windows of the dormitory and Kiram could hear the faint sounds of some student practicing scales on a harpsichord.

"The law must not fall across the back of the common man as a flail, having no purpose but to punish," Javier recited smoothly. "Instead, it should enfold him as a cloak, which comforts and keeps the cruelest elements at bay."

Kiram glanced to Javier. He looked so relaxed. It was hard to believe that less than an hour ago he had been lying like a corpse in his arms.

"I've never heard that quote before," Kiram said at last.

"It's one of Bishop Seferino's more obscure statements." Javier smiled and Kiram could see that he was pleased with himself. "I found it in a treatise called *Concerning Natural and Unnatural Ardor*. A little more racy than the bishop's more popular works but not without its charms. I should lend it to you sometime."

"I'd like that," Kiram replied.

Javier reached out and casually brushed his hand through a curl of Kiram's hair. His fingertips just traced the curve of Kiram's neck. The sensation rushed over Kiram, making his breath catch and his heartbeat quicken.

"Leaves in your hair," Javier said. "Those curls of yours really hold onto things, don't they? They're like gold vines."

Kiram flushed and looked down at the beds of pumpkins and squash.

"I should get it cut," Kiram said.

"No, this length suits you. Lends you an air of a creature that has not yet been tamed. I'm sure Master Ignacio hates it." When Kiram glanced up to see his expression he realized that Javier wasn't even looking at him. Instead, his eyes focused on the dormitory.

Three windows on the first floor had been propped open. The oil lamps inside lit the room perfectly. It had to be one of the kitchens. Large tables stretched across one wall, while two big ovens occupied another. Two men pulled racks of small pastries from the ovens and spread them across wire racks to cool.

The smell of butter and warm bread wafted on the air and slowly curled around Kiram.

"I'm starving," Javier said.

"We could ask for something for you to eat. I'm sure they'd understand if they knew you missed dinner."

"I'd rather not have to tell my sad story to a room full of servants. Particularly not ones who will just panic at the sight of me and then spend the whole night washing down all the vegetation with blessed waters to purge it of my demonic influence." Javier gestured at the bowing vines of dark green gourds. "Who knows what accursed dishes could arise if the squash were infected by a hellfire?"

"You know," Kiram said, "sometimes you don't sound like you believe in the white hell yourself."

"Oh, I believe, but I also know it can't be caught like a cold. It takes much more than that." Javier returned his gaze to the kitchen windows. "They're putting pies out on the sill to cool. Surely that is a sign from heaven."

"I doubt it."

"Of course you do. You doubt everything." Javier turned back to Kiram and gave him a look of serious consideration. "But I think if you truly searched your heart, you would find that you want me to have one of those pies as much as I want me to have one."

Kiram had to suppress a laugh at Javier's mocking tone of piety. He really did sound like some priest. He even held his hands up in just the perfect manner.

"Fine," Kiram agreed, "but if we're caught…"

"I will take full responsibility," Javier assured him. "You just curl up like a little pill bug and roll under a cabbage or something."

"I'm sure no one would take the slightest note of that."

"Probably not if they saw me first," Javier murmured. "All right. Once I get close to the window, the light will make me too easy to see. I'll have to stay down below the line of the window, so I won't be able to see what the cooks are doing. You'll need to watch them for me. When they both have their backs to the window, give me the sign to advance." Javier glanced to Kiram and clearly saw his confusion. "Hold your right hand up at a right angle to your body."

Kiram held his right arm out.

"Just like that." Javier gave him a pleased smile. "If they start to turn then warn me with your left hand. Got it?"

"Right hand: advance. Left hand: retreat."

"Good. I'm counting on you."

"But wait, if you will be able see me from the window, won't the cooks be able to do the same?"

"They won't be looking for you. People almost never see what they're not expecting."

Before Kiram could point out the flaw in that logic, Javier was away.

For a man as tall as he was, Javier folded himself down into a surprisingly low crouch. As he moved, his dark form melted into the silhouettes of rosemary shrubs and chamomile flowers. He slunk across the grounds and slid against the wall of the dormitory. He crouched just below an open windowsill like a cat beneath a birdbath.

Kiram watched the cooks inside the kitchen intently. For a while he felt that they might never turn their backs to the windows at the same time. He wondered if their behavior could be purposeful, a defense intended to keep pilfering students at bay. Maybe the pies were placed out on the windowsill as some kind of trap?

Surges of nervous energy played through his muscles, preparing him for sudden flight.

Thinking reasonably, Kiram could see that the men were simply assembling ingredients. He'd watched his mother's cook often enough to recognize the hurried movements from one cupboard to another. A minute later both cooks had heaps of flour, dry goods, and a large bowl of eggs gathered on the long work table. Both of them turned their backs to Kiram as they mixed and kneaded large masses of dough.

Kiram lifted his right arm immediately, expecting Javier to spring into action at once, but apparently Javier shared none of his nervous urgency. Very slowly, Javier snaked his bandaged left arm up over the edge of the windowsill into the blazing lamplight. His long fingers curled rim of a pie tin and slid it off the sill in a single fluid movement.

Kiram waited for Javier to bolt back to his side. Instead, Javier reached up and took a second pie. Kiram stared at Javier in disbelief. The cooks were sure to notice two entire pies missing.

One of the cooks turned and wiped his face with the back of his hand. Kiram instantly lifted his left hand and Javier stilled. The cook sneezed and snuffled and then turned back to rolling out long sheets of dough.

Kiram raised his right hand. He squinted hard into the darkness and then almost shouted out when Javier suddenly rose up from the shadows of the pumpkin leaves just beside him.

"Here, this one is yours." Javier held out one of the pies. "The tin is still hot so use the cuff of your jacket to hold it."

"I didn't want one," Kiram said, but he still took the pie carefully. Even with his jacket protecting his hand, the metal was almost too hot to hold.

"The pulley lift is just a little further. Come on." Javier started towards a small shed built up against the west wall of the dormitory.

The savory scent of meat and mushrooms rose up off the pie. He'd never been served anything this nice in the dining hall, nor could he imagine the cooks making enough meat pies to satisfy a hundred hungry students. He wondered if the pies had been intended for the scholars or the war master.

If so, Kiram sincerely hoped that he was stealing Master Ignacio's breakfast.

Once inside the shed, Kiram realized that it had no roof. Instead, a series of pulleys and heavy chains dangled down from the third floor.

"There's a trap door up there. Scholar Donamillo has the staff haul his mechanisms up there with this." Javier sat down, carefully placing his pie to his right side. He gave the pulley chains a tired look. "How strong are you feeling?"

"I doubt I could haul us both." Kiram paused as he studied the pulleys more closely as well as the shadowy shapes of gears, high above him. "You ass. This is a gear lift. An infant could haul us up so long as the counterweight was properly set. Is it?"

Javier sighed. "Yes. I should have known you'd know what it was right away."

"Of course." Kiram set his own pie down beside Javier's and then located counterweight release. He couldn't see them clearly in the gloom but his hands knew them by feel.

"I helped my father build two gear lifts when I was fifteen." Kiram gently eased the release open. The hand crank turned smoothly. Someone took good care of the mechanism. The chains whirred as the counterweight slowly descended, causing floor beneath them to rise. The lift was surprisingly quiet and Kiram couldn't help but admire its creator. He wished that he had a lamp so that he could examine its engineering more closely. He glanced back to Javier. "How heavy is the counterweight?"

"Heavy. I've cranked it back up by myself before, but it's damn hard work."

"It shouldn't be. A gear lift this well built shouldn't be hard to reset," Kiram thought aloud. "Are you sure you had it in the correct gear when you cranked the counterweight back up?"

"I believe that my ignorance about the lift even possessing different gears is all the answer you need," Javier confessed and Kiram smiled at his honesty.

They rose to the underside of an overhang below the third floor of the dormitory. Javier worked the trapdoor above them open. He hefted himself up into the darkness inside the dormitory.

A second later he lowered an iron rung ladder. Kiram handed up the pies and then climbed blindly up into the pitch blackness. The floor beneath him felt like solid stone. The stagnant air smelled of machine oil.

He heard Javier close the trap door. Then a flicker of pure white light flashed up, momentarily illuminating Javier's raised left hand as well as the rows of machinery surrounding them. The light died and then flared back up, flickering across several huge, faceted, glass spheres. Slowly, the light in Javier's hand steadied to a dim, undulating flame.

They were in a windowless store room. Most of the space was neatly packed with the pieces of mechanical cures. They looked old and broken down. Spatters of rust etched the arching iron ribs. Many of the glass panes that made up the enormous spheres looked chipped. Some were blackened, as if coated with soot. Kiram could barely discern the shadows of the leather harnesses and wires hanging inside the spheres.

"The counterweight is here." Javier held his hand over the lift gears mounted in the store room floor. His expression was intent and Kiram imagined that it took a great deal of his concentration to maintain the even glowing light that danced over his palm.

Kiram worked quickly, shifting the gears and then cranking the counterweight back up into its housing.

"Done," Kiram said at last.

"Good." Javier crouched down at the heavy iron base of one of the mechanical cures and the light in his hand guttered out. Total blackness enveloped Kiram again.

"Are you all right?" Kiram asked.

"Fine," Javier replied. "Just catching my breath."

Kiram sat down to wait. A minute passed and the silence began to worry Kiram. He wondered if Javier really was well. Could he have collapsed again?

"Javier?"

"Yes?" Javier's voice was strong and relaxed. Kiram felt foolish for worrying. "What is it?" Javier asked after a moment.

"Oh," Kiram said, and then a genuine curiosity came to him. "I was just wondering if you've ever been in one of these mechanical cures?"

"Once. My first year here Scholar Donamillo wanted to test one on me."

"What was it like?" Kiram couldn't imagine being strapped into one of the huge contraptions. As much as he loved mechanisms the mechanical cures unnerved him.

"It was much like a catastrophe," Javier sounded amused. "Scholar Donamillo buckled me into the harness and closed the orb and then just when he had cranked the handle fast enough to begin building a current the glass blew out. It blackened and shattered. Then the iron supports broke apart. I think the remains are up here somewhere."

"You weren't hurt?"

"Not badly. But I'd rather not ever do it again."

Kiram couldn't help but remember Fedeles' howls and the mechanical cure in the infirmary.

"What do you think it does to him?" Kiram asked and then he realized that Javier couldn't know who he was talking about. "I mean Fedeles. How does the mechanical cure help him?"

Javier said nothing for a long while and Kiram realized that the subject was probably too close for Javier to talk about. He wished he could take the question back.

"It eases his suffering a little." Javier's voice was soft and humorless. "The treatments exchange one kind of madness for another. He isn't terrified or screaming after the treatments but he isn't well either. The mechanical cure makes him happy, but it can't lift the curse. Holy Father Habalan is certain that it's helping to protect him from being consumed, though, so I suppose it's worth it."

"He was cursed? Nest—someone said that the white hell attacked him."

"People say a lot of things. But they don't know shit about the white hell or the Tornesal curse. They don't know shit!" Javier almost spat the last word.

"I'm sorry. It's none of my business. I shouldn't have asked—"

"No, it's not your fault. People start rumors. They know we Tornesals are linked to the white hell by our bloodline and so they assume that it is the cause of all our infamy and misfortune. But it wasn't the white hell that attacked Fedeles or killed my father. The white hell is in me and I would have known if it had touched either of them. Something else attacked them. I don't know what, but I've felt it. I..." Javier was silent for several moments, then sighed heavily. "I'm too hungry and tired to talk about this, that's what I am."

"Do you think you're rested enough to make it to our room?" Kiram asked.

"I've been fine for a while. I was just stalling for time to remember where I put our pies."

Kiram laughed, mostly out of relief to hear a note of humor return to Javier's voice.

Once they located the pies, the two of them raced through the narrow tower halls to their room.

They washed their hands and faces together but Kiram left the bathroom when Javier began to strip off his clothes. While Javier bathed Kiram found a knife and sliced his pie into quarters. When he made an experimental slice in the pie Javier had been carrying he discovered that it was filled with cherries. If they shared, they'd both have a decent meal.

Javier returned from the bathroom wearing his dark blue dressing robe. He looked exhausted but clean. He brushed a wet lock of his black hair back from his face and Kiram caught a glimpse of his left wrist. The wound had closed, leaving that same raw red scar that Kiram remembered seeing the very first day he had met Javier. If he did regular penance then that wound must have been opened over and over again. It must never really heal. Disgust curled through Kiram at the sheer barbarity of the Cadeleonians, but he hid it when Javier pulled a chair up to Kiram's desk in order to inspect the pies.

"We're going to have to eat with our hands, you know," Javier said after a moment.

Kiram shrugged.

They ate messily, sitting side by side, grabbing handfuls of pie and licking gravy and cherry filling from their fingers. Kiram's mother would have been horrified. Actually he couldn't think of many civilized people who wouldn't have been appalled at the sight of the two of them.

When Javier leaned over and sucked a blob of cherry off of Kiram's thumb the action seemed innocent and indecent at once.

"How do I taste, Lord Tornesal?"

"I think I would need another sample to form an opinion."

There was a moment, with Javier so close, that Kiram almost leaned into him, almost kissed his mouth.

Then the night warden's voice boomed through the quiet hallway. He pounded on the door and both Javier and Kiram bolted apart.

The warden pushed the door open and peered in. Kiram shouted out a little too loudly in response to his name. Javier simply rolled his eyes and glared at the old man.

"Lights out," the night warden snapped, then slammed the door closed.

Kiram's heart hammered. What had he nearly done?

He was no longer in the Haldiim district of Anacleto. He wasn't in the company of the young men he had grown up with. He was in the very midst of a Cadeleonian institution with a man who he hardly knew and certainly didn't trust.

He wanted to believe that Javier felt something for him, that Javier was somehow immune to the hatred and prejudice of his society, but he couldn't be sure. From what he did know of Javier, he would be as likely to laugh at Kiram as to kiss him. Either way he would probably confess everything when he attended chapel. That could get Kiram thrown out of the academy or worse, put on trial for corrupting a Cadeleonian.

Kiram stood quickly. "I should wash my hands."

Javier stared at him for a moment and then simply bowed his head.

"Scrub hard and use lots of cold water. You don't want the cleaning women wondering how your sheets got so sticky," Javier called after him.

When Kiram returned from his bath, Javier was already in his own bed, feigning sleep. Kiram wished him goodnight but wasn't surprised when Javier said nothing in response.

Chapter Eleven

It took Kiram a few days to fully realize the importance of Javier inviting him to the third table. It wasn't just a matter of better servings of meat or glasses of red wine every Sacreday. It signified his allegiance with the men at that table. It meant that the other students at the academy, from first year to fourth, now considered him one of Javier's circle, one of the Hellions.

No one attempted to trip him as he passed and no one taunted him to his face. At the same time, some youths who had been cautiously friendly towards him no longer engaged him in debates during law class. Watching two of them slink away as he sat down at a study table in the library, Kiram couldn't help but feel uneasy about his new alliance.

Nestor was delighted. The fact that his mother would have been incensed seemed to make it all the more exciting.

"She'd be furious if she knew Elezar and I were called Hellions." Nestor smiled as he glanced up from his sketch of a man in armor. "She's a very religious woman, you know. Doesn't allow anyone in the household to have sweets the entire week of Our Savior's Misery. She would piss blood if she found out."

Kiram's own mother had apparently laughed when she received his letter informing her that he was now considered a Hellion.

Along with her letter, Kiram's mother had sent a package of fresh pen nibs, dried tea, and hard candies. Beneath the satchel of candy was a note from his father.

It congratulated him on making friends and fitting in so quickly with the Cadeleonians, but also warned against getting any tattoos that he would regret later. Apparently one of his cousins was now wearing long sleeves to hide the bare breasted mermaid emblazoned on his forearm with the words 'wet fuck' written beneath her. His uncle Rafie was looking into the removal of the image.

Then, in closing, Kiram's father had encouraged him to keep up his good grades.

Kiram sucked on one of his apple candies and scowled at the thought of grades.

He was doing very well in most of his classes. Now that he was training daily with Javier, he was even beginning to improve in the war arts. Master Ignacio no longer scowled at the mere sight of him. But in history he seemed unable to score the kind of grades he was used to.

He had worked harder on his essay analyzing the reign of King Nazario Sagrada than he had ever worked on any assignment. He'd spent a week combing through the library for original source material. He'd searched through old diaries and ancient tax records.

It had been with a sense of triumph that he had detailed and documented, on page after page, how Nazario Sagrada's excessive violence and persecution of even his own nobles had set in place all of the elements of the civil war that unseated his heir. He had even felt confident enough to point out that the divisions that Nazario had created had later contributed to certain noble families choosing to support the Mirogoths against their fellow Cadeleonians during the invasion nearly a hundred years later.

Kiram had never been so proud of an essay. It seemed nearly as perfect as one of his mechanisms.

And then it had been returned with the lowest mark Kiram had ever received. The ugly red note scrawled across the last page informed him that his lack of understanding of his subject obviously revealed the failings of his earlier Haldiim education.

A month before, such a comment would have made him want to weep. Now—he didn't know if this was a result of constant battle training or just the extent of his outrage—he wanted to beat Holy Father Habalan to a pulp.

He had been so angry that he had paced through the room ranting while Javier sat at his desk, looking on in amusement.

"Would you like me to kill him?" Javier offered offhandedly.

"No, I'd like to kill him myself."

"You can hardly wrestle Nestor to the ground by yourself," Javier replied. "Holy Father Habalan is about three times Nestor's weight."

"I'll roll him into the lake."

"He'll just float on the water like a bloated pig bladder," Javier said. And Kiram laughed in spite of his anger.

"You've got to consider these things when you plan a murder, you know," Javier had added.

A little later, after Kiram calmed himself by bolting together a small housing for a miniature glass boiler, Javier had tossed him an essay of his own.

"What's this for?"

"To keep you from failing Holy Father Habalan's class." Javier hadn't looked up from the book he was reading. Calixto Tornesal's diary. Again.

"I can't just copy one of your essays."

"I didn't say that you should. Read it. Then write your own."

Kiram had read the paper and several others of Javier's since then. They were the funniest and most scathing criticisms that he had ever encountered. Javier described King Nazario Sagrada's reign entirely in terms of the advances made in chastity belts and dog breeding during the king's lifetime.

Kiram remembered snorting with laughter as he read the conclusion:

While other rulers may have contributed more to the art, science, medicine, law, irrigation, architecture, agriculture, political stability and economy of our great nation, it is Nazario Sagrada to whom so many a virginal girl owes her greatest happiness as she cuddles one of this nation's many three-to-seven pound lapdogs.

The genius of it was that it was all true and all written glowingly, as though Javier were really in awe of the literally miniscule contribution of lapdogs.

Kiram couldn't manage the same level of sarcasm, but he had realized that if he wanted to pass Holy Father Habalan's class then he would be wise to resort to minutiae.

Since then he had turned in an essay on the advances in saddles during the civil war and was rewarded with his highest score so far. Another paper detailing the numbingly dull history of the southern warhorses brought his overall grade back up to passing.

But now the class had reached the era of the Mirogoth invasion and Kiram was determined to write his next essay on Yassin Lif-Harun. He already suspected that he would receive low marks for his efforts.

Holy Father Habalan didn't really understand Yassin Lif-Harun's contribution to astronomy or navigation, and he always looked annoyed when the subject came up. There was a chance that he would fail Kiram simply for making him aware of his own ignorance.

It frustrated Kiram that he could write a perfect essay and still be failed, simply because the scholar grading him didn't like his ideas or worse yet, just couldn't comprehend the subject. Things were so much more straightforward with machines. Either they worked or they didn't. Anyone using one knew which it was.

Kiram flipped through the pages of an old diary, scanning for any mention of Yassin. He'd found only one reference so far and it was buried in a list of men who had joined Calixto Tornesal's boar hunt.

"Yassin Lif-Harun was an acknowledged genius at the age of sixteen, and all this idiot can think to write about him is that he wears his hair a little too long for a proper gentleman."

"I'm telling you," Nestor gazed at Kiram over the rims of his spectacles, "Calixto Tornesal is the one to write about."

"Everyone writes about Calixto."

"That's because everyone wants to pass the class."

"I know. But honestly, what's left to say about Calixto? He killed two of his own cousins in duels, opened the white hell, killed every Mirogoth within a hundred miles, fathered a son, and then killed himself. Every other action he took seemed to be killing."

Nestor shrugged and studied his drawing, then he glanced back up at Kiram. "You think Javier wrote about him when he took the class?"

"No, he probably wrote about the nation's brief but shining romance with hard-ball candy, or something."

"You think?" Nestor asked. "That almost sounds…you know…obscene."

"Yes, then I'm positive that's what he wrote about."

Javier loved to provoke the people around him. His jokes could turn quite cruel if he disliked the person, particularly another student. Often Master Ignacio and other instructors turned a blind eye. They expected malice and audacity from Javier; after all, he had no soul.

"Oh, speaking of candy." Nestor interrupted Kiram's thoughts. "You don't have any more of those delicious apple candies left, do you?"

"Dozens." Kiram handed one of the gold candies to Nestor.

"I'd write an essay on these if I knew anything about them," Nestor commented as he sucked on the candy.

"I'd tell you everything I know but it isn't much." Kiram scanned through a long description of dice tricks Calixto Tornesal could preform. "My mother will only share her recipes with my sister."

"That's stupid, isn't it?" Nestor asked. "You're the one who will be inheriting the business, aren't you?"

"No. We Haldiim pass property and businesses through the women. So my eldest sister will take over the candy shop after my mother."

"Doesn't that leave you out in the cold, then?"

"My father has money of his own that he gives to us boys but eventually I'll have to support myself."

"Or marry a rich wife," Nestor suggested, though even as he said it he frowned slightly as if the idea sounded wrong even to him.

"I'm planning on supporting myself."

"That's probably a good idea," Nestor agreed. "Not that you couldn't attract a wife, but you know, if it didn't work out…"

"I understand," Kiram assured Nestor. "It's best to be able to take care of yourself."

Nestor nodded and Kiram returned to his fruitless research. Now and then he glanced up to watch Nestor fill out the details of Calixto Tornesal's cold expression and shining armor.

It was only later that day, as Kiram watched Javier flip through the pages of hellscript that filled his ancestor's diary, that Kiram wondered what Javier actually thought of Calixto Tornesal's decision to bind his bloodline to the white hell.

For the rest of the students, Calixto's decision was only relevant as history. His defeat of the Mirogoths made dramatic fodder for an essay, probably for hundreds of essays. But for Javier, Calixto's actions had personal ramifications. They bequeathed both burden and power to him even before he had been conceived. The very core of Javier's identity seemed forged by the hell-brand his ancestor had taken a hundred years before. Kiram couldn't imagine what it would be like for Javier to know that there was one man who was so directly responsible for all the power and all of the isolation in his life.

"I have to write another essay for Holy Father Habalan," Kiram said casually.

Javier glanced at him, then went back to his book.

Kiram added, "We're studying the era of the Mirogoth invasion."

"From the year 1242 up until 1250," Javier said thoughtfully, "the silky native Cadeleonian thickening agent used for most puddings suffered a significant decline and was almost completely replaced by a clumpy foreign imitation. Some of our best desserts might never have been recovered had it not been for the tireless effort of a short, balding cook named Vences Aniparo. Little is remembered about the man himself but his legacy remains with us today, as a variety of viscous gravies and glutinous desserts."

Kiram laughed and felt oddly sad at the same time. He had known Javier would not mention Calixto.

Even among the Hellions, Javier never spoke of anything that troubled him. Listening to his banter and watching him both bully and amuse the other young men, it would have been easy to believe that Javier lived without a care.

Yet Kiram knew that something drove him to seek penance nearly every morning. And Kiram couldn't forget the pain in Javier's voice when he had spoken of the curse that had killed his father and left Fedeles a half-wit.

There had been one night when Kiram could not sleep and had found himself staring at the white beams of moonlight falling across Javier's pale body. Then Kiram had seen Javier raise his hands over his face and almost claw at his own skull as if he couldn't bear the thoughts inside. Javier had opened his mouth as if to scream but no sound escaped.

But the next morning Javier had sat with the Hellions, taunting and inciting them as he always did. He had bitten Morisio's ear but only hard enough to make the other man flush and sputter. Then Javier and the rest of the Hellions had laughed uproariously. Kiram had realized that Javier would never allow any of them a deeper glimpse of his true self than this.

Elezar aside, Kiram doubted that any of the Hellions would have believed that Javier cared in the slightest about his ancestry. Certainly none of them would have imagined that he spent so many nights pouring over Calixto's worn leather diary. Kiram imagined that Javier had the entire book memorized by now, and yet he returned to it again and again, the way another man might turn to a consoling scripture.

Kiram sighed. Contemplating Javier wasn't going to get him any farther with his essay. Kiram stared down at the page of pitiful notes. After three days of searching through old academy records and decayed diaries he had managed to glean little more than was common knowledge about Yassin Lif-Harun.

He had been widely known as the bastard son of Demolia Helio by a Haldiim mistress. At an early age Yassin had shown amazing talents, particularly at mathematics but also in his mother's holy garden. If his father had not decided to send Yassin to the academy as a study companion for his legitimate son, then Yassin would have become a Bahiim.

As it was, he had charted the courses of the stars while the Mirogoth invasion advanced towards the academy. He finished the last of his calculations only two days before the Mirogoth forces reached the academy walls. They had come intending to seize the last living Sagrada heir and everyone in the academy knew as much.

Yassin had been among the students who volunteered to defend the academy while the war master secreted the young prince to safety. Few of the students survived, though they succeeded in keeping the Mirogoths from discovering that the prince had already fled.

Yassin had died sometime during the second night of the ensuing three-day siege.

Kiram wondered if Yassin had lived long enough to know that Calixto had opened the white hell. Had he seen it happen? Surely someone had documented it, most likely Calixto. And then suddenly Kiram wondered if Calixto might not have also mentioned Yassin in his diary.

Maybe now that they were on good terms he could convince Javier to let him have a look at that book. It was worth a try, anyway.

"Does Calixto's diary mention Yassin Lif-Harun? He was one of the defenders of the academy," he said casually.

Javier studied Kiram over the top of the book.

"I believe I already explained the fee I would require for access to my deranged ancestor's autobiography."

"Don't be an ass," Kiram replied. "I need the information for my history essay."

Javier leaned back in his chair and stretched out his long legs. "I imagine that only increases the value, then."

"I'm not selling you my soul."

"What about your body?"

Kiram felt his entire face flush red, not because he was shocked by Javier's suggestion, but in shame at his own desire to accept. This was just the way Javier played with the people around him. Kiram knew that, but Javier's slow, suggestive smile still affected him.

Kiram lowered his face, pretending to look over his notes one more time.

"I don't even know if you have anything of value in the book," Kiram said primly.

"My God, Kiram." Javier laughed. "I never expect you to take me up on these things. You seem so demure most of the time."

"I'm not demure. I just have some self-restraint."

"But not, it seems, when it comes to the pursuit of knowledge. You're willing to sell your body for a look at a book." Javier held the diary up as if it were a shimmering enticement.

"No, I refuse to sell my body." Kiram was a little amazed to realize that he'd grown used to these kinds of exchanges with Javier. "Unless you can guarantee that your book has any information that would be of use to me."

Javier bounded up from his chair and sat down on the edge of Kiram's bed, leaning in close. "If that's the case, then I propose a little demonstration of quality on both our parts."

"What do you mean?" Kiram tried to sound calm, but Javier's nearness flustered him.

"I'll give you a sample; you give me a sample." Javier slipped behind Kiram, wrapping his arms around his waist and placing the diary on Kiram's lap. He spread the pages of the book open. "I'll let you read a page and you let me—"

"—have one kiss." Kiram didn't wait to hear what Javier would suggest for fear that he would agree. "One kiss. That's all."

"All right." Javier sounded far too pleased and Kiram suddenly wondered if he'd offered too much. "You drive a hard bargain but I accept."

Kiram pulled away just slightly. "I want to read a page in the diary first. And it had better say something about Yassin."

"Don't worry. It's all there. You'll get to give me that kiss."

Javier flipped back two pages. A diagram of radiant lines illuminated the left side, while crumpled black hellscript filled the right.

"I can't read it," Kiram said.

"Not yet." Javier wrapped his arms around Kiram's chest, pulling him closer. "Relax a little. Lean into me."

"Why?" Kiram couldn't help but suspect that Javier was toying with him.

"You'll be protected while you're touching me," Javier said. "The closer the better."

Kiram leaned back but tried not to simply melt against Javier. The heat of Javier's arms and the scent of his body seemed to soak into Kiram. Javier bowed his face close to Kiram's. His lips almost brushed Kiram's ear. Kiram felt unreasonably aware of where the fine stubble along Javier's jaw brushed against his own skin.

"You're taking advantage—"

Before Kiram could finish his sentence, white bolts of light crackled up from Javier's chest and burst through his own body. Kiram expected pain and he almost jumped away but Javier held him tightly. A hot, liquid sensation flooded Kiram. He felt lightheaded, almost drunk. Strange, unfocused shadows filled the edges of his sight. He could no longer see his desk or even the corner of his bed. Bright white sparks flickered across his skin. The lights sprang along Kiram's hands and spread across the open pages of the book.

Before Kiram's eyes the diagram seemed to spread and rise from the page. What had been flat, straight lines slowly unfolded into the curving, organic form of a stylized tree, with wildly twisting branches and roots connecting through a braided trunk.

He had seen a design like this on Bahiim holy books. Across the facing page, the hellscript also stretched out, spreading into beautifully ornate Cadeleonian script.

"Do you see?" Javier's voice sounded as if it were coming from inside Kiram's head.

Kiram wanted to respond but he couldn't think of how to open his mouth, how to move his lips or form words. His entire body seemed lost somewhere between the flickering light and Javier's hard muscles.

"You shouldn't stay too long. Read it quickly." Again Kiram heard Javier as if the thoughts were his own. He felt the urgency and slight worry in them and at once he focused on the diary.

As the weeks pass I pray less and listen to Yassin more. He is not the child I thought him to be. He has seen death firsthand and does not fear it.

Beside him the holy father is a doddering coward. When we speak of death he can only think of the hells and cringe in horror. But I have seen the white void open. I felt its pull at my very soul as I lay bleeding on the dueling field.

Yassin knew what I spoke of at once. He told me that I had been on the threshold of a shajdi. It is a place where death feeds into life and life is devoured by death. It is a place of immense power.

Before Nazario's rule the Haldiim knew a way to hold these shajdi open, but the wisdom is either lost or hidden. Yassin does not know how it was done. But it is enough to know that it was accomplished. It can be done again. We will continue our attempts.

Kiram wanted to turn the page. He tried to lift his hands but he only managed to spread his fingers across the surface of the page.

"That's enough, Kiram."

No, Kiram thought, but he couldn't say the word.

Javier suddenly lifted his hands away from him and all the warmth and light seemed to be ripped from Kiram. The words and image in the book collapsed to unintelligible scrawls. Then the book itself seemed to go dark. The edges of Kiram's vision dimmed and then the whole room went black.

When Kiram opened his eyes he was lying back on his bed. Bright gold shafts of late summer sun glowed across the walls. Javier knelt beside him.

"Yassin was part of it." Kiram's voice felt rough, as if he'd just woken after a heavy slumber. He cleared his throat. "Yassin helped Calixto open the white hell. He was part of the whole thing."

"I know. How are you feeling?"

"You knew. You knew all this time and you haven't told anyone. Why?"

"Calixto never wanted Yassin's name dragged down by association with the white hell and demonic magic," Javier said. "He wanted him remembered for his genius."

Kiram sat up slowly, still feeling off balance.

"So together they found some way not only to open a shajdi, but to keep it open."

"Exactly so."

"Is it always like that? I mean, for you. Is everything so—" Kiram wasn't sure of how to describe what it had felt like to have the shajdi open all around him, "—distant?"

"Nothing about the white hell is distant for me. If you had been directly exposed to it without my protection, it would have burned your senses hollow."

It sounded so dramatic that Kiram half expected Javier to be joking but his expression was serious.

"You still look a little groggy." Javier offered Kiram a cup of water and made him drink it all. A few minutes later Kiram's head began to clear.

The diary lay in its usual spot on Javier's desk. It seemed deceptively small, almost insignificant. Then Kiram's gaze fell to the dozens of hellscript markings drawn all across the floor. What larger forms lurked within those simple dark lines? Somehow he couldn't get the idea of huge sea creatures floating just beneath the ocean's surface out of his mind.

Then he realized that he was remembering an image from a Bahiim holy book that Alizadeh had read to him when he was a young child. The caption had read: ***A world deeper than the one we know, where great forces move beneath us like sea serpents coiling below tiny boats.***

Kiram had the uneasy feeling that many of the superstitions he had summarily dismissed might be more true than he previously thought.

"Feeling better?" Javier seated himself on the bed beside him.

"I wasn't expecting the shajdi to be like that." Kiram noticed his notes lying on his desk and then remembered that he still had a page of equations to go over. The thought was relievingly mundane. Everything was just as it had been. "I'm fine, actually."

"Good." Javier moved closer so that his mouth almost brushed Kiram's lips. "Because I would hate to take advantage of you when you were feeling weak, but you still owe me something."

Kiram opened his mouth but he knew that there was no point in arguing; he had set his own price for seeing the diary. And it was only one kiss, after all.

He started to lean forward to kiss Javier's lips but Javier drew back.

"I haven't decided yet just where it is I want to kiss you," Javier said. He gently pushed Kiram back down onto the bed. "I want to see what my options are."

"That wasn't what I meant," Kiram protested. Javier placed his finger against Kiram's lips and gazed down at him with a strange intensity.

"When you deal with a Hellion you should know that he'll hold you to your word, no matter what you intended." As much as it embarrassed Kiram, he couldn't think of anything but the sensation of Javier's touch.

"I'm going to take the kiss you promised me," Javier whispered over him. "There's no point in fighting me about it."

Kiram closed his eyes. He could only hope to maintain his dignity, to keep from giving Javier a reaction that he could laugh at and taunt him with. He tried to imagine that this was just another day of battle practice, when Javier's body pressed close against his own, when Javier's warm hands touched his bare skin. But Javier never would have lingered so long or caressed him so gently in battle practice.

Javier's fingers traced the curve of Kiram's lip and then dropped to the base of Kiram's throat. He unbuttoned Kiram's shirt to expose his chest and abdomen.

Kiram shivered as Javier stroked the muscles of his bare shoulders and then brushed his fingers over Kiram's nipples. He hated Javier for dragging this out and at the same time his body ached to feel more than just the gliding hints of Javier's fingertips.

Javier stroked the flat plane of Kiram's stomach. He tugged the loose waist of Kiram's pants farther down, exposing his hips. The feeling of Javier's warm breath so near his groin sent a hot ache through Kiram. He folded his arms over his face in humiliation.

"Don't do that." Javier pulled Kiram's arms aside. "Look at me."

Kiram opened his eyes, expecting to see Javier gloating over him. Instead Javier's expression was gentle and strangely serious. He bowed down and kissed his lips.

His mouth was hot and pungent with the tastes of cardamom tea and honey. Kiram opened his lips to the pressure of Javier's tongue. His entire body responded to the sensation as Javier thrust into his mouth. Kiram curled his hands through Javier's thick black hair and pulled him closer.

He felt Javier's thigh between his legs, and the intense heat of Javier's groin against his own hip. Kiram wanted desperately to arch up against him. But the slightest sliver of common sense fought against the idea. He had promised one kiss and was giving much, much more.

Kiram shoved Javier back, harder than he intended. Javier almost fell off the bed but caught himself. He looked momentarily stunned and then he took in Kiram's expression and laughed.

"Don't glare at me. I'm not the one who interrupted your pleasure."

"We agreed to one kiss. That was all." Kiram pulled his legs up, though he was sure Javier knew just how aroused the kiss had made him.

"That was all for a page of the diary." Javier wrapped his hand around Kiram's bare ankle and slowly slid his palm up along the inside of Kiram's thigh. "But we could have a little more for ourselves, don't you think?"

"No." Kiram pried Javier's hand off his leg.

"And why not?" Javier demanded. He was still smiling but his voice had an angry edge. "You think I can't see that you want me? Every inch of you is up for me."

"Whether I'm aroused or not is none of your business, Javier." Kiram tried to sound firm despite his embarrassment. "I'm not a toy for you to play with and I'm not one of the whores at the Goldenrod whose body you can buy with a few pennies."

"No, you charge much more and put out far less." White sparks jumped across Javier's left hand but Kiram refused to be intimidated.

"I gave you exactly what we agreed upon." Kiram returned Javier's hard stare. "In fact, I gave you better than you gave me. You know I'm not going to dishonor Yassin's name by writing about what you showed me."

"Oh, I see. So, you won't spread your legs unless I can give you something that will get you a better grade."

"No! You are not going to pretend that I'm just a greedy whore." Kiram was shocked at his own anger. "That is not why I stopped."

"No, I'm sure it wasn't the only reason." Javier suddenly stood and glared down at Kiram. "You like to pretend that you aren't afraid of what I am but when it comes down to it, you're as much of a coward as Holy Father Habalan."

"Are you some kind of moron? I'm not afraid of your twinkly little sparks of hellfire!" Kiram was rewarded with a look of surprise from Javier. He took advantage of it to get to his feet. He met Javier's glower with his own unflinching stare. "You want to know what scares me? It's your shallow-minded Cadeleonian law and your bigoted Cadeleonian church. You like to pretend that they don't mean anything to you but you still go to penance every single day." Kiram jabbed Javier in the chest with his forefinger. "I may find you handsome and I may enjoy your touch but that doesn't mean that I want to be lashed or imprisoned for corrupting you with my Haldiim ways. And you know *I'm* the one who will be blamed if we're caught. No one is going to accuse you. You're the Duke of Rauma. So, yes, I am scared. But I have every reason to be scared and I have every right to refuse you."

Kiram felt suddenly exhausted as if he had expelled all his strength and fury with those last words.

Javier stood where he was, his expression drained of anger. He studied Kiram as if he had somehow become a new person.

"You've got quite a temper," Javier said at last.

"You aren't exactly sedate yourself."

"I know. I'm too used to getting my way." Javier shrugged. "Not many people are willing to refuse the Duke of Rauma, you know."

"Yes, I gathered that."

For a long moment Javier studied Kiram in silence. Then he looked down at his hands.

"So, this is how it has to be between us?"

"I think so." Kiram could no longer meet Javier's gaze. He looked down at his bare feet and at the coiling symbols on the floor. He wanted to say something else, to somehow tell Javier that if circumstances were different, then…

There was no point; the circumstances were exactly what they were.

He wished suddenly that he had never asked about Calixto's diary. The knowledge, like his desire for Javier, did him no good and yet he could not forget it.

"I have to find something else to write about for my history essay," Kiram said at last.

Javier walked back to his desk and sat down. He didn't pick up Calixto's diary. Instead he took out his penknife and cut a new tip for his quill. "If it has to be a biography, you might try Nusrat Kir-Miakah. He was the guide who escorted the Sagrada heir and his war master to safety all the way from the academy to the western hold."

"Was he Haldiim?"

Javier nodded. "There's a little biography on him filed with the hunting and trapping texts in the library."

"I'll read it. Thank you for—"

The rest of his words were drowned out by a loud beating against the door. An instant later Elezar shoved the door open and leaned in from the hallway, though he came no farther, since even he was hesitant to step into the room where Javier slept.

The arbitrary nature of Cadeleonians' superstition was absurd, Kiram thought. They would eat and wrestle, ride and fight with Javier but were terrified of what might lurk in a room where he slept, as if his dreams might leap out from under a pillow and grasp them. Normally Kiram found it all amusing, but this afternoon it only irritated him.

"No need to look so dour, my friend." Elezar's voice boomed through the room. "Master Ignacio has invited us out for a ride."

Kiram rolled his eyes. Javier said nothing but he pulled on his riding boots and began lacing them.

"A ride to the Goldenrod, no doubt," Kiram murmured. Elezar's ecstatic expression told him as much. A week ago Upperclassman Atreau had informed Kiram and Nestor that Master Ignacio's afternoon rides were, often as not, an excuse to visit prostitutes. Apparently, the war master had taken it upon himself to ensure that the older students' physical desires found release, lest they resort to desperate acts of abnormal carnality.

"Who knows how far we may wander in the pursuit of healthy male exercise," Elezar responded happily. "Don't be sullen about it, Kiram. Once you've been blooded in a tournament you may be asked out on a ride as well."

"I just can't wait," Kiram muttered.

He didn't watch Javier leave with Elezar. Instead he sat down at his desk and wrote a letter to his father assuring him that he was staying out of trouble and doing all he could to keep his grades up. After he was done with it, Kiram ripped it apart and threw the shreds into the cold grate of the fireplace.

Chapter Twelve

Battle practice with Javier the next day was incredibly difficult. Kiram struggled not to notice the heat of Javier's hands on his bare chest, or feel a thrill as the two of them grappled in the wrestling ring. More than once he completely lost his concentration while gazing at Javier's mouth and remembering his insistent kiss.

If the same desire troubled Javier, he gave very little indication of it. Only once, as Kiram arched beneath him struggling to break a hold did he notice a strange catch in Javier's breath. But then Javier pinned him down—hard—against the mat and stepped back, calm and collected.

Kiram wondered at Javier's ability to so completely sublimate his desire. Of course, being Cadeleonian, he'd doubtless had a lifetime of practice. There was also the fact that he, unlike Kiram, could turn to the prostitutes at the Goldenrod for relief.

That night Kiram left the Hellions' table early and found respite in the cold pistons and bolts in his work shed. He returned to the room he shared with Javier just before the night warden rang the last bell.

If Javier thought anything of Kiram's absence he said nothing and Kiram guessed that Javier understood that keeping a distance between them was for the best.

The next day Kiram claimed illness to avoid another frustrating battle practice, but that only resulted in Javier appearing in the infirmary to inform him that they would now have to make up for the practice on Sacreday—just the two of them and Master Ignacio.

From Javier's scowl Kiram knew he'd made a poor decision and even Scholar Donamillo shook his head, as if nothing good could come of a private session with Master Ignacio.

He had not feigned sickness again. Instead he got through the next week of battle practice by focusing on his technique. He met Javier's gaze as little as possible and took care not to stand close when they weren't training. Up in their shared room during the evening hours, Kiram found himself staring at Javier and obsessively brooding on the memory of his touch. Every time Javier glanced up from reading, Kiram felt the blood rise in his face.

If he stayed here, he was going to make a fool of himself, or worse, endanger his entire future. He had to distract himself from Javier's effortless temptations.

He spent the next two weeks in self-imposed exile in his work shed assembling his Crown Challenge mechanism. Each night he wandered back to the dormitory exhausted and simply dropped down to his mattress, still reeking of gear oil and ash. Twice he missed curfew while struggling with the proportions of his steam chambers. The night warden dragged him up to his room and threatened to report him if it happened a third time before slamming the door and leaving him fumbling toward his bed in the dark.

"Only an idiot would get himself caned for a mechanism." Javier's voice floated through the stillness.

"I'm not an idiot," Kiram assured him.

"Then don't act like one." Javier sounded petulant and Kiram wished he could see his expression. "You don't have to hide from me. I'm not going to attack you."

"I know." Kiram pressed his face into his pillow. "But who's to say I won't assault you?"

Javier's soft laugh was the last thing Kiram remembered before he fell asleep.

The next afternoon Javier and most of the other Hellions went riding with Master Ignacio. Kiram knew he had no right to resent the excursion, and yet he did. He decided a walk would do him good. He chose the path through the orchard.

The crisp autumn air was colder than the more southerly climate Kiram was used to. Many of the apples in the orchard were turning gold and red. They reminded Kiram of the sunset skies over Anacleto. It had been a long while since he had simply walked among the trees and felt the ground beneath his feet. He was half tempted to pull off his boots as he would have in one of the sacred groves at home, but he wasn't among Haldiim and any Cadeleonians coming across him would probably think he was suffering from a brain fever.

Kiram contented himself to walk along the white pebble path that cut through the orchard and curled around the chapel. He listened to the songs of birds and crickets and tried not to feel homesick. He'd chosen to come to the academy, knowing that it would be strange and challenging, he reminded himself. This was what he wanted—what he needed to do, if he was going to prove himself.

Distantly he heard the gurgle of the stream and the voices of first-year students splashing through the cold water. As he wandered, the apple trees thinned to stands of white birch and oaks. Sprays of wildflowers and brambleberry bushes spread between the trees.

Then he came across a delicate, wrought iron fence and beyond this a wide field of red clover and gravestones. The two graves nearest Kiram were engraved with doves and the words *Loyal* and *Faithful*. Kiram couldn't help but think that the words seemed more appropriate to pets than to people. A third grave was inscribed with a Cadeleonian woman's name and the designation of *Academy Cook*. Kiram wasn't sure if the dates below represented her lifespan or the duration of her employment.

A loud peal of laughter drew Kiram's attention farther down the neat rows of graves. A lean young man dressed in the academy blue crouched on the mound of a grave. His black hair hung over his eyes and he shoved it back brusquely.

For an instant Kiram thought it was Javier and he was unreasonably glad to see him. But as soon as the thought came to him he discounted it. Javier never laughed like that. It had to be Fedeles.

As if to confirm Kiram's thought, the young man broke into wide grin and crowed out the names of several horses. Then he swung up a silver trowel and plunged it into the earthen mound of the grave. He hurled up a spray of dirt and mangled clover.

Alarm shot through Kiram as he realized that Fedeles was digging up a grave, desecrating the dead.

"Fedeles! You can't dig there."

Fedeles glanced briefly to Kiram but then returned to his work as if utterly unaware that he was breaking common Cadeleonian law. Kiram raced across the field, jumping over the low mounds where bodies lay. He reached Fedeles quickly but not before Fedeles had opened two large holes directly beneath the headstone. There were flowers all around Fedeles' feet. Most of them looked as if they had been recently ripped from the ground. Their roots still gripped dark clods of dirt. The name on the headstone was Victaro Irdad, the groom who had died the previous year.

"Firaj," Fedeles sang out to Kiram.

"What are you doing?"

"Flowers," Fedeles cooed and he stroked the head stone with a muddy hand. "Flowers for Victo. He won't see them but I brought them. I brought them…" Fedeles' expression went slack and he leaned against the headstone allowing the trowel to fall aside.

Kiram remembered Nestor telling him that a groom had been torn to pieces. Secretly, everyone blamed Javier but no one had seen it happen. When Nestor had first told him the story, Kiram had simply accepted that Javier was responsible, but now he had seen how well Javier could restrain himself and the white hell. He couldn't believe that Javier had killed the groom, not even by accident.

But it unnerved him to think that someone had and that no one at the academy spoke of it.

"Was Victo a friend of yours?" Kiram asked Fedeles gently.

Fedeles dug into his jacket pocket and brought out a small wooden figurine of a horse. It fit in Fedeles's palm.

"Lunaluz," Fedeles said quietly. "I made it for Victo but he's gone now."

"You carved this?"

"Haldiim murdered him," Fedeles whispered the words through his gritted teeth.

"What?" Kiram couldn't quite believe what he thought Fedeles had said.

Fedeles' expression jerked again and for a moment he seemed unsure of where he was.

"I brought flowers for Victo." He turned away from Kiram and quickly gathered the uprooted flowers. He pushed them into the holes he had dug so that their roots were sticking up, exposed to the air and the blossoms were down in the dirt. "Victo can see them now."

"Fedeles," Kiram watched him closely, "you said something about Haldiim just now. What was it?"

Fedeles shook his head as if dismissing Kiram's question completely. He lay down on top of the grave and nestled his face into the red clover and earth. "I want to go."

"You should." Kiram straightened. "We both should."

"No," Fedeles replied. "I want to go down there. I want to tell him, I didn't mean it."

"You didn't mean what?"

"It's a secret." Fedeles rolled onto his side and gazed at Kiram. For a moment he looked calm, almost at ease. Kiram was always surprised by how strongly Fedeles resembled Javier when his features weren't contorted with grins and grimaces. The two of them could have easily passed for brothers.

"I shouldn't have told him." Fedeles closed his eyes and lay still.

"We can't stay here," Kiram said at last.

Fedeles opened his eyes and smiled as if he were only half-awake.

"Firaj." Fedeles patted the ground, inviting Kiram to sit down beside him.

In other circumstances, Kiram might have sat down with Fedeles and attempted to make some sense of his words. But today he had no desire to linger in a graveyard or risk being accused of disturbing the Cadeleonian dead.

He turned away.

"I'm leaving whether you come or not," Kiram called over his shoulder. He heard Fedeles scramble to his feet. By the time Kiram had reached the fence, Fedeles had fallen in alongside him. He gently nudged Kiram's elbow to get his attention.

"What?" Kiram tried not to sound annoyed but he wasn't sure he succeeded.

"Look." Fedeles stepped off the path and pushed aside the thick mass of wild grasses at the base of a tree. Kiram was surprised to see a small horse carved into the tree trunk.

It wasn't just a simple outline cut into the bark, but a delicate bas-relief, like something that he would have expected in a temple.

"That's really well done, Fedeles." Kiram looked at him. "Did you do it?"

"Yes." Fedeles grinned, looking genuinely pleased.

As they walked back to the academy Fedeles pointed out other carvings of his. All of them were small and hidden from casual sight. But they were each masterfully formed and not all of them were horses. Dogs and birds as well as a few tiny human figures peered down from the branches of trees and peeped out from knotholes.

Kiram smiled at one man who was clearly picking his nose.

"Does anyone else know about these?" Kiram asked. He thought Nestor would love them. Fedeles shook his head.

"It's a secret." Fedeles suddenly lowered his voice. "Keep secrets or you get killed."

Kiram frowned and would have asked why but Fedeles didn't give him the chance. He let out a gleeful howl and raced towards the dormitory where clusters of first-year students were lounging. The boys looked up at Fedeles and then scattered apart. They laughed and shrieked excitedly as Fedeles chased them around the grounds in a game of tag.

Forgotten by even Fedeles, Kiram slunk away to find Nestor.

Chapter Thirteen

Kiram found Nestor in the library, drawing as always, and settled down into a chair opposite him.

"Something bothering you?" Nestor asked.

Kiram nodded but didn't know exactly how to approach it. His encounter with Fedeles had been strange and troubling. To his relief Nestor didn't prod him. He waited patiently while Kiram gathered his thoughts.

"Can I ask you about Fedeles?" Kiram asked at last.

"What about him?"

"Is he…" Kiram paused, weighing his words carefully. "Could he hurt someone?"

"On purpose?" Nestor raised his brows, as he met Kiram's gaze. "No. Never. He's simple and a little lost, but he couldn't harm a living soul. That's not in him, never has been, not even when he was…well. If you could have seen him before, you'd know. He was always speaking up for me—or anyone—when Javier and Elezar got too rough." Nestor shook his head sadly. "He was great fun. Everyone loved him."

"But he's not the same now."

"No, he's not. But under all that madness, he's still Fedeles. You can see it when he's with the horses and when he plays with the other boys. He's just not mean."

Kiram picked up a book that another student had left on the table; a slim volume of Bishop Seferino's musings. He still had not found the book that Javier had told him about, *Concerning Ardor.* Instead Kiram read through *On the Nature of Vice and Virtue.*

"Why do you ask?"

"He was putting flowers on that murdered groom's grave and saying…things."

"They were friends, up until…you know," Nestor said.

"Until the groom was murdered," Kiram responded. "Why doesn't anyone seem to care about that?"

Nestor flushed slightly.

"You can't tell Javier that I told you about this, all right?" Nestor leaned across the table, dropping his voice to the softest murmur.

"Told me what?" Kiram too lowered his voice.

"Victaro was too…friendly with Fedeles." The flush coloring Nestor's cheeks darkened to scarlet and he lowered his gaze down to his hands. "There were rumors that he took advantage of Fedeles' innocence."

"You mean he raped—"

The alarm in Nestor's face silenced Kiram.

"I'm just saying that there might have been a good reason for Javier to do what he did, but talking about it would only humiliate Fedeles. Do you understand?"

Kiram nodded slowly. It was all so very Cadeleonian and Kiram wasn't sure he believed it in any case. Fedeles had clearly stated that murdering Haldiim had killed the groom. And why would he be placing flowers on the grave of a man who violated him?

But Kiram knew it would be no good to press Nestor further. Instead, he nodded to the papers tucked into the textbook at Nestor's elbow. "How's your math assignment coming along?"

"Very slowly," Nestor confessed.

"Can I help?"

"You know you can." For the next hour Nestor labored over his mathematics and Kiram offered explanations and answers. Later, when Kiram finally found an opportunity to ask Nestor if he had ever noticed any carvings in the trees near the stream, Nestor said, "They're devils that come out of the trees at night. Everybody knows that."

"I didn't."

"Well now you do." Nestor finished his class work and stretched in his chair. He studied Kiram for a moment, absently sketching him on a parchment, and then noted that neither of them fit into their clothes so well any more. Kiram had to agree. Nestor had lost enough weight to require several tucks in the waist of his trousers. Kiram's shirts were tight across his shoulders. "You're going to end up bigger than Elezar."

"I doubt it, but you just might," Kiram replied.

"He did have to lend me a couple of his shirts," Nestor said and Kiram could see that he was pleased to be favorably compared to his older brother. "You know, my arms are getting bigger." Nestor flexed his bicep.

"Did Elezar have the shirts washed before he gave them to you?" Kiram asked, as casually as he could. "Or have you stopped taking baths?"

Nestor flushed bright pink as only a pale Cadeleonian could. "I washed yesterday—no two days ago, but it's not that bad…Is it?"

"It's a little bad."

Nestor sighed. "Well, I suppose I ought to go wash before bed. Otherwise the stench might kill Upperclassman Atreau."

While Nestor retired to the second floor dormitory, Kiram remained in the library, skimming through the Bishop Sefarino's cautious contemplation of ardor. The numerous floral and gastronomic euphemisms the bishop employed to avoid any reference to actual copulation, while still expounding upon the pleasures of 'that most physical act' struck Kiram as funny and kept him reading. This was exactly the sort of book Javier would like. He wondered if he should bring it up to their room. It wouldn't be long before last bell.

At last, he closed the book and stretched. Then suddenly he realized that Javier was there. Javier leaned against the doorframe and watched him. Kiram felt stupidly happy to see him.

He said, "I was just reading this book—"

Then Elezar and Atreau rushed up. Elezar grabbed Javier around the neck, playfully throttling him and Javier had to turn away to fight him off. Atreau lounged against the wall, yawning and occasionally critiquing Elezar's style.

Kiram felt a surge of annoyance. Elezar was always like this after Master Ignacio took the Hellions out riding. Elezar wouldn't stop grappling with Javier until the night warden called for lights out. Leaving the book behind, Kiram waited until the two of them lurched clear of the door and then slunk out of the library and up to the tower room where he gladly embraced the oblivion of sleep.

Chapter Fourteen

That night something terrible haunted Kiram's dreams. Above him, dark shadows crawled across the ceiling like seeping tar. Droplets struck Kiram's face, spattering his mouth and eyes. He tried to move away only to find himself sinking deeper into an engulfing black. The harder he struggled, the deeper he sank until oily fingers curled over his face and dragged him into a suffocating cold.

He jerked upright and nearly collided with Javier, who knelt at his bedside. Kiram couldn't be sure but he thought Javier looked worried.

"What are you doing?" Still only half-awake Kiram blurted the words out in Haldiim.

"You called out for me," Javier spoke the Haldiim words with a slight accent and Kiram stared at him, not sure if he'd heard correctly or if this was the lingering of his dream.

"Was it bad?" Javier asked and this time his words were clearly Cadeleonian.

"I was suffocating, I think." Kiram wiped his face, as if he could scrub his dazed confusion away. "I can't really remember it now."

"Probably for the best." Javier stroked his back once, lightly, and then stood. A thin shaft of moonlight briefly illuminated the naked expanse of his chest as he headed for his own bed. "We should get what sleep we can. The morning bell will be sounding soon enough."

Kiram didn't think he could fall asleep again, and yet in a few moments he slipped back into another dream.

Again a dark weight lay atop him, but this time it felt warm and living. The mass became flesh. Naked skin pressed against his own. Thick black hair fell across his face. Soon it became Javier's body thrusting down onto him, pinning him to the bed.

Kiram woke up embarrassed, erect and alone. Javier had already left for his morning penance. Kiram spent most of the morning in a daze, trying not to think of Javier and yet unable to think of anything else.

After lunch, Kiram was so distracted that he walked directly into Scholar Blasio. He apologized and offered to help carry a few of the books that he had dashed out of the Scholar Blasio's arms. Blasio accepted and made polite conversation as they walked to the mathematics lecture hall. When Kiram shelved the books incorrectly twice, Scholar Blasio inquired if something was wrong.

"I'm just distracted," Kiram said quickly and this time he shelved both books properly.

Scholar Blasio straightened a stack of papers that the first-year students had piled up on his desk. "How are things going for you with the other boys?"

"Fine, I think." Kiram wasn't certain what Scholar Blasio meant.

"It's just that you were forced into Javier Tornesal's company and he runs with a very… energetic crowd of young men." Scholar Blasio awkwardly flipped through the stack of papers teetering at the edge of the desk.

"Upperclassman Javier has done well by me." Kiram shrugged. "Most of the Hellions have."

"Yes, but you're very different from them. You have such potential, and the Hellions have so little—" Scholar Blasio seemed to suddenly realize that he was deriding a duke and at least two noble heirs. "I mean, intellectually speaking. They aren't great thinkers, and Master Ignacio doesn't really encourage development in the academic realm—"

Suddenly the papers slid out from beneath Scholar Blasio's hand and spilled to the floor.

"Damn it," Scholar Blasio muttered.

Kiram helped him gather the papers. Scholar Blasio seemed embarrassed. He turned to the bookshelf against the far wall and picked up a heavy, wooden bookend that he plunked on top of the papers and as if some gust had been to blame for the earlier fall. The bookend had been beautifully carved into the shape of a dove.

"I suppose I'm just trying to warn you," Scholar Blasio said at last. "It may seem exciting to drink and fight and be one of those kinds of young men, but I hope it doesn't come at a cost to you. I hope you don't feel like you have to behave that way just to fit in with them."

"No, sir, I haven't been out drinking with them and the only fighting I'm doing is in Master Ignacio's class." Kiram was only half thinking about the conversation; instead he was observing the bookend. It strongly resembled the carvings Fedeles had shown to him.

"I'm not so good at fighting that I would engage in a brawl as recreation," Kiram added. He was rewarded with a smile from Scholar Blasio.

"No, you're no Elezar Grunito. You're not like any of the young ruffians in that group. I know that Master Ignacio would have it otherwise. More than likely he'll exert as much pressure as he can to reshape you into the kind of brute that he can impress. But you should know that outside of the academy there are quite a few thinking men who do not share Master Ignacio's values."

It struck Kiram suddenly that Scholar Blasio was probably speaking from his own experience as a student at the academy. Scholar Blasio wasn't really that much older than Kiram. Master Ignacio could well have been one of his instructors. Kiram couldn't imagine Scholar Blasio excelling in Master Ignacio's classes or commanding much respect from his fellow students.

For an instant Kiram thought that there was even a kind of resemblance between Scholar Blasio's nervous, awkward interactions and the uneasy exchanges Ladislo attempted from time to time. Kiram chose not to consider the comparison too closely.

"When I was a student here I had my brother to confide in," Scholar Blasio said. "I just want you to know that if you need it, I will always make time to talk with you."

"Thank you, Scholar Blasio." Kiram did feel touched by Blasio's offer, though he doubted that Scholar Blasio would remain so friendly if Kiram described the details of the dream that had been distracting him all day.

A silence hung between Scholar Blasio and himself for a moment and Kiram realized that the scholar was expecting some kind of confession or confidence.

All Kiram could think of was a question.

"I was wondering where this carving came from?" Kiram touched the smooth surface of the dove's neck.

"That?" Scholar Blasio looked a little relieved that Kiram hadn't actually dredged up his personal troubles. "My brother made that. He's quite accomplished at carving."

"You mean Scholar Donamillo?"

"Yes, yes. Scholar Donamillo." Scholar Blasio looked amused at the formality. "He doesn't carve very often anymore. He's much too busy. But I think you can still see his artistry in his mechanical cures. They're actually quite beautiful."

Kiram nodded. Though he rarely considered the question of beauty in a mechanism, he had to admit that the luminous panes of glass and beautifully etched supports of Scholar Donamillo's machines made the mechanical cures seem like works of art.

Still, Kiram judged them on their performance. A machine that functioned perfectly was lovely to him even if it stank and looked like a heap of refuse. And there Scholar Donamillo's mechanisms were more than pretty objects; they were inspiring.

He had personally seen the difference they made in calming Fedeles and relieving him of his bouts of paranoia and strange anxiety. Kiram couldn't help but wish that one of his own mechanisms could someday do so much so well.

"You might mention your admiration for his carving to Scholar Donamillo." Scholar Blasio's words brought Kiram back to the subject at hand. "Solstice isn't all that far away and who knows? You might just get a gift from him."

"I wouldn't want to trouble him," Kiram replied. He hoped that Scholar Blasio didn't think he was one of those boys who complimented someone's belongings just in hopes that they would be given to him.

"I don't know that it would be too much trouble," Blasio replied. "He likes you, you know. We both do."

"Thank you, sir." Kiram couldn't help but feel both pleased and shy at the same time. "I should probably get to my riding class."

"Yes, but be careful." Blasio glanced up at him. "Don't fall on your head attempting some mad leap."

Kiram assured him that he wouldn't and then hurried out. He had no desire to irritate Master Ignacio by arriving late. Of course, he managed to irritate Master Ignacio in countless other ways throughout most of the class period. And then, near the end of class, he made a spectacular error.

Kiram shifted his weight in the saddle and twisted his leg against Firaj's side. At the same time, while reaching to scratch his knee, drew back a little on his reins. Somewhere in the chaos of Kiram's motions Firaj picked out something familiar to him.

Firaj went stock-still. Then slowly, and very mechanically, the big black horse began to prance backwards across the arena. Kiram was utterly shocked. He hadn't thought a horse could be trained to walk backwards, much less prance. He could tell from the tension playing through Firaj's body that this was not a simple maneuver.

Firaj held his head high and twisted his ears back, straining for any hint of what was behind him. Kiram sat like a stuffed doll atop Firaj, too worried about startling his horse to move. Once they reached the center of the arena, Firaj came to a halt and gave a soft, pleased noise as if he were extremely proud of his performance.

All around them other students sat atop their mounts, staring. Then Nestor laughed and it seemed to release a torrent of snorts and giggles from the other students. Kiram flushed.

He patted Firaj, assuring him that he had done well—whatever he had done.

Only Master Ignacio remained stony faced. He ordered Kiram back to the other riders with a loud shout.

Throughout the rest of the class, Master Ignacio was relentless in his growling criticisms. He barked out angry reprimands at every one of Kiram's motions.

If Kiram was down in his saddle properly, then Master Ignacio snapped at him to pay attention to what he was doing with his knees. His hands were moving too much. He wasn't watching his surroundings. He was sitting too far back, and then too high up. Master Ignacio's constant recriminations destroyed Kiram's concentration and soon he was making mistakes that he had overcome months ago.

He prayed that some other student would attract Master Ignacio's wrath but Kiram was not so lucky. Even after he dismounted and turned Firaj's reins over to a groom, Master Ignacio wasn't through. He gripped Kiram's elbow and pulled him to the side of the arena.

"Do you know what your problem is?" Master Ignacio demanded. Kiram knew the question was rhetorical, and so he suppressed his response: at the moment Master Ignacio was his problem. Master Ignacio continued, "You are exactly the kind of distraction that gets soldiers killed! I don't ever want to see you show off like that again, do you understand?"

"I wasn't showing—"

Master Ignacio struck Kiram across the face so hard that Kiram stumbled back and almost fell to the arena floor.

"Yes or no?" Master Ignacio growled. Kiram remembered Javier saying nearly the same thing to Genimo.

"Yes," Kiram managed to reply. His entire jaw felt as if it had been ripped from its ligaments.

"Good." Master Ignacio took in a deep breath and only then seemed to become aware of the other second-year students lingering around the arena, gaping.

"Get to your classes and mind your own business!" Master Ignacio shouted.

Kiram saw Nestor start forward towards him, but when Master Ignacio stepped between them, Nestor fled with the other second-year students.

Master Ignacio turned back to Kiram. "I expect you to take my classes seriously. I'm not instructing you in some nonsense of numbers or dates. I am teaching you how we Cadeleonians make war. These skills have protected and maintained our kingdom for generations. This is how the greatest Cadeleonian men have lived and how they have died! You understand that? My instructions make the difference between life and death."

Master Ignacio had never lashed out at Kiram like this before, despite the fact that Kiram had made far worse mistakes in his classes. In fact during the first weeks the master had ignored Kiram, allowing him to fumble ineptly through his training. But Kiram had not been one of the Hellions then. He suddenly wondered how deeply that must have vexed the war master. A skinny Haldiim mechanist fraternizing with his brutal, muscular favorite students. His great Cadeleonians.

Kiram could hear the voices of men coming closer. The third-year students were gathering for their lessons. Master Ignacio glanced to the doors of the arena. "Haldiim genius or not, I expect you to take my instructions seriously. Do you understand that?"

"Yes, sir," Kiram responded.

"Good." Master Ignacio turned his back on Kiram. "Now get out of my sight."

Kiram was glad to leave. And he wasn't surprised to find Nestor waiting for him outside the stables.

"Are you all right? I thought your head was going to come right off."

"Genimo hits harder," Kiram said. It wasn't true but the lie was the only revenge Kiram could take against the war master.

Nestor grinned. "You've got balls, Kiram. Really."

"Thanks."

Though the rest of Kiram's afternoon classes were less eventful, a feeling of alienation clung to him. The bruise on his face was slow to darken but it ached. Kiram decided that he would rather not see the other Hellions at dinner and instead retreated to his shed to tinker with his mechanisms and feel more in his element.

Blue light streamed in through the small window in the north wall. The smell of machine oil settled around Kiram and instinctively he felt safer.

He turned a long, threaded bolt between his fingers and wondered just who had first realized that the threaded shaft would offer a stronger anchor than any nail.

Someone who could see a place for innovation, Kiram imagined, as he fed the bolt into place and tightened its nut. Someone who knew that he could make something better than anything that had come before him.

Kiram smirked at the train of his thoughts. He was describing his ideal version of himself, of course. His ancient inventor was probably just a thick-headed bastard who wanted to sink a support without bothering to get up and find a hammer.

Kiram stepped back and studied his boiler. It looked good. Its glossy, black, iron mass filled a third of the cramped shed. The secondary steam chamber had yet to be assembled. The pistons and rods lay on a shelf. The condensation chamber only existed as a heap of iron plates leaning against the wall and a series of measurements in Kiram's mind.

But it was coming together, slowly taking shape. For a moment Kiram imagined the finished mechanism. All that fire and steam driving pistons with force and precision. It would be beautiful. He could almost hear the roar of the fires inside the big boiler. He gazed up to where the first steam chamber would sit atop the boiler. It would be…

Kiram frowned. It would be too tall for the shed, that's what it would be.

He would have to remove a huge section of the roof, unless he wanted the pistons smashing through it the first time he tested his mechanism. Doubtless the sight of that would thrill the academy scholars and groundskeepers.

Kiram sighed and sat back on the cool dirt floor. It seemed like nothing would come easily for him here at the Sagrada Academy. Not his classes, not his classmates, and not even the simple, stupid proportions of a damn shed. It was like a curse.

Not a terrible, malevolent curse like the ones that filled so many holy books, but a petty, annoying vexation of a curse. A curse that was like the pain in his jaw and the hunger in his belly, slow growing and persistent.

"Where is Javier with a pie when I need him?" Kiram whispered to himself and then he wished he hadn't, because he knew where Javier was. He was at the Hellions' table, laughing and tossing dice in that hearty, arrogant Cadeleonian manner that doubtlessly pleased Master Ignacio.

"**Kihvash** to Master Ignacio," Kiram muttered to himself. He returned to working on the valve that would eventually feed cold water into the condensation chamber. It would need to endure intense heat and then sudden influxes of cold. He had used a double casing to insulate the valve in his miniature version but he didn't know how the material would hold up on a much larger scale.

Kiram heard someone knock lightly at the door but he ignored it. There was a second series of much louder knocks. He thought they might even be kicks.

"I'm busy," Kiram shouted. "Go away!"

"You're missing dinner." Javier sounded annoyed.

"I'm not hungry." As soon as the response was out of his mouth, Kiram realized how childish and petulant he sounded. It was the kind of thing a spoiled six-year-old shouted at his mother when he didn't receive the gift he wanted for Solstice.

"Well, that's too bad because I brought you something to eat," Javier responded. "Now open this damn door."

Kiram sighed. He could sulk when he was alone but with Javier standing outside, having brought him food, Kiram just felt petty. He got up and unlocked the door.

A halo of gold afternoon light poured in around Javier, accentuating the hard lines of his body and casting his face into shadow. He stepped into the shed and closed the door behind him.

The shed suddenly seemed dark, illuminated by only the dim light that fell through a small northern window and the few yellow shafts that filtered in from between the cracked planks of the walls. Kiram was very aware of how close the confines were. Javier thrust a warm bundle into his hands and turned to study the completed boiler.

"So, this is what you're always working on, is it?"

"Yes." Kiram opened his bundle and found, wrapped inside the square of cloth, a stuffed roll and a hot apple pocket.

"Fresh from the kitchen windowsill," Javier commented.

"Thanks." Kiram felt a rush of pleasure, knowing that Javier had gone out of his way to bring these things to him, and embarrassment at the same time because he'd just spent the last hour resenting Javier and the rest of the Hellions.

Kiram bit into his stuffed roll. Thick cuts of pork slid into his mouth along with a warm mustard sauce. He hadn't really realized how hungry he was until he tasted food. He tore into the remainder of the roll.

While Kiram ate, Javier circled slowly around the boiler, studying it. He opened the heavy door where the fire would burn and then peered at the valves that would eventually feed up into the first steam chamber. Kiram watched him move. There was something fascinating about the way the light filtered through his white shirt, exposing the shadows of the body beneath.

Javier turned to the unassembled pieces of the condensation chamber and the cooling valves and Kiram dropped his gaze back down to his own hands. He ate the last of his roll and then wiped the mustard sauce from the corners of his mouth with the cloth Javier had brought him.

"So, what is it?" Javier asked at last.

"A steam engine. At least it will be if I ever get it done."

"You know that the royal mechanist presented the king with a steam-driven engine five years ago, don't you?"

"Yes, but mine is an entirely new kind of steam engine. Mine will work, where the royal mechanist's simply functions."

"Really?" Javier raised a dark brow.

"Yes, really," Kiram replied. "The royal mechanist's steam engine has a boiler and a single steam chamber. When pressure builds from the boiler, it drives steam up into the chamber and that forces the piston up."

Kiram tapped one of the huge pistons on the shelf beside him. "To drop the piston back down into its starting position, the steam chamber has to be cooled so that the steam condenses and dribbles back down into the boiler. Then the entire process has to start again. The boiler has to build heat back up and warm the steam chamber all over again before the piston can make a second stroke. The process requires an absurd amount of time and fuel."

"And your engine is different?" Javier frowned at the boiler. Kiram guessed that Javier couldn't perceive his innovative design, but it didn't bother him. Mechanisms weren't Javier's strong point.

"Once it's finished, the engine will have a second steam chamber inside a condensation chamber, which will buffer the boiler and the first steam chamber from cooling, so there won't be a delay in the drive of the primary piston." Kiram gazed lovingly at his work. "It's designed so that a second piston will be driven by the contraction of steam in the condensation chamber."

Kiram watched Javier mulling all of this over then after a moment he asked, "So what does all of that mean?"

"It means that my steam engine will do twice the work of the royal mechanist's but only burn half the fuel."

"But what will this mechanism actually do?"

Kiram suddenly realized what it was that Javier wasn't asking about the means so much as the end result.

"Anything you want it to." Kiram grinned. This was where

he excelled and he rarely had any opportunity to flaunt it. "The miniature engine I built for my father powers our private mill. But an engine this big could pump water out of a deep mine or grind grain for a whole town. It could pound redbark or pulp linen. It could power almost anything. Riverships, siege engines, forge bellows, smithy hammers…It could do anything."

"Anything but ride a horse, I would suppose." Javier leaned back against the shelf next to Kiram. "Were you planning on staying out here all night?"

"No, I just didn't feel like eating at the Hellions' table." Kiram wiped a smear of oil off one of his wrenches. He'd almost managed to forget about his humiliation in riding class. "I suppose Nestor told everyone about what happened with Master Ignacio."

"No, he didn't say anything, but every other second-year student in the dining hall was jabbering about it."

"They ought to mind their own business."

"If people did that then I wouldn't need to keep my hands to myself, would I?" Javier pushed a curl of Kiram's hair back from his face. Kiram flushed and he could tell from Javier's smile that this was the response Javier had wanted. "They were saying Master Ignacio laid you out flat."

"I never hit the ground." Kiram wasn't sure why it mattered but it did.

Javier caught his arm and gently led him toward the window. He frowned as he studied the left side of Kiram's cheek and jaw.

"Looks like it hurt some," Javier said.

"Yeah, some." Kiram didn't want to complain about an injury to Javier. "I didn't make a scene on purpose. I just…I don't know, did something that made Firaj think I wanted him to perform this strange backwards prance."

"Motesdo steps," Javier supplied. "Not too many horses know them."

"Well, Firaj does. And he was pretty proud of it too, but then the next thing I knew Master Ignacio was furious with me. When I tried to explain that I hadn't done it on purpose he hit me."

"That's not like Master Ignacio," Javier said.

"What's that supposed to mean?"

"It's not like him to lose control in front of an entire class." Javier seemed to disregard the challenge in Kiram's tone. "What else did he say?"

"I don't know," Kiram replied. He pulled out of Javier's grip and returned to the shelf to put his wrench away. "He just ranted about how his teachings were the ways of the greatest Cadeleonian men and that he didn't care if I was a Haldiim genius, I still had to respect him."

Kiram glanced back to Javier. He seemed to be assessing Kiram.

"How bad is your riding?" Javier asked at last.

"What does that have to do with anything?"

"Aside from the fact that the whole matter took place during a riding class, and was provoked by your riding? Oh nothing. I'm just making conversation." Javier shook his head at Kiram. "I think Master Ignacio must be really agitated about you riding in the tournament race. I can't see any other reason that he'd lash out like that."

"Not just because he's a jackass, perhaps?" Kiram suggested.

"He's never struck a student out of sheer rage before."

"Maybe that's because he's never had a Haldiim student before." Kiram gave Javier a challenging look. Javier didn't reply and Kiram could see that the thought troubled him. Master Ignacio was important to Javier, as few other people were. Suddenly Kiram did not want to tear down Javier's hero.

"I'm a terrible rider," Kiram admitted. "I'm easily the worst in the entire class. If Firaj weren't such a well-trained horse I would probably have already been trampled."

"It's not the horses, is it? Do they frighten you?"

"It's not fear, just inexperience. I'd never ridden a horse before I got to the academy."

"Never?" Javier looked genuinely startled at this revelation.

"No, never."

Javier was quiet for a few minutes, simply staring at the shafts of light that cut across the floor of the shed.

"We're going to have to do something about that," Javier said at last. Then he straightened and started for the door.

"Wait, Javier?" Kiram called to him and he turned back.

"What is it?"

"I…I was wondering if you'd be back up in the room before the last bell?" Kiram hoped that the pleading feeling in him didn't carry through to his words. Javier bowed his head, so that his dark hair hid his eyes.

"No, I'll stay away. You don't have to hide down here in this shed." He turned back and opened the door. Kiram had enough time to tell him that he didn't want him to stay away, to tell Javier that he'd missed his company and even his arrogant humor.

But he said nothing, because it was the only wise thing to do, for both their sakes.

He watched as Javier stepped outside and the door fell closed behind him.

Chapter Fifteen

When Javier shook him awake early the next morning, Kiram wasn't ready to greet the day. His eyes clenched closed. He rolled over and Javier jabbed him in the back.

"Up," Javier said firmly. "Get up."

"No," Kiram moaned. "First bell hasn't rung yet."

"We aren't going to lounge around waiting for the bells. You have a riding lesson. So get up." Javier's hand slipped under Kiram's blankets. His fingers caressed Kiram's shoulder and then closed around Kiram's nipple. The sensation was delicious at first but then Javier pinched him harder. Kiram jerked upright and shoved Javier back.

"Fine, damn it!" Kiram was so groggy he almost fell out of the bed. "I'm getting up. Damn you, you—I can't even think of a Cadeleonian obscenity that's filthy enough for you, right now."

"Khivash?" Javier suggested.

Kiram pulled his eyes all the way open and regarded Javier. Not only did he look annoyingly refreshed and well dressed but now he was speaking Haldiim. It hadn't been just a dream the previous night.

"Where did you learn that word?" Kiram demanded.

"I must have picked it up somewhere or other." He offered Kiram a smug little smile.

"It was in Calixto's diary, wasn't it?" Kiram slowly staggered up out of the bed. Faint predawn light filtered in through the windows.

"His friend Yassin was the last Haldiim anywhere near this area for centuries, I'm sure." Kiram scrubbed at his eyes trying to get the sleep out of them.

"You're correct in your first deduction but wrong in your second." Javier tossed Kiram his riding clothes. They hadn't been washed yet and the pungent odors of sweat, horses, and saddle leather wafted up.

"Wait a moment," Kiram said as Javier's comment slowly sank in. "There are other Haldiim here?" Kiram wondered if they would sell him some adhil bread or spiced lamb. It would almost be worth putting on these rank clothes and enduring a morning ride, if he could eat lamb ground with cinnamon served with thick yogurt.

"A troupe of Haldiim performers travel this far north for the autumn tournament. They tell fortunes, sell charms, and pretty much steal anything they can get their hands on. They're none too friendly, nor too clean, either. I doubt they'd know what to do with a nice boy like you."

"Do they keep crows?" Kiram asked.

Javier nodded.

"They sound like Irabiim, not Haldiim." Kiram wasn't surprised that Javier didn't seem to recognize the name. Few Cadeleonians understood that the descendants of Jhahiim were not one group but more than a dozen separate tribes. Generally, Cadeleonians referred to them all as Haldiim, a practice that infuriated Kiram's mother.

"The Irabiim tribe broke off from the Haldiim a long time ago," Kiram told Javier. "They're much more nomadic than we are. A lot of them are thieves and worse. My grandmother used to say that the Irabiim bring trouble to a town and leave the Haldiim to settle it."

"She might have had something there. Last year there was a huge fight between several of them and some of our grooms over a missing horse."

Suddenly Kiram thought of the dead groom and Fedeles' comment about Haldiim murderers. He doubted that Fedeles knew the difference between Haldiim and Irabiim either.

Kiram asked, "Was Victaro Irdad involved in this fight?"

"Who told you about Victaro?"

"I saw his grave. Fedeles told me Haldiim murdered him. Do you think he could have meant the Irabiim?"

"I doubt it. Victaro was killed during the spring break. The Irabiim—am I saying that correctly?" Kiram nodded and Javier continued, "The Irabiim had been gone since autumn. They would have been several counties away."

Kiram frowned in disappointment at the loss of a neat solution.

"You probably shouldn't tell anyone else about what Fedeles said," Javier told him.

"Why not?" Kiram stripped off his nightshirt and tossed it back onto the bed. He didn't miss the way Javier gazed at his naked body.

"You said it yourself earlier. Most people are just looking for an excuse to act on their prejudices. An accusation of murder against the Irabiim might be all it takes to get them killed. They may be dirty but I don't think they should be blamed for Victaro's murder, do you?"

"No, of course not." Kiram staggered to the bathroom and washed his face. He scrubbed at his teeth with a paste of pumice and clove oil then spat it out. "I just can't figure out why Fedeles would tell me that."

Javier walked to the doorway of the bathroom. "I don't know. He says a lot of things but they can't all be taken seriously."

"I know." Kiram accepted the shirt Javier handed him. It was cleaner than the pants. "But I don't think everything he says should be dismissed either. Someone really did kill that groom."

"Nestor can't have failed to inform you about the culprit," Javier said.

"He told me. Everyone thinks you did it." Kiram looked directly into Javier's face. He saw the momentary hurt in Javier's expression and then that almost challenging look of amusement returned.

"If I did, he wouldn't be the first man I've killed."

"You didn't kill him," Kiram replied flatly. He walked past Javier to the dresser and retrieved his stockings.

"You'll want to wear your riding boots," Javier told him. Kiram grabbed them. He sat down on his bed to pull the tight leather boots on. Javier studied him for a moment.

"How do you know I didn't kill Victaro?" Javier asked at last.

"Just consider yourself as a criminal. What kind of crimes do you commit and how do you commit them?"

Javier frowned in puzzlement, which pleased Kiram, so he continued with his analysis.

"You don't seem like the kind of man who would leave a lot of evidence. When you were just stealing a pie you still took care not to get caught. It just doesn't seem in your nature that you'd be so messy or so willing to let everyone think you had killed Victaro if you really had."

"So, you're saying that the fact that I won't deny killing Victaro means I didn't do it? That doesn't strike me as the most indisputable of arguments I've ever encountered," Javier replied.

"No, but it doesn't make me wrong either. You didn't kill him. You're taking the blame because you know that your title will shield you from prosecution. That means that not only do you know the killer's identity but that it's someone whom you wish to protect."

Javier gazed down to his hands, frowning, and Kiram knew he had to be right. He could only think of one person whom Javier would protect so staunchly. Javier defended him so fiercely that he had free run of the entire academy. But allowing him to murder a groom? Kiram didn't know if he could believe that either.

The purely intellectual aspect of Kiram wanted to force the subject, to corner Javier and make him to admit what he knew. But a deeper, wiser instinct kept him quiet. He didn't think he was ready just yet to know what Javier was truly capable of doing to protect his cousin.

And for all he knew Fedeles had acted in his own self-defense, if the groom really had assaulted him…Kiram just didn't know and for the first time in his life he thought he might not have the right to ask. This wasn't a philosophical curiosity, or a mathematical problem; it was Javier's and Fedeles' private lives.

Javier made the choice for him. He strode to the wardrobe and tossed Kiram a heavy jacket. "The sun's hardly up. It's going to be cold outside."

Kiram followed Javier down through the dormitory and across the grounds to the stables.

Outside, the air was cool and only faint rays of sunlight passed through the surrounding orchards. Deep blue shadows stretched across the cobblestone walkways and pooled in the recesses of the buildings. Kiram expected the grounds to be deserted but dozens of servants clogged the paths and scurried between the buildings. Scullery boys dashed from the gardens with baskets of vegetables, while housemen hauled buckets of water from the well to the dormitory. Smoke already pumped up from the smithy. And in the distant shadows of the woods Kiram thought he spied the figure of a groundskeeper returning from his hunt with sacks of dead rabbits, or perhaps quail.

In the stable, the grooms hauled fresh hay to the stalls, changing out feed and water, and leading horses to the farrier. They kept clear of Javier as he strode through the stable. Kiram noticed that many of the grooms watched Javier's approach with intense fear. After he passed by they shot hateful glances at his back.

If Javier noticed any of this, he gave no indication. He walked through the stable as if he had the building all to himself. Kiram followed him, suppressing his apprehension at the thought of so many grooms glaring at his back.

At last, Javier stopped in front of a stall. Almost immediately Firaj poked his big black head over the door. His ears pricked up slightly and Kiram hoped it was a sign of the horse's interest, not annoyance.

Javier held out the back of his hand and Firaj drew in a deep snort and then sighed out a soft, pleased noise.

"Today I thought we'd take a slow walk around the academy grounds." Javier's voice was so soothingly gentle that Kiram suspected he was addressing the horse as much as him. "Does that sound all right to you?"

"I guess…I've only ridden in the arena."

"After three months Firaj is probably bored with that routine."

"Horses get bored?" Kiram couldn't imagine an animal that was content to stand in a pasture grazing for hours on end being bored by anything.

"Of course." Javier stroked Firaj's cheek. "They feel as much as any man does and they aren't above playing pranks to alleviate their tedium."

"You don't think Firaj pranced backwards just because he was bored, do you?"

"I don't know, but I think he might enjoy something new so long as it isn't too startling." Javier glanced back at Kiram and smiled. "He's a little like you that way, I think."

Kiram was sure that if it hadn't been so early he would have had a retort, but as it was he just rolled his eyes at Javier.

Javier showed him how to saddle and bridle Firaj. Previously the grooms had always done this for him. Kiram hadn't thought it took so much work. Somehow he'd imagined that the grooms just tossed the saddles on the horses' backs and buckled them up and everything was ready. Instead he discovered that he had to work slowly, warming the bit in his hands and tightening the girth incrementally so that neither device caused Firaj undue irritation.

"You have to show him that you'll be good to him, or he won't trust you to direct him. Though that doesn't mean letting him get away with anything he likes." Javier gave Kiram a meaningful glance.

"I'm not a horse," Kiram responded.

"Of course not," Javier replied but then he smiled. "Though there are similarities between horses and men."

Kiram pulled the girth another notch tighter. Firaj seemed to hardly notice. He had given himself up completely to Javier's firm strokes and scratches. He brought his head down happily to accept the bridle when Javier slipped it over his nose and buckled it behind his head.

"A mount must acknowledge that the rider is in charge, first and foremost." Javier sounded a little more serious. "There are any number of ways to convince a horse of that. The fastest is to simply beat him when he resists. But that tends to produce a mount without courage. He will run for you but only because he's afraid not to. If he comes up against something he fears more than you then he will disobey. Fear only goes so far. If you're going to ask something truly difficult of him, like carrying you into battle or taking a blind leap, then he can't just fear you. He has to trust you and love you."

"I don't think Firaj trusts, fears, or loves me," Kiram said.

"No, probably not. He's just met you. I think you still have to teach him to respect you." Javier checked the girth and then handed the horse's reins to Kiram. "Why don't you lead him out?"

"How do I do make him trust me?" Kiram asked Javier as they walked through the stable.

"Be kind but firm with him. Stop him when he goes too far. Just don't let him take advantage of you." Javier glanced at Kiram. "Treat him the same way you treat me. You'll do just fine."

"Very funny."

Once they were outside, Kiram swung up into Firaj's saddle. He was happy that he had mastered this one aspect of riding if none other. He could mount and dismount smoothly.

"So, where to now?" Kiram asked.

"We'll follow the orchard trail. I'll walk alongside you."

In the orchard, the branches of the apple trees hung low with fruit. Kiram could hear the stream far ahead. A brilliant blue jay screeched at them as they passed. Kiram watched as the bird flitted from one tree to the next and then it disappeared back into the shadows of the orchard.

"The jays in Anacleto aren't nearly so bright," Kiram commented. "Their heads are completely black, so they look like they've all singed their faces from looking down chimneys. My grandmother used to call them soot-beaked spies." Kiram had expected this ride to be more of an ordeal, like the lessons he took with Master Ignacio. But Javier seemed content to simply stride along as if he were taking a morning stroll.

"The jays in Rauma are blue like these, but much bigger and louder. I've never liked jays. Might be one of the reasons I'm not so fond of the color blue either," Javier commented.

"You must get pretty sick of these uniforms then." Kiram glanced down at Javier. "What color do you like?"

Javier looked back up at him. His expression seemed so relaxed that Kiram wondered if he might still be a little sleepy.

"I like gold and yellow," Javier said. "Your hair is almost exactly the perfect color."

Kiram wasn't prepared for such an artless compliment from Javier. Somehow it touched him more deeply than any of Javier's innuendos. He felt his cheeks flushing a bright red.

This once Javier didn't gloat over Kiram's reaction. He seemed more concerned with Kiram's riding.

"Try to sit up a little straighter," Javier said. "If you hunch like that your back will take a pounding. It'll really hurt after a long race."

"I'm not going to be racing...am I?"

"This year you'll only be in the opening competition, but next year, who knows? Either way you'll be more comfortable if you straighten a little more. That's it." Javier studied him for a moment. "You've got decent posture for someone who's never ridden before."

"It's from dancing, I think."

"Maybe. Or you might have picked up more from Master Ignacio than you think. Rein Firaj to a stop and have him stand at attention while you pick a few of those apples."

Kiram followed Javier's instructions. He had a little difficulty keeping Firaj from grazing but at last succeeded and picked four apples from an overhanging branch.

"At the end of the ride you should give him an apple."

"Would you like one?"

Javier nodded. "Hand it to me though, don't throw it. Horses can spook if there are things flying around behind their heads."

Kiram did as he was instructed and Javier peeled the red skin from one of the apples with his penknife. Kiram was impressed with how quickly and cleanly he did it. He wondered if an affinity for carving ran in Javier's family.

"Has Fedeles ever shown you any of his carvings?" Kiram asked.

"Carvings?" Javier frowned. "He carves?"

"He said he did. He showed me several figures cut into trees near the stream."

"Do you mean all those birds and that little man picking his nose that looks just like Holy Father Habalan?" Javier asked.

"I thought he looked something like Holy Father Habalan too," Kiram admitted.

Javier didn't look amused. "Fedeles didn't carve that or any of the others. They were here when we arrived at the Academy three years ago. He must be playing some kind of joke on you." Javier cut a wedge out of his apple and handed the piece to Kiram.

"What's wrong with him?" That wasn't quite what Kiram wanted to know, but he didn't think Javier would answer him honestly if he asked whether Fedeles was getting worse.

"I told you, he's cursed." Javier stared out into the deep blue shadows of the orchard.

"But cursed how? I mean, do you know what this curse does?" Kiram took a bite of his apple. A sharp, fragrant taste filled his mouth. He guessed that most people would have preferred something sweeter, but he liked the edge to the flavor.

"The curse burns into your body like a fever and fills your head with nightmares," Javier said softly. "At first you hear screams but they sound like they're far away and they don't come often.

You start hearing them more in the evenings, especially when you're lying in bed just on the verge of falling asleep. You get stomach aches and strange, piercing pains. You begin to dream of dying. Night after night you dream of iron pikes splitting up through your body, and the weight of your own flesh driving you further down onto them. Soon the dreams spread into your waking hours. The pain becomes unceasing and all you can hear are screams, hundreds of screams. You can't speak. You can't eat. You can hardly think. All you want is to die."

Javier shoved his hair back from his face, his expression strangely tense. "It came for me when I was seven. It would have killed me if my father hadn't passed the white hell to me then. He saved my life but it left him no defense of his own. The curse took him last year and now it's killing Fedeles."

Javier glanced up at Kiram. His dark eyes were too bright and though he had shed no tears, Kiram thought he must have come close. Javier made an effort at one of his unconcerned smiles.

"The thing is, I can save Fedeles. I know how. All I have to do is give the white hell to him. It will burn the curse out of him."

"But then you wouldn't have any protection," Kiram stated.

Javier nodded and dropped his gaze from Kiram.

"I love Fedeles but I'm just too much of a pig to die like that, even for him." Javier hurled his peeled apple away violently. A jay shrieked as the apple struck a tree branch. Firaj gave a slight shake of his head but didn't seem alarmed by the sudden motion or noise.

They traveled a little further in silence, crossing a second bridge over the stream and wandering slowly back towards the academy. Kiram wished he could think of something to say but there were no words he knew of that could make any of what Javier had described seem less terrible.

For the first time in his life he wondered what he would really be willing to sacrifice for his own brother or sisters. Would he be willing to suffer and die the way Javier described for any one of them? He loved his family and yet he didn't know that he would be able to make that sacrifice.

At last, Javier glanced to Kiram.

He said, "You're slouching again."

Kiram straightened.

"And don't look so serious."

"What do you mean, don't look serious? That curse is terrible!"

"Believe me, I know. But many things are terrible. You can't let yourself brood on them, especially not the things you can't change."

"But maybe this curse could be changed. Maybe there's a solution that—"

"That no one but you has thought of?" Javier's expression was one of amused skepticism. Kiram suddenly realized just how arrogant the suggestion had been. "This curse has hunted my family for eighteen years. Trust me, any solution you could imagine, some desperate Tornesal has already attempted. There have been dozens of exorcisms and pilgrimages. Vows, penances, bribes. The cathedral my uncle funded is still being built, and he's been dead seventeen years now. Before my mother died there were shifts of priests who prayed day and night for her safety. There have been blood sacrifices and even black magic. So far only Scholar Donamillo's mechanical cures have had any effect at all. And it's still no real salvation."

Kiram frowned down at the reins in his hands. He had nothing to offer. Still he hated the thought of simply giving up.

"And in any case, this is my concern. Not yours," Javier told him firmly. "You have your own problems to worry about."

"I don't have any problems as dangerous as yours."

"You may think so, but Master Ignacio might just kill you if you don't improve your riding. So I'd concentrate on that if I were you." Javier gave him one of his hard smiles.

Kiram let the subject drop. He knew Javier didn't want to discuss the curse and wouldn't be goaded. At the same time it wasn't as if Kiram could simply forget that some strange, cruel curse was hunting his upperclassman's family.

He couldn't help but wonder what had caused the curse. What gave it its power, and most importantly what could destroy it? The fact that a mechanism had impacted it—at least protected Fedeles to some extent—made Kiram think that perhaps he could find some solution. Perhaps Scholar Donamillo could use his help if Kiram could approach him in the right way.

"More jays," Javier commented.

Kiram watched them pass overhead. He forced his attention back to his riding lesson, keeping his weight down in his saddle and working into the rhythm of Firaj's long gait. Javier corrected his posture once more as they continued the ride.

When they reached the academy, bright golden sunlight illuminated the grounds and the low boom of the first bell reverberated from the chapel. None of the house servants were anywhere in sight and most of the grooms were out exercising the horses.

It was quiet in the stable. Javier showed Kiram how to brush a horse down and reminded him to offer Firaj the apple he'd picked. Firaj seemed to appreciate the treat. Though Kiram wasn't good at grooming him, Firaj endured his ministrations patiently.

"It's good to touch him. He needs to grow accustomed to your physical presence as much as you need to get used to his," Javier commented as Kiram finished brushing Firaj's coat. "When you're comfortable together it will be easier to trust each other."

Kiram glanced back. Javier returned his gaze for a moment and then reached out and tucked a curl of Kiram's hair back behind his ear.

"You'll get a little less afraid of him as time goes on," Javier said. "And he'll want to please you more and more."

Kiram knew Javier was taking advantage of the moment but this once Kiram didn't admonish him. He didn't know if it was the gentleness of Javier's expression or simply that he seemed to deserve some kind of comfort.

Kiram knew that if Javier pulled him close, kissed him, or even slipped his strong hands into his clothes, he would have allowed it. More than allowed it.

But Javier only smiled and then turned away to the door of the stall.

"Wash up before breakfast," Javier told him and then he left the stable. Kiram was both irritated and relieved. Then Firaj lifted his tail and dropped a tremendous pile of pungent excrement only inches from Kiram's boot.

"You beast," Kiram muttered to the horse. It seemed to him that Firaj looked quite pleased with himself.

Chapter Sixteen

The next month Kiram kept so busy that he could hardly remember a time when he didn't ride, train, or spend long hours poring over medical papers that Scholar Donamillo handed him in response to his many questions about Fedeles' condition.

As crisp fall winds set in and the days grew shorter and the nights long and cold, Kiram began to see certain advances.

He became familiar with Firaj's sense of humor, as well as the gelding's favorite places to be brushed, his preferences in apples, and the astonishing amount of filth he could accumulate in his hooves.

Kiram's riding skills improved as well, though it was not always obvious in Master Ignacio's classes. At times when Master Ignacio sneered at him and snapped criticisms ceaselessly, Kiram's nervousness undermined him. He tended to confuse the command for a trot with that of a prance. At least once a week he and Firaj were out of step with the other riders.

But now Kiram didn't allow small mistakes to panic him. That was the one thing he had learned from observing Javier handle Lunaluz when they went riding together each morning. No matter what happened, whether Lunaluz was obstinate or nervous, Javier remained calm and firm. His collected manner always settled his mount.

That knowledge served Kiram well. He controlled Firaj with more and more consistency each day. None of the few errors he made enraged Master Ignacio enough to strike him again.

He improved in battle practice as well.

When pitted against his fellow second-year students his focus rarely wavered and his speed gave him an edge. He managed to best both Ollivar and Ladislo two falls out of three. The week after that, Kiram even managed to pin Chilla and then Nestor, which resulted in Nestor calling him 'a wily beast' and another exchange of coins between Elezar and Javier.

Then they'd advanced from hand-to-hand combat to duels with wooden swords. Javier made every motion look easy, when he demonstrated the sword stances. In reality Kiram discovered that it was a challenge just to make himself aim his blows at his opponent's body and not his blade. The whole idea of it—that he was teaching himself to drive a sword into another man's heart—appalled him. Kiram couldn't delude himself about the nature of swordplay. Men trained with swords for the single purpose of hardening their bodies and minds to the cruelty of killing.

Kiram hated the idea, particularly when his opponent was Nestor.

He simply could not take any pleasure in exploiting Nestor's poor vision to murder him, not even when the mortal wound was no more than a tap across his chest or neck. Nestor unfailingly complimented him on his strikes and that only made Kiram more uncomfortable.

At times Kiram found it frightening to watch Javier and Elezar demonstrate techniques. They were both skilled with blades and though they were friends, when they fought neither of them held back. They had both drawn blood on more than one occasion.

Elezar struck with so much force that he often cracked the tip off of Javier's wooden blade. He charged in with a shout and always took the offensive. His raw, muscular power drove his attacks. Sometimes Kiram thought nothing could wear Elezar down.

"He's like a bull," Nestor whispered. "You hit him and it just makes him madder."

Kiram nodded, though his attention was focused on Javier.

Unlike Elezar, he rarely relied on sheer muscle and he never overextended his thrusts. He looked so relaxed and his smile was so assured that his hundreds of parries and strikes seemed effortless. But when Kiram really studied Javier's form he could see that Javier was constantly working at Elezar's defenses. He was constantly moving around him, testing and pushing him. Javier was a master of footwork. He never stood still, but always edged subtly in and out of Elezar's strike range.

He drew Elezar out, slowly wearing him down with precise blow after blow. He didn't underestimate Elezar's speed the way Atreau often did. Instead he restrained himself, patiently whittling away at Elezar's energy, waiting for him to get clumsy and make a mistake.

When that moment came, Javier's entire demeanor changed. His smile dropped. He lunged past Elezar's wide swing and punched his cracked blade into the thick padding that protected Elezar's heart. Almost instantly he jerked back out of Elezar's reach. In that moment, just as he pulled back from the killing strike all of the strain of the fight showed in his face. Javier looked both sick and stricken. Then he was smiling again.

"You're dead, my friend," Javier told Elezar.

"You barely..." Elezar looked down at the chest of his padded jacket. A thick white lump of wool protruded from the gash in the canvas. "Well, damn it. Who's going wed those six pregnant whores now?"

"I'm sure they'll manage to find some other dolt," Javier replied.

Nestor leaned a little closer to Kiram and whispered, "Mother would kill Elezar if that really happened."

"How do you know it hasn't?"

"Oh, I'd know," Nestor assured him and Kiram took his word for it. After all, Nestor had a knack for collecting all the whispers and rumors that circulated around the academy. He had kept Kiram apprised of all of the love letters that Atreau received, as well as the rumors of Holy Father Habalan's affair with a milkmaid.

And surprisingly, he was also one of the only reliable sources that Kiram could find for information concerning the curse that plagued the Tornesal family .

Later, when they sat side by side in the library studying, Kiram decided Nestor's insights might be just as good as anyone else's.

Kiram had expected to uncover dozens of references to the curse in academy diaries and biographies. Certainly every other minor affliction of the powerful Tornesal family had been noted. Letters and journals abounded with mentions of *fever passions, congenital cruelty,* and *bloodlust.* But until the most recent writings there wasn't a single suggestion of a curse destroying the Tornesals.

The curse was apparently a new phenomenon. According to Nestor, it had first struck one of Javier's uncles eighteen years ago. The curse never afflicted the Sagradas or the Fueres despite the fact that they had intermarried with the Tornesals extensively. At the same time it hunted down inheriting women like Fedeles' mother even when they had married out of the family.

"It's like it knows which of them could inherit the dukedom and goes after them. Doesn't that seem suspicious?" Kiram studied a painting of the Tornesal family tree. The vast branches narrowed to a single line bearing Javier's name.

"Maybe the dukedom is what really makes them Tornesals. You know, like cured ham and goose fat makes a prince's pie. Without them, it's just bean stew in a crust." Nestor turned a page of his own book and Kiram caught sight of the title: *One Thousand Royal Feasts and Banquets.* "I overheard Holy Father Habalan saying that if Javier would only turn the power of the white hell over to the royal bishop then the curse would be lifted."

"What do you think he meant by that exactly?" Kiram wondered. "It sounds almost like blackmail or a threat."

Nestor blanched and then shook his head.

"I'm sure that's not the way he meant it. He probably thinks, like a lot of people do, that the white hell has gotten a taste for Tornesal blood and now it wants them all."

"Why would it wait eighty-two years for that?"

"Maybe Tornesals are an acquired taste, like tomatoes," Nestor had replied. "I used to hate tomatoes when I was young but just yesterday I had one and I thought it didn't taste so bad."

"I'll take that into consideration," Kiram replied.

"Doesn't sound likely?" Nestor asked.

"Not from what I've read."

Kiram had dredged through hundreds of Cadeleonian texts searching for mentions of curses. All the descriptions bore striking similarities. They were dated from the time of King Nazario Sagrada or earlier, and curses were always described as Haldiim in origin. They were always acts of retaliation for a wrong done.

One fragile text described how the souls of two murdered Haldiim children had become a curse and ravaged the house and lands of the baron who killed them until a Haldiim witch—Kiram recognized the description as a Bahiim—had trapped the curse and bound its fury into the wood of a great oak tree where it could do no more harm.

The mention of a Bahiim dispelling the curse had offered Kiram some hope that he could, at last, get accurate information regarding curses. He'd immediately written to his uncle's husband, Alizadeh, to ask what he knew, but he'd not yet received a response.

The next two weeks offered Kiram no time at all to contemplate curses or even mechanisms. In addition to riding with Javier, constant battle training, and learning the formal rules of engagement, his time had recently been taken up by fittings for the leather cuirass, byrnie, and gauntlets he would be wearing for his fights; he was also drilling on horseback for the opening parade through the city of Zancoda.

The last two weeks before the tournament the majority of scholars had given up their class times to allow Master Ignacio to keep the students in constant training. Only Scholar Blasio and Scholar Donamillo refused. Scholar Blasio gave extensive lectures, but also tolerated a great deal of napping. Kiram guessed that it was just to spite Master Ignacio and he warmed to Scholar Blasio more for it.

However the last week before the autumn tournament Scholar Donamillo also excused his class. Though he asked Kiram to help him carry several books from his classroom to the infirmary.

The air smelled of liniment and sweat. Dozens of young men sprawled across the medical cots. Most sported ugly bruises and cuts or wore bandages over their various sprains. Many seemed to be sleeping, though one fourth-year student looked perfectly healthy and seemed to be using the time to read. Kiram felt a little awed that Donamillo had managed to teach his classes for so long and still treat all the bumped, bruised, and sprained youths in his infirmary.

"This way, to my office." Donamillo led Kiram past the cots and between two huge black screens into the space where he kept not only his hulking mechanical cures but also a desk and shelves overflowing with books and medical instruments. Light glinted off the glass panes of his mechanical cure, lending a radiance to the scholar's deeply lined face.

"I hope you're managing to find time for the Crown Challenge." Scholar Donamillo laid several tomes down on his already cluttered desk. He indicated with a wave of his hand that Kiram ought to rest the books he carried anywhere on the wooden shelves.

"Not so much right now." Kiram glanced away. He hadn't worked on his steam engine for nearly a month. The Tornesal curse was just so much more important than winning a challenge. People had died because of the curse. Fedeles was going mad because of it.

"I know it isn't a classroom subject, but I was wondering if you could tell me a little more about your mechanical cures?" Kiram asked.

Scholar Donamillo offered him only the hint of a smile.

"Hoping to get out of Master Ignacio's grip for several hours?"

"No, sir. I really do want to know more. I've been trying to work it out on my own, reading all the texts you've recommended but—"

"I think it might be allowable. Just this once, you understand." Scholar Donamillo gave him a stern look.

"Yes, sir." Kiram almost bowed and Scholar Donamillo's countenance softened slightly. When he relaxed, Scholar Donamillo's resemblance to Scholar Blasio increased. For a moment Kiram imagined that he could see just what Scholar Blasio would be like fifteen years from now: far less permissive, but still intelligent and kind.

"Look here." Scholar Donamillo beckoned Kiram closer to the two huge mechanical cures. "Study them and tell me what you can."

Kiram spent the next two hours with Scholar Donamillo, examining the faceted spheres of the mechanical cures and studying the stacks of copper plates that generated the mechanisms' charges.

While both mechanisms were very similar Kiram noticed that one of them contained a harness while the other had none. The thick panes of glass that made up one of the spheres seemed darker than the other. The edges looked sooty and black. The glass of the other mechanical cure looked milky. Kiram also noticed that the markings etched into the metal supports of the two mechanisms differed greatly.

At first Kiram had thought that they were marks to aid in the assembly of the mechanisms, but as he looked closer he realized that they resembled the symbols drawn across Javier's floor.

"What are these?" Kiram asked at last.

"Prayers," Scholar Donamillo replied, as if it were a perfectly reasonable response.

Kiram stared at him. "Prayers?"

Scholar Donamillo nodded.

"That's completely contrary to the philosophy of mechanism." Kiram frowned at the black lines. "It's turning science back into superstition."

"Half of medicine is faith, Kiram. I have immense admiration for mechanism. It's a great achievement to create tools that will serve all people regardless of their breed or religion. But these mechanical cures must do more than be admirable." Scholar Donamillo traced a sinuous black symbol. "These mechanisms keep Fedeles Quemanor alive. That's all that matters in the end."

"I didn't mean to criticize." Kiram gazed at the fine, flowing black symbols and the thin copper wires that threaded through the harnesses.

Now he couldn't help but feel a little excited and curious about why this particular union of science and faith had proved so effective when previous mechanical cures had done nothing for the Tornesals. But then neither had other prayers. Even holy invocations issued by bishops had failed to stop the curse.

"What do these prayers say?" Kiram asked.

"It would be easier to tell you what they do than what they say."

"What do they do, then?"

Scholar Donamillo stepped a little closer to Kiram, his expression grave.

"Are you willing to keep a secret, Kiram Kir-Zaki? Can I trust you?"

Kiram nodded. Scholar Donamillo smiled just a little.

"Do you know anything about transfusions?" Scholar Donamillo asked in a whisper.

"I read a mention of a physician who tried to treat a dying boy by siphoning blood from his mother and father down into his veins. The boy lived for a short while but eventually died of blood poisoning."

"This is a different kind of transfusion, but similar in concept. Every month or so, I give a little of my life to Fedeles. I believe it disguises his Tornesal blood and keeps the curse at bay. It isn't a cure…not yet. He still has an extreme reaction but I have seen improvements in him over the last three years. He's talking more now and he even has moments of rational thought."

"You give him your life?" The magnitude of it stunned Kiram. Wasn't that what Javier had said a month ago? The only way he could save Fedeles was to sacrifice his own life? Kiram would never have expected anything like this from Scholar Donamillo. He'd always seemed so reserved and distant.

"It's the best I can offer him for the time being." Scholar Donamillo kept his voice low. "At first I had thought that Javier might be a better match for him but Javier isn't…compatible with the mechanical cures. Needless to say, what I'm doing is not something that Holy Father Habalan or many of my colleagues would approve of. So you must keep this a secret. They may tolerate the white hell when it's wielded by a duke, but here in the northern counties they still hang common men for witchcraft."

Kiram blanched at the thought of Scholar Donamillo being dragged to a scaffold and hanged.

"I won't tell anyone. I swear on my life," Kiram whispered.

Scholar Donamillo seemed amused by Kiram's unsolicited oath and he felt suddenly embarrassed. It was something a little boy would have said.

"Do you think there's any way I could help you, sir?"

"In fact I have been thinking about that for some time now. That mechanism that you're building, it's an engine of some kind, isn't it?"

"Yes, sir."

Scholar Donamillo pointed to the large hand cranks at the bases of the mechanical cures.

"Right now I have to crank these mechanical cures by hand or have Genimo do it for me. But if I had an engine, that might make all the difference. I might be able to maintain the treatment long enough to actually drive the curse out of Fedeles." Scholar Donamillo gazed intently at Kiram. "Would you be willing to become my accomplice, Kiram? I will understand if you aren't willing to take the risk…"

"I'd be honored to help, in any way I can, sir."

"Good." Scholar Donamillo patted Kiram's shoulder and when he smiled at Kiram the deep wrinkles at the corners of his mouth lifted so that he looked much younger. "I knew I'd made the right decision about you."

Kiram would have thanked him for the compliment but his words were cut short by the sound of Javier hissing his name across the infirmary. Scholar Donamillo indicated that he should go with just a wave of his hand. Kiram stepped out from behind the black blinds and picked his way between the cots of sleeping students.

Javier stood in the middle of the infirmary, still dressed in his riding clothes.

"Nestor said Scholar Donamillo had to take you to the infirmary." As Javier closed the distance between them his gaze moved over Kiram's body, searching for some sign of an injury.

"I was feeling nauseous," Kiram said. "I'm better now."

"Really." Javier stepped closer. The deep scents of leather and sweat wafted over Kiram. When he had first arrived at the academy he had found the smell of men's sweat overpowering, but now it was familiar, almost comforting.

"Nestor said you hurt your arm," Javier murmured to him. "The two of you should really get your stories straight."

"My arm hurt so badly that I felt nauseous."

"You're a terrible liar." Javier still looked slightly concerned. "You really aren't sick, are you?"

"No. I'm not. Scholar Donamillo just..." Kiram shrugged. "I guess he took pity on me and let me hide in the infirmary. I've been looking at his mechanical cures and we were discussing how my engine might help power them." Kiram felt he could say that much without betraying his promise to Scholar Donamillo. "I'm really not sick at all."

"Good, because a huge package just arrived for you and Nestor is so sure that it's crammed with more of those candies that your mother always sends that he's overcome all fear and is guarding it up in our room."

When Kiram reached the tower room he discovered that Nestor was indeed there. His hair was stringy with dried sweat and he sat on the floor with his shirt hanging half open. He looked exhausted. A huge wooden crate towered up behind him.

"Nestor, I can't believe that you came in here." Kiram grinned at him. To his surprise Nestor shot Javier an irritated look and shoved his spectacles up on his nose imperiously.

"He made me help him carry it up. Three flights of stairs!" Nestor complained. "And once I was here what would the point be of running off? If the white hell is going to take me then at least I ought to get a few of those sweets your mother sends first. Don't you think?"

Kiram chuckled and said, "Yes, absolutely."

Javier might tease him for considering selling his soul for knowledge, but Nestor was obviously willing to give it up for candy. Though when Kiram considered the amount of weight Nestor had lost and how much he'd grown over the last four months, Kiram supposed he might just be desperate for anything to eat.

"Well," Javier said, "let's get it open and see what's inside."

"You don't think that there could be one of those autumn meat pies in there, do you?" Nestor asked. He sounded almost delirious. "I'm really not going to be devoured by the white hell, am I?"

"No." Javier began to pry the crate open. "You're under protection as a courier."

Kiram rolled his eyes at this.

"I don't know if I believe that the white hell recognizes the king's protection of couriers," Nestor replied.

"You'd be surprised what it can recognize." Javier wrenched a wooden crossbar off of the crate and tossed it aside.

"I've got a small pry bar down in the shed, you know," Kiram informed him.

"You can't possibly make Nestor wait that long for his reward," Javier replied. They both glanced to where Nestor sat on the floor. Nestor still seemed lost in some mix of thought and exhaustion.

"I've always been curious about what it was like up here." Nestor flopped back on the floor. "It's nice, really. You have so much space and all this light just pours in."

"Don't get too settled in," Javier said as he jerked another crossbar free. "I'm not looking for another underclassman." He pulled a third wooden bar free. "Are either of you going to help me with this crate?"

Kiram shrugged. "I offered to get a pry bar and you turned me down." His attention still lingered on his discussion with Scholar Donamillo. He would need to remove the roof from the shed as soon as possible. If only this damn tournament was over, he'd have some free time. As it was he'd just have to endure another week of training and then the week of the tournament itself before he could get back to work on his steam engine. His thoughts were interrupted by Javier waving a board in front of his face.

"Kir-Zaki, you have absolutely no enthusiasm. Look at this crate. It could have anything in it. Aren't you desperate to tear it open?"

"I am," Nestor moaned from the floor, "but I'm just so sore from carrying the damn thing up the stairs."

"Why didn't you use the gear lift?" Kiram asked.

"The gear lift is only for scholars' use," Nestor grumbled. Javier smiled at that and then ripped the last cross bar free. One entire side of the crate fell aside. Javier caught it before it hit the floor and leaned it up against the wall.

"I smell honey cakes," Nestor said. "Honey cakes and roast pheasant."

"He's out of his mind," Javier commented to Kiram.

Kiram helped Javier unpack the individual wooden boxes from inside the crate. They stacked them on the floor around Nestor. Outside the bells sounded from the chapel. It would be time for dinner in an hour.

"Isn't Master Ignacio going to notice that the three of us are missing?" Kiram asked.

"You're in the infirmary and Nestor is assisting me," Javier replied. "Master Ignacio won't expect any of us back today."

"What's Nestor supposed to be assisting you with?" Kiram eyed Nestor's prone body. Then he picked up one of the smallest boxes and cut through the cord that held it closed.

"Cleaning my armor. Bringing it up to a high polish," Javier said. "I finished it myself last night."

"I don't remember you polishing any armor." Kiram frowned at Javier.

"You wouldn't. You sleep like a log."

"I do not—"

"I definitely smell a honey cake!" Nestor sat up suddenly and leaned over the box Kiram had just opened. His delighted grin collapsed as Kiram lifted out a dozen beeswax candles.

"Sorry," Kiram said. He unpacked five deep-red cakes of sealing wax and then fished out a linen satchel.

"I'm going to starve to death," Nestor said. "I really am."

Kiram opened the satchel. Nestled among countless dried rose petals were six marzipan pears. Kiram guessed that each of the boxes would have similar treats hidden in it. He could be generous.

"Here." Kiram handed the satchel to Nestor. "Leave one for me and Javier."

Nestor's face lit up as he discovered the pears.

"One each or to split?" Nestor bit into a marzipan pear and closed his eyes as if he were in a kind of ecstasy.

"One each," Kiram told him.

"Oh God," Nestor murmured. "These are so good. Oh God." He let out a low moan.

"Damn, Nestor, you sound like you're ten inches down some trollop's throat." Javier shook his head and he took out his penknife.

"I don't care." Nestor sighed. He bit into another pear and gave another groan of pleasure.

Kiram wasn't sure if it was Javier's crude language or Nestor's moaning but he could feel his cheeks growing warmer. Javier crouched down beside him with a rectangular box. He cut through a cord holding a box shut but didn't open it. Instead he pushed it over to Kiram.

Kiram lifted the lid and gazed at the contents. For a moment he thought it was some kind of amazingly embroidered winter blanket. Then he lifted the silky yellow cloth out and realized that his mother had sent him a formal jupon to wear over his leather armor. Simple leaf designs embroidered in red thread decorated the collar and hem of the long jupon. But a single black silk sun blazed across the back. Kiram stared at it. The black sun was the Tornesal crest.

How had she known? He hadn't mentioned the tournament in any of his letters for fear that she'd worry about him. His letters were always unfailingly happy, concerned with his classes and often verged on being entirely fictional.

"I assured your mother that since you are under my protection it would be appropriate for you to wear my emblem," Javier said.

"You assured my mother…" Kiram thought about this for a moment. "You wrote to my mother?"

"She wrote to me, actually." Javier glanced down at the empty box. Kiram imagined that he was attempting to appear sheepish, but it wasn't working. Javier looked as smug as ever. "I've just been replying to her letters."

"You—how long? What did you tell her?" Kiram cut himself short despite his sense of outrage, remembering Nestor's presence.

"Her first letter arrived a week after you did. She thanked me in advance for looking after you and asked me to write to her should you need anything. She's only written four more times since then, but she's always very polite. Very refined. Even her script." Javier smiled a little and Kiram suddenly realized that Javier wasn't trying to disguise an arrogant grin, but to hide a look of fondness.

"Don't worry. I didn't give her anything to fret about." Javier pulled the jupon from Kiram's loose grip and held it up to the late afternoon light. Tiny gold threads glinted all along the length of the yellow silk.

"You don't think Atreau writes to my mother, do you?" Nestor suddenly asked. "That isn't something all upperclassmen do, is it?"

"What on earth could Atreau tell your mother that she doesn't already know?" Javier asked.

"She doesn't know I beat off," Nestor furtively replied.

"She's married to your father and has eleven sons, Nestor. She knows men beat off." Javier laughed. "How could she avoid it, with Timoteo in her house?"

"I thought that was what he was doing up in his room," Nestor said. "But then he always claims that he's praying."

"Praying his pillow grows a cunt, maybe," Javier replied. "Hopefully he'll be able to get his fingers off his dick long enough to take his holy vows for the priesthood. I imagine the sacred chalice might be a little sticky after he hands it off, though."

Nestor seemed both scandalized and thrilled. Kiram imagined that he was trying to memorize the offhanded way that Javier tossed out obscene words like "cunt."

Javier held the jupon up against Kiram's chest and nodded as though what he saw pleased him.

"You'll look like you're made entirely of gold." Javier's tone was soft and Kiram imagined that if Javier's hands hadn't been full he would have reached out and touched Kiram's hair, as he often did when they were alone. But Nestor was with them and Javier simply dropped the jupon back into its box.

"No candy in that one," Javier said to Nestor. "Let's try another."

The three of went through the boxes, unpacking winter clothes, mechanist tools, one of Kiram's bows, a clay talisman Kiram's little nephews and nieces had made for him, rounds of waxed cheese, dried figs, and to Nestor's utter delight, honey cakes and four dry-cured sausages.

"Do you mind if I have a little of it?" Nestor asked.

"Help yourself. You should have some of the cheese as well." Kiram opened a last box, which contained several Haldiim books and his mother's sheaf of correspondence.

While Kiram read the letter, Nestor devoured slices of sausage and cheese and Javier considered several of the tools Kiram's father had sent with a look of uncertainty that almost bordered on suspicion.

The news from home was comfortingly normal. Two more of his cousins had become fathers and thus assured their places in their wives' houses. His brother Majdi on the other hand had once again failed to find a woman willing to take him and had again set sail aboard the *Red Witch*. Kiram's mother wondered if she hadn't made a terrible mistake purchasing the ship for Majdi, as she now feared he would never settle into a secure marriage.

At home his sisters, Siamak and Dauhd, were attempting to entice his mother to offer Cadeleonian cookies in the candy shop. His father was still tinkering with designs for mechanical birds. Most of them were very pretty and few of them could remain airborne for more than a few moments. Several had crashed into the henhouse and the cook was eyeing Kiram's father with annoyance.

Kiram smiled at his mother's obvious affection for his father despite his eccentricities. He was disappointed to find that the questions he had written to his uncle's husband had gone unanswered. Both his uncle Rafie and Alizadeh were traveling. She didn't expect them back until midwinter, weather permitting.

Kiram glanced down to the stack of books in front of him and then to Javier.

"She says she sent the books you asked about," Kiram said. "Though she doesn't want you to think that we're all so superstitious as these Bahiim writings would make you think."

Javier looked pleased and Nestor squinted at the books.

"What do they say? I can't read them at all," Nestor complained.

"This one is called *Red Blossoms from a Fallen Tree* and this one is *A Beast Cries in the Sacred Heart of the Night* and the last is called *A Longing That My Bones Will Remember.*" Kiram pointed out each of the books as he spoke. "They're poems written by two famous Bahiim mystics. They talk quite a lot about the sacredness of all aspects of life, even those that seem base and animalistic."

Kiram hadn't read any of the books all the way through but he knew the more famous poems, as most Haldiim did. They were quite old and Kiram could only guess that Javier had gotten the titles from Calixto's diary.

"Thank her for me, will you?" Javier picked up the three books and took them to his desk. Kiram nodded and continued to skim the gossip from Anacleto. There was news of his friend Musni. Kiram took it in with a sense of loss, frowning at the letter.

"What's wrong?" Nestor asked.

"What?" Kiram looked up at him. "Nothing. Nothing at all.

It's just that one of my close friends has decided to marry a girl." Kiram realized how this sounded and quickly added, "I liked her as well, so I'm happy for him but sad about the marriage."

"Did he know you fancied her?" Nestor asked.

"Yes, he knew." Kiram accepted a slice of sausage from Nestor. It was spicy and tasted of juniper and cloves. For a moment he couldn't keep from wondering whether Musni would have refused to marry if he hadn't left for the academy. He sighed again, realizing that he would have left even if he had known that he would lose Musni.

"Not much of a friend if you ask me," Nestor grumbled. "It's pretty low to steal a man's girl while he's gone away to school."

"He didn't steal her," Kiram replied. Nestor handed him a piece of cheese. He ate it and felt better. He couldn't have cared that much about Musni, he supposed, if a slice of sausage and a bite of cheese could console him so easily.

"She liked him and he comes from a poor family, so taking a wife is a good choice for him. Her mother owns two mills. Musni will be well taken care of."

"Still doesn't make it right," Nestor said, frowning.

Kiram shrugged. He glanced down to the box and realized that he'd missed a satchel. He opened it and discovered his favorite taffy, packed with mint leaves. He shared a piece with Nestor and then turned to offer one to Javier.

He didn't know why, but Javier's expression seemed almost stricken. Then he gave Kiram a quick smile.

"You have an entirely different life waiting for you back in Anacleto, don't you?" Javier accepted the taffy but didn't eat it.

"We all have other lives outside of the academy," Kiram replied.

"Not really." Nestor's expression turned thoughtful. "Not like you do. I never considered it before, but all of us Cadeleonians are going to be dealing with each other like this for the rest of our lives. Not with upperclassmen and all that but we do the same things here as we do at home, eat the same food, know the same people. You come from an entirely different place..." Nestor spoke as if this idea just occurred to him and he found it somehow troubling. "When you're done with academy you're not just going to disappear back behind the Haldiim wall to your other life, are you?"

"I have to go home sometime."

"But you're going to write to me and come visit and invite me to visit you, aren't you? My family house is in Anacleto, less than an hour from the Haldiim district."

"Of course." Kiram smiled at Nestor. "After a few days back at my mother's house I'll be desperate to get out. I'll be visiting you everyday. Honestly, escaping from home was half of why I came here in the first place. I wanted to see something new and meet different people."

"Well, you've certainly met different people, I'll bet!" Relief rang through Nestor's voice. "And you've ridden horses and learned to fence, and you're going to win dozens of ribbons in the tournament. When that girl sees you she's going to break down in tears because she missed her chance at you."

Kiram laughed at the thought of any girl crying over him, much less Musni's new wife. Briefly Kiram wondered what would happen when they were both back in Anacleto. If he ever did find a husband, how would he introduce the man to Nestor?

Nestor nodded happily. "You won't care because by then you will have had your fill of women from the Goldenrod and half of them will be writing you love letters the way they write to Atreau."

"Yes," Javier said tiredly. "It will be a glorious future for all. But for now I think we ought to go down for dinner."

"The bell hasn't—" Nestor began but then the seventh bell sounded from the chapel.

The three of them joined the flood of other students filing down to the dining room and Kiram's brief, troubled thoughts of his future were forgotten as the smell of beef and fresh bread beckoned him.

Chapter Seventeen

When the day of the tournament finally arrived, the students at the academy rose early and ate quickly before mounting up and riding in a tight procession into the town of Zancoda. Nervous excitement pervaded the air, and neither Kiram nor Nestor was immune. As Kiram reined Firaj alongside Nestor's mount he noted the pink flush of Nestor's cheeks and felt certain that anyone close at hand could hear the pounding of his own heart.

Students from the Yillar Academy would be approaching from the opposite direction. Once the two great schools of Cadeleon had converged in Zancoda's center, the race to the gold pavilion would begin.

Kiram hadn't known what to expect beyond that, but he certainly hadn't imagined anything like the spectacle surrounding him. Crowds of people lined the road even far outside of town. As they entered the city gates the display amazed him. When he had last passed through Zancoda on his way to the Sagrada Academy the town had struck him as dull and colorless. The buildings were old and the stonework had been weathered to a lifeless gray. The few inhabitants he had seen from his carriage had looked as pallid and plain as their surroundings.

But now brilliant blue banners and vibrant green flags hung from the balconies. Flags emblazoned with colorful crests of noble families were waved from poles and chapel bells rang out wildly over the shouts and cheers of the gathered crowds.

Men and boys thronged the streets, cheering as the academy students rode past. Every so often Kiram spotted an older matronly woman amidst the crowd holding a young child on her hip and helping the child wave. Kiram often waved back.

Younger women, with their dark hair still braided and held up in combs, threw flowers and perfumed kerchiefs from overhanging balconies. Groups of onlookers stared out from open windows. Everyone, regardless of age or sex, wore bright paper flowers pinned to their clothes or waved shimmering ribbons.

Kiram could not believe the sheer number of people who had come out just to watch the students of the Sagrada Academy ride two abreast through the streets. The inns appeared to be bursting with visitors, all waving from windows or leaning out on the steps. Some onlookers had even positioned themselves up on the roofs.

From time to time, especially where the streets were narrow and the crowds were close, Kiram would feel a small hand reach out and touch him or Firaj. He realized that parents were holding out their children as if the passing riders were lucky stones to rub. At first he feared that an excited grasping child would spook Firaj or cause him to strike out with one of his hooves, but Firaj remained calm. At times he seemed to enjoy the attention. Even when a youth stumbled out and collided with his hindquarters, Firaj only released a hard snort and stamped once in warning. The youth scurried back into the crowd.

"There are even more people here this year than last year!" Nestor shouted over the noise of the crowd. "The stands around the tournament arena are going to be packed!"

"They can't all be from around here," Kiram yelled, surprised at how little impact his voice made upon the turbulent roar of so many other voices.

"No." Nestor shook his head. "Merchants and nobles from all over the country come to see the autumn tournament. Even the princes come. This year the heir himself is supposed to attend."

Kiram couldn't help but feel a slight dread at the mention of a royal Sagrada. Though Nazario Sagrada's atrocities were long past, it was still Kiram's first association with the name "Sagrada". If he won the Crown Challenge he would have to attempt to change that. He would be expected to demonstrate his mechanism to the king and entertain the royal family with its many uses. He couldn't be brooding over the infamous impaler while cheerfully serving the man's descendants.

Then a downpour of pink rose petals from the balcony above distracted him. A white kerchief, embroidered with yellow butterflies, fluttered down and landed across Nestor's arm. Nestor flushed bright red and clutched the token. Kiram joined him in gawking up at the shy Cadeleonian girls on the balcony.

"Might be the one with the butterfly combs in her hair," Kiram shouted to Nestor.

"Do you think?" Nestor peered at the girl and she ducked quickly back into the shadows of a bright blue banner. "She was pretty, wasn't she?"

"I think so," Kiram replied, though he hadn't really seen much of her, but she had certainly possessed the deep curves and lustrous dark hair that Cadeleonian men seemed to desire.

"It smells like jasmine." Nestor carefully tucked the kerchief into his riding glove. "Not too much further to the town center. You ready?"

"Not at all. I'm terrified."

"Me too."

Under other circumstances Kiram thought he would have found it funny that both he and Nestor were screaming out their fears. But now the irony of the situation didn't amuse him. He was too nervous about the race that was to come, once they met the Yillar students at the town center.

The students of both schools would circle the city fountain once and then race madly down six narrow avenues out of the town and to the tournament grounds. The first student to reach the gold pavilion would receive a favor directly from the Sagrada prince.

Countless bets had been placed within the academy and in the town as well, Kiram imagined. Both the Helio twins were thought to be contenders, as was Javier.

Apparently Javier had finished second last year, only a neck behind Hierro Fueres of the Yillar Academy. Elezar had placed a huge wager on Javier and made it clear that he would personally take it badly if any other rider from the Sagrada Academy cost him his money.

Kiram had no illusions about his own chances of winning. He hoped only to survive. He clenched his fists around Firaj's reins. Last night Elezar had recounted stories of students who had taken terrible falls in the race from the fountain. He'd described young men being trampled by their own horses, or becoming tangled in their stirrups and being dragged against the hard cobblestones of the street.

Kiram's thoughts were so focused on his possible impending death that for an instant he failed to register the familiar voice calling his name from the surrounding crowd.

"Hey! Kiri! Kiram Kir-Zaki!"

Kiram turned slightly in his saddle and was shocked to recognize his uncle Rafie waving from the midst of dozens of pale Cadeleonians. The sight sent a thrill of joy through him.

Despite Rafie's elegant Cadeleonian clothes he stood out starkly from the rest of the crowd. His slim Haldiim build and smooth skin lent him the appearance of a tall youth but his close-cropped hair was nearly white and deep smile lines etched the corners of his mouth. Days of summer travel had deepened the natural cinnamon tone of his skin to a rich walnut color, making his pale blue eyes seem to blaze in contrast.

Rafie ducked between two big Cadeleonian men, slipped through the crowd with fast graceful twists, and was soon jogging alongside Firaj.

"We're staying at the Laughing Dog!" Rafie called to him in Haldiim. ***"We'll see you this evening. Take care!"*** Rafie tossed a small bundle into Kiram's lap, then ducked back into the relative shelter of the crowd.

"Who was that?" Nestor called out.

"My uncle Rafie." Kiram clumsily opened the satchel with one hand. Inside he found a Bahiim lotus medallion on a fine gold chain.

"He came all this way to see you in the tournament?" Nestor looked happy. "That's nice."

Kiram nodded. He guessed that Alizadeh was here as well and had probably blessed the medallion personally. Kiram pulled the chain over his head. The weight of the medallion felt amazingly comforting.

Chapel bells boomed over the streets in double time, and Kiram realized that the riders at the front of the procession must have arrived at the city center. A few moments later he and Nestor rode into the huge square with a massive fountain at its center that featured a sculpture of three stallions rearing up in the spray. Carved across the base of the fountain were the words: *Faith, Honor,* and *Strength.*

A church rose up on one side of the square, and ranks of Yillar students, dressed in deep green uniforms, gathered there. Kiram guessed that there were nearly two hundred of them, forming a veritable wall of armed men and glossy warhorses. A gnawing anxiety clutched at his stomach and he had to look away from them.

The last students from both schools filed into the square. Like Kiram and Nestor, they each took their positions as they had drilled countless times in the months earlier.

Master Ignacio rode his stallion from the front of the Sagrada Academy ranks to the fountain where he met the war master of the Yillar Academy. Ignacio was the younger of the two and far more serious in appearance. The Yillar war master was plump with a big white beard. He smiled like an indulgent grandfather at Master Ignacio's grim salute and returned the gesture as if it were nothing more than a wave.

Once the salutes of engagement were exchanged, riders from both schools surged into action all around Kiram.

"Good luck!" Nestor shouted, and then his roan stallion lunged ahead into the fray of riders and horses.

First-year riders forced their way forward and suddenly strangers surrounded Kiram. One rider attempted to force Kiram into the wall of a guild building. Firaj snorted angrily and sprang ahead. Kiram clung to his reins. He lost sight of Nestor. Then suddenly Yillar riders surged up from behind him. Kiram spurred Firaj forward to keep from being trampled in their charge.

Though Kiram had hated every moment he had spent with Master Ignacio, he was suddenly glad for the practice. Without it he would already have fallen.

Now his heart pounded madly in his chest but he urged Firaj ahead faster and the big gelding responded. His hands shook, but he kept his grip on his reins and focused himself on staying in his saddle.

Somewhere in the crush of uniforms and horses, Kiram heard shouts of pain and animal screams. Firaj bounded between two other horses and a big student in Yillar green swore at Kiram and swung his riding crop. Firaj suddenly bared his teeth at the man's mount and the other horse reared back, nearly throwing its rider. Firaj and Kiram raced ahead.

Kiram completed his circle of the fountain just behind the bulk of other riders and took the nearest of the six avenues leading out of the town. Stone buildings rose up on either side of him like walls and dust churned up from the street in choking clouds. From the balconies above, spectators screamed other men's names and hurled flowers.

Suddenly the closeness of the crowd and the constant downpour of flower petals became unbearable. Kiram swatted rose blossoms away from his face as if they were flies. He couldn't slow, much less stop, without being trampled by the riders behind him. They drove Kiram ahead faster but could not pass him. The street was too narrow. All of them raced to escape the confines of the town walls and tight streets.

The sight of harvested fields and wide open tracts of fallow land came as an overwhelming relief.

Even in the fields there were spectators. Groups of young boys sat atop stone walls and waved. Milkmaids and farmers leaned against fences watching. Ahead, an entire fairground of tents and bright flags spilled out from behind a huge yellow pavilion.

The open field allowed him the space to slow. Other riders urged their mounts ahead and Kiram let them pass. Firaj seemed to hate the sight of another horse racing past him and each time another rider sped by, he made an attempt to give chase. Kiram always reined him back to a reasonable pace.

He just wanted to reach the gold pavilion in one piece; he had no interest in risking his life to be counted among the finest riders, though he could tell that Firaj would have liked to be among the finest horses.

As he neared the huge gold pavilion Kiram caught sight of Nestor, racing across the field on his roan stallion. Kiram slowed Firaj further to allow Nestor to catch up.

Kiram waved. But Nestor didn't respond and Kiram guessed it was because Nestor couldn't see him. He'd obviously lost his spectacles somewhere earlier in the race.

However as they both drew closer to the gold pavilion, Nestor squinted at him and then waved ecstatically. Kiram rode up next to him. Nestor's face was streaked with road dust and the bridge of his nose appeared to be bruised.

He shouted, "It's madness this year!" by way of greeting.

Then they both passed beneath the yellow silk ropes decorating the entry to the tournament grounds and they were done. Grooms wearing blue armbands took their horses and told them what place they had taken in the race. Kiram was the hundred and forty-eighth rider. Nestor was the hundred and forty-ninth.

"I don't see why anyone keeps count after fifth, except to embarrass us," Nestor commented. Kiram wondered briefly how Javier had fared in the race. He hurried after Nestor into the gold pavilion.

Inside, sunlight glowed through the luminous yellow silk walls, lending a gold cast to the hundreds of onlookers gathered in the wooden stands. The center of the silk tent, however, was open and hard morning light poured down over the dirt floor of the arena, illuminating every detail of the filthy students gathered there.

Two men with silver horns blew out sharp notes as Kiram and Nestor walked in. A young man shouted both their names. When Nestor was announced a roar of cheers went up from the stands and Kiram realized that most of Nestor's family had to be here. The Grunito crest of a red bull on a blue field hung from ten raised box seats where dozens of big Cadeleonians waved and shouted out Nestor's name. A tall woman with shoulders as broad as Kiram's and a nose like a hawk's beak hurled a bouquet of red and blue ribbons to Nestor. It slapped into Nestor's chest and he gripped it tightly. His dirty cheeks took on an embarrassed flush.

"God save me," Nestor whispered as he squinted up at the box seats. "I'm never going to hear the end of this. I come in one hundred and forty-ninth and then get a bouquet from my mother."

"It's not so bad." Kiram said. "There are plenty of riders behind us."

"Yes, but my mother isn't going to throw them bouquets."

"Your mother isn't the only one who threw you a favor, though," Kiram reminded him.

"That's true." Nestor smiled slightly. "She really was pretty, wasn't she?"

"She was," Kiram assured him.

The two of them joined the other Sagrada Academy students in the center of the arena. Elezar was the easiest to pick out in the crowd, simply because of his size. The vestiges of a bloody nose stained his upper lip and mud spattered the entire front of his shirt. Almost immediately after finding Elezar, Kiram caught sight of Javier.

He wasn't with the rest of the Sagrada students but instead he leaned up against wall of the stands with his neck craned back. He shouted something up to a group of people in a box seat on the second level. A green and yellow banner hung from the box. Fedeles was up there, along with half a dozen other very well-dressed people. None of them resembled Fedeles as much as

Javier did but Kiram still guessed that they were Fedeles' family, the Quemanors. One elderly woman gazed at him with that particularly adoring expression that Kiram always associated with grandmothers. When her gaze shifted to Javier, however, her expression was one of undisguised hatred.

Fedeles bounced in his seat and appeared to be singing something. Kiram couldn't hear him over the pressing roar of hundreds of surrounding conversations. Elezar was recounting his own worst failure in a race to Nestor, but Kiram was only half listening. Every now and then a trumpet blast announced more riders and cheers went up through the crowd.

A giddy feeling of joy and relief washed through Kiram. It had been a mad ride but he had survived it. Briefly, he thought that he would do it all again just for this rush of happiness at the end. The notion was crazy, but it filled him with a strange kind of joy. Kiram thought he might be grinning as wildly as Fedeles right now.

Up in the stands, Fedeles threw a wad of black and white ribbons down at Javier and then suddenly leapt up from his seat and pointed directly at Kiram.

Kiram returned his enthusiastic wave. He received a cold stare from Fedeles' grandmother, but he hardly cared. Javier pulled the black and white ribbons from his dusty hair, then he turned and started towards Kiram. As Javier drew closer Kiram caught sight of the bloody, matted black hair dried to the right side of his face.

Suddenly Kiram's pleasure turned cold. "Are you all right?"

Javier only smiled at him.

"He took first place!" Elezar crowed. "Flat out beat Hierro Fueres this year."

"What happened to his head?" Kiram asked. Javier seemed oddly unaware of the question.

"He got clipped. His right ear is full of blood." Elezar pointed to Javier's head.

Javier nodded. "I can't hear out of my right ear. It's full of blood."

"Shouldn't he see a physician?"

"He'll be fine," Elezar responded. "It's just a graze. Bled like hell though. He looked completely bitched when I first came in. Bastard had the gall to tell me I looked bad."

Javier watched Elezar's face intently as he spoke and then nodded.

"I said you looked like shit," Javier said to Elezar and then he turned his attention back to Kiram. "I didn't hear them announce you."

"You can't hear anything, can you?"

"No, I'm fine," Javier responded.

"He can't read lips for crap either." Elezar stepped closer to Javier. "Do something about your bloody ear."

"I think it's nice and quiet like this." Javier shrugged.

Kiram saw the faintest spark flicker over Javier's right ear. It guttered out almost instantly. Another spark trembled to life only briefly and then it too went out.

Kiram frowned. It wasn't like Javier to put up with an injury, not even to annoy Elezar.

"Did Holy Father Habalan administer muerate poison to Javier?" Kiram asked Elezar.

"Of course. It's the only way to make sure he doesn't cheat during the tournament. He still took first—" The rest of Elezar's words were lost in the loud blast of a trumpet. More riders were announced. The crowds in the stands cheered as the dirty students made their way to the center of the arena. The last students seemed to be arriving nearly all at once. Few of them showed any injuries, though one young man in a Yillar uniform had clearly been bombarded with flowers. Rose petals and straw flowers were still falling out of his hair and clothes as he walked across the arena.

"Well, I did better than Ladislo," Nestor said. "He was two hundred and thirty. What about you, Elezar?"

"Thirty-three," Elezar replied proudly. "I came in right ahead of Morisio. Genimo took fortieth. He's helping Scholar Donamillo treat a first year who took a nasty fall."

"What about Atreau?" Nestor asked. "I thought he'd be here by now." Kiram hadn't thought to look for anyone but Javier but now he noticed that of all the Hellions only Atreau was unaccounted for.

"Poor bastard got completely fucked by some crazy girl who threw herself at him on the street." Elezar shook his head.

"Is he hurt?" Nestor looked suddenly worried.

"No, he kept his seat, but he was pretty much out of the race once he had some love-struck trollop in the saddle with him. He said something to Morisio about riding her hard and putting her away wet." Elezar flashed another of his crude grins.

Kiram had no idea what Elezar was referring to. He glanced askance at Javier but then realized that Javier hadn't heard any of the conversation.

"Atreau ought to show up soon," Elezar said. "Ahh, look! What did I just say? There he is."

Elezar pointed just as the trumpet sounded and Atreau was announced along with the last two other riders. Wild, feminine screams tore through the pavilion as Atreau walked past the stands. Gaudily-dressed women in the lowest row of the stands hurled flowers at him as well as kerchiefs. Kiram even thought that one woman had thrown out a pair of underpants.

"The whores do love him." Elezar shook his head.

"It's not just whores," Nestor said. "Lots of ladies write him letters."

"I imagine that the number would drop significantly if they knew they would have to spend their wedding night queuing up in line for a turn at him," Javier commented.

"So, you can hear again," Elezar said.

"Sadly, yes. It's louder than it was last year." Javier surveyed the hundreds of people in the stands, then turned to Kiram. "I'll take you around the fair after we're done here. The fighting doesn't usually last past third bell. After that, actors take the arena. You can see those Irabiim I was telling you about."

"All right, but I have to find the Laughing Dog—"

"Wait! What's this?" Elezar broke in on them, scowling. "We should celebrate your win at the Goldenrod."

Javier looked genuinely annoyed. "Not tonight. Master Ignacio won't allow any indulgences until after the tournament. And in any case, Kiram and Nestor can't—" The rest of Javier's reply was drowned out by the resounding noise of several trumpets blasting out a piercing melody.

"All bow before His Royal Highness Prince Sevanyo!" A man called from the pavilion entry.

A sudden, perfect silence fell over the entire gathering. An instant later the quiet rustle of cloth became a reverberation through the pavilion as hundreds of people bowed down. It struck Kiram as strange to hear such a slight noise magnified so intensely by the sheer number of people making the same motion at once.

Immediately, Javier caught his hand and pulled him down to kneel beside him. The Cadeleonians were all so much more formal than his own people. There was no nobility among the Haldiim and not even the oldest grandmother would demand that others kneel in the dirt before her.

Javier kept his face lowered, not even glancing at Kiram. But he didn't release Kiram's hand either. His skin felt icy—an effect of muerate poison. Even so it seemed singular to Javier and made Kiram very aware of how long Javier's fingers lingered, pressing against his own, and also of the precise moment when Javier released him.

It was exactly as six young men dressed in violet liveries emblazoned with the white Sagrada stallion marched into the pavilion. The gold buckles on their highly polished boots jingled like bells. Kiram stole a glance up at them. They wore dueling swords, but also carried golden bowls full of flowers, from which they scattered fistfuls of rose petals across the ground. Behind them came six mounted guards, wearing light armor and riding black chargers.

The trumpets raised a resounding note as the prince rode into the pavilion on a white stallion. Six more pages followed him on foot, carrying large gold globes, and behind them came another six mounted guards.

Kiram studied the prince. He inspired so much awe and wielded so much power. If he wished he could elevate or destroy any man, woman, or child in this pavilion. He could do it on a whim.

Kiram knew that many of his fellow students were nobles as well. In their own lands they could decide the fates of entire populaces with a few words, but at the academy they attended classes and took tests just like everyone else. They obeyed the rules of common scholars and accepted punishments for their misdeeds.

The Sagrada heir was not restrained in any such manner. He had left his academy days far behind him. Kiram thought suddenly that Javier too would leave the academy. After next year he would be free to bring hundreds of people to their knees with his mere presence. Kiram wondered if he would choose to do so.

Prince Sevanyo's pale skin and dark eyes were testaments to his close relation to both Javier and Fedeles. There was resemblance in his long build as well. But the prince was not a young man; deep lines creased his forehead and the corners of his mouth. The sharp bones of his cheeks jutted up over gaunt hollows. White streaks shot through his black hair.

As he shifted, surveying the gathered crowd, his entire body seemed to glitter. The crown on his brow shone, gold stitching flashed up and down his dark violet clothes, and dozens of cut jewels gleamed on his gloved hands.

He hardly moved, but his mount immediately drew to a halt. For a moment, the prince surveyed the bowed heads of his gathered subjects up in the stands. His expression was distant and contemplative, as if he were regarding a foreign landscape. Then his gaze shifted to the students kneeling in the arena.

Kiram quickly bowed his head, as the prince looked his way. He didn't dare to look up again.

"You may rise, faithful subjects." The prince did not need to raise his voice. His words carried effortlessly through the silence.

As everyone straightened, the pages standing behind the prince opened the gold spheres they held, releasing dozens of white doves. The royal prince sat in gleaming gold and darkest violet as white wings rose all around him, ascending into the heavens. It was a startlingly beautiful image, but also obviously contrived.

"Where's a cat when you really need one?" Javier whispered. Kiram stifled his laugh. Javier smiled at him with such open affection that Kiram had to look down at his feet to keep from blushing.

"Javier Tornesal," Prince Sevanyo called out over the noise of beating wings and dove calls.

Javier stepped forward. His uniform was gray from road dust and blood and dirt clung to his hair. Still, there was something in his bearing—his utter ease—that made Kiram think he looked as regal as the prince.

He paused to allow the prince's stallion to nuzzle his bare hand. The horse clearly knew him.

Prince Sevanyo smiled at him benevolently. "Well, cousin, I understand that I am to offer you a favor, but I cannot imagine what the Duke of Rauma would want for."

"Nothing so much as the royal prince's health and happiness," Javier said.

"I am both well and greatly pleased," Prince Sevanyo said. Then the prince pulled a massive ring from his right index finger and handed it to Javier. "Attend me for a little time."

Javier inclined his head slightly.

"It would be a pleasure, but I beg for a dismissal. I have an obligation to the academy."

"The nature of this obligation?"

"This is my third year and I am required to mentor an underclassman, my prince." Pride carried through Javier's voice. Prince Sevanyo's expression showed both surprise and amusement.

"You have an underclassman?" The prince raised his dark brows. "Is the boy without human fear or an unmitigated idiot?"

"I assure you, he is no idiot," Javier replied with a pleased smile. The prince studied Javier as if he had offered him a challenging riddle.

"I must see this underclassman," Prince Sevanyo pronounced at last. "Bring him. You will both attend me."

Kiram's stomach clenched like a fist. Nestor gave a quiet gasp and Kiram looked at him.

"As you wish, my prince." Javier turned back to Kiram and beckoned him with a gesture, appearing utterly unconcerned.

For a moment Kiram felt too afraid to move. All he could think of was King Nazario, and the countless Haldiim he had murdered. But then he forced himself forward. Javier watched him intently, as if his mere gaze could draw Kiram to him.

He walked to Javier's side and bowed deeply before the resplendent prince. The prince blinked at Kiram for a moment and then laughed.

"A Haldiim! How clever." The prince swung down from his saddle and a page led his horse out of the pavilion. Just standing near the prince, Kiram was intensely aware of the dust, sweat, and grime that clung to his own body. While a rich fragrance of vanilla wafted off the prince, Kiram was sure his own scent was much more rank.

Fortunately two of the prince's pages brought basins of water and washcloths. Javier and he cleaned up quickly. The half-healed laceration running across Javier's right ear and up into his scalp stood out strongly against his clean, white skin.

"Let us take our seats," Prince Sevanyo said. For the first time he seemed to take note of the pavilion of silent onlookers. "Certainly a tournament should be getting underway in this arena."

The words released everyone from their frozen silence. The war masters called their students to attention and marched them off the arena grounds and into the low stands reserved for them. There they hurriedly stripped off their uniforms and pulled on their leather fencing armor. Master Ignacio shouted out the orders while grooms handed out blunted dueling blades.

All flurry of action and noise seemed muted and distant to Kiram. The prince's guards surrounded them and they ascended the stairs up into the stands. The pages trailed behind them.

The seats in the prince's box were padded with purple velvet. The surrounding wood walls were gilded and painted with images of horses and armored men in battle. As soon as the prince seated himself, a page knelt to wipe the dust from his boots, while another page brought wine and a small pastry of some kind. Javier sat beside the prince and pulled Kiram down next to him.

Not wanting to be caught staring at the prince, Kiram averted his gaze down to the arena below. First-year students from both schools assembled for the first contests. Six fencing rings had been drawn up and Kiram guessed the fights would be quick. The best of the first years would go on to challenge the second-year students.

"So how did this come about?" Prince Sevanyo asked Javier, though he indicated Kiram with his wine glass.

"This is Kiram Kir-Zaki. He won the Silver Leaf Challenge last year." Javier stretched out in his seat. "Scholar Donamillo was so impressed with him that he petitioned for Kiram to be invited to attend the Sagrada Academy. Kiram accepted and now he's my underclassman."

"I had heard that a Haldiim won the Silver Leaf, though I hadn't imagined that he would be so young… " Sevanyo studied Kiram, frowning slightly. "You are young, are you not? It's hard to tell with you Haldiim. You all look like boys."

"I am seventeen, sir—Your Highness." Kiram was horrified at his own gaffe but the prince just laughed.

"Now, why do I know the name Kir-Zaki?" the prince asked.

"His family makes the Kir-Zaki candies in Anacleto," Javier replied.

"Of course." Prince Sevanyo looked delighted. "I am told that I have them to thank for the proliferation of Grunitos throughout the kingdom."

"Yes." Kiram tried to sound steady. "Nestor Grunito says as much himself."

"You must get Javier to eat more of those candies, then. We are in need of Tornesal heirs, you know."

"The world needs more Tornesals like it needs another great flood," Javier said.

"I would be greatly displeased if Rauma fell into my brother's hands, Javier." The prince sounded suddenly very serious. Javier nodded.

"It will not. Fedeles is my heir."

"Fedeles is not fit."

"He's improving steadily," Javier replied. "And I have no intention of dying any time soon.When I do, Rauma will pass to Fedeles' children in the Quemanor house. Your brother, the royal bishop, will not have it."

Prince Sevanyo sighed. A page refilled the prince's wine glass. He offered a glass to Javier as well but Javier waved it aside.

Another page arrived and offered Prince Sevanyo a silver tray stacked with small pieces of creamy paper. Each of them bore the seal of some noble house or a merchant's name. The prince chose several of them but told the page not to extend the invitations just yet.

Kiram stole another glance down to the arena below, where pairs of first-year students dressed in thick leather cuirasses fought with blunted silver blades. Only the crests on their gauntlets designated which school they came from. Judges in white coats walked between the contestants, calling fouls and strikes. The fights were fast and most ended amiably. Javier watched them intently but the prince was obviously bored.

Prince Sevanyo leaned forward a little to study Kiram. He didn't quite look at Kiram's face but instead seemed to be gazing at his hair.

"It really is quite an amazing color," Prince Sevanyo commented. He reached past Javier and caught a curl of Kiram's hair. Kiram froze in place. The prince pulled the lock of hair straight and then released it to bounce back into a spiral.

"You know, one of my ancestors had a cloak made entirely from Haldiim scalps," Prince Sevanyo said quietly. "I used to play with it when I was a boy. It really was the most beautiful thing. The leather was soft as silk and the hair looked just like long curling ribbons of gold. I loved it madly. When I turned ten I was told where the hides had come from."

A cold sick feeling gripped Kiram. Javier scowled at the prince but said nothing.

Prince Sevanyo took another sip of his wine. "I cannot tell you how horrified I was to discover how that cloak had been made. I could not bear to even look at it, much less touch it again. I burned it and then I cried all night. To this day I am not sure whether I was crying because I lost something I loved or because I had loved it in the first place."

Kiram had no idea what to say in response. But the prince didn't seem to expect any answer.

"I have not met many Haldiim in my life but whenever I do I am always struck by the thought that I am at last admiring those lovely curls as I ought to have in the first place. It's as though I am seeing the owners of those scalps reborn into better lives. That's what your priests would say, isn't it?"

Kiram wasn't sure but the prince seemed intent on this so Kiram nodded and the prince smiled.

"Even if you Haldiim are denied our holy heaven, I would like to believe that your souls can find some kind of peace." The prince sat forward again but to Kiram's relief he didn't reach for his hair. "I am told that your dead are reborn into other forms and if they have been wronged they can return as a curse."

"Yes." Kiram wished that Javier would say something but Javier just leaned back in the seat and looked tired.

"How do you Haldiim lift these curses?" Prince Sevanyo's expression was intent and his tone very serious. "Without the solace of heaven how can you put an angry soul to rest?"

Kiram glanced to Javier, but Javier only shrugged.

"I don't know," Kiram admitted. "I'm not from a religious family, Your Highness. We never discuss these matters. I'm sorry."

"Not religious?" The prince looked stunned for a moment then gave a short laugh. "Did you hear that, Javier?"

"I did," Javier replied. He gave Kiram a quick apologetic look.

"Tell me," the prince said to Kiram, "if you are not religious, then what do you make of Javier and the white hell, young Haldiim?"

"I…I don't know," Kiram replied.

Beside him, Javier sighed. "When he thinks of me at all, he thinks I'm an ass who keeps interrupting his work for the Crown Challenge with annoying, superstitious babble."

Prince Sevanyo raised his brows.

"Really?"

"Really," Javier replied firmly and something unspoken seemed to pass between Prince Sevanyo and Javier. The prince sighed and took another sip of his wine.

"The Crown Challenge. That will be quite an accomplishment." The intensity dropped from Prince Sevanyo's voice leaving only a polite interest. "I suppose it's good then that you are receiving a proper Cadeleonian education. My father loves to retain geniuses at his court. No doubt he will want you there. He is quite sure that we are moving into a new age of mechanist wonders, but I cannot help but find them eerie—mechanisms without life or souls, moving about like living things."

Kiram had heard the same sentiments before, generally from older people. He considered his reply, but then Javier caught his arm and pulled him forward to the edge of the box.

"Watch out for this one, Kiram." Javier pointed to a young man in one of the fencing circles. He looked tall for a first-year student and his face was oddly expressionless.

"Ariz Plunado?" the prince asked.

Javier nodded.

"Bland thing, isn't he?" Prince Sevanyo commented.

Kiram found himself in agreement with the prince. Not even the reddish tint of Ariz's hair lent any character to his appearance. He moved quickly, but without grace or emotion.

He lunged forward. His opponent easily parried his strike, but then suddenly stumbled and fell to the ground. Ariz placed his blade to the fallen man's heart and was immediately declared the winner. Only then did Ariz allow himself a small, satisfied smile.

"Well, there is something to him after all, isn't there?" Prince Sevanyo commented.

"Did you see what he did?" Javier asked Kiram.

"No," Kiram admitted.

"All the time that they were fencing Ariz kept tripping his opponent until he finally brought him down. It's the second time he's won that way. Keep your feet in close when you're up against him. Make him overextend to get at you."

"I'll try," Kiram replied, though he had no idea how he would manage any such thing.

The three of them watched another pair of first-year students duel. Kiram's attention wandered and he found himself searching the stands for his uncle.

"Tell me, Kiram, have you thought of conversion?" Prince Sevanyo asked.

"What?" Kiram looked up quickly.

"Have you considered converting to the Holy Cadeleonian Church?" Prince Sevanyo briefly glanced to another of his pages and accepted two more papers with noble seals embossed upon them. "If you are to attend the royal court you ought to do so. Otherwise you'll have half the courtiers spreading nasty rumors about your private habits before they've even laid eyes on you.

Taking a Cadeleonian wife would help as well. Probably one of those charming merchant girls. You aren't already engaged, are you?"

"No," Kiram said, though he immediately regretted it.

"One of my bailiffs has a daughter who would be just about the right age..." The prince nodded as he considered the prospect.

Alarm shot through Kiram.

"I...I really couldn't marry right now," Kiram managed.

"Of course not now," the prince replied. "You must finish your schooling first. But it's always wise to have your plans in order, you know."

Kiram wondered how it was possible that a Cadeleonian prince could fill him with the same cold, trapped fear that his mother often inspired. He thought that it had to be something about older people. So many of them seemed intent upon planning his future for him. Both the prince and his mother seemed so sure of what would be best for him that they were already working out the details.

Conversion. Marriage. Living at court. Taking over his father's shop. Living at home for the rest of his life.

He didn't want either of the lives they planned for him.

"The first years are almost done," Javier announced. "We should get back down to the rest of the students. Kiram still needs to change into his cuirass and byrnie."

"It's good to see you take a responsibility so seriously, Javier," Prince Sevanyo commented.

"A man must serve his obligations. Though I won't deny that I have a sizable wager on Kiram to best Elezar Grunito's underclassman."

Javier stood, as did the prince, and they embraced.

"Thank you for coming, Sevanyo," Javier said into Sevanyo's shoulder.

"Of course. It's always a pleasure to see you. But do take care of yourself, Javier." Prince Sevanyo stepped back reluctantly. He looked at Kiram. "I look forward to seeing you again, Kiram Kir-Zaki. Look after Javier for me, won't you? Slip him some of those candies when you can."

On the stairs outside, dozens of well-dressed men stood waiting to be admitted in to attend the prince. They bowed their heads respectfully as Javier passed but several of them glared at Kiram as if his presence among them was distasteful.

"Ignore them," Javier whispered over his shoulder.

When they reached the lower stands where the rest of the academy students were gathered, Kiram flopped onto a hard seat of the bench next to Nestor. Javier remained standing, leaning against a wooden support. The nearest pair of combatants on the arena floor were only a few feet away. Kiram could hear them gasping for air and smell the sweat pouring down their arms and legs.

Javier studied them like a cat watching swallows. Other students glanced up from time to time but most were involved in their own preoccupations. The only change came when a winner was announced. Every Sagrada Academy student cheered for one of their own. Defeated students were greeted with disinterest. Master Ignacio hardly even glanced to them.

Farther down the bench Elezar stood close to two other third-year students and Kiram was sure he glimpsed money pass between them. Elezar was collecting winnings from his wagers already.

Kiram wondered if Javier had actually placed a wager on him. He hoped not.

"So, how was it?" Nestor asked Kiram. "What did the prince say?"

"He wants Kiram to convert, marry a nice Cadeleonian girl, and come live at court," Javier said.

"Convert and marry and move to the court?" Nestor rolled his eyes. "Why doesn't he ask him to shave his head and buy a monkey while he's at it?"

One of the judges on the arena floor signaled a win for the Sagrada Academy, waving a small blue banner over the head of a winded young man. Kiram had no idea who he was but he cheered along with the rest of the academy students.

It had been the student's fifth duel and he would not be expected to fight again today. The exhausted first-year student staggered back to the stands and collapsed onto the bench.

"Prince Sevanyo means well. He just doesn't know when he's asking too much of someone or even telling them too much." Javier glanced to Kiram. "He didn't offend you, did he?"

"No, he surprised me. I guess I wasn't expecting…Well, I didn't know what to expect." Kiram looked up to where Javier stood. "I wish I could have answered his questions."

"What questions?" Nestor asked.

"He wanted to know about the Haldiim religion," Kiram replied. "I couldn't tell him too much because my family isn't religious."

"Lucky." Nestor sighed. "My mother made us recite a verse of her choosing before she would let us sit down to dinner each night. I memorized the entire *Book of Redemption* just for the love of a hot meal." Nestor shook his head. "I still don't know what half of it is supposed to be about."

"Redemption, I'd imagine," Javier said.

"I guess, but every time I hear a verse all I can imagine is piping hot roast beef."

"Chapel sermons must be oddly appetizing for you," Javier remarked.

Nestor nodded. "I always leave hungry."

"Maybe you should convert to my faith," Kiram said. "On the Highest Holy Days the Bahiim prepare huge feasts and anyone who comes to the Holy Gardens is fed and offered honey wine."

"You all just eat in church?" Nestor stared to Kiram as if this were unbelievable.

"Of course. The two Highest Holy Days are celebrations of compassion and generosity. Even my family puts gifts out for the poor on the Highest Holy Days."

Nestor looked like he was going to ask something more but Javier leaned between them.

"I'm not sure how wise it is for you to be seen and heard at this public gathering, converting Nestor to your faith."

"I wasn't serious," Kiram objected.

But Nestor, too, looked worried. "He's right, Kiram. It's just what Holy Father Habalan is always warning us about in chapel. If word were to get back to him it could be bad for both you and me. The holy father hasn't got much of a sense of humor."

"I guess not." Kiram frowned out at the arena. The white salt circles of the fencing rings were spreading into the dirt, blurring and distorting the way smoke rings dissipated.

Several grooms worked their way down the length of the stand distributing leather armor and fencing blades to the second-year students. Kiram imagined his own face reflected Nestor's queasy pallor. It would be them out in the arena soon. Everyone in the stands would be watching.

The leather of Kiram's cuirass fit tightly across his back and chest though it hung loosely over his stomach. The byrnie he pulled over it draped down to his groin. The thick scales of leather overlapped like snake skin.

He laced his blue gauntlets tightly over his forearms and then tested his grip on the blade he had been given. The armor felt hot and heavy. Kiram could already smell his own sweat soaking through his under shirt and into the cuirass. He had no idea how men managed to move, much less fight while wearing the much heavier armor required for the tournament's final duels.

"Here." Javier handed him a black ribbon. "Tie your hair back."

Kiram did as he was told. Next to him Nestor sat back on the bench, scowling at the dueling sword he'd been given.

"I was out right away last year. It wasn't so bad really." Nestor sighed heavily and then glanced up at Javier. "You don't think Elezar's put any money on me, do you?"

"Of course he has. We both know how much you've improved over the last four months. You're going to take the wind out of your opponents before they know what hit them."

Nestor straightened slightly. "I have gotten a lot better. Though I wish I had my spectacles."

"You never wear them while you're fighting," Kiram said.

"I know. I just think it would settle my nerves if I could see how nervous the other boys look."

Kiram nodded. In a way he thought Nestor might be the lucky one. None of the students left on the arena floor looked nervous. All of them had already fought and won several duels. They looked dirty and some wore bandages, but all of them wore hard, assured expressions.

The last remaining pair of first-year duelists stepped into a nearby ring. They were both Yillar students and their armor was covered in nicks and dust from previous duels. A judge raised his hand and then swung it down indicating the beginning of their combat. Both students stood still with their blades drawn and then one of them simply knelt and the other touched his chest lightly with his blade.

Kiram gaped at them. "What was that?"

"Yillar etiquette, I guess," Nestor said. "When they're evenly matched one Yillar student will forfeit to another of higher rank instead of dragging out a real fight."

"We're allowed to forfeit?" It made sense. Why should two students from the same school exhaust themselves fighting each other? And it offered Kiram some relief. Rather than take a brutal beating he could simply forfeit.

"No," Javier said firmly. "They can forfeit. We at the Sagrada Academy do not."

"Master Ignacio would kill you if you did," Nestor said. "A chain is only as strong as its weakest link or something like that."

"Master Ignacio will not tolerate cowardice," Javier continued. "It's his philosophy that it is better to fight and be beaten than it is to simply surrender. No war was ever won through surrender."

"None was ever won by being beaten into bloody submission either," Kiram replied.

"True." Javier smiled at him. "So, I wouldn't advise that you do that either."

Master Ignacio shouted out the names of the second-year students who were to take the floor of the arena. They were the worst combatants of the second year: the ones who would face first-year challengers and both Kiram and Nestor were among them.

As Kiram started to go, Javier caught his shoulder and leaned close to his ear.

"Bring them to their knees," he whispered and his breath sent a thrill over Kiram's skin. Then Javier gently shoved Kiram out into the arena.

Kiram's heart hammered in his chest as he took his place inside the salt circle of the dueling ring that Master Ignacio indicated.

"Hold this ring," Master Ignacio told him. "Hold it five rounds. Do not fail me."

"Yes, sir," Kiram responded but the war master had already turned away. Moments later the first-year combatants took their places. Kiram's first opponent was a stocky young man from the Yillar Academy. He had a blunt little nose and a snorting, aggressive sword style. The first time his blade crashed against Kiram's it sent a jolt through Kiram's wrist.

Fortunately months of training with Javier had honed his defenses. Even utterly flustered, Kiram reflexively sidestepped the Yillar student's second thrust and brought his own blade down across the Yillar student's exposed shoulder.

"Haldiim bitch," the Yillar student snarled. An instant later Kiram deflected another thrust and the Yillar student's sword arm swung wide out. Kiram pounced forward, slamming his blade against the Yillar student's chest. Taken off guard and suddenly off balance, the Yillar student fell to the arena floor.

The judge called the win in Kiram's favor and a cheer went up from the Sagrada Academy stands.

Kiram's entire body trembled with a rush of exhilaration and shock. He hadn't expected to win. Now he would have to fight again. His heart was beating so fast and hard that he thought he could hear his own pulse pounding in his ears.

He faced another Yillar student. This one was faster and he scored a bruising strike across Kiram's left forearm, but the blow cost him his balance. Kiram brought him down with a two fast thrusts into his stomach and chest. The judge held his banner over Kiram and another cheer went up. Kiram's muscles felt molten. The air of the pavilion seemed cool against his skin.

Kiram's third opponent was a first-year student from the Sagrada Academy. Kiram exploited his clumsy footwork, pressing him hard to the right then suddenly shifting his thrusts to the left. The young man finally tripped over his own boots. Kiram dispatched him with a quick strike.

Excitement and fear rolled through Kiram's entire body. His breath came in deep animal gasps. He held the ring. He brought his opponents to their knees. But with each triumph came the realization that he had to do it all again and his next opponent would be better.

By his fifth and final duel, Kiram's body was slick with sweat. His nerves felt tremulous as spider silk; his muscles were soft lead.

A tall Yillar student stepped into the ring. Locks of chestnut colored hair were plastered to his face by sweat. He gazed at Kiram with a blank, almost dead expression. Kiram wondered how long he'd been fighting. He looked like he might collapse any moment.

The judge signaled for them to begin. Kiram tested his opponent's reflexes with quick thrusts. The Yillar student blocked, but just barely. Kiram moved in closer, pressing the attack. He thrust for the Yillar student's stomach, but suddenly something caught his foot. Kiram stumbled backwards. Instantly, the Yillar student struck for Kiram's heart. Kiram blocked the blow with his left forearm. The blade tore into his gauntlet with shattering force.

Kiram fell and rolled just as the Yillar student slammed his blade down again. The sword slashed across Kiram's left shoulder, ripping through the leather scales of his byrnie.

Kiram bounded back up to his feet, gasping for air and shaking. The Yillar student regarded him with that same dull, dead gaze.

Through the din of the roaring crowds in the stands, Kiram suddenly picked out a single voice shouting at him. It was Javier. Kiram couldn't make any of his words out clearly, but he didn't have to. Javier had already warned him, already told him what to do. He had just been too exhausted to remember the one Yillar student Javier had specifically pointed out to him. Ariz Plunado. Kiram felt like an idiot for not recognizing that bland face immediately, but Ariz was simply so forgettable.

Now he circled Kiram slowly, testing Kiram's defenses with quick jabs. All the while his feet darted in, kicking at Kiram's steps. Pain shot through Kiram's left arm as he pulled it in close to his side. Dark red rivulets of blood trickled from under his gauntlet and dribbled down his hand.

"If it hurts you can forfeit." Ariz's voice was as colorless as his expression. His lips hardly moved.

"I—"Before Kiram could make his response, Ariz kicked his ankle hard and lunged for Kiram's chest. Kiram leapt to the side.

Ariz spun on him. "You look like you should see a physician. You're bleeding a lot."

Kiram was expecting the attack this time but it was still brutal. Ariz lunged to strike Kiram's left arm and when Kiram shifted back Ariz landed a hard kick on Kiram's knee. Kiram's leg buckled. He caught himself but hardly had time to block Ariz's thrust for his stomach.

"You look pale, Haldiim." Ariz drove him back toward the blurred white edge of the fencing ring. If he stepped back across it this could all be over. He would be disqualified. His arm hurt so badly he could hardly think. One misstep and it would be over. Javier would be so disappointed. Every bigoted Cadeleonian in the stands would be pleased, though.

Kiram forced himself to attack Ariz again, jabbing hard and fast. His muscles screamed from the effort and when his strength failed him, Ariz sprang after him, lashing out with his blade. Kiram didn't attempt to block the blow. Instead, he spun to the side as if he were dancing. Momentum carried Ariz a step past him. Kiram planted his shoulder in Ariz's back, shoving forward as hard as he could. Ariz skidded forward then spun back. But it was too late. He had crossed through the salt ring.

The judge swung his blue banner up over Kiram. Screams and cheers erupted from the Sagrada Academy stands, but he could barely hear. His own pulse hammered through his ears. His left arm hung like a limp rag and muscle cramps bit into his legs. Slowly, Kiram sank to his knees on the ground. He felt numb, utterly thoughtless. Then he was lying on his back staring up at the blue sky above the pavilion. Three back silhouettes passed over him. Crows, he thought.

A few moments later two of the judges dragged him from the arena back to the Sagrada Academy stands.

Chapter Eighteen

"You're going to have a great scar," Nestor proclaimed. From deep inside a haze of duera, Kiram gave him a slow, distracted nod. He had never had cause to drink the painkiller before; how completely it altered his perception surprised him.

Rambling corridors of vending wagons and open tents spread out in every direction around Kiram. Many of the tents served as small theatres. Several brightly-costumed musicians accompanied masked actors, and others played for acrobats as they flipped and twisted. Now and then the odd dancing bear or trained monkey was brought on stage. Once Kiram glimpsed a scantily clad woman holding a large snake around her waist. Then a man in a velvet coat pulled the tent flaps closed.

Between the theater tents, merchants' stalls brimmed with countless diverse goods. Just in the small area Kiram had explored so far there were cut flowers and bolts of cloth, strings of beads, garlands of garlic, powdered saints' bones, horse shoes, red squash, arrowheads, chests of spices, ivory dice and jars of pressed sunflower oil. Men in piebald coats and extravagant hats wandered the open grounds hawking dueling knives, exotic perfumes and decks of blessed cards. Their offers hardly carried over the noise of the surrounding crowds.

The wild shouts of the fair criers, bartering merchants and music blurred through Kiram's drugged thoughts. The vivid colors of the painted sign and red striped tent in front of him seemed to jump and waver before his eyes.

A man brushed past Kiram leading his newly purchased goat. A few yards away, two youths shouted out enticements as they held up squealing black piglets. A dog raced past with a haunch of roasted lamb in its mouth and two plump women came running after it shouting insults and threats, which Kiram doubted would help to attract the dog. He took a breath and thought he could smell every creature that had ever lived.

Beside him, Nestor held his kerchief and studied the yellow butterflies embroidered in the corners. He looked almost guilty when he noticed Kiram watching him and he quickly tucked the kerchief back into the pocket of his academy uniform.

"Your arm's not hurting you, is it?"

Slowly, Kiram's attention drifted down to his own forearm. A long red seam of broken skin was surrounded by a wide expanse of deep purple bruises. Black silk stitches laced the wound closed like the ribbons of a lady's dress. It was almost pretty, though it looked like it should hurt.

"I'm not feeling a thing." Kiram swayed and Nestor braced him.

"Steady now," Nestor said. "Scholar Donamillo gave you a very strong dose. Maybe we should find a place to sit down."

"No, I'm fine." Kiram shook his head. The sensation of his hair swinging against his neck distracted him; then he focused his concentration. "We have to see the fair with Javier. We're going to meet dirty Irabiim and have our fortunes told and probably get robbed."

"I'd rather not be robbed," Nestor commented.

"Where's Javier?" Kiram suddenly demanded. He stared around him. Three girls hurried after their mother with piglets clutched in their arms. A group of Yillar students passed by and then ducked into a striped tent. But Javier was nowhere to be seen.

"He's getting us some food," Nestor said. "He's only been gone a few minutes, you know."

"I know. I know," Kiram said and suddenly he had the urge to be completely honest with Nestor.

"I want to see him. But can I? No. Who could? I mean, I honestly want to, but it's just so stupid. Look at where we are." Kiram waved vaguely at a man with puppets on his hands. "Is this the kind of place for that?"

"Puppets?" Nestor didn't seem to have really grasped Kiram's confession. Kiram tried again.

"This isn't Anacleto," Kiram pronounced firmly. "And even if it were, Javier is still going to have to buy a damn monkey and —my god! Look at that pig!" All of Kiram's thoughts of Javier's obligations to wed and his own duties to his family instantly dispersed before the amazing girth of a huge black boar with painted gold tusks. The colossal animal trailed behind an old woman who led it by a chain attached to a ring in the end of its nose. Despite the packed crowd, people stepped aside giving the woman and her boar a wide berth.

Nestor grinned. "He's big, isn't he?"

"He is one of the old gods brought low by mortal flesh!" Kiram pronounced. The idea felt amazingly profound. A moment later, with the boar out of sight, Kiram forgot it completely.

"Where's Javier gotten off to?" Kiram demanded.

"He's gone to the kingdom of Yuan."

"What? That bastard!"

"Oh, look, there he is." Nestor pointed past the pig sellers, to a tall man with jet-black hair. An older, bland-looking man and two women stood with him. One of the women looked about sixty and wore a widow's veil over her white hair. The younger woman resembled the man in her plain features but Kiram guessed she was only sixteen or so. All three of the people wore black bands of mourning around the sleeves of their fine silk clothes. The black-haired man was dressed in a blue academy uniform and smiled widely up at the sky.

"That's Fedeles," Kiram said.

"Is it?" Nestor squinted intently. Fedeles caught sight of the two of them and waved both his arms in the air as if he were flagging down a passing ship. "Yeah, that's Fedeles all right."

Fedeles pushed and danced his way through the crowd. The Quemanors followed him, though they looked annoyed by the effort. Fedeles easily outdistanced them, having no inclination to either apologize for or excuse his intrusions.

"Firaj! Firaj!" Fedeles shouted and he hugged Kiram to him with bruising force, shoving his face into Kiram's hair with the rough propriety of a dog snuffling someone's crotch.

"Careful, Fedeles." Nestor pulled him back. "Kiram's hurt."

Fedeles looked shocked and quickly disengaged. He peered at Kiram's stitches and whimpered. Then he patted Kiram's head. "Don't run away. It hurts but don't run away."

"I won't." It was surprising how much Fedeles resembled Javier physically and yet his mind was so different. Though there were moments, just instants, when Kiram thought he could see Javier's expressions on Fedeles' face. A thoughtful frown would flash across his sharp features only to be engulfed in a maniacal grin.

It was almost like Kiram's thoughts right now, as he floated through a drugged haze. There were moments of clarity, which the duera distorted and consumed, so that he could hardly communicate. Was that how Fedeles felt?

"You are trying to tell me something, aren't you?" Kiram asked.

"Yes, yes!" Fedeles hugged Kiram to him again fiercely, hissing into his ear. "He wants to kill Lunaluz. Help us."

"Who?" Kiram demanded.

"Pretty!" Fedeles released his grip on Kiram and lunged after a flower seller. Nestor sprang forward and caught his arm.

"Fedeles. No!" Nestor said. "Look, your family is here. See?"

Fedeles' grandmother gazed at him with a look of long suffering affection. Fedeles smiled, but sadly, as if he knew how his behavior horrified her, as if some sane, dignified aspect of himself was trapped within his madness, witness to all this humiliatingly childish activity but utterly helpless to stop it.

Kiram wondered if being drugged really was offering him an insight into Fedeles' mind or if the idea was itself a delusion of the duera coursing through his bloodstream. At the moment it felt like genuine insight.

He turned to Fedeles and clutched his hand.

"Don't give up, Fedeles," Kiram said. "I'll find a way to get you free. Nestor and I, we're both looking for a way."

"Brave ponies!" Fedeles threw his arms around both of them.

"Lord Quemanor." Nestor pulled free of Fedeles' grip and bowed his head to Fedeles' father. "It's good to see you at the tournament. We missed you last year."

"Thank you for your compliments, young Master Grunito. Your good manners lead me to believe that you will understand why we have no wish to remain in your company at present."

Kiram wriggled free of Fedeles' arm, scowling at Fedeles' father. What had he just said? It had sounded like a kind of insult but Kiram wasn't thinking well enough to be sure.

Then out of the corner of his eye he caught sight of Javier. He stood back in the shadows of a theater tent just watching them all. There was something in his expression that stopped Kiram from calling out to him, though he wanted to.

Beside him Nestor bowed slightly to Fedeles' father.

"Of course. I understand, sir. Your family has my deepest sympathies."

"Thank you. Though I am sorry to be told that members of my extended family have been offered far more of the Grunito sympathy than have those of us who suffered the greater loss."

Kiram had no idea what the man was talking about but Nestor seemed embarrassed by it.

"Come, Fedeles." Fedeles' grandmother took his hand. "Shall we go look at the horses in the auction?"

Fedeles nodded vigorously. She led him away without a further word to either Nestor or Kiram.

"That was ugly," Nestor said.

"What was he talking about?" Kiram asked.

Nestor squinted around at the surrounding crowd, then he stepped closer to Kiram and lowered his voice.

"Lord Quemanor may always hate Javier but he's just cutting himself out of society when he refuses to socialize with any of Javier's acquaintances. If it comes down to it, who in his right mind is going to side with Quemanor against the Duke of Rauma?"

"Side with him over what?" Kiram asked.

"Hasn't anyone told you?"

"You're the only one who tells me anything, Nestor."

"And I didn't mention the duel over Fedeles?"

Kiram shook his head.

"Well, it's not exactly table conversation. But you ought to know," Nestor said quietly. "Javier killed Fedeles' older brother in a duel two years ago."

"Was it during a tournament?" Kiram could easily imagine something going wrong in one of the fencing circles.

"No, it was a real blood duel. Prince Sevanyo sanctioned it. Herves Quemanor made some nasty claims about Fedeles and Javier challenged him to a duel."

"Why would Herves insult his own brother?"

"That's just it." Nestor lowered his voice to the faintest whisper. Kiram had to lean in to hear him. "After Fedeles went mad, Herves claimed he wasn't his full brother. He said that the rumors about Javier's father having an affair with their mother were true. He called Fedeles a foul, illegitimate product of Tornesal incest."

"What a rotten brother." It was the first thing Kiram thought, though almost immediately he wondered if Herves' claim could have been true. It would explain why Fedeles, of all the Quemanor children, was the only one afflicted by the Tornesal curse.

"People claim Fedeles never really understood what was happening but I think he did. I think it hurt his feelings pretty badly when Herves started talking about having Fedeles disinherited. That's when Javier challenged him to the blood duel and killed him."

Kiram glanced over Nestor's shoulder to where Javier lurked in the shadows of the theatre tent. Now he realized why his first impression of Javier had been that he resembled the mercenary street snakes of Anacleto. There was a cold assurance to the way Javier met other men's glances. He knew he was capable of killing and his gaze conveyed that.

Javier met Kiram's gaze and his grim countenance changed completely. He offered Kiram a warm, almost boyish smile. He stepped out of the shadows, swiveled between two men, and sidestepped an old woman. He held up a fistful of roasted meat skewers. In the other hand he held a reed basket full of some kind of bread.

"Are those the chips all you Cadeleonians eat?" Kiram asked.

"What?" Nestor asked.

"That basket of chips Javier's bringing." Kiram pointed.

Nestor spun around. "Good eyes, Kiram. Yeah, they're casocres. God, he's nearly here. I would have still been babbling about him when he came up, if you hadn't seen him."

Nestor was always so willing to compliment another person. Kiram felt a sudden warmth for him and his effortless generosity of spirit.

Javier reached them, handed the basket of casocres to Nestor, and frowned at Kiram. "What's the happy occasion?"

"What do you mean?" Kiram accepted a beef skewer.

"You were grinning like an idiot just now," Javier said. "Relief from Lord Quemanor's company couldn't have left you that happy."

"No." Kiram took a bite of the thinly sliced beef. It was salty and greasy and just a little sweet. He took another bite.

"I was just thinking of how lucky I am," Kiram said at last. "I could have had the worst time at the Sagrada Academy these last four months but I haven't. I've been really happy."

"Have you?" Javier handed a skewer to Nestor.

"Well, not when Master Ignacio berated me or when he struck me or when Genimo cropped me, but other times…with the two of you. I've been happy and it's because you're good people. Don't give me that look, Javier. You are a good man."

The smirk didn't drop from Javier's face but he managed to look somewhat contrite. "Has he been like this the whole time?"

"More or less. He's a nice-tempered drunk, that's for sure." Nestor ate several of the crispy chips.

"I'm not drunk," Kiram objected.

"Not exactly sober either." Nestor handed Kiram the basket of casocres. Kiram took one of the small triangular chips. A thin layer of cheese had been melted over it, and there was a strong scent of mustard on it as well. The chip was amazingly crisp and it tasted delicious with Kiram's beef skewer.

"Try these with the meat." Kiram offered the basket to Javier. "They're amazing."

"Really?" Javier gave him an amused look.

"You already knew they went well together, didn't you?"

"I had reason to suspect so, yes. I'm glad to know that you agree though." Javier turned to Nestor. "So, what did Quemanor have to say?"

Nestor floundered, so Kiram answered for him. "Apparently, he came over to tell Nestor that he wasn't going to talk to him. Quemanor said it nicely enough I suppose but it was still a rude thing to do and I didn't understand what was going on at all because I didn't know about your duel with Fedeles' brother."

"Odd that you'd mention it without knowing it took place," Javier said.

"Well, I know now." Kiram finished his beef and tossed the wooden skewer aside. "Nestor just told me."

"Of course he did." Javier gave Nestor a reproachful glance.

Nestor flushed guiltily. "Everybody at the academy knows. I didn't see any reason Kiram shouldn't."

"I suppose there isn't any." Javier ate the last of his beef and tossed his skewer on top of Kiram's. "So, Master Kir-Zaki, are you feeling up to a stroll through the fair or should I take you back to my townhouse?"

"I want to see the Irabiim and Nestor says there's a Mirogoth performer who comes every year and turns into a wolf."

"I wouldn't say he turns into a wolf so much as he steps behind a curtain and shoves a rangy dog out onto the stage," Javier replied.

"No," Nestor objected. "You have to have an open mind about it to really appreciate the transformation. You hear all these terrible noises coming from behind the curtain and then a wolf steps out. I swear it's a real wolf, Kiram. And it has the same color eyes as the Mirogoth man. It's shocking."

It didn't take them long to find the tent where a red-haired woman was selling tickets to witness her brother reveal his beast-soul. Signs painted with huge wolves stood outside the small tent and the woman's wild hair was tied up to resemble two long ears flopping down over her shoulders. Though the woman was clearly of Mirogoth descent, she spoke flawless Cadeleonian.

Most of the people buying tickets were parents, escorting their young children inside. From time to time the red-haired woman gave a wink and reassured a mother that her wolf-brother attended chapel every Sacreday.

Javier bought tickets for all three of them and they filed into the dark confines of the tent. Two lamps at the foot of the stage provided the only light. The three of them kept to the back of the tent, so as not to block the views of the many children assembled inside. As the space filled up Javier stepped slightly behind Kiram, allowing several children to squeeze in closer.

The performance itself was rather simple. A red-haired man walked onto stage, explained in an exaggerated Mirogoth accent, that among his people there were those who walked as men but could assume the forms of beasts.

Few could bear to witness the transformation directly, the Mirogoth man warned them gravely. The sight had driven horses mad and turned milk sour. For their own sakes, he told the children, they should not look too closely.

Then he picked up one of the lamps and stepped behind a curtain. His terrible change was all a matter of strange noises and silhouettes cast up on the curtain by the flickering lamp. Nestor watched with rapt attention.

Kiram hardly noticed the performance. All of his attention focused on the sensation of Javier's hand touching his own. His fingertips sent a thrill up Kiram's right arm. He traced the delicate skin of Kiram's palm and wrist. His touch was light and flirtatious.

Kiram returned Javier's motions. He pushed his fingers between Javier's and Javier clenched his hand around Kiram's, gripping him tightly.

Javier leaned closer, his thigh brushing the back of Kiram's leg. As their hips brushed together an aching desire pulsed through Kiram's groin. He longed to press into Javier, but Nestor was standing only a breath from them. Dozens of children were gathered all around them.

Kiram pulled away but he didn't release Javier's hand. Not yet.

A theatrical howl rose up from behind the curtain. Then the lamp there suddenly went dark, leaving only the single flame illuminating the empty stage. A lanky, reddish dog padded out from behind the curtain. Gasps and squeals escaped the children. Nestor leaned forward.

"That's definitely a wolf." Nestor peered intently at the animal.

Kiram had never seen a wolf and had no idea if this animal was one, but it looked too thin to somehow encapsulate the entire mass of the man who had stood on the stage earlier.

The would-be wolf regarded its audience and then suddenly bucked up onto its hind legs and awkwardly tottered back behind the curtain. Children gaped in amazement. A moment later there was another howl and the man returned. He bowed and thanked them for their time and attention.

Then, on cue, the flaps of the tent were pulled open and blinding afternoon sunlight poured in. Javier dropped Kiram's hand instantly. The man on the stage bounded back behind his curtain and the show was over.

Nestor, Kiram, and Javier wandered out onto the fairgrounds along with several dozen dazed and excited children and their laughing parents.

"It's genius!" Nestor said. He seemed nearly as delighted as the children. "He's hiding in plain sight! That performance was so obviously false that it had to be real."

"What?" Javier asked. He sounded more annoyed than Nestor's proclamation merited. Kiram himself was feeling a little frustrated, but it had nothing to do with the performance. Nestor didn't seem to notice.

"Exactly!" Nestor said. "It looked like a shoddy performance to disguise a genuine transformation."

"Or," Javier replied, "maybe it looked like a shoddy performance because it was. You can't honestly believe that a real Mirogoth shapechanger would march out to the middle of Cadeleon, advertise himself, and sell tickets."

"Probably not. But on the other hand, what's the harm in believing it?" Nestor shrugged. "It makes the whole fair more interesting. And I think it could be true. You have to admit that it would be a clever way to hide himself."

"There's a point when something clever just becomes stupid. I'd say that hiding in plain sight is that point." Javier sighed as if he was releasing some deep frustration. He glanced to Kiram. "What do you think?"

"Well, if we're going to assume the Mirogoth really is a shapechanger—"

"Let's assume he is," Nestor said and Javier just shook his head but appeared resigned to the idea.

"Then, I guess that it would depend on how well he could disguise his true nature," Kiram said. He didn't look at Javier as he responded, but he was thinking of the way Javier teased men and made lascivious insinuations. "If there were aspects of himself that he couldn't suppress then maybe it would make sense for him to flaunt them and make them a kind of joke. People would laugh and never suspect that he was showing them the truth all along."

"Exactly," Nestor said.

"But it would be a very dangerous way to live his life." Kiram glanced to Javier.

"You're sounding more lucid than before," Javier commented. "How does your arm feel?"

"It aches, but it's not bad. I'd like to see the Irabiim before it gets too late. Then I need to find the Laughing Dog—" Kiram cut himself off as a figure in the surrounding crowd caught his attention.

A group of five well-dressed girls walked primly between the stalls of flower sellers and cloth merchants. All but one of them wore their braids up in maiden's combs. Most were decorated with floral designs but one was painted with butterfly wings.

"Yellow butterflies." Kiram nudged Nestor. "Yellow butterflies! She's coming this way."

Kiram pointed as discreetly as he could.

Javier's lip curled as he caught sight of the girl. "What do you care about her?"

"She threw a favor to Nestor."

"Oh, I see." The edge of anger disappeared from Javier's expression immediately. "Do you still have the kerchief, Nestor?"

"Of course!" Nestor responded.

"Well then, take it to her," Javier said. "Tell her that you noticed that she had dropped it and you've been looking for her all this time to return it."

"But, what if it's a mistake? I mean, what if she didn't mean it for me? What if—"

"Just do it. It always works for Atreau. You can't go wrong acting the part of a gallant gentleman. Now, go get her." Javier shoved Nestor forward.

Nestor seemed dazed. He stumbled ahead, digging the kerchief out of his pocket. As Nestor drew closer to the girl, she caught sight of him. Her expression was so excited and nervous that it made Kiram smile. Then Kiram noticed the tiny pair of spectacles perched on the bridge of her nose. She reached up, removed them, and secreted them in her small yellow silk purse.

She was staring wide-eyed when Nestor reached her, and they both blushed deep red as Nestor offered her the kerchief. She pressed it back into his hand.

In a matter of moments the rest of the girls crowded around. Nestor said something that made them all laugh and then they started after him back towards the transforming Mirogoth's tent. The girl with yellow butterfly combs clung to Nestor's arm.

Javier touched Kiram's shoulder.

"Let's go before Nestor feels he has to introduce us. He'll make a better impression without a hell-branded duke flustering his little flock of hens."

"Are you sure?" Kiram didn't want to abandon Nestor.

"Positive," Javier replied. "I'm poor company for giggling girls like those ones. They put me off and I put them off. And you're hardly likely to win Nestor any compliments either."

"What's wrong with me?"

"You're a Haldiim for one thing." Javier pulled Kiram back slowly as he spoke. "And you're not available to them for another."

Kiram didn't bother to argue. He'd been caressing Javier's hand and pressing against Javier's thigh only a few minutes ago. He gave a quick wave, turned, and followed Javier through the fair.

They passed tanners' stalls where beautifully tooled saddles and bridles were displayed along with deerskins and bull hides. Despite the strong smell of leather Kiram picked out a familiar scent. The aroma of the sharp spices, which perfumed adhil bread, briefly floated over Kiram but when he looked around him all he saw were stocky Cadeleonian men, testing the stirrups or bartering over the cost of calfskins.

"Is something wrong?" Javier asked.

"I was just thinking that we must be close to the Irabiim."

"Oh?" Javier cocked his head slightly, studying Kiram. "How did you know?"

"I can smell them," Kiram said. "Not in a bad way, but their food. Someone must be frying adhil bread. Our cook used to make it for us on cold mornings."

"I haven't ever heard of it."

"It's delicious, though it's not really bread at all. It's more of a thin pancake. The batter is fried in a pan, flipped out and eaten right away."

"It sounds good," Javier commented but he seemed distracted by other thoughts. "Here, let's go up around this way. There are fewer people."

Kiram followed him through a narrow lane of rickety stalls and drab tents. They walked past a stall offering spurs and twisted bits. Kiram glanced away from the jagged edges of metal. He was glad that Firaj was already trained and didn't require such brutal tools to be controlled.

Just behind the stalls Kiram could see a poorly-repaired stone wall and beyond that stood thirty or more brightly-painted traveling wagons circled in the shadows of a stand of large, twisting trees. Black crows perched among the branches on the wagon roofs. Blue-tinged smoke rose up from at least four cooking fires.

As Kiram gazed at the red and gold designs on the walls of the wagons and at the shabby figures crouched around the fires, the sense of familiarity that the aroma of adhil bread had nurtured in him withered.

The Irabiim really weren't Haldiim.

They were filthy and their horses were rangy-looking creatures with rough, spotted hides. The women standing watch over the cook pots wore dark circles of kohl around their eyes and their blonde hair was tied up in what looked like strips of rag. The men carried fighting knives tucked into their belts, wore no shirts, and jangled gaudy bangles from their wrists.

Kiram's uncle Rafie had told him that each of the bracelets identified an Irabiim man as the son or husband of a particular matriarch and that because Irabiim mothers exchanged their sons like they were trading dice, only those bracelets prevented daughters from wedding their own brothers.

The wagons were decorated with morbid warnings to trespassers. Gilded human skulls hung from the roofs like wind chimes. Kiram felt his stomach clenching as he stared at them. No Haldiim would have treated his ancestors' remains that way, much less allowed crows to grow fat picking away the strips of flesh.

Kiram retreated into the shadow of the stone wall.

Javier asked, "What is it?"

"I always thought my uncle was exaggerating about them." Kiram didn't want to tell Javier that he was frightened, so he said, "They're filthy."

"Well, cleanliness doesn't seem to be a ruling tenet among them." Javier appeared unfazed by the skulls and obscenities on the wagon walls. "They breed some of the fastest colts you can buy and of course there's also the matter of having your fortune read."

"I don't believe in fortune telling."

"If you don't want to meet them, that's fine with me." Javier leaned against the wall beside Kiram so that their shoulders just brushed together. His hand hung down, almost touching Kiram's. "But I don't feel like wandering around in a crowd right now."

"Neither do I." If Kiram had been thinking more clearly he knew he would never have moved. As it was, he shifted slightly, leaning into Javier's shoulder. The weight of their bodies balanced. Kiram closed his eyes, letting the familiar scents of sweat and leather encompass him. He imagined that he could feel Javier's heart beating through his own body.

Kiram twined his fingers between Javier's and held his hand tight.

Javier said, "You don't make it easy for me to stay away from you."

Kiram kept his eyes closed, fearing his resolve would collapse if he looked into Javier's eyes. Then he'd kiss his mouth. He'd run his hands over his chest and down to his thighs. His body ached just thinking of the mistakes that he longed to make. Kiram started to pull his hand back but Javier tightened his grip. Kiram relented too easily.

"I want to be with you. But then you know that. Does it please you to know how much I want you?" Blatant hunger edged Javier's voice. "That I lie awake, staring at your sleeping body, thinking of how close you are and how easily I could reach you? How easily I could tear off those flimsy white clothes you wear and have you? Some nights I hardly sleep at all."

Kiram opened his eyes. He expected some trace of resentment in Javier's expression but instead there was only that familiar look of rueful amusement.

"I'm sorry."

"Don't be. I managed to use the time to get my armor to a high polish. It just gets cleaner the dirtier my thoughts get. But I wish I could inspire a few restless nights myself. You don't seem too easily inspired, though." Javier's gaze seemed to burn into Kiram. A lock of inky black hair fell across forehead. "If only I were some exquisite machine. Do you think you might miss a little sleep over me if I were made of gears and pistons?"

"I'd wonder who built you so well." Kiram wanted to tell Javier that he spent most nights dreaming of him. Some mornings he despised waking because it meant leaving the rapture of his fantasies.

"Do you think you'd be tempted to tinker with me?"

"Of course I would." Kiram pushed the lock of hair back from Javier's face.

"Was there really a girl you liked in Anacleto?"

"What? No." Kiram laughed at the thought. "I was talking about a man named Musni. He and I were close. But I always knew that it wouldn't work for us."

"Why not?" Javier asked the question so directly that Kiram wasn't quite sure how to respond. He and Musni had not been suited to each other for a dozen reasons. But one in particular had always kept him from committing his heart to Musni.

"I always knew that he would marry into a wealthy woman's household someday. He just liked being comfortable and normal too much not to. And his mother wouldn't have been happy until he did."

"You think your mother will be happy if you don't?"

"My mother knows I will never take a wife. She used to complain that it was a waste of my good breeding, but I think she secretly likes the idea that she'll never have to hand her baby boy over to another woman."

"But she doesn't care that you're..." Javier seemed unable to find a word for what he wanted to say. "You're with a man?"

"That would depend on the man, I suppose. She wasn't all that fond of Musni, but that had more to do with his mother than anything else. On the other hand, there's a pharmacist, Hashiem Kir-Naham, who she constantly points out to me."

"And does this Hashiem Kir-Naham interest you?"

Four months ago he might have. Kiram stole a sidelong glance at Javier, taking in the long, sinuous muscles of his shoulder and neck, the hard contrast of his tousled black hair and his delicate pale features. He was scowling, filthy, and he wore his dueling sword like he planned to make his living with it, and Kiram still found him appealing.

Kiram shrugged. "Maybe."

"Well, what is he like?" Javier pressed. "Short, ugly, old? Missing his teeth?"

"Not at all." Kiram laughed at the idea of any mother choosing such a man for her son. "He's older, thirty, I think. He's about my height. Very slim, and very formal. An only child, so he'll inherit his mother's pharmacy. His aunt owns several medicinal gardens, so he's well established in Anacleto."

Even as he described Hashiem Kir-Naham, Kiram felt a trapped dread spreading through him. Hashiem Kir-Naham was a perfect partner. Wealthy. Stable. Established.

Dull.

He would never ask Kiram to leave for the kingdom of Yuan in the dead of the night. He wouldn't dream of traveling into the Mirogoth lands or sailing across the White Sea. He certainly wouldn't hold him in his arms and open the white hell for him.

"He's nice," Kiram said, then seeing Javier's scowl deepening he quickly continued, "but he'll never leave the Haldiim district of Anacleto. I want to see more. I want to travel."

"Well, there is certainly much more of the world to see. I'd like to travel myself, someday." Javier looked almost wistful. "If you could go anywhere, where would you choose?"

"The kingdom of Yuan." Kiram decided after a moment of consideration. "My uncle Rafie told me the musicians there sharpen their thumbnails like knives and wear bright blue wigs."

"I'm not sure about the fingernails," Javier said, "but my family once entertained an ambassador from Yuan. Several of his attendants wore wigs like that. The ambassador himself had a long white wig, made of bird feathers."

"Did he invite you to take steam with him?"

"No, he didn't say anything to me. I was just a child at the time. Is steam one of their mystical potions?"

"I think so. Alizadeh took steam in Yuan. He said that it opened the world of dreams and allowed him to enter them while he was still wide awake."

"I'm not sure I want more chances to enter my dreams." A teasing expression flickered over Javier's face. "I am curious about yours, though."

A guilty flush flooded Kiram's cheeks and Javier leaned close and whispered, "Are they dirty?"

"I don't remember any of them," Kiram lied. "What about yours?"

"Filthy," Javier replied with a salacious smile. "You'd be shocked to see the things you do in my dreams."

"How can you just admit that?" Kiram asked. "Don't you ever get flustered or embarrassed?"

"Why would I be embarrassed? You're the one who can't keep his clothes on in my dreams." Javier's fingers gently curled along the curve of Kiram's neck and he accepted it as easily as he would have accepted one of Musni's caresses. It seemed natural to rest his hand on Javier's hip, hooking his thumb under the supple leather of Javier's belt and leaning in close to him.

The muscles of Javier's body went taut at Kiram's touch. The confident smirk dropped from Javier's mouth; his lips parted just slightly as he caught his breath. He stared at Kiram almost as if he were powerless to look away, a soft pink flush spreading across his cheeks.

Kiram wanted to kiss him. And he almost gave into that desire, but out of the corner of his eyes he caught a movement at the edge of the Irabiim camp. Javier saw it too and pulled back immediately, dropping his hand down to the sword hanging from his belt. Kiram turned just as the approaching figure waved at them.

And then Kiram realized he knew the man.

Alizadeh so perfectly looked the part of an ancient Bahiim that his appearance could have graced a Haldiim scroll from two hundred years past. His honey-blonde hair hung in spiraling curls down to his waist. Flashes of his dark bronze skin showed through the fine white cotton of his flowing prayer clothes.

The orange wrap that he wore over one shoulder and tied at his hip was heavy and in ancient times it would have served as the only shelter a Bahiim could depend upon while crossing the desert. For the same reason, all Bahiim carried water skins, short bows, and hunting knives. Alizadeh's looked like they had been used often.

His leather sandals were past their prime. The strap wrapping around his right ankle looked as if it had been recently mended. Kiram could easily imagine his uncle Rafie doing the careful stitching while commenting that Cadeleonian boots didn't have these kinds of problems.

"Well met, Kiri!" Alizadeh called. Kiram waved back at him.

Javier studied Alizadeh with an expression somewhere between wonder and suspicion. "You know him?"

"That is Alizadeh, my uncle's partner. The one I told you about."

"The Bahiim." Javier nodded.

Kiram made introductions. Javier gave a curt bow and Alizadeh responded by holding up his palms in a sign of formal blessing. A flock of black crows swept out from the Irabiim camp, passed overhead, and then scattered out over the fair. Alizadeh watched the birds then returned his attention to Kiram. "I see Rafie got the lotus medallion to you."

"Yes, it's already brought me lots of luck. I did better in the fencing circles than I expected anyway. And I think some of it rubbed off on Javier. He won the race this morning."

"Congratulations." Alizadeh studied Javier for a moment then glanced back to Kiram. When he spoke again it was softly and in Haldiim. **"Do not take the medallion off, Kiri. This place may not be safe. The shadow of an old evil lingers here and it will not be made to rest."**

Kiram knew that Javier understood more of the Haldiim language than he admitted to and clearly from the way his body tensed at the mention of an old evil, he understood Alizadeh's words, and doubtless took them to mean the white hell.

"Anything I can do? Perhaps show you and your partner around?" Javier's tone remained polite, but his face revealed his tension.

"No, thank you." Alizadeh gave Javier a cool, priestly smile. "Kiram's uncle and I just want to catch up with him and make sure that he is doing all right. He's never been this far away from home before and he's been missed."

Kiram frowned at hearing something so dismissive coming from Alizadeh, who as a rule was so welcoming.

"Yes, he was saying something like that just a few moments ago." Javier's expression shifted to mild disinterest, a sure sign that he had withdrawn into Cadeleonian reserve. "I imagine that you all have things to catch up on, and I ought to check on Lunaluz."

"We could go with you." Kiram wanted Javier to make some effort to stay with him.

But Javier had retreated to the impenetrable guise of a bored Hellion. Kiram wanted to assure him that he didn't need to, that Alizadeh wouldn't see him as a soulless aberration. He'd understand that Javier was a man—a friend. Only Alizadeh wasn't treating Javier with the warmth of a friend.

He regarded Javier with a cold formality that the Haldiim reserved for only their least loved neighbors and Cadeleonians. He said, "We shouldn't impose on your upperclassman any longer, Kiram."

“Master Ignacio will expect us at the city stables by the sixth bell,” Javier told Kiram. “I’ll see you then.” And with that he left them.

Chapter Nineteen

Alizadeh kept one hand clamped on Kiram's shoulder as he hurried him back across the fairgrounds. He glanced to the sky often, watching the crows converge and fly apart.

"*What's wrong?*" Kiram asked but as he took in Alizadeh's grim countenance and remembered his words, he knew the answer—an old evil lingered here. "*You and Rafie didn't just come to see me, did you? You're here because of the curse.*"

Alizadeh gave Kiram a quick assessing look and then nodded.

"*I'm so glad you came,*" Kiram told him. "*They're in real trouble—*"

"*Not here,*" Alizadeh cut him off. "*This is not a safe place to talk. Come quickly.*"

Apprehension gnawed at Kiram's sense of the normalcy of the fairgoers and merchants surrounding him. Suddenly they seemed to be staring too long at him and stepping aside too quickly. All around them children gaped at Alizadeh's long yellow hair and his strange clothes. Adults often made signs of the Cadeleonian church against their chests.

In Anacleto, Alizadeh would have grinned at them and returned the signs. He might have struck up a light conversation with one of the merchants and slowly charmed the people around him. But today he strode past them as if their discomfort wasn't worth noticing.

He led Kiram off the fairgrounds and across the harvested sunflower fields to a stooped traveler's inn at the edge of the city. A sign depicting a grinning black dog hung over the door. Two huge crows called down from the thatched roof. An old dog lay curled up near the wooden steps. Like most animals, the dog rushed to Alizadeh, full of excitement.

"Rafie is waiting for us, as are two of our Irabiim friends. You must be polite to them and don't let their appearances bother you. They're both Bahiim like me." Alizadeh stroked the dog's dusty hide.

"Of course," Kiram replied.

The room Alizadeh and Rafie had rented was directly under the ridge of the roof and so the heavy beams of the rafters slanted down on one wall, while the opposite wall abutted the stone of a central chimney. A single window illuminated a narrow bed where Kiram's uncle Rafie sat. Next to him a lanky Irabiim woman hunched, watching the window. Another more muscular Irabiim woman sat cross-legged on the floor toying with a string of brass prayer beads.

Both women wore their blonde hair long and twisted into thick matted locks. Their clothes resembled Alizadeh's, but the material was much brighter and covered with patches of dark red embroidery. The woman on the bed also wore a necklace that looked like it had been made from bird skulls. Both women gazed curiously at Kiram. Their pale green eyes looked almost luminous against the deep circles of kohl surrounding them.

Rafie said, *"This is my nephew, Kiram."* And Kiram knew from the women's sudden warm expressions that they had already heard quite a bit about him. *"This is Nakiesh,"* Rafie indicated the woman sitting beside him, and then the woman on the floor, *"and Liahn."*

"It's an honor to meet you," Kiram said. Reflexively, he lifted his hands in friendly greeting. A slight pang shot through his left forearm as he moved.

"What's happened to your arm, Kiri?" Rafie crossed the tiny space to Kiram's side.

"He was injured in a duel, apparently," Alizadeh provided.

"A duel?" Rafie demanded. *"How did you get into a duel?"*

"It was just one of the competitions in the tournament. It wasn't anything serious, and a physician took care of it right away."

"A Cadeleonian physician," Rafie commented as he studied the stitches. *"They still use black silk."*

"I'm fine, honestly." After four months of speaking nothing but Cadeleonian, Kiram felt strange conversing entirely in Haldiim again. He heard a difference in the cadence of his own words, as if he had picked up a slight Cadeleonian accent.

"Do you have any other injuries?" Rafie's gaze suddenly fixed on the fine scar on his cheek.

"I'm a little bruised but nothing serious." Kiram pulled his arm out of Rafie's grip. *"I won the duel."* Kiram felt he needed to say as much so that they wouldn't assume he'd just taken a beating.

"Good for you! Come sit here, Kiram." Liahn patted the floorboards beside her. Kiram obeyed and Rafie returned to his seat on the bed. Alizadeh seated himself on the floor and leaned back against Rafie's leg.

Kiram found it amazing that all five of them fit in the room. The smell of strong spices, the sight of familiar faces, and the cadence of the Haldiim tongue spoken so freely made Kiram acutely aware of how genuinely different his own people were from the Cadeleonians. In the past, he could only observe the Cadeleonians as being unusual, but now he could see unique characteristics of his own people. They stood and even sat in a particular loose manner and had an almost sleepy fluidity in their gestures and speech. Kiram wondered if that was how he looked to Javier and Nestor.

Liahn seemed to think he needed cheering up. She held up her right arm so that Kiram could see the long white line running from her elbow to her wrist.

"I took this scar from a Mirogoth shapechanger in the Blue Forest. I took an eye from him in exchange." She grinned at Kiram. Her gums seemed a little too red and her teeth looked a little too long.

"Your uncle stitched her back up," Nakiesh said from the bed. *"And if I remember correctly he stitched what was left of the Mirogoth back together as well."*

"The reward for bringing him in alive was bigger than the reward for his dead body,"Liahn informed Kiram with a wink.

Kiram stole a wondering glance between his uncle and Alizadeh. They certainly hadn't ever mentioned anything like that in the stories of their travels. Rafie looked a little pained.

"The last thing Kiram needs is to hear more tales of dangerous adventure. His mother is going to be horrified by this entire situation as is."

"He's safe enough now." Liahn shrugged. "At least as safe as anyone can be with the shadow of a curse in the air."

At the mention of a curse Rafie leaned forward just slightly and lightly touched Alizadeh's shoulder. Alizadeh offered him a reassuring smile.

Rafie asked, "Did you find it?"

"No, I hunted the entire city and the fairgrounds but I couldn't pin it down. I know that it's cast from the fortress on the hill, and spills down across this entire valley but its vessel seems unnaturally elusive." Alizadeh scowled in frustration. "Something is hiding it, shielding it from sight."

Kiram frowned, trying to follow the conversation. Were they talking about the Tornesal curse?

"I had no luck with the blood calling, either." Nakiesh held up her palm, which was bandaged. "I sent out our sister crows to look at the fortress more closely."

Kiram asked, "Are you talking about the Sagrada Academy?"

Alizadeh nodded impatiently, as though it was obvious. "Before it became the Sagrada Academy it was a fortress. Did you know that there used to be a Haldiim village just north of here?"

"No, I didn't." He couldn't imagine any Haldiim living this far north.

"The desecrated bodies of murdered Haldiim and Irabiim were hung from the walls of that fortress like banners of loyalty to King Nazario." Nakiesh ran a finger lightly over one of the bones hanging from her necklace. "Thousands of us died in that place. If you dig deep enough in the orchards you can still find bones."

"And ghosts," Liahn added. "Ghosts so wronged that their souls became a desolating curse."

"There's no need to frighten him," Rafie interrupted. He turned to Kiram. "That was all a long time ago. The furious ghosts who became the curse of the Old Rage were all put to rest by the Bahiim. They were locked away in the wood of the Ancients. And they are born into new lives with the passing of those old trees."

Rafie looked to Alizadeh for confirmation but Alizadeh's expression was troubled.

"Until I came here I would have thought so. But something is moving up on that hill."

"It feels like the Old Rage. But all we can see is its shadow," Nakiesh said softly.

"Wait, is this Old Rage curse the same curse that's destroying the Tornesals?" Kiram asked.

All eyes turned abruptly his way.

"What are you talking about?" Rafie asked.

"Well, there's a curse on the Tornesal bloodline. It's been hunting them down and killing them for eighteen years now, but it's been most active in the last three." Kiram looked between their faces for a sign of recognition. Rafie nodded slowly.

"A fellow physician from Rauma once mentioned some affliction that plagued the Tornesal dukes," Rafie said.

"Yes, but people are always claiming curses have been placed on certain families," Alizadeh replied. "As a rule it's either plain bad luck or bad choices. Sometimes there's murder involved."

"Or social diseases," Rafie added. Alizadeh, Nakiesh and Liahn all nodded at this.

Alizadeh went on. "But genuine curses don't pursue any single individual or even a blood line. They spread from a physical locus like spilled ink. They destroy people and animals alike."

"Maybe it's not a curse, then, but there is something that's killing the Tornesals," Kiram said.

"I'd bet soft gold that it's a greedy relative with a talent for poisons," Nakiesh replied.

Liahn nodded, looking amused.

"It's not poison," Kiram insisted. "Javier said that it's like some kind of insanity. First you hear screams that become louder and louder. Then you begin to have visions of being impaled that grow worse and worse until you stop eating and drinking. After that you die."

"Javier? The young man you introduced me to?" Alizadeh asked, his expression deeply knowing. "He didn't look like he was in the throes of a curse."

"He isn't now." Kiram felt his cheeks warm. "He was saved from it but his cousin Fedeles is dying."

Nakiesh cocked her head slightly as she gazed at Kiram. The motion struck Kiram as oddly bird-like. "Sounds like poison to me."

"There are poisons which would cause auditory hallucinations." Rafie absently curled a finger through a lock of Alizadeh's hair and then released it. Alizadeh leaned back against him. "Frostvine will do it and cause severe, cramping pain."

"But visions of being impaled?" Alizadeh glanced back to Kiram. "You're sure about that?"

Kiram nodded, remembering Javier's haunted expression as he spoke of iron pikes piercing his flesh.

"He said that he could feel the weight of his own body forcing spikes deeper into him. And it was the same for all of them. All of the Tornesals died believing they were being impaled."

"But no one else around them has died? No friends or lovers?" Liahn asked.

"No," Kiram responded. "No one else."

"Then it can't be a curse. Certainly not the Old Rage. It would take everyone. Everything."

"After Javier described it, I thought that someone might be using some curse to kill inheritors to the dukedom," Kiram said. ***"But I didn't know if that could be done. I wrote to you, Alizadeh, to ask about it but you were gone."***

Kiram was about to explain about how the white hell had saved Javier when Nakiesh suddenly stood up and shoved the tiny window open. The noise from dozens of screaming crows poured in.

"Jays are driving our sisters back," she hissed.

Nakiesh took a step back and Kiram saw the black mass of a flock of crows veering across the sky, chased by a swath of brilliant blue jays. Mobs of jays clutched at the crows, tearing at their wings and pulling them down. Some plummeted to the ground. Others slammed into the stone walls of nearby buildings.

Nakiesh made a low hissing noise and then her entire body trembled. Her arms flew out wide, as if she had been struck. Every one of the crows blinked out of the sky. Simply gone. The jays circled and swept across the sky, calling to one another in piercing shrieks.

Nakiesh slammed the window closed then clutched the windowsill, bowing her head and gasping. Kiram thought she was going to be sick. Then he saw deep shadows rippling across her back. Kiram thought one of the shadows looked like a wing, another like a beak and a bird's skull. Then a yellow eye opened, staring at him. He jerked back and hit the edge of the bed.

An instant later dozens of black wings, curved beaks, and glossy bodies burst up. A storm of crows erupted from the shadows of her body as if they were scattering from the shelter of a tree. The beating of their wings filled the room and their black bodies seemed to darken the entire space. Then they settled, in perfect silence.

Some perched on the bed; others alighted on the floor near Nakiesh. Many of them were injured. One with a drooping wing crouched on Liahn's shoulder. Another, with a bloody gash above its eye settled next to Rafie's thigh.

There had to be nearly thirty crows in the room. Kiram stared wide eyed at the birds and then back to Nakiesh.

She sank down against the wall. Her dark skin was beaded with sweat and looked gray. She exhaled a deep relieved breath.

"*What just happened?*" Kiram asked quietly.

"*Nakiesh brought her sisters in,*" Alizadeh whispered. Kiram realized that he'd asked the wrong question. He had seen what had happened. Thirty crows had flown out of Nakiesh's body. But how had it happened?

"*It's not the Old Rage.*" Nakiesh didn't look at Kiram but instead she gazed intently at Liahn. "*But something in its form. Something with a living intelligence but no passion. It was tearing apart our sisters, looking for us.*"

Liahn slipped past Kiram and knelt beside Nakiesh. She offered her a water skin and then pressed her head against Nakiesh's chest, as if listening to her heartbeat. After a moment Liahn lifted her head and smiled. "*There's no trace of it on you now.*"

"*What about the jays?*" Nakiesh asked.

Kiram looked back out the window and for a moment he thought that the jays had gone, but then he noticed flashes of their bright plumage on the roofs of nearby buildings and in tree branches.

"*They're waiting and watching,*" Alizadeh said.

"*They won't stay long.*" Nakiesh closed her eyes and leaned her head against the wall. "*They'll feel drawn back to the fortress soon. They're being kept as guards and spies there.*"

"*Did our sisters find anything before the jays attacked?*" Liahn asked.

"*The wards binding the Old Rage are intact. They've been nicked at here and there but not damaged. As for the jays, their master is definitely a man and a Cadeleonian, I think. A very ugly soul and very arrogant.*"

"*So, Kiram might be right,*" Rafie said. "*This man is using the Old Rage for his own purpose.*"

"It would seem so." Nakiesh nodded. "I felt a deep hunger for power in his presence. He would have liked to devour our sisters if he could have. But we were not his primary interest. He is focused on exploiting the shadow of the curse towards someone within the fortress."

"A Cadeleonian murdering Cadeleonians." Liahn tilted her head slightly and glanced to Alizadeh. Kiram was still so stunned by what he had witnessed that he almost missed the amusement in Liahn's expression. "Not even using a real curse. Is this really a Bahiim concern?"

"If the Old Rage is awakened it will be," Alizadeh replied.

"But that doesn't seem to be happening." Liahn looked to Nakiesh and Nakiesh nodded. "The wards haven't been disturbed. They've remained the same now for years. Whoever he is, he knows better than to awaken the Old Rage. He's just casting its shadow at his enemies."

"What do you mean when you say a man is casting the shadow of a curse?" Kiram asked. The crow on Liahn's shoulder blinked at him.

"A curse like the Old Rage is immense and so malevolent that even sealed away it radiates a presence," Alizadeh replied. "It lies across its surroundings the way a shadow covers the land. We Bahiim can see the shadow even when the object casting it is hidden from us."

"To control or stop a curse you must stand in its shadow," Liahn said. "But no one can step into the curse itself. That is certain death."

Alizadeh nodded. "This man on the hill couldn't hope to be able to structure a curse as vast as the Old Rage but he can feed his own power into its shadow. The resulting creation will move like the Old Rage. It will come in nightmares and whispers first, then settle. It will even destroy like the Old Rage but it doesn't have any of the Old Rage's power. That he has to provide. Do you understand?"

Kiram thought about it for a moment.

"Do you mean that he's using the shadow of the Old Rage like a mold? He's casting his own curse in its shape?"

"Yes, that's basically it." Alizadeh nodded.

"So, how do we stop him?" Kiram asked.

There was an odd quiet. Kiram was suddenly aware that all the crows seemed to be regarding him, just as Nakiesh was, with a look of pity.

"At the moment it's a question of whether we're required to stop him, not how we will do it," Liahn said. "What one Cadeleonian does to another isn't our concern and getting involved has never served us in the past."

"But he's killing Fedeles and he wants to kill Javier!" Kiram couldn't help but raise his voice. "They're my friends!"

"Calm down, Kiri." Rafie's tone was harder than Kiram had ever remembered it sounding. "This isn't a decision to be made lightly. It's not a matter of who anyone likes or doesn't like. It's dangerous for the Bahiim to make their presences felt here in the northern counties. And no one has invited them to intercede."

"Javier would—"

"Of course he would. But your friend Javier is not who would need to extend the invitation. It would have to be the royal bishop of the Cadeleonian Church," Rafie said firmly. "The Bahiim can legally intercede in Cadeleonian affairs only if they are given the blessing of the royal bishop."

"I imagine that the royal bishop has more than one reason to withhold his blessing," Liahn commented. "Not only would it make his church look powerless, it would defeat his own machinations, wouldn't it?"

"What do you mean?" Kiram demanded.

"He is the end point of all Cadeleonian inheritance," Liahn said. "If a noble family is wiped out, then their lands and titles are ceded to the divine rule of the church. The royal bishop, Prince Nugalo, stands to inherit the dukedom. Why would he ask us to stop that from happening?"

Kiram felt a sudden cold dread and he remembered Prince Sevanyo warning Javier that he didn't want Rauma to fall into his brother's hands. He had meant the royal bishop.

"If this has been going on for eighteen years, as you say Kiram, then the royal bishop has had more than enough time to place a request before a Bahiim council." Rafie gave Kiram a sympathetic look as if Javier were already dead.

"The man on the hill is probably the royal bishop's agent," Liahn said. *"Do they keep priests up in that academy?"*

Kiram nodded. The sick chill clenching his stomach intensified.

"There's a chapel and a holy father. He administers muerate poison to Javier as penance." Kiram's voice trembled as he spoke. It was so obvious. Holy Father Habalan actively poisoned Javier. He bled him and kept him from accessing the healing strength of the white hell. And Javier submitted himself to the ministrations because he trusted his church.

"He gave muerate poison to a student and no one in the academy objected?" Rafie asked.

"It's what they all expect," Kiram replied. *"Javier inherited the white hell from his ancestor Calixto. Everyone expects him to endure harsh penances because he's damned."*

"Cadeleonians and their hells," Nakiesh muttered. She pulled her knees up to her chest. Liahn removed her own heavy wrap and placed it over Nakiesh's shoulders. For a few moments they were all quiet. A few of the crows preened their wings.

"We should return to the wagons soon. I'll tell the Circle of the Crooked Pine what we've discovered," Liahn said. Then she looked at Kiram. *"But they aren't going to intercede in Cadeleonian business. I already know that. I'm sorry, boy. But that's how things are."*

Kiram couldn't meet her pale green gaze. Instead he cast his eyes down at the worn floorboards.

"I'll report to the Circle of the Willow Grove and the Circle of the Red Oak in Anacleto," Alizadeh said. *"They might offer*

their assistance to the royal bishop. There isn't much more they could do."

Kiram nodded. He couldn't stop thinking of that moment when he had found Javier on the chapel grounds, lying there like he was dead.

He couldn't give Javier up. No matter how foolish it might be to intercede in Cadeleonian business he would intercede. He would do something. He had to.

He'd promised Fedeles as much, hadn't he?

After Liahn and Nakiesh and their sister crows had gone, Rafie turned back to study Kiram.

"Don't you get any strange ideas, Kiri. Alizadeh and I are taking you back to Anacleto with us. It's not safe for you here."

"What? No!"

"Yes," Rafie said flatly.

"You can't just take me out of the academy!" Kiram scrambled for any reason. *"Mother's already paid my full tuition—"*

"We both know she'd give up your tuition a hundred times over to keep you from harm."

"But I'm in the midst of the autumn tournament. I've made commitments. I have to serve as squire to my upperclassman and I have another day of duels." Kiram knew he was babbling but the thought of just being whisked away from Javier and Nestor and the academy was too terrible.

"You're not going to be taking part in anything if you get killed." His uncle pinned him with a hard glare. *"This isn't a game, Kiram."*

"You think I don't know that?" Kiram snapped back. *"I've seen Javier lying in a pool of his own blood because of what the holy father is doing to him. My friend Fedeles is being tortured to the point of madness! I know this is serious—"*

"We won't be leaving until the Irabiim are done with their business here," Alizadeh broke in with a calm that silenced both Kiram and his uncle. *"That should allow Kiram time to see out the end of the autumn tournament and say his goodbyes."*

Rafie glared at Alizadeh but Alizadeh simply cocked his head and offered him a crooked smile. **"You'll know where he is this way and watching him compete will give us an excuse to get closer to the residents of Sagrada Academy and see if we can't discover a little more about this shadow curse."**

Kiram saw the muscles of Rafie's jaw clench on an angry retort, and he nearly offered Alizadeh an argument as well. So much anger and frustration churned up inside him that he could hardly think, but he at least recognized that Alizadeh's proposal was an improvement over the immediate departure that Rafie wanted.

Outside the window the city bells rang out. Half past five.

"I have to go and report to Master Ignacio if I'm going to remain in the tournament." Kiram didn't meet Rafie's eyes. He simply bowed his head and waited.

"All right," Rafie said at last. **"But you come back here when you're done."**

He nodded his assent and took his leave.

As Kiram closed the door he saw Alizadeh shake his head at Rafie, his expression somehow both amused and deeply sad.

Chapter Twenty

Kiram arrived at the city stables late but not far behind the bulk of the second-year students. Master Ignacio hardly seemed to take notice, only giving him a hard disapproving glare as he hurried past. Kiram wasn't sure if Master Ignacio was feeling generous towards him for his success in the fencing ring or if the war master was simply too angry with the student who arrived drunk to care about Kiram's tardiness.

The drunken student was held down in a horse trough until Kiram thought he might actually drown. Then he was hauled out, dripping wet, and dragged away by two grooms to do penance in the city chapel.

Kiram quickly took his place beside Nestor among the second-year students in the stable yard. He glimpsed Javier ahead of him, standing next to Elezar, but couldn't seem to catch his attention. Elezar playfully punched Javier in the shoulder several times, until Javier retaliated.

"I was worried when Javier showed up alone," Nestor said.

"I bumped into my uncle and spent the afternoon with him."

"Oh, that must have been nice…" Nestor suddenly frowned. "Is something wrong? You look rather angry."

"I thought my uncle of all people would understand but he didn't. He wants me to leave the academy. He doesn't think I'll be safe here."

"What? No, you can't go!" Nestor frowned deeply. "You've just gotten settled in. Damn it, Kiram, I don't want you to leave!"

"I don't want me to leave either."

"We'll have to convince your uncle that you're just as safe here as you would be at home."

But he wasn't as safe. He couldn't be. Back in Anacleto he would be smothered in security. His family and neighbors insulated him in the familiar and only the most decent Haldiim socialized with him. Nowhere could be as safe as his mother's house back in Anacleto, where he would be shut away from the rest of the world.

"Maybe my mother could talk to your uncle…" Nestor seemed to consider the thought for a moment and then shook his head. "Probably not. She'll end up explaining how battle and injury bring men closer to the true faith. That probably wouldn't mean much to a Haldiim."

"Not my uncle, no." Kiram scowled down at the dirt. Next to him Nestor hung his head.

"When do you have to leave?" Nestor asked dejectedly.

"After the tournament." Kiram glanced back towards Javier and discovered that his attention was returned. For a moment, Javier seemed about to break away from the other third-year students and come to him but then Elezar grabbed Javier's neck and after that all of his attention turned to wrestling out of Elezar's grip.

"So, we've got a week to change your uncle's mind." Nestor continued his strategizing. "Do you think a fellow physician like Scholar Donamillo could convince him?"

"I don't know if anything is going to change his mind." Suddenly Kiram felt like he couldn't stand to dwell on the hopelessness of it for another moment, so he changed the subject. "How did it go with the girl, Yellow Butterflies?"

A flush spread across Nestor's cheeks.

"I'm in love," he said very quietly and very seriously. "Her name is Riossa Arevillo. She draws really well and she loved the Mirogoth shapechanger. And she wants to meet you."

Nestor's afternoon had been so different from his own. At least one of them had enjoyed the day.

"She sounds nice," Kiram said and he meant it.

Nestor's lovestruck expression slipped suddenly into one of melancholy. "I thought today was going to be the happiest day of my life, but now you're going to be taken out of the academy. It just doesn't seem fair."

"It's not," Kiram agreed. He couldn't make himself accept the thought of abandoning Javier and Fedeles to Prince Nugalo. "But what choice do I have? Even if I refuse to go, Rafie would only have to tell my mother that the academy is dangerous and she'll withdraw my tuition."

Master Ignacio shouted out for silence and all conversations immediately ended. Elezar even stopped taking playful swipes at Javier and stood at attention with the rest of the students.

Master Ignacio paced along the long rows of the gathered students, taking roll and demanding to know where they intended to spend the night in the city. Those who didn't answer quickly enough or whose responses he didn't like were assigned beds at the church hostel.

Atreau wasn't even allowed to get his answer fully articulated before Master Ignacio assigned him to the church hostel. The majority of the students were staying with their families, many of whom owned townhouses in Zancoda, which were maintained specifically for the yearly tournaments.

The Grunito family owned one, as did the Helio and Quemanor. There was even a Tornesal townhouse, though only one Tornesal remained to occupy it.

Kiram wondered how Master Ignacio would respond to the idea of one of his students boarding at an inn like the Laughing Dog. For an instant Kiram smirked, imagining the Master's dilemma of either accepting a shoddy inn at the edge of the city or having to assign a Haldiim to a church bed.

Nestor's turn came.

"I'll be at the Grunito townhouse with my—"

"Fine," Master Ignacio cut him off, moving on to Kiram. "And you?"

"I…I'll be staying with upperclassman Javier at the Tornesal townhouse," Kiram said in a rush of defiance. Never in his life had he been so disobedient as to disregard one of his uncle's directives, but he had to warn Javier about Holy Father Habalan as soon as possible.

Immune to the momentous nature of Kiram's decision, Master Ignacio simply nodded, jotted it down in the roll book and moved on.

Once all the students' future whereabouts had been established, Master Ignacio announced that he expected all of them back at the city stables tomorrow morning before first morning bell, adding that if he discovered any of them out on the city streets after eighth bell this evening, he would personally beat them to a pulp. After that Master Ignacio dismissed them to their lodgings for the evening. Kiram and Nestor jostled through the crowd to meet up with Javier and Elezar. Outside, carriages lined the street and groups of students crammed into them to share fares to their lodgings.

"I thought you would stay with your uncle," Javier said.

Kiram could see that he was trying, unsuccessfully, to hide an arrogant smile. Javier clearly gloried in the fact that Kiram had chosen his company. His triumphant pleasure verged on egotism and yet Kiram found him charming.

And that made him feel even more depressed.

"Kiram's uncle is pulling him out of the academy!" Nestor announced, before Kiram could reply.

"What?" Javier's pleased expression collapsed.

"Rafie thinks it's too dangerous for me here." Kiram's throat felt tight. Just saying the words made him feel like he was already leaving, as if it was inevitable.

"Well, that's a hard lump of shit to swallow." Elezar sighed and shook his head as though he had expected something like this to happen. "Just because you got a little cut on your arm?"

"It's not just that but I'm sure it didn't help." Kiram glanced to Javier, but couldn't read any emotion in his expression now. His features seemed set as perfectly as those of a statue.

"God forbid you ever fall down and break a bone," Elezar said. "Your uncle would probably lock you up in your room for the rest of your life."

"There's got to be some way we can change his mind," Nestor protested.

"I don't know." Kiram had expected Javier to rail against this—not just expected, but wanted it. Instead, Javier stared silently at the street ahead, frowned slightly, and then looked to Elezar.

"Are you two taking a carriage to the Grunito townhouse?"

"No, we have to meet our mother at the chapel." Elezar made a sour face. "You coming?"

"Not tonight. My bailiff is expecting me at the townhouse. Give your mother my apologies."

"Sure," Elezar replied. Then, to Kiram, "Sorry you're getting pulled out. At least you'll have one glorious tournament to your name before you go."

Kiram nodded somewhat numbly. Nestor looked like he would say something but Elezar caught his shoulder.

"Come on, you." Elezar gave Nestor an appraising look as they began towards the nearest carriage. "I hear you met a girl…"

"The Tornesal townhouse isn't far." Javier didn't look at Kiram, but instead turned and strode along the raised walkway, forcing Kiram to rush to catch up with him, though once he reached Javier's side he found he had nothing to say that could be said in public, so they walked together in silence.

The Tornesal townhouse stood out from the other nobles' townhouses by virtue of both its size, which was immense, and its simplicity. Onyx inlays of black suns decorated the white marble walls but there were no ornately carved sconces, nor any golden filigree. Surrounded by wildly decorated pleasure houses, it looked grim and ancient. The massive doors, with their iron reinforcements and the narrow windows, remained from an age when peasant riots were common and livestock was kept indoors.

The moment Javier approached the doors two servants in black and white piebald liveries pulled them open.

"Welcome home, Lord Tornesal." The doormen greeted Javier in unison. Javier didn't acknowledge either of them nor did they seem to expect him to, though they both glanced sidelong at Kiram as he followed Javier into the brilliant light of the house.

Inside, hundreds of candles blazed from iron candelabras and the white stone walls seemed to glow with the light. In the entry room, three more serving men greeted Javier respectfully and bowed deeply to him. They peered at Kiram as if he was some kind of strange curiosity, but said nothing to him. One of them bowed out of the room but the other two lingered, occupied by replacing several guttered candles.

Javier abruptly stopped and pivoted around, startling Kiram backward. "I have to meet with my bailiff and with one of my bankers. I didn't think you'd be staying here with me so I scheduled most of the evening with them. You can entertain yourself for a little while, can't you?"

"Yes, but after that I need to talk to you. Alone." His lowered voice seemed to boom through the open space. He felt the presence of the serving men too intensely.

"I'll try to hurry things up. We could take dinner together in an hour or so," Javier said.

"Sounds fine."

Then Javier called one of the servants to him and directed the servants to escort Kiram around the townhouse. When the servant asked what room Kiram would be using for the night Kiram quickly suggested that he'd be happy to share Lord Tornesal's room.

"I realize you weren't expecting me and I don't want to cause all the trouble of preparing another room," he explained more for the servant's sake than to convince Javier.

"Of course, you won't have to spend the night on the floor in my room. This isn't the academy, after all." The frustration in Javier's voice was palpable. "The green room should do. It's near the library."

Javier took his leave and the servant led Kiram on a brief tour of the townhouse. Most of the huge structure was closed up. Furniture was covered, carpets rolled away and fireplaces had been cleaned and sealed up to keep out bats. Nothing was so unkempt as to seem abandoned but a sense of emptiness pervaded the house. Entire suites seemed like preserved historical specimens.

At one time the building had to have been inhabited by more than just staff. Once the Tornesal family had occupied the halls and numerous entertaining rooms. Someone had played the harpsichord in the music room and no doubt many members of the family had sat at the card table.

But now Javier was left alone with this edifice of a house and its huge, desperately attentive staff, who occupied themselves obsessively with the vast minutiae of sweeping, dusting and polishing every surface of the place.

Kiram glanced to the hollow-faced saint chiseled over a stone doorway and absently thought that he'd been told about that particular style of sculpture. Had it ended just before King Nazario's death? He couldn't remember.

He was escorted to the second floor past the library to the green room, which turned out to be a large suite with slit windows that overlooked a small herb garden. The bed was hard and cold, but the deep green linens on it smelled freshly laundered. There was a bath and Kiram used it.

Afterwards he was loath to dress in his old clothes. Instead he wrapped a towel around his waist and lay back on the bed. A fire blazed in the hearth and Kiram stared up a the ceiling, feeling troubled and at the same time too exhausted to do more than lie there and watch the shadows dance above him.

His arm hurt. His head ached. He closed his eyes and if he slept he didn't dream, but when he opened his eyes the room had darkened. Outside, he could hear rain falling.

"We should run away," Kiram murmured to himself.

"Where would we go?" a quiet voice responded. Javier leaned against the doorframe, arms crossed over his chest, skin luminous in the dim, golden light. He'd washed recently and his hair was glossy black.

Kiram asked, "How long have you been there?"

"Not too long." Javier sounded weary. "I was enjoying the view."

"You should have woken me up." A slight breeze fluttered through the room and suddenly he became aware that the towel must have slipped off his hips. Javier watched, with a smile as Kiram reached for but did not replace the towel. He felt a confusing mixture of embarrassment and pleasure at being so ardently observed. Then he heard someone clomping up the stairs and quickly covered himself.

"My valet, bringing clothes for you to wear to dinner," Javier explained.

A moment later, an old man bowed past Javier and laid out the suit of fresh clothes. The pants, jacket and vest were all Tornesal black but not servant's dress. Silver threads decorated the silk vest and the white shirt was flawless linen. The trousers were silk as were the stockings. The clothes fit him decently, but had obviously belonged to someone with broader shoulders and thicker thighs.

Javier watched him dress and the valet waited, pretending to watch nothing. But when Kiram caught the older man's gaze flicker to Javier's face and then to Kiram's own body, he missed a button of the vest and had to unbutton it and start again.

"These clothes are much too nice. They look like they belonged to a prince," Kiram said, as if it were an excuse for his flustered clumsiness.

Javier replied, "They're too small for me anymore. And they suit you."

The valet gave Javier a narrow, disapproving glance, as if he felt that the clothes would have been better suited for a pig to wear than Kiram.

If Javier noticed the look, he paid no attention to it. "Tornesal black is drab on most men but you make it seem magnificent."

The valet lowered his eyes, apparently engrossed in the marble floor.

Kiram couldn't believe that Javier would say such a thing while another man was standing in the room with them. Was he drunk?

Javier swaggered forward to brush some minuscule speck of dust off Kiram's shoulder and gave him a smile. "Now that you're suitably attired, shall we go down to dinner, Underclassman Kiram?"

The ebony inlayed dinner table had clearly been made for gatherings of more than a dozen diners. Even sitting across from Javier, the width of the table made it impossible to whisper to him. And yet, Kiram didn't dare to raise his voice in front of the constant stream of servants that circulated between the kitchen and the table.

They brought small, exquisite foods in ornate dishes. Kiram sampled tender cutlets of veal, rich cream sauces and sharp greens served with fragrant orange and lemon dressing. The food was delicious and yet Kiram hardly ate more than a few bites. Javier ate nothing; he drank a milky, white liqueur from a cut crystal glass and watched Kiram.

"Aren't you hungry?" Kiram asked.

"I'm not as interested in food as I am in getting drunk."

"You shouldn't," Kiram said.

"Maybe not, but I'm going to if I can."

"I need to talk to you." Kiram couldn't help but lower his voice.

"So, talk," Javier said.

A servant slid a plate of pork loin medallions and blood orange segments in front of Kiram. Another servant removed the bowl of soup that Kiram had hardly tasted. A third refilled Javier's glass. Their relentless attention made Kiram uncomfortable. Any of them could be spies for Prince Nugalo or his man on the hill.

"I don't trust these servants," Kiram said in Haldiim. He scanned the men's faces for any sign that they understood his words. Most of them seemed to take no notice at all. Only the man refilling Javier's glass seemed to be listening and he just looked confused. Emboldened, Kiram continued, *"I need to tell you what I found out about the curse that's been placed on your family."*

"All right, tell me." Javier pronounced his words slowly. His accent was very strong, but Kiram was delighted to see that his suspicion about Javier's fluency in Haldiim had been correct.

"My uncle's partner and several other Bahiim tracked the Tornesal curse down to the academy. Someone there is using the shadow of an ancient Haldiim curse called the Old Rage to destroy your family. They think it's an agent of the royal bishop's—"

"Slow down. You're talking too fast for me," Javier said in Cadeleonian.

"A man at the Sagrada Academy is responsible for the curse. The Bahiim think he's an agent for the royal bishop, probably Holy Father Habalan." Kiram spoke as clearly and evenly as he could.

Javier seized his glass and swallowed what remained of the milky white liqueur within. When he set the glass down, the servant refilled it again.

"Is your uncle taking you away because of me?" Javier asked at last.

"Yes," Kiram admitted.

"Does you uncle's partner know how to lift the curse?"

"Maybe..." Kiram gazed at his dish of pork and the dark blood oranges. *"But the Bahiim can't interfere. They have to be invited to do so by the royal bishop."*

Javier laughed at this but in a hard, angry way.

"So, it's hopeless," Javier said in Cadeleonian. "You're leaving me and it's hopeless."

"We could go to Yuan." Kiram couldn't keep the slight quaver of fear out of his voice. He had no idea how they would get there or how they would survive, but if Javier said yes, then he would go. He'd go tonight.

Javier's dark eyes glittered like polished obsidian. Then he bowed his head and his black hair fell over his face.

"I can't leave Fedeles." Javier drained his glass. "And it wouldn't matter if I did, because the curse would follow me. Your uncle is probably right. You will be better off in Anacleto."

"No, I won't," Kiram snapped.

"Yes, you will," Javier said it like it was an order. He slammed his glass against the table. The servant poured the last of the liqueur into his glass and Javier swallowed it like medicine then stood up slowly, swaying on his feet. "Well, it looks like I managed to get drunk after all. It's not easy, you know. The white hell burns the alcohol out of my body like a poison. It never lasts long enough." Javier absently ran his finger along the rim of his empty glass. "It never lasts."

Something in Javier's tone alarmed Kiram. He pushed his plate aside and rushed to Javier's side.

"Are you all right?"

"Not really, no." Javier leaned against him and draped an arm over Kiram's shoulder. The heat of his body radiated through Kiram's clothes. "I'm blind drunk and talking to myself. The least you could do is offer to take me to my bed, don't you think?"

Kiram didn't miss the hunger in Javier's voice, nor did he think that it was a coincidence that Javier got drunk enough to need help getting to bed.

"Should I summon the footmen to assist His Lordship?" a servant asked.

"No," Kiram answered. "I'll take him. Thank you."

Javier directed him to the master bedroom, which had the requisite spells inlayed in the floor. He stepped over them without concern and propped Javier up on the curtained bed.

"Close the door," Javier said quietly.

Kiram closed it and locked it. When he returned, Javier had already pulled off his jacket and was unbuttoning his shirt. His motions were fluid and graceful.

"You're not drunk at all, are you?" It seemed unbelievable, considering that he'd emptied an entire bottle in less than an hour.

"A little, but it'll burn off in a couple of minutes." Javier threw his shirt aside. He reached out and pulled Kiram close to him. "Stay with me tonight."

A rush of excitement surged through Kiram at the feel of Javier's hands finally on him. They might never have this chance again. He had already wasted so much of the time he had with Javier.

Kiram slid his arms around Javier's bare back, feeling the heat of his skin and the taut muscles beneath. Javier was so tense that he was almost trembling. He stared at Kiram, his dark eyes wide, his lips slightly parted. Kiram leaned in and kissed him. The taste of anise and alcohol passed from Javier's lips to Kiram's, the sensation both sweet and hot.

Kiram traced the tip of his tongue over Javier's lips. Javier's mouth opened to him and the heat of Javier's tongue touched and stroked his, the sensation soft and hard at once. The thrusts aroused a deep pang in Kiram's body.

As the kiss deepened, Javier's hands slipped under Kiram's shirt, stroking the small of his back, working against his belt. Kiram pulled back from the kiss, breaking them apart, though all he wanted was more. Breathlessly, Kiram pulled off his jacket, vest and shirt. Javier's hands caught the heavy buckle that held Kiram's belt closed. A tight ache pulsed through him as Javier removed the belt and began unfastening the pearl buttons of Kiram's pants.

Javier was so close that Kiram could feel his breath brush over every inch of his newly exposed flesh. As Javier's lips grazed the tender skin of Kiram's hip, heat and desire flooded Kiram's groin. He ached to pull Javier's mouth to him, but the tremor in Javier's hands made Kiram aware of how unfamiliar this must be for Javier. No doubt whores had gone down on their knees and pleased him but Kiram couldn't imagine Javier ever kneeling on the floor before another man.

"You don't have to—"

"I want to." Javier touched a curl of Kiram's blond pubic hair then slowly cupped Kiram's hot erection, his touch careful but not tentative. He bowed his head and took Kiram into his mouth. Waves of ecstasy rolled over Kiram, and he had to fight to keep his senses, to gently run his hands through Javier's hair and not grasp him too tightly or thrust hard into that wet heat.

When Javier drew back, catching his breath, Kiram almost swore out of frustrated longing. But Javier's hopeful expression touched Kiram even more deeply than his passion.

"Am I doing this right?" Javier asked.

"You're perfect," Kiram replied and it wasn't entirely a lie. What Javier lacked in experience he made up for with sheer desire. Kiram drew in a deep breath, wishing he could think clearly. All he wanted at that moment was his own satisfaction, but that was hardly fair to Javier. If this was his first time making love to another man then it ought to be more than this.

"Come to the bed," Kiram forced himself to step back. "The floor is too cold."

Despite the aching need pounding through his body, Kiram waited for Javier to completely undress and join him on the bed.

Javier was beautiful naked. Kiram had known as much for months but now the physical reality of it riveted him. The whiteness of Javier's skin allowed him to see even the minute pink blush that spread across his cheeks and colored his tight nipples. Javier's erection jutted up, straight and shockingly scarlet.

He watched Kiram intently and there was something in the way that his natural poise tempered his uncertainty so that even now he seemed proud.

"Lie here close to me," Kiram said.

They touched experimentally, stroking one another's skin, feeling the curves of ribs and the tension of muscles. Every nerve in Kiram's body craved contact. Even the softest caress of Javier's fingertips shot through him, down deep into his loins.

Kiram felt his breath coming too fast, his control slipping away as Javier stroked him. Kiram caught Javier's hand and lifted it away from his thigh. Javier looked momentarily worried, but his expression relaxed as Kiram kissed each of his fingers.

Kiram leaned forward, kissed his lips once gently and then flipped around so that his head rested against Javier's hip. He kissed Javier's flat stomach. Javier's breath caught and his muscles tightened in anticipation. Slowly Kiram took Javier's erection in his mouth. Javier gasped, his entire body flexing into Kiram.

Kiram gripped Javier's hips firmly, reminding him, almost as he would have reminded Firaj, that he would set their pace. Javier responded immediately, restraining his powerful thrusts.

Kiram pressed his own body closer to Javier's and a moment later Javier seemed to realize the opportunity the position offered. He tentatively nuzzled Kiram. The teasing brush of his breath, the contact and withdrawal of his lips drove Kiram half mad. But he waited for Javier to take him in his mouth again.

Javier's lips were soft, his tongue teasing, and his mouth hot and velvety. He echoed Kiram's hungry pressure, taking him slowly, but deeply. Their bodies rocked in a mounting rhythm. Kiram gave up control over his own driving thrusts and Javier's.

A desperate pleasure flooded Kiram. He could feel nothing but Javier, both in him and on him. The smell of him, the taste of him, the voracious heat of his mouth, sang through Kiram, engulfing his senses. He wanted more of Javier and yet he could hardly bear the wild shocks of ecstasy pounding through him.

Just as Kiram felt his senses burning beyond his endurance, Javier arched hard into him and a hot gush of semen spilled into Kiram's mouth. Kiram's own pleasure peaked with the exhilaration of taking so much of Javier's passion and control, feeling it surge into him and become his own, bursting into Javier's mouth.

Kiram rolled back, flopping against the ivory sheets. His heart pounded wildly. Heat radiated from Javier's body. While they both lay on the bed in spent silence, Javier's breathing slowed and grew steady. Kiram was suddenly aware of the sweat clinging to his skin. He shoved a damp coil of hair back from his face.

The dying fire in the hearth cast deep gold shadows across the room. Kiram stared up at the ceiling, watching the way the light flickered over the black invocations chiseled into the stones above, then he propped himself up onto his elbows and gazed at Javier, who lay with his eyes closed. He wore a deeply thoughtful expression as he slowly lifted his hand to touch his own flushed lips. Then he opened his eyes, studying Kiram's face intently, worried.

When Kiram smiled at him, overwhelming relief flooded Javier's expression. He pulled Kiram into a hard embrace.

Kiram held on with all his strength. "I'm not going to leave you. I won't."

"Of course you will. That's why you're here now giving me something to remember you by."

"No." Kiram withdrew only far enough to see Javier's face and Javier let him go. It had been Kiram's intention to have this night as a farewell but now that he had been so close to Javier he couldn't imagine letting him go so easily.

Javier didn't meet his eyes.

"You'll be safe with your family in Anacleto." Javier sat up and swung his legs off the bed, turning his back to Kiram.

"I don't care where I might be safe," Kiram growled. He grabbed Javier's shoulder. "I'm not leaving."

"How can you stay if your family decides to take you back to Anacleto?"

"I'll run away," Kiram decided. "I'll find somewhere to stay here and I'll work."

"No one in Zancoda is going to board or employ a runaway, underage Haldiim." Javier gently pushed a lock of Kiram's hair back from his face. "And even if someone did—if I kept you here—your family would find you. You don't exactly blend in with the populace of the city."

Kiram knew Javier was right, but he didn't care. He wrapped his arms around Javier, holding him tightly and then finally drawing him back down into the warmth of the bed.

The chain of Kiram's charm tangled with Javier's medallion and for a moment they occupied themselves working the two apart. For the first time Kiram noticed that the design of Javier's medallion, which he'd always thought was a sun, resembled the circle of lotus petals embossed into the face of his own charm.

"Is this a blessing?" Kiram asked.

Javier nodded. "My father gave it to me when he passed the white hell to me. It belonged to Calixto and was supposed to have protected him."

The gold was warm from Javier's body and heavy in Kiram's hand. He wished that he had the skill to press his own desire to protect Javier into the soft gold, but he wasn't a Bahiim. All he could do was wish deeply that somehow the two of them could find a way to stay together.

He carefully laid the medallion back against Javier's bare chest and settled beside him, relaxing into the comfort of Javier's nearness. They both slept.

When Kiram awoke he found that he liked the weight of Javier's thick thigh against his own. If he listened closely he could hear Javier release slow, deep breaths.

There was another sound as well—a cry rising through the patter of raindrops, distant but growing increasingly close.

Crows. He could hear them now, just outside the window. Despite the darkness and rain, the birds were flying and calling to each other. Or more than likely they were calling to some Bahiim.

Kiram sat up.

"What is it?" Javier asked. "Is your arm hurting?"

"No." Though in truth his arm ached deeply, but he had grown used to it, almost forgotten about it. "It's my uncle and his partner. I think they may be looking—"

Before Kiram could finish there was a loud rap at the locked door.

"I'm sleeping," Javier shouted, though the response came far too quickly and loudly to be believable.

"I beg your pardon, my lord." Kiram thought it was the same servant who had served Javier his liqueur. "There are two…men here, relations of your guest's. They seem to have some urgent news for him. I looked for him in his room but then I recalled that he had helped Your Lordship to bed."

Javier glared at the door and then glanced questioningly to Kiram. Kiram had no doubt that Javier would have Rafie and Alizadeh thrown out if Kiram wanted him to. He also knew that neither Rafie nor Alizadeh were likely to go quietly and a public spectacle was the last thing he wanted.

"I better go." Kiram started up but Javier caught his hand.

"We'll both go," Javier said softly, then, to his servant, "Show them to the sitting room. We'll be there directly."

"Very good, my lord."

They dressed quickly and in silence. Kiram wanted to again assure Javier that he wouldn't leave, and at the same time a fear crept through him that if he spoke he might be lying. He buttoned the vest Javier had given him, while Javier laced his boots. At the door, Kiram caught Javier's hand meaning only to offer a reassuring touch, but Javier immediately pulled him into his arms. They kissed deeply and desperately, as if they both knew that this opportunity would never come again.

Then they descended to the small sitting room, which was furnished with several plush chairs as well as a card table and harpsichord. Neither Rafie nor Alizadeh had taken a seat. They stood just a little apart from each other in front of the fire, both soaking wet. Straightened by water, Alizadeh's blonde hair hung nearly to his knees. Rafie glared at Kiram with an expression that was as much disappointment as anger, while Alizadeh maintained the calm countenance of a Bahiim, though Kiram noticed that his gaze lingered on Javier.

Javier studied Rafie and Alizadeh with the cool appraisal of a prince surveying a newly conquered land. Kiram had lived with him long enough now to know that this proud countenance was a reflex imparted by noble Cadeleonian upbringing. Even Nestor assumed the same upright posture when he was unsure of his surroundings. Javier resorted to it rarely. At this moment, however, his hard gaze and arrogant frown looked like they were carved from a column of white marble.

The room was silent except for the crackle of the fire. Then a quiet clink sounded as a footman placed a tray of porcelain mugs and a pitcher of mulled wine on the card table. Kiram had hardly noticed the footman when he and Javier had come in. The servant glanced nervously between Javier and the two rain-soaked Haldiim, bowed to Javier and then fled.

"I'm sorry that you had to venture out into such terrible weather," Javier said. "It must be a matter of some importance that brought you."

"We came to find Kiram." Rafie only gave Javier a cursory glance before turning his attention to his nephew. "I thought I was very clear when I told you to return to the Laughing Dog."

"That was my fault, I'm afraid," Javier replied. "I arranged with War Master Ignacio for Kiram to stay at the Tornesal townhouse."

"I mean no offense, Your Lordship," Rafie replied easily, "but Kiram knows his duty regardless of what others may have arranged for him. He knew we were expecting him and he chose not to return."

"I have decided to stay with Javier," Kiram said firmly.

"Do you have any idea of what you're saying?" Rafie demanded in Haldiim.

"Yes, and I mean it," Kiram replied. He tried to stop the slight quaver in his voice. He'd never seen Rafie look so angry. **"He's my...friend and I'm staying with him."**

"Your friend?" Rafie narrowed his eyes. **"Musni is your friend. Hashiem is your friend. This man is some Cadeleonian you just met. Do you really expect me to let you risk your life at that snake pit of an academy just so you can ogle his firm ass and bulging cock?"**

The sudden red flush that colored Javier's cheeks made it immediately obvious that he had understood Rafie's words, though Kiram was somewhat surprised at Javier's embarrassment. After all he said far more provocative things to his fellow Hellions every day before breakfast. But then, Kiram thought, Javier had never had the experience of being the subject of this sort of remark before.

"You discover so many new turns of phrase when you learn another language." Alizadeh gave Javier an almost warm smile.

"That's quite true," Javier replied.

"Did you know that the Mirogoths have a single word which means to put your foot into the excrement of an animal?"

"I didn't." Javier picked up two of the mugs of mulled wine and offered one to Alizadeh.

"That is not why we are here," Rafie snapped.

"No, it isn't." Alizadeh accepted the wine with a slight bow. "But it's late and the weather is foul. It seems a waste of energy to drag Kiram back through the mud and rain to the Laughing Dog. Especially when His Lordship seems so generous with his hospitality."

Alizadeh gave Javier a pointed look.

Javier seemed to grasp the opening being offered. "You are both welcome to stay here, if you like. I can have rooms prepared."

"We're all family. We can share Kiram's room," Alizadeh said. "We wouldn't want to put you out any further."

"Of course," Javier replied.

Rafie scowled but didn't argue. He grudgingly accepted a mug of mulled wine. Kiram took his from Javier, feeling obvious and foolish for being so aware of Javier's fingers as they brushed his hand. Javier stepped back from him self-consciously and sat down in one of the chairs. Kiram drifted towards the hearth.

"There's white pepper in this, isn't there?" Rafie took another sip of the mulled wine. Kiram knew from his tone that Rafie was trying to recover from his earlier gaffe and make the best of the situation.

"I think so," Javier replied. "It's hot enough, isn't it?"

"It's good." Rafie took another appreciative drink. "You wouldn't believe the things they'll serve a man on the Mirogoth border."

"Oh?" Javier asked and Rafie began to describe the numerous, unctuous drinks that he'd forced down his throat while traveling in the frozen north.

Kiram stole a quizzical glance at Alizadeh, wondering what had softened him towards Javier so suddenly. But Alizadeh had turned back towards the fire, his head slightly raised, studying the ceiling where the firelight flickered and cast deep shadows on the now familiar Tornesal invocations.

Alizadeh waved his hand just slightly and the firelight crackled and spat briefly. Suddenly the shadowy forms of the invocations were gone, and Kiram found himself gazing at a simple pattern of filigree.

"In Yuan," Alizadeh whispered to Kiram, *"they have a word for a man who fights a darkness he cannot defeat."*

"What is It?" Kiram asked.

"A fool," Alizadeh replied. He gave Kiram a pitying smile. *"Everyone knows that."*

Chapter Twenty-One

The next morning was overcast and the cobblestone streets glistened with rain. Out on the fairgrounds masses of bright yellow straw had been scattered over the paths to stabilize the sinkholes of mud. Under the gold pavilion, fine wood shavings and black grit filled the salt rings of the fencing circles.

The footing was still bad. More than once Kiram slipped as the soil beneath him slid away. Fortunately his opponents had no better luck than he did.

But neither the poor weather nor the filthy streets seemed to dampen the enthusiasm of the crowd. The stands were brimming with onlookers. Shouts and laughter as well as jeers spilled out in a constant cacophony. There were so many bodies and faces that Kiram could almost lose sight of Rafie and Alizadeh. But the glints of golden hair and dark skin always caught his eye. Anytime he looked, they were watching him.

He'd seen almost nothing of Javier this morning. They hadn't spoken more than a few words at breakfast and once they reached the city stables Javier had left him to ride with Elezar.

Kiram stole another quick glance to where Javier stood in the stands. Elezar, Moriso and Atreau lounged next to him. Elezar was repeating some joke, Kiram could tell just from his stance and gestures. Javier smiled but looked tired. He glanced to Kiram and their eyes met.

Kiram felt a breathless flutter in his chest and an ache deep in his stomach. Javier blinked and then looked away. He said something offhandedly and the Hellions gathered around him laughed. For a terrifying instant the fear that Javier and the other Hellions were laughing at him seized Kiram. He didn't know why he thought it, except that Javier had turned away from him so coldly, as if he could hardly stand to look at him.

Kiram wiped a thick mass of mud from his boot. His left forearm hurt badly. The pain had made his motions clumsy during his last fight. He'd won but it hadn't been pretty. Beneath his leather gauntlet, he could feel the wet heat of blood welling up from where his stitches had torn open.

The Hellions were still laughing and Kiram didn't look their way.

He wished that he knew Javier well enough to be sure that he wouldn't brag about his conquest. When the two of them were alone he did feel that he understood Javier well. An easy honesty existed between them. But Javier was different when he was with the Hellions—shocking and almost cruel, and they loved those qualities in him. Kiram wished that he could somehow forget this realization the moment that he'd had it. But it was so obvious, watching Javier smirk at Elezar and roll a coin over his knuckles. With the Hellions Javier completely disresembled the man who had pulled Kiram into his arms and held him desperately the night before.

A new opponent entered Kiram's circle, his fourth today. The Yillar student looked clean assured and well rested and Kiram fought hard because it would have been too humiliating to simply drop his blade and walk away, but he knew he wouldn't win.

When the judge finally raised the Yillar banner that signaled his defeat, Kiram pulled himself up from the mud and staggered back to the stands where the other filthy, beaten students sat. He collapsed down beside Nestor who, despite being defeated in his first round, appeared to be in good spirits. An open sketchbook lay across his lap.

"Don't look so glum, Kiram," Nestor said. "You did your best. Nobody expected you to last one round much less four. You've really improved in the last few months, you know."

Kiram nodded. He wasn't sure if he could speak without sobbing. Beneath the leather gauntlet, his stitches had burst, and his arm hurt so badly, worse than anything he'd ever felt in his life. How did professional soldiers do this day in and day out? How did they go to war or fight blood duels? How did they endure so much pain?

Red rivulets coursed down Kiram's fingers. Nestor squinted at him. "Are you all right?"

"I'll be fine. I didn't get much sleep last night."

"Me either." Nestor stared out at the crowd in the stands opposite them. "I hardly slept at all. I kept thinking about Riossa and then about you having to leave the academy. I spent the whole night just tossing and turning between good and bad."

"Yes, me as well." Kiram was glad to have Nestor beside him right now. "I thought maybe I'd run away and hide in Zancoda."

Nestor cocked his head, considering this latest plan. "Would you still come to classes?"

"I don't see how I could," Kiram replied.

"Maybe I could sneak notes down to you and take your papers back up to the academy," Nestor suggested, a playful expression on his broad, honest face. "Or maybe we could disguise you somehow and enroll you as a foreign prince. We could say you were from the kingdom of Yuan. You'd have to wear a live bird on your head, or something, but it would be a small price to pay."

Kiram laughed out loud at this.

Nestor smiled. "For what it's worth, my mother's agreed to speak with your uncle if you think that will help. I told her that you're the reason that my math scores have been looking so good this year. And Prince Sevanyo invited you into his box. That has to count for something, don't you think?"

"With my uncle?" Kiram asked. He tried very tentatively to flex his left hand into a fist. A deep, ragged ache shot through his forearm.

"Seriously, Kiram, are you all right? You just went white. Which for you is pretty shocking looking."

"My cut broke open again."

"Should you take the gauntlet off?" Nestor leaned closer, peering at the leather laces. "It looks like the blood has soaked into the laces and swollen the knots tight. We'll have to cut it apart, but I've got my penknife."

"Just leave it for now," Kiram said. He leaned back, resting his left arm across his stomach. His muscles felt stringy and limp. The sweat clinging to his skin began to turn cold and Kiram shivered as a breeze washed over him. "I don't know what to do about my uncle."

"Neither do I." Nestor absently resumed his sketching. "But, you know, we can't give up."

Kiram spied Rafie working his way down to the second level of the stands with Alizadeh only a few steps behind him. No doubt they had decided to collect him immediately after the third year duels ended. They seemed to think that they had won the whole argument about him leaving already. And there Javier was, acting as if Kiram had already left when they still had a week to fight for him to stay. His lackluster capitulation suddenly infuriated Kiram and the ensuing rush of anger was a relief from his earlier feeling of rejection.

He'd been so distressed and confused today that he'd lost sight of what it was that he needed to fight for. Yes, he wanted to stay with Javier but there was also his friendship with Nestor and his goal of being the first Haldiim to graduate from Sagrada Academy. He wanted to honor Yassin Lif-Harun, who had been killed before he fully proved himself. And he had sworn to help Scholar Donamillo to save Fedeles—a matter of life and death.

This wasn't just Javier's fight. If he wanted to have one night and then give up he could, but Kiram wouldn't.

He wondered if all endurance was this simple. Whether it was physical pain or complex calculations, a person had to push through it if they wanted to win. Winning just had to matter more than exhaustion or hurt. Kiram thought of how Fedeles kept fighting even though a curse tortured him relentlessly. Compared to that, a disapproving uncle seemed manageable.

Kiram searched the stands for Fedeles and found him in the Quemanor family box along with his father, sister and grandmother. He returned Kiram's gaze as if he'd been waiting for Kiram to look at him all day. He grinned and waved wildly. Kiram smiled back at him and gave a brief salute with his right hand.

By the time the third-year students entered the dueling ground, the sun had broken through the clouds and humid warmth filled the gold pavilion.

"We'll see some real fighting now," Nestor commented.

Despite Kiram's disgusted frustration, he couldn't help but look up when Javier's name was called. He watched as Holy Father Habalan used a small dagger to open a shallow cut in Javier's wrist and then administered several drops of a black fluid to the wound. Javier grimaced as the holy father bound his wrist and then laced his gauntlet over the wound.

Kiram stole a quick glance to Rafie and Alizadeh, to see what they made of the holy father's ministrations, and found Rafie openly scowling at the sight, disgust plain on his face while Alizadeh shook his head sadly. Good. Let them see what Javier endured and then still refuse to help or even allow Kiram to try.

Javier strode across the filthy arena and took his circle. Despite the poison, he held the ring five rounds without seeming to even break a sweat. Only after the fighting was done, as he and the other third-year champions left the arena, did Javier offer Kiram a warm, longing smile that sent a rush of desire through him. Then Javier bowed his head and went to the benches with Elezar.

Seconds later Rafie and Alizadeh swooped down on Kiram, intent on escorting him throughout the rest of the day. Kiram introduced them to Nestor, who joined them out on the fairgrounds. Shortly after that Riossa and her friends flounced around them in a giggling cluster of silk and ribbons. Nestor's imposing mother, Lady Grunito, and her five attendants manifested moments later. Kiram began to feel like he was walking in a parade. He smiled, because he could see from Rafie's set expression that he had not planned to spend the afternoon in this manner, but had no way of politely extricating himself without leaving Kiram.

Lady Grunito stood as tall as Alizadeh and had a large, angular body which neither her flowing silk skirt nor her velvet coat could soften. Next to her, Rafie looked even more boyish than usual. His delicate features and slender body were only emphasized further by his white hair and muted, Cadeleonian clothes.

"My son Nestor speaks quite highly of your nephew Kiram." Lady Grunito gazed down at Rafie like a hawk contemplating a rabbit.

"I'm glad to hear that Kiram has made a good impression, but I think he might be a little too young to be attending the Sagrada Academy. He's been more sheltered than most boys his age, I think."

"More sheltering is rarely an antidote for too much in the first place." Lady Grunito gave Kiram a piercing glance and then cocked her head just slightly at Rafie. "And to be honest, your nephew seemed to do quite well for himself out in the arena today. He certainly held his own with the other students."

"He stayed on the grounds longer than me," Nestor admitted easily, though he stole an uncertain glance at Riossa. She just smiled at him and then stepped a little closer to him, under the pretense of showing him the drawings in her small sketchbook.

While Lady Grunito continued to lecture Rafie on the value of a Sagrada Academy education, Nestor and Riossa walked close together, discussing inks and brushes and seeming oblivious to everyone else.

Alizadeh complimented Riossa's friends on the perfumes and flowers that they bought from vendors. The girls blushed and smiled nervously; obviously unsure of how to behave toward a Haldiim they fell back on emulating Lady Grunito's polite demeanor.

For his part, Alizadeh never stood too near any of the girls, nor did he speak with any of them too long. Often he simply walked quietly beside Kiram, watching the sky.

"Is something wrong?" Kiram spoke in Haldiim but still kept his question to a whisper.

"No." Alizadeh's gaze moved through the crowd of fairgoers and brightly-dressed vendors. *"It is all very normal, as if the shadow had never fallen here at all. He knows we're looking for it. I wonder how he hides it so well and where?"*

Kiram couldn't even begin to guess the answer to Alizadeh's question and was distracted from thinking about the matter by the breathless whisper of one of Riossa's friends.

"Look, it's the Duke of Rauma." The thin girl pointed with a quick flick of her lace fan.

Javier strode through the crowd with Elezar and Morisio. Atreau followed a little behind them, a young woman with long, loose hair and a low cut dress clinging to his arm.

"He looks so brooding," another of Riossa's friends murmured. "I'd be terrified to be introduced to him, much less make conversation."

Kiram thought Javier looked bored and tired.

"They say he glows in the darkness with the light of the white hell," the girl added.

"He doesn't glow or breathe fire or eat people's souls or anything else you've heard." Kiram watched as Javier pushed Elezar off him. The muerate poison was still hurting him; Kiram could tell from the stiff way he moved his right arm. Javier paused for a moment and turned as if he could feel Kiram's attention.

At the same moment Kiram became acutely aware of both Alizadeh and the surrounding clot of girls observing his study of Javier.

"He's just a man," Kiram said as offhandedly as he could. "Some nights he even snores."

The girls laughed in an excited and scandalized manner.

When Kiram glanced back through the crowd, Javier had slipped out of sight. Kiram tried not to feel disappointed that Javier had not come to join them.

It wasn't long before Rafie made his apologies to their companions and led both Alizadeh and Kiram away, explaining that he needed to see to Kiram's injured arm. Kiram hadn't thought Rafie had even noticed but he'd obviously been wrong.

In their small, warm room at the Laughing Dog, Rafie carefully cut away the leather laces and then peeled the blood-caked gauntlet off of Kiram's left forearm. Kiram flinched when he saw the jagged red wound, with its tattered black stitches jutting pointlessly up from his flesh. The skin was swollen and feverish red. Mottled green and black bruises discolored the rest of Kiram's forearm.

"*There's no point in trying to sew it back up now,*" Rafie said. He held Kiram's arm firmly as he poured a stinging alcohol over the open wound. "*You should have stopped fighting the moment you felt the stitches pull.*"

Kiram gritted his teeth as the alcohol burned deep into his raw wound.

"*I didn't notice when it happened.*"

"*Anyone looking at you could have told that something had happened. You turned white as snow,*" Rafie replied. "*You should have stopped.*"

"*At least he beat four of those Cadeleonian boys,*" Alizadeh said. "*Who knew he was such a fighter?*"

Rafie dried and bandaged Kiram's arm then asked, "*Will you keep it in a sling if I make one for you?*"

"*For today,*" Kiram agreed.

Rafie tied a sling and fitted it around Kiram's arm and neck. His touch was sure and quick. After he was done, and he had thrown out the bloody gauntlet, Rafie sat next to Alizadeh on the floor and accepted a cup of peppery, spiced tea.

Kiram lay on their bed, tired but not willing to sleep so early in the day. He listened as Rafie and Alizadeh discussed their plans for the next year. Rafie needed meet with one of his colleagues who had just returned from Yuan with new medicinal herbs. Alizadeh complained about the tedium of the city, but in a teasing manner that made Kiram think that he was perfectly content to stay in Anacleto for a time.

Kiram's own thoughts drifted in memories of his mother's garden and his father's workshop. He closed his eyes. The scent of Alizadeh's tea roused the half-forgotten longing for cardamom cakes, served at the Autumn Dances. He imagined that Musni was attending one of the dances right now, probably with his new wife.

Kiram wasn't sure when he fell asleep but it was nearly twilight when his uncle Rafie woke him and took him to the city stables to again check in with Master Ignacio. Nestor greeted Kiram warmly, but didn't miss the fact that his uncle stood waiting for him at the gates of the stable.

"He's not taking any chances, is he?" Nestor asked.

"Rafie never makes the same mistake twice."

Nestor scowled. "You think my mom helped any?"

"I don't know. She certainly gave Rafie a long enough lecture on the importance of education."

Nester smiled and nodded as if he had much experience with this. "Your uncle may come around. We've got until Sacreday."

Before Kiram could say anything more, Master Ignacio called them to order and took a quick roll. He reminded them of the eighth bell curfew. Then he announced who would be riding in tomorrow's races. Kiram was neither disappointed nor surprised that he was not among those chosen. Javier on the other hand would be expected to compete in two of the three events, as were the Helio twins.

Kiram tried to catch Javier's attention several times but Javier avoided him, and at last Kiram gave up. He left with Rafie without even saying a word to Javier.

They didn't stay the night at the Laughing Dog, as Kiram had expected, but instead crossed the empty fairgrounds to the Irabiim camp. Nakiesh and Liahn greeted Kiram as if he were a longtime friend and wrapped him in a deerskin cloak while he sat by their fire and waited for his supper. At least thirty crows perched around him. The dusty hound that he'd seen at the Laughing Dog wandered over and flopped down next to the fire.

Kiram patted the animal and it licked his hand briefly, before settling down to sleep.

A few Irabiim girls with their black-kohled eyes watched Kiram curiously from the fires they attended. And several of the young men found reasons to walk near him and ask if he would be traveling with them, as his uncle and Alizadeh often did.

"I don't think so," Kiram replied. *"I'm enrolled at the Sagrada Academy and I'm planning on staying there."*

His response made Rafie frown at him.

Alizadeh laughed. *"He's as stubborn as you."*

Liahn gave Kiram a hot disk of adhil bread and a hollowed gourd full of fragrant stew. When he thanked her, she simply inclined her head and then returned to Nakiesh's side with her own meal.

Rafie sat down beside Kiram with his own gourd full of stew. Alizadeh joined them a few moments later. He tossed a few pieces of his bread to a crow and Nakiesh jokingly warned him that he was going to win himself another lover.

"Well, you know, I can't help but be attracted to the difficult types," Alizadeh replied. Rafie just rolled his eyes. Alizadeh glanced to Kiram and then frowned slightly. *"Don't look so sad, Kiram. Nakiesh's cooking isn't as bad as it looks."*

As a reply Nakiesh sent small clump of adhil bread sailing into the back of Alizadeh's head.

"The food is wonderful," Kiram said quickly. *"I've been missing this kind of meal for months. It's nothing like that."*

"He's moping because his duke has forgotten about him. He didn't even look at Kiram when they were at the stables this evening." Rafie folded his bread and used it to scoop his stew from the gourd. *"It's just as well, Kiri. At least this way it won't be so hard for you to leave."*

"I'm not leaving," Kiram replied.

Rafie's placid expression hardened. *"I know you're young and full of romantic notions, but it is dangerous and foolish to link your fate to that of a Cadeleonian. They aren't like us. They can't free* themselves from the bigotry they're brought up in." Rafie sighed heavily before going on. "He may say he's different. He may want to be different. He may even go so far as to become your lover. But he'll always feel guilty and dirty. He'll be ashamed to be seen with you and try and blame you for his own desires. He'll claim you seduced him or that you are somehow irresistible because you're Haldiim. If the two of you are discovered together, he'll press charges against you to save himself. That's how Cadeleonian men are."

Kiram just stared at Rafie, wondering if all of this had happened to someone he knew.

"A Cadeleonian man can't just accept love and be happy," Rafie said sadly.

"Well, your Cadeleonian man couldn't, but not everyone is Rubio," Alizadeh said. Then, to Kiram, "You uncle had a sweetheart before me, you know."

Kiram hadn't known and he found it a little disquieting to consider. Rafie had always been with Alizadeh for as long as Kiram could remember. They were like twin stars fixed, side by side. He couldn't imagine either of them ever being in love with someone else.

"I'm not just talking about Rubio," Rafie objected. "It's the way all Cadeleonians are brought up."

"Not all of them are brought up the same way, any more than all Haldiim are," Alizadeh replied. "But I grant you that any relationship between a Haldiim and a Cadeleonian is bound to be hard. Between two men, it's nearly impossible unless the Cadeleonian converts, and that happens rarely. For a nobleman, it would mean losing his name and abdicating his title. It's never happened as far as I know."

Kiram felt a deep pain in his chest, as some half-formed wish ripped apart in the face of Alizadeh's pragmatism. But Kiram refused to acknowledge how much the realization hurt him. He had a higher goal than romance.

"I understand what the two of you are saying but none of that matters. I don't want to stay at the academy just to be near Javier."

Kiram wasn't sure that he was telling the truth but it was what he needed to believe at the moment. *"I want to stay because of Nestor and for Fedeles and because I want these Cadeleonian noblemen to see that a Haldiim is just as strong and smart as they are."*

He didn't bother to list breaking the curse among his reasons, as he already knew none of the Bahiim present seemed to think it was a problem worth solving.

Rafie said, *"You'll have plenty of other opportunities to prove yourself in Anacleto."*

"I'm going to stay here," Kiram stated.

"How?" Rafie demanded.

Kiram started to answer and then scowled up at Rafie.

"I'm not going to tell you." Kiram was a little insulted that Rafie would expect him to give away his plans. He was also irked that he'd almost responded. *"You'll just have to find out along with everyone else."*

Rafie looked deeply annoyed but Alizadeh laughed out loud, earning himself a hard glare from Rafie.

"It's not my fault that he's so much like you, now is it?" Alizadeh addressed his attention to his dinner, murmuring, *"Ah, the irony."*

Rafie just shook his head.

After they had eaten, Nakiesh and Liahn offered them the shelter of their wagon for the night. The space was cramped and smelled of sweat and rich spices. Kiram wasn't sure if it was a pleasant perfume or not, but the wagon was warm and his family was close. Despite the strangeness of the deerskin bedding and the soft sounds of birds' wings all around him, he slept soundly.

Chapter Twenty-Two

The sharp cries of crows woke Kiram. He sat straight up, staring into a deep darkness, trying to find Javier. An instant later he remembered he was in an Irabiim wagon, far away from the tower room he had shared for so many months in the Sagrada Academy. He bowed his head against his legs, and wished the absence didn't hurt him so deeply.

Kiram could hear Alizadeh's voice somewhere outside the wagon. Uncle Rafie was gone too—probably outside. Crows shrieked and dogs barked. The wagon's small, wooden door creaked open.

"Did the crows wake you, Kiri?"

Kiram could only make out a vague shape in the darkness of the wagon, but he knew Rafie's voice.

"Is something wrong?"

"Nothing that you or I could do anything about," Rafie said. Kiram didn't find the answer at all reassuring.

"What is it that's got them so alarmed?"

"No one is quite sure," Rafie replied. *"Alizadeh and the other Bahiim all felt a shock of some kind. Something very powerful triggered all of their wards."*

"The shadow curse?" Kiram couldn't help but fear the worst. Had it awoken and taken Fedeles? Had it assaulted Javier?

"No, it wasn't a mere shadow. This was something different. Much more powerful, I think." Rafie sat down beside Kiram. He was cold and his clothes were damp from rain. *"I really can't tell you much more. I only know that Alizadeh woke up like lightning had just struck him and then the crows started screaming. Alizadeh, Liahn, Nakiesh and both the old mothers are outside now, replacing*

the wards that burned up. They're trying to trace the source of the assault." Rafie patted Kiram's shoulder gently. "You think you can get back to sleep?"

"No," Kiram said.

"Me either." Rafie sighed heavily.

"Are they going to be all right?" Kiram asked. "I mean Alizadeh and Liahn and Nakiesh. They aren't in danger, are they?"

"I don't know." Fear tinged Rafie's voice. That, more than anything else, frightened Kiram. He had always held Rafie in such esteem that he had never been able to imagine anything disturbing him. "Whatever burned through the wards, it was stronger than any of the Bahiim, and it was searching."

"What for?"

"For Alizadeh probably. Nakiesh says it was concentrated very close to the Laughing Dog when it struck."

"Did it hurt him?" Kiram asked.

"No. It just struck powerfuly but blindly, though it seared through every ward anywhere near it. Liahn thinks it was meant as a warning from the man on the hill. He doesn't want any Bahiim involved in his business."

Kiram scowled at the surrounding darkness. "None of them are involved in his business."

"Both Alizadeh and Nakiesh breached his domain yesterday. Maybe he felt threatened enough to send out a warning." Rafie sighed and then straightened. "It's nearly sun up. You want to help me with breakfast?"

"Help? You mean, cooking it?" Kiram had never cooked anything in his life.

Rafie laughed, sounding more himself. "Yes. That great mystery: cooking. Come, I'll show you how to burn adhil bread and scald mare's milk."

Kiram dressed in the dark and then joined Rafie outside. The sky was pale with predawn light and a humid wind whipped Kiram's hair into his face. Most of the Irabiim were awake also. Women stoked their fires up to bright yellow blazes. Boys yawned and trudged out to their rangy horses, with brushes and bridles. Kiram guessed that they would be taking the animals to auction at the fair in an hour or so.

Kiram didn't see any of the Bahiim. When he asked, Rafie said that they were out in the woods, anchoring their wards in the wood of the trees. As he spoke Rafie frowned at the deep shadows of the forest then turned back to Kiram with a determined expression.

"Well, let's see about your first cooking lesson."

He kept Kiram running all over the camp, trading spices with Irabiim mothers and begging mare's milk from an older man with dozens of brilliant bangles on his wrists. Rafie taught him to mix adhil batter and cut onions. The sun peaked over the distant hills and the last of the night bells rang over Zancoda. People would be up and about their business in the city soon.

Rafie heated oil in an iron skillet and fried the bread. He flipped the thin disks of bread with a flick of the pan. Kiram watched, feeling his awe of his uncle grow. Rafie cracked several eggs into the pan, stirred black salt and spices into them and tossed in the onions. After a few minutes he turned the eggs and onion out onto the bread.

Kiram ate quickly, noting the fragrant spices but still too hungry to savor them.

Rafie ate his own breakfast much more slowly. *"You need to be back at the city stable soon, don't you?"*

"Master Ignacio wants us there by the first morning bell," Kiram said.

Rafie frowned into the deep shadows of the woods again.

"I can go by myself," Kiram said. *"You should be here for Alizadeh, in case he needs you."*

Rafie studied Kiram closely. Kiram could see him weighing his desire to be near Alizadeh in case he or any of the other Bahiim were injured against his need to prevent Kiram's escape.

"I won't run away," Kiram assured him.

Rafie studied him for a moment. *"I need to have your word."*

Kiram sighed, nodding his resignation. As clever as it might be, he just couldn't bring himself to use Rafie's fear for Alizadeh for his own gain. And in any case where would he run away to?

"I swear on Mother's blood," Kiram said. "I'm just going to check in with Master Ignacio and then attend the tournament races. If you don't come for me after the races then I'll come back here, all right?"

"All right," Rafie agreed. He ruffled Kiram's hair lightly. "Be careful."

Kiram hurried back toward Zancoda. The moist wind tossed his hair into his face and sent shudders across the back of his neck. He pulled up the collar of his coat, wondering if it would rain again today and what would be done should a downpour foul the race course. The sky looked both pale and gloomy, white clouds diffusing the sunlight into an eerie glow.

As he passed the Laughing Dog he paused to look for signs of the night's disturbance. At first he saw nothing unusual. The small stone building and its plank stable stood just as they had two days before. Crows perched in the nearby trees.

Kiram bowed his head from the wind and began to walk again. Then he noticed a few black lines cracked through the flagstones just outside the stable. The stone seemed glassy in places and when Kiram stepped back he saw that the black cracks formed a perfect circle around him. A wave of fear washed through Kiram and he quickly stepped out of the circle.

As he did so he noticed a crumpled dark form at the corner of the stable and nearly called out in alarm. His sharp gasp brought the shadowy form suddenly up into the shape of a man. Kiram recognized Javier with relief but didn't feel any less surprised.

He had no idea what Javier was doing here or why he had been hunched like broken firewood against the stable wall. Javier whispered something but Kiram didn't hear the word over the wind. Then Javier rushed forward and pulled Kiram to him, clutching him desperately.

"You weren't at the inn and I thought they had taken you away," Javier whispered into Kiram's neck. His skin was like ice.

"We stayed with the Irabiim," Kiram said. For a moment he let himself relax into Javier's embrace. He had wanted to be held like this yesterday. And it had been this nearness that he had longed for when he woke this morning. But now, feeling himself melt into Javier's arms, he couldn't help but resent Javier's importance to him and how Javier had withheld this closeness all of yesterday.

Kiram pushed him back. Javier released him immediately, glancing up and down the street for any sign of onlookers. There was no one. Javier jammed his hands into his coat pockets and eyed Kiram with an uncertain expression.

"What are you doing here?" Kiram demanded.

"I couldn't sleep. I thought I would meet you at the inn and we could walk together to the city stables."

"So that you can ignore me once we're there?" Kiram had wanted to sound cold and controlled, but instead the words came out sounding so hurt that it embarrassed Kiram. A wave of disgust at his own weakness washed over him.

He turned, bowing his head before the wind, and stalked towards the city stable. Javier fell in beside him. Only a few vendors were out, loading carts with their wares for trade at the fair. The merchants paid little attention to either of them as they passed.

"I thought that if I didn't bother you, if I kept away, it would be easier for you to leave," Javier said quietly.

"Easier? Why are you here, now, if you want it to be so much easier for me?"

"Because I don't really want you to go. Can't you understand? I'm selfish. I don't want to be, but I can't help it. I want to keep you with me even though I know you should be somewhere safer." There was a long pause and Kiram wanted to look at Javier but he didn't trust himself. It was too easy to be won over by him and he wasn't yet willing to relinquish his feeling of righteous outrage.

"I'm not making a lot of sense right now, I know that," Javier said. "But I came here to tell you that I'm sorry."

Kiram sighed, finally meeting Javier's eyes. There he saw the other man's exhaustion and vulnerability. He had not changed his clothes or slept. Blue shadows filled the hollows of his eyes—eyes that hunted for some sign of Kiram's forgiveness. At that moment, he had Javier completely at his mercy.

"It's all right." He let his hand brush against Javier's. The tips of their fingers touched and then parted. "And just so you know, I don't intend to leave."

Javier smiled his familiar, slow smile.

"Not just because of you," Kiram said but Javier's pleased expression didn't change.

"Of course not. We both know how much you love Holy Father Habalan's classes."

Kiram just rolled his eyes.

"I promised Fedeles that I would help him, and I happen to enjoy a good number of my classes," Kiram said primly.

"Yes, you do so love riding and fencing instruction."

"I adore my mathematics and natural science classes."

"It's all right to just admit that you like me, you know," Javier said softly.

Kiram's breath caught in his chest, but he still managed to say, "Yes, I do."

They passed a row of bakeries. The smells of fresh bread perfumed the cold air.

"I have enough money to pay your tuition, easily," Javier said in a thoughtful tone. "But there's still the problem of your family's consent. If you were just a half a year older…"

Kiram shrugged. Nothing but time was going to change his status as a minor. "We'll figure something out."

As they continued to walk through the wind, Kiram's thoughts turned over possible ways to elude Rafie. Not for the first or last time he pondered fleeing to a foreign land. That was futile fantasy, and he knew it. Neither he nor Javier could leave Fedeles to the mercy of the man on the hill and his creeping shadow curse.

Another thought occurred to Kiram, suddenly. "You were at the Laughing Dog this morning. When that…thing struck. I think it might have been hunting you." Rafie had said that it had been searching. But what if it hadn't been seeking Alizadeh or any of the Bahiim, what if it had been after Javier?

"What thing?" Javier asked.

"Did you notice that scorched circle in the flagstones near the stable?"

Javier arched a black brow. "Is this a trick question?"

"What? No. No, it's not. There was a circle—"

"I know there was a circle," Javier cut him off. "I made it. I got so frustrated and I thought I wouldn't ever see you again and I lost my grip on the white hell. It was just for a moment."

"You." Kiram stared at Javier, remembering Rafie's grim expression and his fear. "You did that?"

"It was just some stone." Javier shrugged. "I didn't harm anyone. I wouldn't have."

"I know. That's not what I meant…The Bahiim all around the Irabiim camp felt it when the white hell opened. I think you scared them pretty badly."

"The white hell scares most people, or at least the ones with any common sense." Javier gave Kiram a teasing glance.

"Superstition is not common sense," Kiram went on before Javier could get in a retort. "And that's not my point, in any case. I just realized that they didn't recognize the white hell. They didn't know what it was."

"Why would they? The Haldiim don't have hells."

Kiram frowned at this. They didn't believe in hells, but certainly they would have their own understanding of Javier's power. Kiram had his own theory that it was some link to a shajdi. Calixto's diary had hinted at the same thing. But Kiram had hoped that a Bahiim like Alizadeh would recognize the white hell and provide an explanation for it. Maybe he did but hadn't had time to explain it to Rafie. Maybe Rafie hadn't bothered to tell Kiram.

He wondered if he would ever be old enough that his uncle Rafie would take him into his confidences. Remembering last night's lecture he imagined it would be a long time coming.

"How's your arm?" Javier asked.

"Sore," Kiram admitted. "The stitches tore out yesterday."

"I thought that might have happened. You looked bad when you came out of the fencing circle."

"I didn't think you noticed," Kiram replied and a little of his old resentment briefly flared up.

"Of course I did. You were white as a sheet and glaring at me like it was my fault." Javier studied Kiram, and for just an instant he looked deeply sad and then he went on. "You ruined my concentration. I should have wiped the floor with my first opponent but my focus was a wreck. I kept trying to get a look at you without you seeing."

"You succeeded pretty well, I guess. Anyway you ripped through all of your fencing opponents."

"Not nearly as cleanly or as quickly as I should have." Javier smirked at Kiram. "You're going to ruin my reputation."

Kiram rolled his eyes. "Oh yes, next thing you know people will be saying that you read books."

"I do read books."

"Not nice books," Kiram replied. "They'll be saying you read stories about ducklings and apple blossoms. The Hellions will be saying that you've gone soft and have foresworn eating kittens entirely."

Javier smirked at this and then leaned close to Kiram and whispered, "Why would I touch any kind of pussy when I can have the taste of you in my mouth?"

Kiram felt heat roll through his entire body as he flushed. "I wasn't referring to ladies."

"Weren't you?"

Kiram hadn't meant the comment in that way, but now suddenly he realized that he should have. If he was going to stay with Javier, then he wanted some assurance of Javier's commitment to him in return.

A bellowed greeting from Elezar destroyed any possibility of such a conversation. Javier waved and both Elezar and Nestor hurried from the gates of the city stable to meet them.

"Cutting it close, aren't you? It's nearly first bell." Elezar grinned at Javier. "Why are you out wandering the streets when you should be inside, communing with that finicky horse of yours. I've got money on you, you know?"

"I've got money on me too." Javier didn't move away from Kiram but his stance shifted just slightly and Kiram could feel him distancing himself.

"For all three races?" Nestor asked.

"I expect to be in the top five for the short run. But Lunaluz won't take second to any other horse on either of the long runs. We could take those jumps in our sleep, we practiced them so many times." Javier spoke with such assurance that Kiram found himself feeling that he must be right.

The four of them joined the other students gathered inside the courtyard of the stable. Atreau and the other Hellions all informed Javier of the bets they'd placed on him. They slapped his back and issued absurd threats for his failure. Kiram watched them, saddened by the insight that this was the only way that these Cadeleonian men could offer him their affection.

Master Ignacio arrived and all of the students quickly arranged themselves in rows according to their years. As always Nestor stood beside Kiram.

"I noticed your uncle isn't here today," Nestor whispered hopefully.

"There was an incident at their lodgings and he had to stay in case someone needed a physician." Kiram was aware of how vague his reply was but Nestor accepted it without concern.

"So he hasn't changed his mind about taking you back?"

"Not that I know of."

They both went quiet as Master Ignacio walked through the ranks of second-year students, assigning them their duties for the races. Both Nestor and Kiram were in charge of keeping onlookers from crossing the track just before the finish. Kiram couldn't imagine anyone who would rush out past two lines of ropes at oncoming horses and he guessed the job was something just to keep them in one place and accounted for.

Once Master Ignacio was done with roll and assignments, the grooms brought the horses out from their stalls. Kiram stroked Firaj's muzzle. Firaj drew in a deep breath of Kiram's hair. He seemed excited to go for a ride, despite the wet chill of the morning.

By the time they reached the tournament grounds the sun had burned through most of the cloud cover. A fine mist hung in the air, catching the light and flaring briefly into rainbows.

Groundsmen had hauled bales of hay out across several fields and strung up rope barricades along side them. The hay bales formed a wide corridor, looping around stone walls, and circling out into a thinly wooded glade, marking the racecourses. Taking in the route firsthand, Kiram felt relieved that he wouldn't be competing but also worried. There were at least three walls and two wooden fences that the horses would need to clear in addition to whatever other obstacles lay out in the woods.

Kiram observed Javier, remembering how he had first seen him riding Lunaluz across the summer fields. He had looked so handsome and assured. This morning he still radiated beautiful strength, but shadows of exhaustion hollowed his eyes. The knowledge that Javier had spent the night searching for him instead of sleeping gnawed at Kiram.

Onlookers, both wealthy and poor, already gathered around. They thronged the rope barricades. Many of them had brought tall wooden stools, and some had hired men to wave banners displaying the colors of the riders they supported. Groups of girls clustered under bright parasols.

The only covered shelter was a dais near the starting line. Royal banners hung from the roof and armed guards stood at attention at the foot of the dais. Kiram thought he caught a glimpse of Prince Sevanyo sitting in the shadows, among his attendants and courtiers.

On the grounds, the black and yellow Helios' colors were well represented, as were the red and white stripes of the Fueres family. As the crowd grew the numbers and variety of banners and ribbons increased. Kiram had no idea who some of the more wild assortments represented. There seemed to be countless shades of blues, reds, yellows and violets and scattered throughout were simple flags displaying either Sagrada blue or Yillar green.

In the sea of color Kiram noticed the absence of the stark black and white of the Tornesal house. He wondered if it saddened Javier that no one flew his colors. Kiram searched the growing crowd for Fedeles but didn't see him anywhere. Then to Kiram's surprise he caught sight of two huge banners displaying the white field and black sun of the Tornesal crest. Lady Grunito stood between them, surrounded by attendants. She wore a magnificent golden fur coat that made her look almost like a bear. She waved at Javier and he waved back.

"I knew my mother would come through for him," Nestor said. "Elezar wouldn't stop nagging her about it all last night."

"I'm glad he did," Kiram said.

"It's not like she wasn't going to support Javier all along. She had the banners made months ago but she wouldn't let Elezar know that. She likes to tease him."

Kiram nodded. He could see how someone might want to give Elezar a hard time. He warmed to Lady Grunito, though he knew very little about her; she had cajoled his uncle on his behalf, no doubt to please Nestor—and she had brought banners for Javier knowing that Elezar would want them. For all her appearance of ferocity, Kiram imagined that she was in fact a very loving mother.

"By the way." Nestor reined his roan stallion a little closer to Firaj's side. "I had an idea about how to keep you at the academy last night during prayer service. It's a little crazy but I think it would work."

"Great. What is it?"

"You convert."

"Convert?" Kiram was so stunned by the suggestion that he initially thought he misunderstood Nestor.

"You convert and then request sanctuary at the academy chapel. There's no way your family could get you out of there."

"If I converted they wouldn't even want to. They'd never speak my name again. My mother would never forgive me."

"Is it really that serious an offense?" Nestor asked.

"How would your mother feel about you becoming Haldiim?" Kiram asked back.

"Very poorly," Nestor admitted after a moment of thought. He sighed. "Well, I thought I'd at least mention it."

"Thanks for trying. Who knows, if it comes down to it…" Kiram couldn't even bring himself to say that he would consider it.

He and Nestor took up their positions near the finish line. Now and then Kiram shouted at a curious boy who had ducked under the rope barricades. He guessed that he looked a little imposing atop Firaj because the boys fled away and nearby parents hauled their children back from the ropes as well. The judges took their positions beside the green and blue ribboned finish line. Far across the field the riders from both schools lined up at the start. They saluted Prince Sevanyo and then the starting bell rang out. The pounding thunder of horses' hooves was instantly drowned out by the roars and cheers of the crowd.

Kiram's entire body tensed as he watched Javier push to the front of the riders. He saw crops slash and the rain soaked earth slide from beneath the horses' hooves. His stomach felt like a clenched fist when an animal stumbled. Each time Javier neared a jump or rounded a tight turn Kiram looked away, scanning the rope barricades. He felt like a coward but he was terrified of seeing Javier fall.

Then suddenly the riders were storming past both him and Nestor. The cold air smelled of sweat and horses. Wet clumps of sod and mud flew through the air and spattered the hay barricades.

The first race had been the short run. Javier took second, just behind his cousin, Hierro Fueres. The Helio twins took third and fourth, though Kiram wasn't sure which twin had won which place.

Javier looked flushed and happy, grinning and leaning close to Lunaluz's neck. He stroked the stallion's jaw and whispered something in his ear. Lunaluz pranced back to the starting line with his head held high.

While the groundsmen adjusted the bales of hay for the next race, Kiram thought he heard someone calling his name. He searched the crowd and caught sight of Alizadeh approaching. Rafic was nowhere to be seen.

Alizadeh glanced to where the riders were still gathering at the starting line and then ducked under the barricade and quickly strode to where Kiram sat atop Firaj. Alizadeh offered Firaj a sniff of his hand and the gelding seemed won over, allowing Alizadeh to stroke his shoulder and neck.

"Is Rafie all right?" Kiram asked.

"He's fine. He just stayed back at the camp." Alizadeh scratched a little harder as Firaj leaned into him. "One of the boys fell and hurt his arm. The ground is really slick right now."

"I know." At the thought of a rider falling, the sick dread in Kiram's stomach returned. He focused on Alizadeh instead. "Did you figure out what happened last night?"

"I have an idea," Alizadeh said. His expression turned grim and Kiram needed suddenly to reassure him that he and the Bahiim weren't in danger—or if they were that they hadn't been attacked the night before.

"I think I know what happened." Kiram leaned down, lowering his voice. "It wasn't the man on the hill who disrupted your wards. Javier was looking for me and he opened the white hell."

Alizadeh gave him an amused, disbelieving look. "And you think that your duke's Cadeleonian hell affected the Bahiim wards?"

"Yes," Kiram insisted, annoyed by Alizadeh's apparent dismissal of his theory. A horn sounded as the riders of the second race were called to the starting line. "I'll explain when I'm finished here."

"Yes, I'd be interested to hear the finer points of your argument." Alizadeh cast his gaze out over the racecourse, as if he'd just noticed it. *"So, races today? Anyone I should cheer for?"*

"Javier. He's there on the white stallion."

"He does cut a fine figure," Alizadeh remarked.

Kiram felt his cheeks warm slightly. *"He has a good chance of taking first place in the next two races."*

"Well, I'll cheer for him as loudly as I can. Is there somewhere in particular that I should stand?"

"Anywhere as long as you keep behind the rope barricade. It's my job to keep people back, you know."

"In that case I'll slink away as quickly as I can." Alizadeh quickly slipped back behind the rope barricade. Kiram watched him go, wondering what it would take to convince Alizadeh to take his side and help him stay at the academy. Then the loud clang of the starting bell captured all Kiram's attention.

Javier and Hierro Fueres took the lead immediately. But even before the second lap Kiram could see Hierro Fueres' mount tiring. The Helio twins steadily gained ground. One of them edged into third place and the other fell in just behind his twin in fourth.

Lunaluz cleared the last stone wall, but Hierro Fueres' horse shied from the jump and the Helio twins surged ahead. The first of them cleared the wall but the second didn't.

A sick horror flooded Kiram as both rider and horse crashed down, half across the wall half over it. The horse let out a wrenching scream and the Helio twin's body flipped through the air and then smacked into the muddy ground. Two men in Sagrada colors rushed past the barricade and pulled him up to his feet. He hung between them, sobbing as they dragged him back off the field.

Hierro Fueres turned his mount aside and jumped the wall a little to the left of the convulsing horse. The five other riders followed his example.

The fallen horse thrashed in a revolting, spastic manner. Its hindquarters collapsed over the wall. The horse tried to stand but its legs splayed out, buckling like broken sticks. Its head twisted at a wrong angle and still it cried out. Firaj folded his ears back and shivered in seeming sympathy.

The surrounding crowd went silent and motionless as the horse's cries carried over the course. Kiram felt like he might vomit but he forced his revulsion back. He couldn't believe that the horse was still alive, or that the race was still going on.

Then suddenly Javier wheeled Lunaluz around. He cut across the field, riding back to where the horse lay, thrashing and crying. Lunaluz balked as they drew near, shaking his head and whinnying. Javier swung down from his saddle and ran to the fallen beast.

Terror coursed through Kiram as the horse flailed, nearly striking Javier with its hoof. Riders raced past Kiram, crossing the finish line, but Kiram hardly noticed them. He stared at Javier and the pathetic, trembling ruin of a beautiful roan stallion.

A tiny flicker sparked up between Javier's hands and then it spread into a luminous glow. Javier held his hands out, basking the horse in the white light and the horse quieted. It stared at Javier, shudders still passing through its body but it made no noise. Javier moved closer, kneeling beside the animal's head.

Javier lowered his face and whispered something to the horse. Then the soft light between his hands crackled like lightning and a blinding bolt shot straight down through the horse's head.

The horse went entirely limp, its head falling into the mud and its legs drooping like hot taffy. Javier returned to Lunaluz and stood for a long moment, stroking the stallion's neck. Then he rode back to the starting line, clearly forfeiting.

Neither of the Helio twins took their places for the third race, and Kiram was shocked that the war masters hadn't canceled the final race. The remaining riders were called to their places and the bell rang.

The start was slower than either of the two before and the cheers from the crowd were thin and subdued at first. But after the second lap, as Javier and Hierro Fueres rode neck and neck, voices rose and groups of men chanted in booming voices. Elezar managed to shout over everyone, howling out Javier's name and taunting Hierro Fueres.

Kiram was silent, just watching and dreading the moment Lunaluz approached the last stone wall. He didn't want to look and at the same time he couldn't pull his gaze away. A red smear colored the gray stones. He tried to convince himself that it was just mud.

Then Lunaluz leapt and soared over the wall. Javier came charging towards the finish line. His expression was set in that arrogant smile, as it often was in duels. But for an instant he glanced to Kiram and Kiram saw his entire countenance slip like a mask. He looked overwhelmed with sorrow. Then he glanced away and his satisfied smirk returned.

He and Lunaluz tore through the ribbons of the finish line a full length ahead of Hierro Fuere. The last five riders came through the line in quick succession. Kiram watched them, feeling both numb and raw. He wanted to be able to roar Javier's name in triumph, but he couldn't stop thinking of the terrible heavy thud of the roan stallion's body breaking over that stone wall and how little it seemed to have impacted anyone else. It disturbed him that a living creature could have suffered so terribly so recently and that the crowd of Cadeleonians would already be cheering and hooting.

Prince Sevanyo presented medals to the winning riders. Javier took a silver and a gold with a fixed smile. Hierro Fueres accepted his gold and two silvers with a grin that reminded Kiram a little of Fedeles in the grip of near madness. Cocuyo Helio received his gold, and a bronze medal in his brother's stead. He managed a thin smile for the prince. The remaining medals, two bronzes, were presented to a Yillar student who Kiram didn't know, but he wore a bright orange ribbon on his sleeve.

Kiram suddenly wondered what it took for a Cadeleonian to admit weakness or to express open sorrow. Did they always force a confident smile and charge thoughtlessly ahead like brave soldiers? Maybe that's what made them such great warriors, but also such terrible intellectuals.

"Are you needed for anything else?" Alizadeh once again ducked under the rope barricade and stood beside Firaj. He wasn't smiling and Kiram found it relieving to know that at least he hadn't forgotten the fallen horse.

"No," Kiram said. "Master Ignacio just signaled our dismissal. One of the grooms is already on his way to take Firaj back to the stables. After that I'm free until sixth bell."

"Good." Alizadeh said nothing more as the groom drew closer, but the tension that Kiram had noticed the first day he'd seen Alizadeh had returned to his bearing. He glanced up at the blue jays circling overhead. Kiram stroked Firaj's jaw for a few moments before handing his reins over to a young groom. The entire time Alizadeh's disquiet seemed to increase.

Alizadeh stepped closer to Kiram. *"Do you know what it is that your friend Javier did to that fallen horse?"*

"He opened the white hell and...killed it..." Kiram glanced quickly to the bloodstained wall and then back to Alizadeh. *"He had to, it was suffering."*

"I have no doubt that it was a merciful killing. That is not what concerns me," Alizadeh said. His gaze flickered to the throng of Hellions surrounding Javier and he lowered his voice to a whisper. *"It wasn't a hell he opened. That was a shajdi. The same one that opened this morning."*

"That's what I was trying to tell you before the race," Kiram said. *"I think that the white hell is actually a shajdi."*

"This changes things," Alizadeh said. He turned his attention back to Kiram. *"We have to go now."*

Alizadeh caught his hand in a tight grip.

"But I haven't gotten a chance to talk to Javier or Nestor," Kiram protested. *"I should at least tell them where I'm going."*

"I'm sorry Kiram, but we do not have time to argue. Not now and not here." Alizadeh hissed a word that Kiram didn't recognize. Suddenly a throbbing sensation shot through Kiram's arm, as if he'd been stung by a bee. Kiram tried to pull his arm

back from Alizadeh but a wave of numb surged through him. He stepped forward in a daze.

Kiram was aware that he walked beside Alizadeh. His body moved like some mechanism, striding ahead regardless of Kiram's will to stop. He recognized banners and bright tents as he passed them. He even heard Javier call his name. But sounds, sights and sensations came to him as if he were in the midst of another man's dream—he marched onward, little more than a mute puppet in Alizadeh's grip.

Soon he and Alizadeh reached the Irabiim camp. Horses were already hitched to wagons. Only embers and thin trails of smoke remained from the cooking fires.

They were leaving.

Chapter Twenty-Three

Kiram resisted with all his will. He concentrated on flexing the muscles of his legs and digging his heels into the wet ground. Focusing all his strength, he managed to slow the strides of his body to clumsy stumbling steps.

"You willful Kir-Zakis never make it easy, do you?" Alizadeh grumbled as he dragged Kiram forward into the Irabiim camp. Irabiim women watched them with curious expressions. Young men looked away as Kiram staggered past. Rafie met them a few feet from the wagon where they had slept the night before. He glanced briefly between Alizadeh and Kiram and then scowled.

"Kiram, you swore you wouldn't try to run away," Rafie said.

"He didn't," Alizadeh replied. *"At least he hasn't yet."*

"Then why are you're holding him in a thrall?"

"Bait to trap for a certain duke," Alizadeh replied. Kiram had expected a different answer and clearly so had Rafie.

"What do you want with the Cadeleonian duke?"

"He opened the shajdi this morning." Alizadeh didn't release his grip on Kiram's wrist as he sagged back against the wall of the wagon. Sweat beaded his brow.

"That's not possible, is it?" Rafie asked and then he lowered his voice to a whisper. *"You told me yourself that the craft of forging portals was locked away by the Bahiim."*

"It was and it remains so." Alizadeh's voice was equally low. *"Somehow Calixto Tornesal discovered the secret, found a sacrifice, and forged a portal. That's what the Tornesal's white hell is."*

"So that's what the man on the hill is after," Rafie said quietly. *"Not just a dukedom but the power of a shajdi as well."*

Alizadeh nodded. *"We can't allow a shajdi to fall into the hands of the Cadeleonian church, especially not the royal bishop."*

Hope surged in Kiram's heart. Maybe Alizadeh would intercede on Javier's behalf after all.

"Hopefully the duke is young enough that his link with the shajdi is weak and I'll be able to break it," Alizadeh said.

Hope turned to horror. The white hell—the shajdi that powered it—was all that protected Javier from the curse. If Alizadeh broke that then Javier would die just as his mother and father had.

Kiram concentrated on jerking his arm back from Alizadeh's grasp. He felt his forearm flex. A shudder passed through Alizadeh.

"Something wrong?" Rafie asked Alizadeh.

"Your nephew's not any easier to enthrall than you were when we were in Hidras," Alizadeh said to Rafie.

"We're a stubborn family." Rafie glanced to Kiram. *"You shouldn't fight Alizadeh. He's doing what's right."*

"N...no." Kiram's lips felt like lead slabs as he struggled to form words that eventually emerged as a groan. *"You'll...kill...Javier."*

"Should I fetch Nakiesh or Liahn?" Rafie asked.

"No..." Alizadeh frowned out at the distant groups of Irabiim. *"They really might kill the duke. It would be the easiest way to close the portal and the Irabiim could flee to other lands before the Cadeleonians mounted a reprisal. No, we need to keep this among ourselves."*

"So, what can I do?" Rafie asked.

"A draught to put your nephew to sleep would help me greatly." Alizadeh looked out past Kiram. *"I don't think I'm going to have much time to prepare before the duke arrives and I'm going to need my strength."*

"I'll mix a few drams of duera. That should take Kiram off your hands."

"Thank you, my dear." Alizadeh smiled and Rafie leaned close to kiss his cheek.

"Don't scowl like that, Kiram," Rafie said gently. *"This is for the best, and honestly you look like you could use the sleep."* Then Rafie turned and bounded into the wagon.

Kiram struggled to pull out of Alizadeh's grasp. He didn't have much time if he was going to make his escape. Alizadeh's grip tightened around his wrist and his fingers suddenly felt like brands of fire.

Be calm, Kiram. I will not harm you or your young duke. Alizadeh's voice filtered through Kiram's thoughts.

Yes, you will! Kiram could only think the words. He trembled with the frustration at his numb, mute body. He wanted to scream at Alizadeh. *You'll strip Javier of the only protection he has against the curse and he'll die. He'll die in agony!*

"If he no longer possesses the white hell then the man on the hill may not bother to maintain the curse," Alizadeh answered though Kiram had said nothing aloud.

You don't believe that. Kiram concentrated on Alizadeh, and the burning sensation of Alizadeh' grasp seemed to roll up from his arm to engulf his entire body. He had felt something like this, when Javier had opened the white hell for him. Javier's presence in his mind had been hot as well, but sensual and inviting. Alizadeh was a scouring flame, searing into Kiram's thoughts.

Despite the discomfort, Kiram pushed his consciousness into the scorching presence and thought hard.

I can tell from your expression. You know you're condemning Javier. You're condemning him the same way that Nazario Sagrada condemned innocent Haldiim to their deaths. You're as bad as him.

"Perhaps, but Kiram," Alizadeh looked suddenly deeply tired and Kiram was glad to have affected him, *"there is more at stake here than one man's life. A shajdi is not some plaything. It is a locus where all death becomes life. It is power, pure and formless. The very soul of creation. When a shajdi comes under the dominion of humanity it changes. Over time it takes form, becoming what they will it to be. The shajdi that your friend possesses is probably*

already deeply corrupted by the generations of Tornesals. It is becoming the hell they have imagined it to be. If it remains in your friend's control it will bring forth the devils of his religion. He will give them form and the shajdi will give them life. They will enter our world. They will be a plague upon all living things. That must not happen. Do you understand?"

Kiram did understand, but he still couldn't accept the sacrifice of Javier's life.

Alizadeh seemed to see Kiram's resistance. His green eyes narrowed in anger.

"Do you know why King Nazario Sagrada tortured and murdered so many Haldiim, Kiram?" Alizadeh didn't wait for Kiram's response. *"He and his bishops wanted to possess a shajdi. Had they succeeded in their quest they would have brought the tortures of the Cadeleonian church out into this world and conquered all nations. Countless Bahiim died to keep that from happening. We endured his tortures and we destroyed our own writings. At the very last we locked the knowledge away, depriving even our own people of the shajdi's healing powers rather than allowing them to become perverted. All those deaths, all that sacrifice can't have been for nothing. This shajdi must not become a Cadeleonian hell."*

Kiram thought: *But you're condemning Javier for something that he hasn't done. You don't know how he sees the white hell. I do. It isn't full of devils. It's light and beautiful. I saw a Bahiim tree there and words but nothing else. Javier isn't creating some terrible Cadeleonian hell with the shajdi. It's a refuge for him. If anything, that's what he'll make it into. A place of peace. Please, Alizadeh, you have to believe me.*

For the first time Alizadeh looked uncertain.

"You have been inside the shajdi?"

Yes, Javier shielded me while I read a script that could only be seen in the shajdi's light.

Alizadeh nodded, apparently familiar with such script. Again, the burning sensation seemed to surge through Kiram's body. Unwillingly, Kiram's memory of that afternoon arose. Kiram felt

Alizadeh searching through them as one might leaf through a book. Kiram struggled to escape Alizadeh's grasp before the sensations of that day—the feel and taste of Javier's body—rushed over him again. His resistance made no impact. In seconds, Kiram basked in the light of the white hell and read Calixto's words. Then he felt Javier's warm lips and insistent tongue and flushed with embarrassment, knowing that Alizadeh could see his pleasure in the sensations.

Then suddenly a chill swept through Kiram and he was once again standing in front of an Irabiim wagon. Alizadeh still held his wrist, but not with the enthralling grasp he had used earlier.

Alizadeh released Kiram very deliberately.

"All right, Kiram. I believe you," Alizadeh said after a moment. *"But I still need to see the shajdi for myself. I'll need your help."*

"The duera is prepared." Rafie stepped out of the wagon with a porcelain vial in his hands.

"There's been a change of plan," Alizadeh called to Rafie.

"Oh?" Rafie asked. *"Well you'd better tell me about it quickly because I think I just caught sight of the duke and he looks like he has a few friends with him."*

Across the open field Kiram spotted Javier in the midst of cleared the stone wall that surrounded the fairgrounds with Elezar close on his heels. Nestor followed behind them a little more clumsily. The three of them strode across the open field, heading towards the remains of the Irabiim camp.

"I'm putting a great deal of trust in you, Kiram," Alizadeh said.

Kiram nodded, overwhelmed with relief. He thought he might agree to anything if it meant that Javier would be safe. *"I know and I can't thank you—"*

"Just listen." Alizadeh caught the lotus medallion that Kiram wore. *"Rafie and I will ask the duke to take you home with him—a little duera will ensure that you look worn out. Once you have the duke alone you'll need to convince him to allow*

you into the shajdi again. I'll be able to see the extent of the shajdi's corruption through you."

"And if you decide that the shadji is contaminated, then what?" Kiram asked.

"Then I'll have to strip the shajdi from the duke by any means possible." Alizadeh glanced to Javier briefly. Then he returned his attention to Kiram. *"I don't want to harm your duke—"*

"He has a name," Kiram said.

"Javier, then," Alizadeh conceded. *"I don't want to harm him. If I find that the shajdi is still intact, then there may even be a way that I can help him to destroy the shadow curse. But I must see the shajdi myself to know."*

"If you're lying—if you're using me to hurt him, I won't ever forgive you."

"No, I can't imagine that you would." Alizadeh smiled for the first time since they'd left the fairgrounds. *"Fortunately for us both I'm telling you the truth. So, will you help me or not?"*

"Yes," Kiram said.

"Good." Alizadeh suddenly leaned close and lifted the lotus medallion to his lips. He whispered a strange word and a shudder passed through his body. Then he let the medallion fall back against Kiram's chest.

Alizadeh swayed and then caught himself. His face paled but his expression was calm. Rafie came to his side, placing a supporting hand casually on Alizadeh's back.

"Drink a just a little of the duera," Alizadeh told Kiram. He gazed up into the sky.

Kiram hesitated only an instant before he accepted the vial from Rafie and took a quick sip. *"Now what?"*

"Sit down," Rafie said. *"Before you fall down."*

Kiram took his advice and leaned back against the wagon as the familiar, lightheaded feeling of the duera came over Kiram. He didn't try to fight it. Instead, he watched Javier approach. He strode past groups of heavily bangled Irabiim youths and they averted their gazes. In the trees overhead crows took flight.

Javier's dark eyes scanned the camp and in an instant Kiram found him staring straight at him. His intense expression softened and a slight smile curved his mouth.

Kiram lazily lifted his hand and waved. Nestor waved back at him enthusiastically and then rushed ahead of both Javier and Elezar.

"Kiram!" Nestor shouted. "We've been looking all over for you." Nestor bounded out of the way of a sleeping dog and then skidded to a stop in front of Rafie and Alizadeh. He bowed to them.

"It's good to see you again, young Master Grunito," Rafie said in flawless Cadeleonian. Alizadeh smiled at Nestor but said nothing.

"Good to see you as well, sirs." Nestor beamed at them but frowned when he turned his attention to Kiram. "You look done in."

"His arm was hurting him," Rafie said. "I gave him a little duera for the pain but I think he may need to rest as well."

"What's this? Kiram's injured his arm?" Elezar asked. He and Javier had just reached the edge of the cooking fire. Thin trails of smoke drifted from the dying embers. Elezar waved them away from his face. Javier simply stepped past. Even in the squalor of the half-abandoned Irabiim camp, an air of elegance seemed to surround Javier. Kiram tried to remind himself that this giddy enchantment was just an effect of the drug.

Javier offered Rafie and Alizadeh a cursory half bow and Elezar followed his example. Kiram found his gaze drifting back to Javier's lips and remembering the soft heat of them against his skin.

"Now what's happened to your arm, Kiram?" Elezar demanded. Kiram opened his mouth but didn't quite trust himself to reply.

"He was wounded the first day of the tournament fighting Ariz Plunado. You lost three crowns to me in the wager, remember?" Javier glanced at Kiram with a slightly worried expression.

"I remember losing the money," came Elezar's sulky response.

"My arm started to act up again this afternoon," Kiram explained.

"You should have mentioned it," Nestor chided him.

"I didn't want to be a bother."

"It's not a bother," Nestor said. "Except that we had no idea why you vanished so suddenly. I was worried that…something… had happened to you. So were Javier and Elezar."

"I'm feeling better already," Kiram said though he thought the words came out a little slurred. He straightened and addressed his uncle. "Do you think it would be all right if I went to look around the fairgrounds with my friends?"

Rafie nodded, his expression one of quiet concern.

Alizadeh turned his attention to Javier. "You are his guardian, Lord Tornesal, so I would ask you to please look after him. You must not leave him alone while he's in this state."

Javier stepped closer to Kiram. "Of course, I'll stay beside him."

"We had planned to lodge with the Irabiim this evening but obviously that will not be possible." Rafie waved his hand at the three remaining travel wagons of the dismantled Irabiim camp. "Kiram will need somewhere to spend the night."

"He is welcome at my home," Javier offered quickly. "As are the two of you. I would be honored if you would stay at the Tornesal townhouse with me."

"We would be delighted." Alizadeh's smile became predatory. Neither Javier nor the Grunito brothers seemed to notice.

"We would be glad to accept your hospitality later this evening," Rafie said. "For now, we still have some business to arrange with our friends here. We should be able to join you before the fifth bell."

"Very good," Javier replied. "Kiram and I will see you then."

Again Alizadeh gave a pleased nod.

"Take care," Rafie told Kiram. He placed a soft leather coin pouch in Kiram's hand. ***"Buy yourself something to eat. It will steady you."***

"I will." Kiram slipped the pouch into his pocket. *"Thank you."*

"No chance of Labara wine, I suppose?" Elezar asked once they were back on the fairgrounds.

"Not today," Javier replied. He caught Kiram's elbow and pulled him back from a fascinatingly large boar.

"I've seen him before," Kiram said.

"Yes, you're old friends, no doubt," Javier replied. "Duera goes straight to your head, doesn't it?"

Kiram would have disagreed but then a brilliantly plumed bird caught his attention. Javier laughed at him but Kiram was sure the bird gave him a knowing wink.

Most of the afternoon passed in a relative haze. Kiram ate several rolls stuffed with cabbage and pungent meat and he purchased an assortment of odd, glittering trinkets that struck him as wonderful gifts for his friends in Anacleto. At one point he suggested that Nestor could make a small fortune selling pictures of Javier to the gaggles of young women who were always eyeing him. Then he challenged Elezar to a game of ring toss and proceeded to throw his rings everywhere but onto the mounted bull's horns.

As the afternoon grew late, he and Javier returned to the Tornesal townhouse. When they were alone in Javier's bedroom, Kiram asked Javier to open the white hell so that he might read another passage from Calixto's diary. Javier laughed and reminded him of the price they had agreed to. Kiram pulled Javier close, kissing him deeply.

Javier embraced him tightly and Kiram was not sure if the rush of heat was the white hell or the surge of his own passion. Then the luminous depth of the white hell opened around him. From the center of his chest, just where the lotus talisman lay, an icy chill sparked and spread through him with a terrible, cold blackness. Kiram tried to grasp Javier, but he couldn't see him. He tried to call his name but nothing came out. Kiram's legs buckled. He fell but did not feel his body strike the ground.

Chapter Twenty-Four

He woke in Javier's bedroom, tucked beneath warm blankets. Golden firelight outlined Javier's silhouette, casting his features into shadow. Strands of black hair fell into his eyes and he flicked it aside.

"You need to get a haircut," Kiram remarked. His voice sounded strange and weak.

"Kiram?" Relief sounded through Javier's voice. "You're awake?"

"Yes." Something about the darkness of the surrounding shadows and the quiet made him suddenly think that it must be night. He remembered falling when Javier had opened the white hell but it had only been late afternoon then. "What happened?"

"You collapsed." Javier touched the edge of the bed and for a moment Kiram thought he might take his hand. Instead his fingers clenched around the corner of the comforter, crumpling it. "I couldn't wake you."

"The duera was probably too strong," Rafie said from across the room. Startled, Kiram rose up onto his elbows. He had been so focused on Javier that he hadn't noticed either his uncle or Alizadeh sitting before the fire only a few feet from the foot of the bed. Firelight glinted along the long spiraling curls of Alizadeh's hair. He gave Kiram a sly wink. Rafie's expression was more troubled. He rose from his chair and went to Kiram's side.

He touched Kiram's forehead lightly and then placed his warm strong fingers against Kiram's throat, checking his pulse.

"Do you have any pain?" Rafie asked.

"Not really." Kiram sat up. He felt oddly groggy. *"My arm hurts but not badly. I'm a little tired."*

"I think he could use a glass of bitter water. Do you have anything like that here?" Rafie asked of Javier.

"I'll have some brought up to him at once." Javier gazed down at Kiram for a moment and his concern seemed so obvious that Kiram had to drop his own gaze to the clean surface of his blankets. Javier turned away and left the room.

The moment the door closed behind him, Alizadeh bounded from his seat to Kiram's side. He caught hold of Kiram's lotus medallion and held it against his palm, where it glowed dully from between Alizadeh's fingers. As the medallion grew luminous, the dizzy sensation in Kiram's head faded; then at last Alizadeh laid the medallion gently against Kiram's chest. Then he stood silently with his eyes closed and his head bowed.

Seconds passed while Rafie nervously eyed the door. *"Young Lord Tornesal will be back soon."*

Alizadeh nodded and opened his eyes.

"Kiram was right. The shajdi has not been contaminated. It is changed, more linked to this physical realm, but its essence is pure. I should have been able to see all of this without harming you, Kiram, but I underestimated the defenses your duke has placed around himself." Alizadeh gestured to the vast expanse of symbols drawn across Javier's floor and inscribed into his ceiling. *"I'm sorry if I pained you."*

"It's all right. I needed the rest anyway."

Kiram was far too relieved by Alizadeh's assessment of the white hell to complain about the brief, terrible chill that had swept through him just before he had lost consciousness.

"He's very attentive, your duke," Alizadeh said.

"Too attentive," Rafie added. *"We couldn't get him to leave your side, until just now."*

Kiram couldn't help grinning at the rush of happiness he felt upon hearing this.

"I did tell him that you were entrusting Kiram's wellbeing into his care," Alizadeh commented to Rafie.

"Yes, but who thought he'd take you so seriously? He's what...eighteen? You'd think he'd be bored by staring at Kiram after a few hours."

"I don't think he would." Alizadeh still gazed at the symbols on the floor. "The more I find out about Lord Tornesal the more I'm inclined to agree with Kiram. We should do what we can to protect him."

"Really?" Hope made Kiram's voice rise almost childishly. "You'll break the curse that's been set against him?"

Alizadeh frowned. "I told you before, it isn't a curse. It's something else disguised as a curse."

"Wouldn't that make it easier to destroy than a real curse like the Old Rage?" Kiram asked.

Alizadeh just shook his head.

"I understand curses," Alizadeh said. "I know the very essence of them, but this is something very different. It moves like the Old Rage but it feels empty. If it has no pain or anger then I have no way to appease it or to bind it." Alizadeh scowled at the floor. "I've never encountered anything like it and I would be a fool, risking my life as well as your duke's if I attacked blindly."

"But you said—" Kiram began.

"I said that there might be a way to save your duke. And there may be." Alizadeh laid a hand on his shoulder. "I have to meet with the Circle of the Red Oak in Anacleto. If this shadow curse has been active for nearly eighteen years then someone may well have knowledge of it."

"If they don't?" Kiram asked.

"Then we'll have to depend on the information that you can gather here at the duke's side." Alizadeh shrugged. "It's the only way."

"He's just a boy," Rafie said with a pained frown. "And not even a Bahiim."

"The shajdi must not fall into the hands of the man on the hill." Alizadeh's expression was serious. "And to be honest I'm nearly as loathe to leave him here as you are, but he is the only one with access to the academy as well as the duke. He shouldn't be in any danger so long as the man on the hill remains focused upon the Tornesals." Alizadeh gave Rafie a reassuring smile. "And the duke certainly seems dedicated enough to Kiram's safety."

"I don't like this," Rafie replied.

"I know," Alizadeh said. "But it's vital that we keep someone close to the duke. And I don't believe we could hope to place anyone closer to him than Kiram is already."

"He's too young," Rafie insisted. Kiram wanted to argue that he was not, but held his tongue. Alizadeh already supported him, and no one else had as much experience or success convincing Rafie to change his mind.

"We don't have the luxury of being sentimental now, my love." Alizadeh caught Rafie's hand and lifted it to his lips, pressing a kiss into his palm. "You saw how Kiram fought on the tournament ground; he's plainly not a child anymore."

Rafie shook his head but offered no further argument.

Deep pride welled up in Kiram's chest. Not only was he being allowed to stay at the academy, Alizadeh was entrusting him with a mission.

"While you are at the academy you must wear the medallion I gave you at all times," Alizadeh told Kiram. "Once a week hold it over a candle flame until the lotus turns white. If something threatens you or your duke, I'll know and do what I can."

Kiram nodded but had no time to ask more of Alizadeh. Javier returned a moment later. A nervous servant followed him, carrying a tray of powdered bitters and a steaming apothecary pot which he deposited on the bedside table. With a bow that was more of a convulsion of fear, the servant then fled the room, careful to avoid stepping on the profane writing. Kiram thought he saw Alizadeh stifle a laugh at this performance. Javier didn't seem to notice any of it, his attention fully focused on Kiram.

As Rafie stirred the bitters into the pot, sharp, herbal scents rose on the steam.

Javier returned to his bedside chair but didn't sit. Instead he leaned over the back of the chair and watched while Kiram drank the steamed bitters. Kiram tried not to make a sour face as he gulped down the hot, astringent liquid.

"You should get a little more sleep," Rafie told Kiram.

"I can't," Kiram replied. "I have to check in with Master Ignacio—"

"You're nearly two bells too late for that," Javier said.

"What? He's going to kill me." Kiram almost choked on the bitters. "I've got to go."

"He's not going to kill you." For the first time since Kiram had woken Javier's usual tone of mocking amusement returned. "He told me to make sure you were well and rested for the tournament tomorrow."

"He's not angry?"

"I didn't say that, but he knew you were injured and after he saw you for himself he was satisfied that you weren't feigning illness."

"He came here to see me?" The image of the war master scowling down at his unconscious body sent a chill snaking down his spine.

"When neither of us reported he came storming in," Javier replied.

"Into this room?" Kiram couldn't imagine any Cadeleonian barging into Javier's bedroom, not when trained footmen practically pissed themselves just delivering a glorified teapot.

"Up to the threshold." Javier smirked. "He didn't come any further, but he didn't need to. As soon as he saw your uncle redressing your arm he told me not to bother waking you."

Kiram glanced down at his forearm and for the first time noticed that the bandages had been changed. Only a few spots of blood colored the white cloth. "It doesn't look that bad."

"It looked bad enough this afternoon." Javier crossed his arms over his chest. "You were white as clay and cold."

"I feel fine now."

"You boys are so resilient," Alizadeh, who had drifted back toward the fire, commented. "I envy your youth."

Kiram almost laughed at Alizadeh envying anyone's youth. The man hardly looked older than Javier in this flickering firelight.

"Finish your bitters," Rafie said.

Kiram obeyed his uncle, then slowly sank back into the bed. The warmth of the fire and the soft blankets engulfed him. Kiram closed his eyes, feeling both relaxed and satisfied. He'd convinced Alizadeh to take Javier's side. He would be staying at the academy. Relief welled through him like an opiate and he drifted.

"I know that these circumstances must seem terrible." Javier's voice was soft and seemed distant. Kiram thought he must have been talking to Rafie or Alizadeh. "But I assure you that Kiram is safe here. I give you my word that I will devote all my resources to his protection if you just allow him to remain at the Sagrada Academy."

Kiram opened his eyes. He couldn't see Javier's face but looking over his shoulder he glimpsed Rafie's serious expression. Sitting in a chair, Alizadeh bowed his head over a small talisman in his hand. He mouthed soft words but made no sound. He seemed unaware of the rest of them.

Kiram expected Rafie to inform Javier that he had already decided that Kiram would be staying.

Instead Rafie leaned back in his chair, steepling his fingers. "Why do you want him to stay so badly?"

"He..." Javier went quiet and when he did speak again his voice was so hushed that Kiram had to strain to hear him. "He's important to me."

Kiram watched as Rafie studied Javier in silence. Slowly, Rafie's harsh expression softened to sadness. "It won't be easy for either of you, you know."

"I'm not afraid of difficulty," Javier replied.

"Of course you're not." A brief scowl flickered across Rafie's face but then he sighed. "Alizadeh and I will be leaving first thing in the morning, but Kiram will remain here in your care."

Kiram saw the tension drop from Javier's shoulders. "Thank you, sir."

"Wait a year and see if you still want to thank me." Rafie frowned over Javier's shoulder to Kiram. "I may be doing you less of a favor than you think."

Chapter Twenty-five

The next morning Rafie and Alizadeh woke Kiram just after dawn. They remained only long enough to wish Kiram good luck and to admire the gold jupon that Kiram's mother had sent. Kiram slipped it over his clothes. It hung a little loosely, having been fitted to wear over thick leather armor. Still, Rafie looked admiring. ***"I'll tell her that you looked handsome in it."***

Alizadeh blessed Kiram's lotus medallion and warned him to beware of blue jays and befriend any crows he met. Despite the previous days of arguments, Kiram felt a pang of sadness when Rafie released him from a farewell embrace.

"Take care," Rafie told him.

"Travel safe," Kiram replied.

Javier had just wandered down stairs into the entry hall, still looking as if he were half-asleep. His black hair tangled around his face and his expression was soft.

Alizadeh waved to Javier and said, "We will meet again."

Javier simply nodded. Then Rafie and Alizadeh quietly slipped out the door leaving Javier and Kiram alone in the entryway.

"Hungry?" Javier asked.

Kiram nodded.

"Well, let's see what we can scare up." Javier started for the dining room. Kiram walked alongside him. "You feel up to today?" Javier asked.

The question worried Kiram slightly. The last day of the tournament was reserved for third year formal dueling, which meant full armor and squires, hence Kiram's new jupon. He would be out with Javier, carrying his weapons and helping him with his armor.

Kiram knew enough of Cadeleonian culture now to understand that it meant a great deal to stand beside another man in battle. He wanted to be the one beside Javier.

"I'll be fine," Kiram said and he was rewarded with a brilliant smile from Javier.

"We'll be unbeatable," Javier said.

Kiram grinned. He had no doubt of Javier's prowess and having won his uncle and Alizadeh over, Kiram's sense of his own abilities soared. That pride buoyed him through the morning.

Not even Master Ignacio's scowl could perturb him. He felt almost comfortable among his fellow schoolmates listening to the war master's stern lecture and smelling the horses all around them.

As they rode to the gold pavilion Kiram recaptured the sense of excitement that he'd felt the first day of the tournament. He smiled at the gathered crowds and bright banners. The warm sun shining over the clear blue sky seemed to reflect his happiness.

"You're not dosed with more duera, are you?" Nestor asked him.

Kiram laughed, which he knew did nothing to alter Nestor's impression.

"My uncle has gone home. He decided to let me stay at the academy," Kiram told him.

Nestor grinned like a mad man. "That's fabulous! You're staying! Javier must be thrilled."

"Why do you say that?" Kiram couldn't keep from stealing a glance ahead to where Javier rode beside Elezar. Gazing at his lean form the memory of the feel of Javier's skin beneath his hands and the taste of his skin rushed over him.

Nestor shot Kiram a puzzled look as if he was reassessing Kiram's intelligence. "He's terribly fond of you. Haven't you noticed?"

Kiram used the excuse of scratching Firaj's cheek to look away from Nestor. Was he and Javier's relationship really that obvious?

"He takes his responsibility seriously."

"Oh, now you're just being coy." Nestor pushed up his spectacles to itch the thin scratch that ran across the bridge of his nose. "Seriously, Kiram. He likes you. You're smart and different from most of the men at the academy. Elezar aside, Javier doesn't give a crap about most of them but he goes out of his way for you. He never would have spent so much time wandering around the fairgrounds with you half out of your brain otherwise. You're definitely his friend. I think he may be a little fond of me as well, you know, by association."

"I'm sure he is."

"Riossa says that only an ass wouldn't like me." His pale cheeks turned slightly pink. "But you know she's a bit biased."

"Nestor, you charmer." Kiram smiled at Nestor's flushed pride.

"She can draw horses pretty well." Nestor gave Kiram a sly look. "And she kisses really well."

"But the real question is, are you any good at kissing?" Kiram expected Nestor to be flustered by the question but instead he beamed.

"I'm marvelous!" Nestor sounded so exultant that Kiram laughed. Nestor laughed along with him.

At the pavilion grooms took the horses. Students from both the Yillar and Sagrada Academy gathered in the center of the pavilion. Friends, admirers, family members, and countless onlookers cheered and shouted at them from the surrounding stands. Flowers and ribbons fell in showers. Occasionally perfumed favors and love notes drifted down.

A yellow kerchief pelted Nestor's head. Both he and Kiram glanced up to see Riossa and her family sitting in the second tier of the stands. Nestor waved to her broadly and Riossa shyly returned his gesture. An older man standing just behind Riossa scowled at him, but Nestor seemed utterly oblivious to his presence.

Before Kiram could comment, Master Ignacio called them to order. The upperclassmen who had been eliminated from the dueling and their underclassmen were sent into the stands to join their families and cheer their classmates.

Kiram bid Nestor a quick farewell, as he and his upperclassman Atreau made for the crowded boxed seats in the third tier of the stands. The Yillar students, too, were divided and the majority sent to cheer and watch while he, Javier and the other combatants retreated to the lowest stands to dress. Grooms handed out bundles of leather armor to the underclassmen, while teams of housemen brought out the heavier metal armor that the upperclassmen would wear.

"Look here, Javier." Elezar held up his breastplate. A red enamel bull reared across its surface. "I just got it re-enameled so try not to scratch it up while you're clinging to it and begging for mercy!"

Javier hefted up his black enameled groin piece in response. "Just so you know what to kiss when you want me to stop beating your ass."

Kiram dressed in his own armor quickly. He winced as he laced a leather guard over his injured forearm. Then, presented with the sight of Javier's bare back, Kiram utterly forgot his discomfort. Kiram touched his shoulder, feeling the smooth warm skin.

Javier gave him a brief, winning smile and then handed Kiram his chest plate. Kiram expected the chill of the metal but not the sheer weight of it.

"Make sure the buckles are tight. It can't slip while I'm out there." Javier's fingers briefly brushed over Kiram's hand. Then he dropped his hand and picked up his leather doublet.

"Not to worry," Kiram told him. "I've had lots of practice getting girths good and tight. I could probably even warm your bit if you had one."

Javier pulled the doublet over his head and then turned to allow Kiram to lace up the leather guard that protected his throat.

After that, the successive layers of Javier's leather armor, chainmail, and enameled plate armor monopolized Kiram's attention.

While Kiram knelt, adjusting the fit of Javier's greaves to his long shins, Scholar Donamillo and Holy Father Habalan arrived with muerate poison. Javier casually held his left hand out to the plump holy father. Scholar Donamillo opened the glass vial of black poison as Holy Father Habalan dragged his silver blade across Javier's wrist. Kiram felt Javier's muscles tense when the blade sliced into his flesh but his expression remained unconcerned.

Kiram bowed his head to keep the holy father from seeing his contemptuous sneer. Even so he smelled the tang of the meurate and felt a shudder pass through Javier as it entered his bloodstream.

"Kiram." Scholar Donamillo handed Kiram a roll of clean bandage. "Bind the wound, but not too tightly."

"Yes, sir."

"Scholar Donamillo?" Javier's voice was low. "Do you know how Enevir Helio is this morning? I'd heard that his leg was broken."

Kiram reflexively glanced up into the stands where the Helio box stood, conspicuously empty.

"His leg is the worst of his injuries," Scholar Donamillo replied. "But he's a strong young man and I expect that he will recover to a great extent within the next few months. Shall I give him your regards?"

Javier shook his head. The Helios were not Hellions, and therefore did not merit much interest. "I was just curious."

"Yes. Well then. Good luck to both of you." Scholar Donamillo offered Kiram a smile. Kiram appreciated the words, but wished that they had not come with a dose of acrid black poison. He couldn't quite bring himself to thank the scholar. Javier, too, remained silent.

Holy Father Habalan and Scholar Donamillo departed as unobtrusively as they had arrived. Kiram wrapped Javier's wrist. His skin felt icy now. Javier's mouth was pale and he drew his breath with slow concentration.

Kiram laced Javier's leather gauntlet over the bandage, his own arm aching in sympathy. Then he helped work Javier's metal gauntlet up over both. Javier caught his hand briefly in a cold, steel grip. His expression was so drawn that Kiram feared he might collapse. Then Javier released his tight grip. He took up his helmet and pulled it on, hiding his face.

Kiram could hardly make out his dark eyes through the slits of his visor. He was a long expanse of steel and black enamel, like some strange union of mechanism and man.

Most of the other Sagrada students were already armored and standing ready. With the added bulk of enameled steel and chainmail Elezar's large body had transformed into an immense scarlet fortress. Unlike Javier, Elezar shifted, rolling his shoulders and moving his armor as if its weight meant nothing.

"Kiram, you better get your jupon on." Javier's low voice sounded almost hollow from within the armor.

"Sorry." Kiram quickly pulled the jupon over his head and smoothed the yellow silk out over his byrnie. The Tornesal black sun over his chest matched the one enameled across Javier's breastplate perfectly. He hefted up Javier's long sword and his shield the way the other underclassmen held their upperclassmen's weapons.

High in the stands, trumpeters blew out a sharp melody, announcing Prince Sevanyo. By the time the notes stilled, the entire pavilion had gone quiet. In the shaded comfort of his box seat, Sevanyo rose and raised a hand. The large jewels adorning his fingers flashed. "Chosen sons of Cadeleon's great academies, stand before me!"

Kiram followed Javier onto the fighting ground. He held his head up high and looked as proud and confident as he could, though, in truth he was concerned for Javier. Between the muerate and the weight of all this armor Kiram wasn't sure how well Javier would fare. His precise and unusually careful motions were exactly the same as when Kiram had discovered him lying, nearly poisoned to death, in the chapel garden.

In comparison, Elezar seemed comfortable and eager. And across the grounds, Hierro Fueres stood like a golden monument, his breastplate and helmet decorated with white swan motifs. Kiram recognized his squire's auburn hair and plain face. Ariz Plunado walked with the blank expression of a mannequin, though for a moment Kiram thought he might have caught the flicker of a scowl as the young man caught sight of him. Clearly he had not forgotten their duel.

Once they'd taken their places, Prince Sevanyo continued, "Though you gather today to test your strength against one another, never forget that you are sons of one nation and brothers in arms. Any man you stand against here today you may proudly stand beside tomorrow. Fight with honor and pride, blessed sons of Cadeleon."

With that the prince returned to his seat and the combatants were assigned their dueling rings. Javier's first opponent was a Yillar student whose squire kept peering at Kiram as if he'd never seen a Haldiim before. Javier only took his short sword, leaving both his long blade and his shield with Kiram.

"They're too heavy just now," Javier whispered when Kiram offered them.

Javier moved with none of his normal grace. His opponent scored several hard strikes against him and twice Javier barely managed to block fatal blows. This emboldened the Yillar student.

"How'd you even get this far, Rauma? Bribed your opponents?" The Yillar student laughed. His squire looked amused.

Kiram wanted to hurl Javier's shield at the man, but all he could do was watch the Yillar student jab a loose and lazy thrust for Javier's heart. Javier blocked the blow with a resounding crash of steel and then suddenly charged. Taken off guard, the Yillar student retreated but not quickly enough. Javier drove his blade up with such force that the Yillar student's visor snapped from its hinge. With a second fast strike Javier knocked the Yillar student to the ground and pounced on top of him. Javier held his blade just inches above the other man's exposed face. The Yillar student gaped at Javier, white faced with shock.

As the judge raised a blue flag signifying the first Sagrada victory, cheers and hoots rose from the stands. The Yillar student stalked from the ring and Kiram rushed past him to Javier's side. Javier lifted his visor. Sweat beaded his face but only a little color had returned to his cheeks.

"I'm fine," Javier said before Kiram could ask. "But it's a damn oven in this armor and the sun doesn't look like it's going to let up."

He was right. The sun had just risen to the open ceiling of the pavilion and was well below its zenith, but already temperatures were rising inside. In the lower stands, men and women fanned themselves and boys in red jackets hawked cups of cider.

"Get me some water before my next duel," Javier said.

Kiram wove through the circles of dueling students. Dust and wood shavings hung in the air, as did the pungent smell of sweat. Elezar's loud roar carried over even the noise of the crowd and the grunts and curses of other, closer combatants. Kiram looked over his shoulder just in time to see Elezar hurl his opponent from the dueling ring.

For a moment, Kiram was too stunned by the sight to do more than stare. He'd witnessed demonstrations of Elezar's strength during practice, but Kiram had never seen Elezar fighting with unrestrained force. His opponent lay on the ground like a broken toy. Even the judge seemed stunned as he raised the blue Sagrada flag.

Kiram prayed that Javier wouldn't have to fight Elezar next. He simply was not strong enough. He raced back to Javier's side with a skin of cool water. Javier drank a little but then his next opponent arrived. Again, Javier went without his shield and only wielded a short sword.

But where he had previously stood still, Javier now prowled. He circled his new opponent slowly and then lunged in with brilliant speed to score a strike before bounding back out of reach.

Light flared off the shining surface of his silver armor. Javier took a hit across his shoulder, but landed his own strike directly across the enamel emblem over his opponent's heart. The enamel shattered and the judge again raised the blue flag again.

Kiram distinctly recognized Fedeles' joyous crow rising over the cheers and boos from the stands. Javier shoved his visor back and Kiram hurried forward with the water skin. Javier drank, dropped the empty water skin back into Kiram's hands, and closed his eyes.

"Javier?" Kiram asked.

"I'm good." Javier remained exactly as he was, eyes closed, arms hanging so limply that Kiram thought he might drop his short sword. After a moment he opened his eyes. "Have you been watching any of the other duels?"

"A little, but mostly just yours."

"Take a look around for me." Javier's tone was stronger than it had been earlier. "Watch Elezar for any injuries. And if you can, keep an eye on Hierro Fueres too."

A third Yillar student trudged up to Javier's dueling ring and gave a salute, which Javier returned. The man's armor was enameled with golden leaves. Kiram made a mental note to learn more about Cadeleonian crests so that next year he could take an educated guess about the occupants of the armor.

"Can you carry your shield yet?" Kiram whispered.

"I can but I don't think I'm going to need it just yet." He flipped his visor closed and strode out to the center of the dueling ring. He tossed his short sword from hand to hand as his opponent chose his own sword and shield from his squire.

The judge signaled the start of the duel and immediately Javier attacked. His movements were smooth, and while they seemed a little slow to Kiram they obviously were too fast for Javier's opponent. Kiram felt assured enough of Javier's wellbeing to investigate how Elezar and Hierro were faring.

Elezar fought like a battering ram, crumpling shields and shattering blades with the power of his strikes. If he took any injuries he hardly noticed them. His only disadvantage seemed to be the sheer number of times his squire, Ollivar, had to rush to bring him a new blade after he cracked one against his opponent's defenses.

In the time that both Elezar and Javier fought a single duel, Hierro finished two. The first he won through a simple concession. A Yillar student entered Hierro's dueling ring, knelt, and allowed Hierro to take the win with a gentle tap of his blade.

Hierro's second duel was against a Sagrada student. Hierro moved lightly around the Sagrada student, never extending himself into a full attack. Instead, he landed blow after blow on the poorly protected joints of the Sagrada student's armor. His attacks were glancing but they quickly accumulated. Soon the Sagrada student staggered like a cripple, his knees and elbows having been beaten mercilessly. His long sword drooped in his grip.

Kiram found it agonizing to watch Hierro pick and nick the Sagrada student's defenses further. It was like watching a cat play with an injured bird. At last when the Sagrada student crumpled to his knees, unable to lift his sword much less his shield, Heirro delivered a single winning blow.

Javier seized his own victory a moment later and he moved now as if he were dancing, making the swift, triumphant thrust look as easy as a bow.

As soon as the judge declared his victory, Javier shoved his visor up from his face and grinned at Kiram. Kiram went to his side. He took Javier's sword and inspected his armor.

"When you're fighting Hierro you're going to have to guard your joints," Kiram told him. "And Elezar…He's really strong."

"Yes, I have noticed that from time to time." Javier laughed.

"He picked up a man in full armor and threw him out of the dueling ring."

Javier raised his brows and glanced across the dueling rings to Elezar. "Who knew he was such a grandstander? But even he has to tire out sooner of later. Anything else you can tell me about Hierro?"

"He's very precise and doesn't extend himself for a killing strike until he's worn his opponent down. His defense looked really tight. The other Yillar students are conceding to him, of course, so he's probably nowhere near as tired as most of the Sagrada students."

"The usual Yillar strategy." Javier flipped his visor back down and took his long sword from Kiram. "Keep watching them."

A new opponent entered Javier's ring and Kiram hurried out. The next two fights went quickly. Lower ranking students were eliminated and withdrew to the stands, leaving many of the dueling rings empty. Soon, only four undefeated men remained: Hierro and another Yillar student, Elezar and Javier.

Master Ignacio and the Yillar war master called for a parley and met with two judges. Kiram saw them write names onto slips of paper and then hand them over to the judges. A moment later one of the judges approached Javier and bid him to choose from the three pieces of folded paper in his hand. Javier took one, unfolded it, and grimaced.

He read the name aloud. "Elezar Grunito."

Kiram's heart sank. Elezar scowled but both Hierro and his fellow Yillar student grinned at each other. Elezar and his squire, Ollivar, walked to Javier's dueling circle.

"Long sword and shield." Javier's left arm trembled slightly as he accepted the heavy shield. Kiram tried not to think of the wound running along Javier's wrist.

Elezar chose his long sword, which he held in his right hand, and his short blade, wielded by his left. He regarded Javier evenly, then asked, "Sure you're up to this?"

Despite his joking tone, serious worry showed in his expression. He had to know that Javier had been given muerate poison.

Javier arched a brow. "Well, I might suffer a little guilt after I beat your ass into the ground but I think I'll be able to deal with it."

"All right then, Tornesal. No mercy." Elezar closed his visor. Javier followed suit.

The judge gave his signal and they charged each other. Elezar's blade smashed into Javier's shield, embedding into the black sun and driving Javier back several feet. Javier released his shield, letting its weight pull Elezar's long sword down. He lunged forward, aiming a blow at Elezar's chest. Elezar blocked with his short sword and then swung his long sword, with Javier's shield still dangling from it, into Javier's side. The blow sent Javier stumbling and threw Javier's shield out across the grounds. Kiram sprinted out to retrieve it. A roar went up from the crowd.

While Elezar and Javier circled and pounded each other with deafening blows, Hierro and his fellow Yillar student flipped a coin. Hierro remained in his dueling circle. The other Yillar student bowed to him graciously and stepped out of it.

"Shield!" Javier shouted and Kiram sprinted into the dueling ring. He thrust the shield up and Javier raised it just in time to block another of Elezar's resounding blows. Splinters of the shield and Elezar's blade flashed as they flew through the air and fell to the dirt floor.

This close Kiram could smell both sweat and blood emanating from beneath Javier's armor.

"Out of the ring!" Javier commanded. Kiram darted away.

A moment later, Elezar hammered his long sword through Javier's shield, cracking his blade apart as he rended the shield in two. Elezar hurled the broken long sword at Javier and then thrust at him with his short blade. Javier dodged the long sword but barely blocked the thrust of Elezar's shortsword. Sparks skipped across the both Javier's and Elezar's blades as the edges ripped into each other. Kiram and Ollivar raced back to the stands to secure other shields and swords.

Elezar broke blades and cracked shields, but he rarely landed a direct blow to Javier's head or chest. In his own way Javier fought as relentlessly as Elezar. He drove in again and again, enduring the savage blows, to land swift strikes. He moved fast and struck from behind when he could. They crashed together and when their blades broke, they pounded each other with their armored fists.

Kiram watched with growing horror as the duel dragged on. Dirt and blood streaked their armor. Javier's left arm hung in a disturbingly lifeless manner. Elezar limped noticeably. And yet neither of them relented.

Hierro and the other Yillar student both looked bored. Their squires brought them water and little bowls of cut fruit. Some people in the stands roared and cheered but many simply stared in silent awe as Javier and Elezar steadily ground each other to exhaustion.

When the end came it was clumsy and brutal. Elezar punched his blade through the left shoulder of Javier's armor. Javier caught the blade and jerked Elezar forward onto his own cracked short sword. Blood poured from Javier's shoulder, but his blade drove into Elezar's breastplate, shattering the enamel bull there.

"Tornesal!" the judge shouted.

Elezar released his blade at once and stumbled back. Javier fell to his knees, curling his hands around his bloody shoulder.

Kiram rushed into the ring and knelt beside him. He reached out to free Javier from his armor but Javier pulled back from him.

"I'll be fine," Javier said even before Kiram could ask. "It's just a scratch."

"Let me help you back to the stands. Scholar Donamillo should—"

"It's fine!" Javier growled.

"Javier?" Elezar's voice was tremulous, almost frightened. He knelt down beside Kiram.

"What?" Javier snapped his visor open with his right hand. Annoyance more than pain showed on his face.

"I didn't mean to—" Elezar broke off. "I was sure you'd dodge."

"I know. That's why I won, you idiot." Javier rolled his eyes. "For God's sake pull yourselves together, both of you. We still have to beat those smug Yillar bastards."

"Right." Elezar straightened slowly. "We'll take them down."

Javier pushed himself up to his feet and Kiram moved to his side, steadying him.

"I'm fine," Javier said.

"So you've said," Kiram replied. "And I still don't believe you."

Javier winced and pulled his head back slightly.

"You see," Kiram said. "You're hurt."

"No, I'm not," Javier replied. "It was just your medallion. It was flashing right into my eyes."

"Sorry." Kiram caught his lotus medallion. As he tucked it into his collar, bright afternoon sunlight reflected off its golden surface and briefly flashed across the dirt.

"Is there anything you need?" Kiram asked.

"Another long sword but not a heavy one. Ask Master Ignacio for a cielyo. Hurry."

Kiram went and procured the sword, though Master Ignacio gave him an odd look when he asked for it and questioned the wisdom of Javier's decision more than once before handing the thing over.

The ceilyo's hilt and pommel were small, delicate and engraved with a curling ivy motif. It weighed less than even a short sword and just carrying it back across the grounds Kiram felt the thin blade flex and bounce with his steps. Elezar would have snapped such a sword in half. But Hierro fought in a much more restrained manner. And looking at Javier, Kiram knew he was too exhausted to wield the weight of a normal long sword. At the same time a short sword wouldn't offer the range Javier needed to fight a man with Hierro's reach and speed.

"Cielyo blade." Kiram handed it to Javier. "Master Ignacio told me to tell you that it's the only one he brought and you're a fool if you think it will hold up for long against a real sword."

"Did he?" Javier didn't sound surprised. "I suppose he expects me to be dancing around with a broadsword after that match with Elezar."

"If he does then he's an ass." Kiram hated how much Master Ignacio's opinion seemed to matter to Javier.

"Refreshingly honest as always, Kiram."

"Well, he is," Kiram replied but he didn't go on.

Hierro strolled into Javier's dueling ring with his squire, Ariz, following silently behind. When Hierro held out his hand Ariz provided him with a long sword. Hierro waved aside the proffered shield.

"You know, Tornesal," Hierro called to Javier, "there is no shame in accepting second place."

"Of course there isn't, cousin," Javier replied. "If you wish to forfeit to me, I would accept your surrender with the utmost respect."

Hierro smirked at the response and shook his head.

"Some men can't be saved from themselves," Hierro commented.

"No, indeed not," Javier agreed then he turned to Kiram and spoke quietly. "If I call for my shield, I'll need it and my short sword right away."

Kiram nodded, then he and Ariz withdrew from the dueling ring. Across the grounds, Elezar and his Yillar opponent began their duel with a resounding crash of metal. Javier and Hierro, on the other hand, circled each other in silence. Suddenly Javier lunged forward, thrusting in for Hierro's stomach. Hierro blocked the blow. Javier's cielyo blade bowed back and Javier suddenly flicked the blade up, making it strike Hierro's extended arm like a whip.

Hierro jerked back as blood spilled from his slashed palm and wrist. Javier drove after him and for an instant Kiram though he might win the duel in this one attack. Then Hierro took his blade in his left hand and deftly drove Javier back. This time, when Javier flicked the cielyo's flexible blade, Hierro parried before it could touch him. He blocked four of Javier's attacks and then scored two hard blows of his own. The cielyo did little to slow Hierro's heavier sword and Javier was forced to bound back to the edge of the dueling ring to keep Hierro from scoring a deadly blow against him.

Kiram felt a terrible dread, realizing that Hierro was not only better rested than Javier but he was also a master swordsman and apparently ambidextrous. He assailed Javier as precisely as he had his previous opponents, raining blows down against Javier's elbows, shoulders, and knees. All with his left hand. Blood poured from Javier's left shoulder.

"Shield!" Javier bellowed.

Kiram leapt forward and then suddenly something caught his foot. Out of the corner of his eye he saw Ariz, and then he fell. Javier's shield and short sword skidded across the ground. Kiram lifted his face from the dirt to see Javier collapse to his knees. Hierro arched over him, sunlight flashed across the edge of his blade.

Kiram gripped his lotus medallion and turned it to catch the bright light, reflecting it at Hierro's face. He flinched as the light flashed in his eyes and Javier drove his sword into the swan emblazoned over Hierro's heart.

"Tornesal!" the judge shouted. For an instant Hierro seemed too stunned to move. Then he simply bowed his head to Javier and stepped back from him.

In the stands the crowd leapt to its feet with a mighty roar and the prince's trumpets sounded loud triumphant notes.

Kiram scrambled to his feet and went to Javier. As he helped Javier get out of his helmet and onto his feet Javier leaned into him, whispering, "You have to be the sneakiest, most brilliant young man it has ever been my pleasure to know."

Kiram felt as if his chest would burst with pride at Javier's words.

"You're welcome," Kiram replied.

Chapter Twenty-Six

Javier's left arm hung in a sling and dark bruises colored both his hands. Yet he beamed as he knelt before Prince Sevanyo and accepted the gold cloak and circlet of a Grand Champion. Hierro received a silver circlet as did Elezar, both of them winning the title Honorable Champion. The three of them stood and Prince Sevanyo bade the crowd to recognize the brave sons of Cadeleon, the defenders of the kingdom.

Though the throngs of people gathered in the stands were of far different classes, from common laborers and servants, to merchants and nobles, they all cheered raucously. A deafening roar burst across the stands and didn't fade. From his vantage point in the Grunito box, Kiram could see the slightest discomfort in Javier's stance. He was used to being respected and certainly feared, but this kind of broad admiration was not common for him. Kiram shouted his name as loudly as he could. Beside him, Nestor grinned and clapped like a madman.

At last Prince Sevanyo raised his gloved hands and the crowds in the gold pavilion quieted. Javier, Elezar, and Hierro returned to their seats in the stands and the prince spoke briefly on the subject of valor. Javier crumpled down into the seat next to Kiram. Elezar dropped down on the other side of Javier. Both fighters looked exhausted and pleased with themselves. When the prince led the crowd in a prayer, neither Elezar nor Javier opened their eyes, just mouthed the words as if saying them in their sleep.

Kiram bowed his head in respectful silence. He felt Javier's fingers brush against his hand, tracing the sensitive curves of his fingers. The prayer ended and Javier withdrew his touch.

"You're feeling better?" Kiram asked him.

"Good as new." Javier gave him a crooked smile. Kiram was in no way fooled, but the faint white flashes that flickered through Javier's bandages assured him that Javier would soon recover.

"I'm all right too. Thanks for asking." Elezar slowly flexed his bandaged knee and scowled.

"Shouldn't Ollivar be attending you?" Kiram hadn't seen Ollivar since all four of them had dragged themselves to Scholar Donamillo to have their respective sprains, cuts, and bruises treated.

"Scholar Donamillo kept him. He got a nasty bump when that last Yillar bastard flew out the dueling ring and landed right on top of him," Elezar replied with a pleased smile.

"You could have aimed him a little better, don't you think?" Javier asked.

Elezar shrugged. "Too much blood in my eyes. Anyway, Ollivar will be fine. He might miss out on the evening's festivities, but he'll live."

"He might not want to when he finds out he missed his chance to dance with the prettiest girls in the city." Nestor stole a quick glance across the stands to Riossa. "You're coming to my mother's party, aren't you, Javier?"

"I'll be there, despite the pretty girls and their glowering mothers," Javier replied. "I'm bringing Kiram to use as a human shield, in fact."

Elezar snorted and Nestor frowned. Kiram just rolled his eyes.

"Some Grand Champion, hiding behind a scrawny Haldiim from a bunch of girls." Kiram was cut off when Master Ignacio chose that moment to call all of the Sagrada students out onto the grounds. They and their Yillar adversaries marched past each other, briefly grasping hands in ceremonial friendship as they crossed the grounds and left the gold pavilion to a theatre troupe.

Master Ignacio informed them that he expected to see them all back at the school in time for afternoon chapel tomorrow and warned them not to sully honor won in battle with poor behavior off the field. Then, to Kiram's surprise, Master Ignacio dismissed them to enjoy the rest of the day as they pleased.

For Javier, that meant an afternoon nap. Kiram joined him, dozing on the bed fully dressed. As they slept their bodies sought each other. When a servant's knock at the door roused them, they woke with their arms entangled and their faces bowed together. Kiram jerked back guiltily and almost fell off the bed.

"I locked the door, though God knows no one would come in even if it weren't locked." Then he raised his voice and shouted towards the dark wood door, "What is it?"

"You instructed that you should be woken before fifth bell, my lord." The servant called politely through the closed door.

Javier rose and opened the door. "Have water heated. My underclassman and I will both require baths. Oh, and Kiram will need some other clothes to wear to Lady Grunito's celebration. See what you can find of mine that might fit him."

"As you wish, my lord." The servant spoke without lifting his gaze to Javier's face and bowed deeply before departing to prepare the baths.

"I do have clothes of my own, you know," Kiram said.

"Yes, but I'd rather to see you in my colors than the academy's." Javier sauntered back to the bed and dropped down beside him. "Though if I had my choice I'd prefer you naked."

"Lady Grunito would find that delightful as well, I'm sure," Kiram replied.

"Lady Grunito isn't here right now." Javier began to unbutton the front of Kiram's shirt, but Kiram caught his hands. It was the middle of the afternoon and he could hear servants in the nearby rooms.

Javier gazed at him, with both expectation and uncertainty. His hands relaxed in Kiram's grip. That small submission touched Kiram and he leaned into Javier, kissing his mouth. Javier responded immediately, pushing into the kiss and pinning Kiram back against the blankets. The weight of his body felt good. Kiram was intensely aware of where Javier's hip pressed against his groin. He pulled Javier closer into that contact. Javier gasped, and Kiram could feel his body tensing.

Another knock at the door broke them apart.

"What?" Javier growled.

"The baths are ready, my lord." It was the same servant. "And cook was wondering if you will be dining here this evening."

"Yes." Javier shoved his hair back from his face and went to the door as Kiram quickly re-buttoned his shirt. Javier wrenched the door open. The servant bowed before him. "Tell cook that Kiram and I will have a very quick dinner here. We'll be leaving just after sixth bell so nothing elaborate."

"Will you want the Veloz carriage, my lord?"

"I doubt we'll need anything larger this evening."

"Very good, my lord." Again the servant bowed.

To their mutual disappointment, the staff had prepared a separate bath for Kiram in the green room. Kiram cleaned his injured right arm gingerly and when one of the servants noticed the wound he fetched fresh bandages. Kiram thanked him but felt a little awkward saying much more while he was standing naked in front of a virtual stranger. The servants in the Tornesal townhouse were much more formal than the intimate staff of his mother's house in Anacleto. Kiram found their constant bowing and lack of eye contact disconcerting.

While Kiram washed, a different middle-aged servant, Javier's valet if Kiram remembered correctly, laid out clothes and fussed with stockings. When Kiram asked for shaving soap and a razor the valet sent yet another servant to supply them. Kiram rinsed fragrant soap from his hair. Wet, his long curls hung down well past his shoulders. If it got any longer he'd look like he'd become a Bahiim.

"Would you happen to know where I could get a pair a scissors to trim my hair?" Kiram asked.

"Of course."

The servant didn't hand the scissors over but instead instructed Kiram to lean his head back and he trimmed Kiram's hair himself. Spiraling, gold locks littered the floor like wet ribbons. Kiram rinsed himself in the warm water one last time and then dried and dressed in Javier's spare clothes.

Feeling the dark silk fall against his skin, he couldn't help but think of Javier's body and how it had filled this cloth. As his fingers brushed over the delicate mother-of-pearl buttons, Kiram imagined how quickly he could have opened these pants and exposed Javier's hard flesh. A single glance at the scowling valet's face deadened Kiram's arousal. He buckled his belt quickly. He and Javier would have the entire evening after Lady Grunito's celebration to spend together. He should be patient and keep his mind on other matters for now.

Javier met him on the stairs. Seeing Javier shaved, clean and dressed immaculately, Kiram had to suppress the urge to tousle his glossy black hair or rumple his perfectly fitted clothes. He'd grown so used to seeing Javier tired and dirty that he'd forgotten what a refined image he could present; how he could look every bit a duke.

"You're staring," Javier commented and he sounded pleased.

A week ago Kiram would have made some excuse for his hungry gaze but today he simply said, "You're good to look at."

At first Javier seemed honestly surprised by the admission and then of course an expression of supreme arrogance settled on his handsome face. Kiram accepted it with amusement. The expression suited him, really.

They ate quickly. Afterward, in the carriage, Kiram chewed a sprig of lemonleaf to freshen his breath after the pork cutlet and roast apples. He tried not to feel nervous. After all he had dueled before hundreds of Cadeleonians only a few days before and today he had been in plain sight as Javier's squire. Still, watching a Haldiim on the tournament grounds—even cheering for him—would not be the same as socializing with him. How many of Lady Grunito's Cadeleonian guests would be willing to talk with him?

And if they did, what would he talk about? He could go on for hours about mechanisms but no one considered relentless lecturing a winning attribute in a conversationalist. And what if his breath stank of pig and onion? Kiram jammed more lemonleaf into his mouth.

The carriage stopped and he felt the blood drain from his face. Javier leaned forward quickly and kissed him lightly on the lips. "You'll be fine."

A moment later a footman dressed in Grunito red opened the carriage door and escorted the two of them into the vast Grunito townhouse. Red marble and gold inlay dominated the interior. Golden candlelight blazed from glittering candelabras, high above them.

Kiram heard the other guests before he saw any of them. Their conversation and laughter poured over strains of Cadeleonian dance music. From the threshold of the ballroom Kiram gazed down the marble steps and took in the brilliant silk dresses of young Cadeleonian women and the elaborately embroidered coats worn by the men. Their elegant forms reflected across mirrored walls, making the hundred guests appear to be a multitude. Far across the ballroom Kiram thought he caught a glimpse of arched glass doors and a flower garden outside.

When the dance came to an end, a servant announced Javier, calling out, "His Lordship Javier Tornesal, the Duke of Rauma, and… " he seemed at a loss when he glanced to Kiram but then added, "and companion."

"Kiram!" Nestor waved from far across the room. It took Kiram a moment to recognize Nestor with his hair powdered black and wearing an elaborate, red velvet coat. He looked surprisingly handsome. Kiram shyly returned Nestor's gesture. It felt like everyone in the entire ballroom had stopped to stare at him.

Javier and he descended the stairs and crossed the ballroom. They both bowed to Lady Grunito who smiled down at them like a benevolent monument.

Neither the soft gold silk of her gown nor the red ribbons braided through her hair did anything to undermine her imposing figure and with her hair blackened and the gold dust powdered across her skin, she truly did look like a cathedral statue come to life. She thanked both Javier and Kiram for attending and made Javier promise to dance with her once before the evening ended.

All around people peered at Kiram. Through the music and rolling conversation he heard soft whispers.

Tornesal's squire. The Sagrada Haldiim. Heathen.

When they reached Nestor, Kiram felt a wave of relief. Elezar and Atreau were with him as was Morisio. He was back among the Hellions and, oddly, that now comforted him.

They too were dressed formally in brocaded suits and ornately embroidered stockings, though Elezar had failed to powder his brown hair, and like Javier, Atreau had no need of powder. Morissio's freckles were hidden beneath the glow of gold dust and a heavy sapphire ring glittered on his right hand.

"That's new," Javier commented.

"Won it off Lord Urvano," Morisio replied with a pleased smile. "The card room is through that little door, just past the musicians." He looked eager to return to the games.

"Fabulous. Now Kiram and Morisio can both count my cards," Elezar muttered.

Rather than adjourning to the card room, Javier scanned the assembled guests. Couples swirled across the center of the ballroom. Clusters of young girls gathered around older women and matrons, while men of all ages periodically ventured into their midst to banter and seek dance partners. "Has Fedeles arrived?"

"You think his father will allow that?" Elezar asked.

"Lord Quemanor left directly after I won the championship," Javier replied. "I told Genimo to bring Fedeles here."

"They haven't arrived yet but the night is—" Elezar cut himself off short as Genimo, two young women in violet gowns, and Fedeles appeared on the stairs. Fedeles was dressed as elegantly as any of the lords. Yellow vines climbed the deep green silk of his coat, while green vines curled across his golden vest and stockings—but there was nothing formal about his bearing. He danced from foot to foot beside Genimo.

When he caught sight of Javier and Kiram, he bounded down the stairs unannounced and plowed through the dancing couples like some child who knew no better.

"Well, Javier, ask and you shall receive," Elezar said. He shook his head at the disruption, but his expression was more amused than embarrassed. Atreau put a hand over his face as if he couldn't bear to witness such poor form. Nestor and Morisio gawked and Kiram imagined his own expression was much the same. Only Javier appeared utterly unfazed by Fedeles' behavior.

"Lunaluz the champion!" Fedeles threw his arms around Javier and hugged him fiercely. Javier returned the embrace gently. All around people openly gaped at the scene. Even the musicians seemed to lose their concentration and for a moment the ballroom was nearly silent.

"Announcing His Lordship Fedeles Quemanor," the red-faced servant on the stairs called out. "Lord Genimo Plunado, Lady Aranya Plunado and Lady Nisa Plunado."

Genimo led the two women, probably his sisters, down into the ballroom and introduced them to Lady Grunito, who pointedly ignored Fedeles' antics. Others followed Lady Grunito's example and in a few moments both the music and dancing resumed.

Fedeles turned his affection on Kiram, pulling him into a fierce and wiggly hug. "Kiri, Kiri. I saw you shining like a star on the battlefield."

"I heard you cheering in the stands."

"Dancing, dancing. Come dancing with me." Fedeles sang the words, still gripping Kiram's hand as he grinned and skipped in place. When he started to drag Kiram towards the dancing couples, Javier interceded.

"You know you can't dance with Kiram, Fedeles. Let go of his hands."

Fedeles stuck his tongue out at Javier, but conceded.

"I'll fetch a girl for you," Javier said.

"Linya Bayezar." Elezar indicated a plain-faced girl in a blue and white striped gown. "Her father is up to his eyes in gambling debts. He'll turn her over to the first rich man who asks according to Lord Urvano."

Javier studied the girl the way he studied an opponent before a duel. Kiram felt a sudden sympathy for her. He would never have wanted to have Javier turn that assessing glower on him. Luckily, the girl remained unaware that she had fallen under such harsh scrutiny. She and two older women laughed together.

"Why don't you let me ask her?" Atreau suddenly offered. "She looks kind, and I'm sure if it was put to her nicely she'd allow Fedeles to dance with her without being bullied."

Javier raised a brow. "Put it to her nicely, then."

"Always." Atreau led Fedeles across the room and after a few minutes of conversation with the older women and Linya, Atreau seemed to win the girl over. She allowed Fedeles to lead her out onto the dance floor when a new tune began. Remarkably, Fedeles danced beautifully, though his gaze seemed far away from his partner.

Atreau led one of the older women out to dance. He smiled at her, said something, and she blushed and beamed as if she were a young maiden.

"Wish I knew what he said," Nestor commented.

"I love prunes," Elezar suggested.

Kiram laughed despite himself.

Genimo soon joined them and introduced his sisters. Morisio escorted the older of the two girls out to the dance floor while Elezar took the younger. Genimo glanced only briefly to Kiram and then excused himself to dance with a plump young lady. The music swelled and the couples in brilliant colors swirled past.

Several lords approached Javier, complimenting him on his success at the tournament and then inquiring about his lands. One wondered how he planned to handle the new church tithes and another asked if the dry spring had affected his crops.

Javier responded with an air of easy, yet somewhat bored, assurance. His tithes would be paid as they always were, from his own coffers. He had no need to increase his rents on the church's behalf. The drought had not been long in Rauma and the harvests were plentiful. He smiled and made polite inquiries of his older peers. Throughout, Kiram couldn't help but note how the conversations always went dead whenever a man mentioned that his niece or daughter would like to meet Javier.

In response to one man who seemed particularly intent, Javier turned to Kiram and Nestor and asked, "Don't you think Ariz Plunado stands a good chance of winning a master's circlet in the next two years?"

"Genimo's cousin?" Nestor's confusion at Javier's sudden change of subject showed in his tone.

"He's really fast." Kiram picked up the thread. "And he's hard to predict."

"Quite," Javier agreed. "Though you did manage to out maneuver him."

At last the older man withdrew.

As a rule the lords who spoke with Javier extricated themselves soon after Kiram joined the conversation, though he didn't know if this was because he was Haldiim or if that's when it became obvious that Javier would not be drawn into meeting their marriageable female relations.

Elezar returned from dancing, but Atreau, Morisio and, surprisingly, Fedeles continued to claim partners from among the noblewomen. Pretty young girls with glittering golden complexions clung to Atreau. Morisio claimed shy young women who seemed delighted with his unexpected attention. Fedeles mostly inspired a motherly affection from middle-aged matrons, who nearly always accepted his outstretched hand. The music rolled on and couples laughed and danced past as Kiram looked on with envy.

He loved to dance, and if this had been a Haldiim gathering he would have been one of the first men out on the dance floor and one of the last to leave. But Haldiim festivities were very different from those of Cadeleonians. Haldiim music was generally much faster and the dancing rarely involved intimate couples. Haldiim dances drew entire families together to form rings or lines, while the music quickened and steps increased in speed.

The Cadeleonian festivities and the dancing in particular seemed to center on couples. Marriageable couples, Kiram suspected. As such, no woman in her right mind would want to dance with him, and he didn't know the steps in any case. Still, it looked fun.

A sunken old gentleman scowled heavily at Kiram as, once again, Javier ignored the mention of a lovely, young granddaughter and asked Kiram if he'd ever been to the Ammej Bridge in the Haldiim district of Anacleto.

"Many times," Kiram replied. Javier had really been serious when he claimed he'd brought him along to be his human shield, he realized. "It's only a few blocks from my family house. I can't imagine any Haldiim in Anacleto who hasn't used the bridge. It's huge. Have you ever been?"

"No, I've only visited Anacleto once and I was quite young. My mother couldn't abide the Haldiim section of the city. I've read about the bridge though and I've always wanted to see it."

"I crossed it once," Nestor said. "Elezar and me both, when we went shopping for sweets for our father." He turned to Kiram. "That would have been at your mother's shop, you know. I wonder if we could have seen each other, then. It would have been four—"

"Five years ago," Elezar corrected.

The old man took his leave with a stiff bow to Javier.

"Should you really have been so obvious about snubbing him?" Kiram inquired.

"Should he have been so obvious in his attempts to insinuate his knock-kneed granddaughter into my bed?" Javier countered and Kiram could see that he was both bored and annoyed.

Before Kiram could respond Nestor gripped his arm. "Look! She's here!"

Riossa Arevillo stood at the top of the stairs, looking small and pale beside the ornately dressed servant. Even across the ballroom Kiram could see that her skin was not powdered; nor was her hair. Her gown was simple and compared to the rich silks and brocades worn by the other women in the room, it looked like it belonged to a peasant. Most surprising was the absence of any escort. She stood on the stairs all alone with her small spectacles clenched in her hand.

Elezar and Javier exchanged a pained look.

"Mother will eat her alive," Elezar told Nestor flatly.

"She won't," Nestor replied. "I'll protect Riossa."

In response, Elezar gave a derisive snort.

"I'll do what I can to distract Lady Grunito," Javier offered. "But what were you thinking, Nestor? And why is she alone?"

"I don't know. Her sister was supposed to bring her." Concern finally registered on Nestor's face.

As the music quieted the servant on the stairs read from a card and announced, "Miss Riossa Arevillo, daughter of His Honor Judge Arevillo."

Lady Grunito's head came up like a hunting hound's. Javier strode across the room, intercepting her before she could reach Riossa while Nestor hurried to lead the girl onto the dance floor as the music once again filled the room. Lady Grunito danced with Javier, though her eyes remained fixed on Nestor and Riossa.

"This could get ugly," Elezar remarked.

"Is it really so bad that she came?" Kiram couldn't quite see why it should be. Riossa was obviously not as wealthy or titled as the other women attending the dance, but she hadn't come uninvited. Her situation reminded Kiram of his own.

Elezar gave Kiram a stern look. "An unwed girl, and she comes, alone, to see Nestor? Either she's an idiot or she's one hell of a conniving little bitch. What if her father demands her reputation and his name be honored?" Elezar scowled at Riossa with the same cold contempt that Lady Grunito shot at the girl. "Nestor's done for."

"What do you mean?" Suddenly icy dread flooded Kiram. "Will her father challenge Nestor to a duel?"

"What? Not likely," Elezar responded. "He'll demand that Nestor marry his daughter."

"Marry?" Kiram repeated, feeling stupid and yet unable to get past the idea. Nestor had only met Riossa this week. How could anyone expect them to wed?

Javier managed to delay Lady Grunito for the entire dance but once it ended she caught the young couple. Riossa looked frightened but Nestor seemed defiant. Kiram expected an argument like the ones he'd often heard ringing throughout his own house when his mother and sister clashed.

Instead, Lady Grunito spoke so softly that the words didn't carry over the music. Nestor's expression weakened as his mother continued to speak. Worry crept into his countenance. He and Riossa both bowed their heads to Lady Grunito and withdrew to a side room, still holding hands. Two of Lady Grunito's maids followed them like prison guards. Guests murmured among themselves. Some laughed, others shared scandalized glances, but couples still took to the floor to dance. As music washed over the hushed speculations, Javier returned to Kiram and Elezar.

"Your mother will do what she can. She's sending for the girl's father. Hopefully, he'll see that no harm has been done to his daughter but who knows? Even being a third son, Nestor's a good catch for a judge's daughter."

"Damn it," Elezar growled. "She came alone on purpose, didn't she?"

"Nestor can always refuse to have her. If it comes to a duel, I'd be happy to stand for him." Javier smiled in that cruel manner that seemed to cheer Elezar though Kiram found it a little disturbing.

"You and me both," Elezar agreed.

"Riossa didn't strike me as the scheming sort," Kiram argued. "She certainly had plenty of other, far better opportunities to be alone with Nestor if she'd been looking for them."

"Possibly," Javier allowed, but he seemed hesitant to give Riossa the benefit of the doubt. "Either way, we aren't likely to know anything more until we see Nestor tomorrow at chapel. And I'm getting bored watching all this prancing."

Elezar grinned. "Master Ignacio is in the card room. He said we ought to come see him when we tire of the ballroom's amusements."

Javier didn't respond directly, instead he just gave a nod. Elezar raised his right hand and flashed two fingers in the sign of the Hellions. Atreau, Morisio, and Genimo left their partners and came to Javier's side.

"Get Fedeles," Javier said told Genimo. Fedeles looked put out to be called from the dance floor but as he caught sight of Javier he grinned.

"Lunaluz," Fedeles murmured to Javier. Then he once again caught Kiram's hand in his own, whispering, "Be brave."

"Fedeles." Javier waved a hand to catch his cousin's attention. "Do you want to stay at the dance or do you want to come out with us and Master Ignacio?"

"Dancing." Fedeles rolled his eyes as if the answer was obvious. He pulled Kiram close. "We will dance all night."

"Don't embarrass Kiram," Javier said firmly. He glanced to Genimo. "Staying with your sisters?"

"I'm their chaperone," Genimo replied.

"Make sure Fedeles and Kiram both get back to my house." Javier gave the sweeping instruction easily.

"I'm to stay here? And what, watch everyone dance? I'd rather—"

"He's right, Javier," Atreau interrupted. "There's nothing for Kiram to do here and besides that, he's been blooded in battle now. He should come out with us." He gave Kiram a conspiratorial wink.

Javier's jaw clenched and Kiram could tell that he didn't want Kiram with them. At the same time, Kiram didn't wish to be stranded at a Cadeleonian celebration, where no one would speak to him much less dance with him.

"I'll return to the townhouse."

"Have a heart, Javier." Atreau spoke directly over Kiram's own words. "It will put Master Ignacio's fears to rest, I'm sure. And the more the merrier. Let Kiram come."

"Atreau makes a good point," Morisio added. "Master Ignacio would certainly go easier on Kiram if he knew he was man enough to ride a whore as well as a horse."

Elezar said nothing and looked none too pleased.

"Look there's no need for—" Kiram began again but Javier cut him of this time.

"Fine. You'll join us," Javier snapped, glowering at Kiram as though he had become some annoyance. "But don't make an ass of yourself over some twat the way Nestor has."

Kiram blanched at the remark but the other Hellions laughed. Atreau slapped Kiram on the back and assured him that the whores wouldn't mind the color of his skin so long as he had money. Morisio assured Kiram that the Goldenrod girls didn't mind anything, not even Elezar's filthy tastes.

They adjourned to the card room where Kiram was surprised to see four more Hellions lounging around Master Ignacio's table. They gathered around Javier, faces lit with excitement at the prospect of the bawdy victory celebration awaiting them. After only a few words to his fellow players, the war master gathered his winnings and escorted them all to the hulking, gilded chambers of the Goldenrod Inn.

Chapter Twenty-Seven

Kiram had never been in a brothel and he did not want to be in one now.

Still, he stared around with anxious curiosity. Just past the dark narrow entry, the building opened into a large foyer. Throughout the room, small clusters of candles protruded from silver and brass plates hung on the walls. They added the scent of tallow to the thick perfume that hung in the air. Dark wisps of smoke rose from the dull yellow flames. Through the luminous haze, the gathered figures took on a soft glow.

Large-breasted Cadeleonian women lounged on dark red divans and sat around small, circular tables talking with the well-dressed Cadeleonian men. Some of the women wore outlandish gowns, cut far too short at the thighs or made only from strips of cloth and glittering beads. All of them wore their hair loose, though some had obviously powdered their tresses black.

Women and men alike glanced up when the Hellions arrived. Men averted their attention, but the women's gazes lingered. Though many of them smiled at Atreau, none would meet Javier's cold gaze. When two women caught sight of Kiram their seductive and coy expressions failed utterly. One woman's jaw dropped; another choked on her wine. He wanted to tell them that he was no more pleased about the situation than any of them were, but that would have defeated the entire point of him being here.

Master Ignacio laughed and, for the first time, his reserve towards Kiram dissipated. He clapped Kiram on the back as though they were sharing a joke at the women's expenses. "Too much for that one to swallow, aren't you, Kiram?"

"Apparently so," Kiram agreed.

A tall woman in her mid-forties rose from one of the red chairs. Scarlet flowers bloomed across the short expanse of her white bodice. Both hips and breasts flashed briefly as she walked towards them. She lifted a dainty liqueur glass to Master Ignacio.

"The Sagrada champions. We had hoped we could celebrate your victories with you." She smiled at the Hellions in an almost maternal manner; though, like the younger women, her gaze lingered a little too long on Atreau and moved too quickly past Javier. Her smile did not falter as she met Kiram's gaze. Nervous dread spread through Kiram as she stepped closer to him.

"You must be Lord Tornesal's underclassman." She caught hold of a ringlet of Kiram's hair. "They say you impressed even Prince Sevanyo." As she pulled her hand back she stroked Kiram's cheek. Her fingers felt warm and slightly moist.

"I'm Kiram Kir-Zaki, madam." Kiram bowed to her just as he would have bowed to any Cadleonian woman. She laughed and Master Ignacio seemed amused. The other Hellions snickered at the misstep, except for Javier, who looked annoyed.

"Such a gentleman," the woman said softly. Then she turned to Master Ignacio. "Padme and Ania would be happy to entertain you privately, good master. And the grand chamber is free for your boys. How many of my young fillies for your Sagrada stallions?"

"Eighteen of your best." Master Ignacio paused, surveying the Hellions. "And a few bottles of white ruin as well. They've done well this year."

With that Master Ignacio strode up the staircase as if the Goldenrod was his own home, calling over his shoulder. "Send Padme and Ania up to the pearl room directly."

"As you wish." The woman bowed to Master Ignacio's back. Then she turned to the remaining Hellions. "Well, you know where the grand chamber is. Make yourselves comfortable. Your entertainment won't keep you waiting long."

As a mass, Hellions tromped and bounded up the stairs, Atreau at the lead and Elezar taking up the rear. Kiram stumbled along, trapped between Javier's even strides and Morisio's impatient push.

Eighteen. That meant two women for every Hellion. A clammy sick feeling spread through Kiram. He couldn't do this but also could not find a way to escape.

They surged through the narrow hall and poured into a humid room. The only source of illumination blazed from the flames of a large fireplace. Light glinted across the silk tassels and strings of glass beads that cascaded down the posts of an immense bed at the center of the room. Scarlet pillows spilled off the huge mattress and lay scattered across the floor. Through the heavy scents of perfume and spices, Kiram still picked up the smell of spent semen and sweat.

Atreau tore off his boots and threw aside his coat. Javier, too, removed his shoes, but with far less enthusiasm. The rest of the Hellions also stripped down to their trousers and undershirts. Kiram followed suit, laying his coat and vest beside Javier's.

Atreau scooped up one of the pillows, sniffed it appreciatively and then he hurled it to Elezar.

"She was a wet one," Atreau called. And suddenly the reality of what they were here for sank through Kiram. He swallowed hard. If he fled now he'd never live it down. Worse, he would probably confirm Master Ignacio's suspicions about him. After the women came in, he thought, the other Hellions would be distracted, then he could slip out.

Elezar hurled the pillow to Atreau and Atreau flopped back on the bed laughing. Other Hellions joined him on the bed. They passed the pillow between them and snickered at its lingering odor.

"You look like a bunch of benders," Elezar told them. Morisio waved his ass at Elezar and Elezar bounded onto the bed and wrestled Morisio into a headlock. Atreau drove Elezar back, playfully smacking him with the pillow.

Javier strode past the bed and picked up a liquor bottle from the mantle over the fireplace. He uncorked it and took a deep drink.

"Hey, what have you got there?" Morisio demanded.

"White ruin," Javier replied after a second drink. He strode to Morisio and pushed the mouth of the bottle between his lips. Morisio swallowed as Javier tipped the bottle back.

"A gift from the previous occupants, no doubt." Javier pulled the bottle back.

"Javier, give some here," Elezar demanded. He leaned forward, allowing Javier to catch his jaw and tip the bottle between his lips.

Kiram wasn't sure if it was just a play of the light but for an instant Elezar's expression seemed to soften, becoming almost tender as he gazed up at Javier. Then Javier pulled the bottle from Elezar and turned on Kiram.

"Come here," Javier ordered. His tone was so harsh that Kiram balked. He didn't want to move away from the door and its implicit promise of escape.

"Come," Javier growled.

Kiram cautiously walked to Javier's side. Though heat poured from the fire, Kiram felt clammy. Javier shoved him onto the bed where he fell half across Elezar.

"To a Hellion's life." Javier held out the bottle.

Kiram started to reach for it but Elezar pulled his arm back. Javier caught Kiram's jaw as he had held Elezar's earlier. He tipped the bottle and a harsh antiseptic tang of alcohol filled Kiram's lungs. Javier pushed the bottle into his mouth none too gently. Scorching liquor spilled across Kiram's mouth. He swallowed to keep from choking, taking deep gulps of the liquor. His stomach rolled and burned. His throat tightened. Just as Kiram started to choke, Javier lifted the bottle.

Elezar clapped Kiram on the back.

"Taken like a man," Elezar congratulated him.

At first Kiram felt nothing but relief, then a wave of disorienting heat rolled over him. His tongue felt numb.

Javier took a quick swig himself and then handed the bottle to Atreau, who drank deeply and let out a whoop. He passed the bottle to the man beside him. Moments later young women, clothed in nothing but gold powder paraded into the room. Several carried bottles like the one Javier had forced into Kiram's mouth. The Hellions howled and hooted as the women ran their hands over each other's breasts and slid their fingers between their thighs and lips.

"White ruin!" Javier shouted. A young girl pranced to the bedside holding a bottle at a provocative angle in front of her groin. Javier snatched the bottle from her hands, nearly pulling her off her feet. The girl fell half on Elezar and half on Kiram. Javier wrenched the cork free and drank more.

More women tumbled and bounded onto the bed. They giggled and squealed as Hellions grabbed their bodies. Kiram evaded jiggling breasts, jutting nipples and closely cropped pubic hair as girls wiggled past him. A strong smell of alcohol and sweat rolled off the girl lying across him. He felt one of her hands grope at his hip. Kiram shifted quickly, rolling her onto Elezar.

"May I have a kiss?" Atreau purred from across the bed. Some dark-haired woman smiled at him and spread her legs wide. Atreau shoved his face into her glistening crotch. A wave of nauseous dread rose through Kiram. He could not do that. No matter how much he wanted to impress Master Ignacio, he just couldn't.

Next to him, the young girl crouched over Elezar's newly bare hips, but leaned forward to where Javier stood beside the bed. She grasped the front of Javier's trousers and opened them with agile hands.

Someone's bare thigh brushed the side of Kiram's face. He rolled closer to Elezar to avoid the contact. Gasps and breathless moans mingled with whispered obscenities. The bed rocked and jerked with so many writhing bodies. Kiram eluded another leg, though his hand came away wet.

And then he realized that Javier was staring straight at him as the girl took him into her mouth. His gaze seemed unbearably intense and Kiram didn't know if it was desire or shame that colored his cheeks. Kiram couldn't help but remember the taste of Javier and the heat of him in his own mouth and yet he hated the sight of this girl taking what should have been his own. He despised the fact that Javier just stood there, looking beautiful and aloof, and allowed it to happen.

Arousal, repulsion, and jealous anger crashed through Kiram. He didn't want to see this. He didn't care if this was what it took to be a Hellion—to impress Master Ignacio or Prince Sevanyo or to convince all these Cadeleonian men that he was worthy of their company—he didn't want any part of it.

Beside him, Elezar's hips flexed and pumped, bouncing the girl's splayed legs against Kiram's thigh. Javier clenched his eyes closed. Elezar pulled himself almost upright, driving deep into the girl but reaching out and grasping Javier's hand. Javier returned his grip but didn't open his eyes.

Some woman slid her hand down along Kiram's chest and dug her nails hard into his shoulder.

"Do you want to fuck me?" The woman's hot breath fluttered across Kiram's ear.

"I…" Kiram could feel the blood draining from his face. No doubt, Javier would have taken the woman. Maybe he still would. The thought tore into Kiram.

"I think I'm going to be sick," Kiram said quietly and instantly the woman's hand retracted. Kiram slipped off the edge of the bed and fled the grand chamber.

He took the stairs in a fast dash, raced through the entryway, and was out the door. Cold night air washed over him on the street. Kiram shuddered. He had taken his shoes but left his borrowed vest and jacket in the Goldenrod.

As he gazed around him he realized that he had no idea of how far he was from either the Grunito house or the Tornesal townhouse. During the carriage ride to the Goldenrod he had been packed between Javier and Elezar and had seen nothing of the streets they traversed.

The black masses of buildings that rose up against the dark skyline offered him no hint of even their architecture. Yellow firelight illuminated many of the windows. He could make out the figures of women coming and going. Just across the street, a door opened and lamp light flared out. Kiram saw the silhouettes of men, staggering and laughing as they entered another brothel. Their merriment augmented his sick misery.

Only a day ago Rafie had warned that he might come to regret staying with Javier, and already Kiram suspected that his uncle had been right. His thoughts slurred with the white ruin and suddenly Kiram found himself reminiscing about Musni. He'd be married by now. Would it have been any easier to see Musni wed than to watch Javier with some drunk whore?

Hot nausea welled up in Kiram. Sick sweat rose and his stomach clenched. He crouched on the curb and vomited.

"Pathetic." Lamplight from a nearby window illuminated the smirk of a passing man and his big-breasted companion. The woman giggled and led the man into an alley.

Kiram spat the sick sour taste out of his mouth and straightened. He half wanted to follow the man into the alley and beat the life out of him. But then his common sense returned. He was far from certain that he would win any fight he picked. He just needed to wash and go to bed.

The sooner he put this night behind him the better.

Night bells rang from far across town. Kiram clumsily navigated toward the sound. The bells would lead him to the church in the town square and from there he would be able to stumble onward to the Tornesal townhouse.

As he wandered beyond the brightly-lit brothels and common houses, the street grew darker and Kiram encountered fewer men. Occasionally a carriage rolled past him, and once an older man with a lamp stopped on the walkway to watch Kiram pass. He scowled at Kiram and placed a protective hand over his coin purse.

"None of your begging here, Haldiim," the old man muttered.

Kiram rolled his eyes and made an obscene gesture.

The old man hurried away and Kiram continued on, grumbling and trying to count the number of things that he hated about Cadeleonian society.

More than once in the darkness he lost his way but then the church bells would sound again and he'd correct himself. By the time he reached the Tornesal townhouse, his bitterness had turned to numb fatigue. Lamps glowed at the entry and yellow light streamed between the heavy curtains of several windows. He wondered suddenly if the staff spent as much of the night as the day cleaning the spotless house. He reached the doors, leaned heavily against the frame, and knocked lightly. A door opened immediately. A footman took a single look at him and smiled as if Kiram were his long lost nephew.

"It is so good to see that you've returned, Master Kir-Zaki. His Lordship was very worried."

"His Lordship?" Kiram had thought that Javier would still be at the Goldenrod, but then he realized his mistake. Javier might have sex there but he couldn't sleep anywhere that wasn't protected with spells.

"Could you inform him that I'm fine and that I'm going directly to bed?" Kiram stepped past the footman and headed toward the green room.

"He will be informed at once, sir."

Compared to the cavernous entryway the green room was comfortingly small, warm, and dark. Only embers burned in the fireplace. The bed looked appealingly clean and empty. Kiram pulled off one shoe. As he worked the laces of the second the door flew open.

"Kiram!" Javier rushed in. "Where in God's name have you been?"

"Walking." Kiram thought that sounded better than saying he'd been lost. "I needed to get out of the Goldenrod and clear my head." He dropped his second shoe beside the first.

Javier gave him a sympathetic smile. "It was a little much all at once, wasn't it?"

"I don't really want to talk about it," Kiram replied. "I just want to go to bed."

"Why don't you come to my room?"

"Because I'd rather sleep here," Kiram snapped and he knew too much anger carried in his tone.

"Look, you've got nothing to be ashamed of." Javier stepped a little closer. Kiram could smell the white ruin wafting off his clothes and body. He offered Kiram a pointlessly reassuring smile.

"The first time Elezar went to the Goldenrod he was so nervous he threw up. There's no shame in running away. No one noticed but me—"

"I'm not embarrassed, I'm disgusted. And I'm angry at you." Kiram cut himself off short. His feelings were still too raw and too tangled with memories of Musni. He wasn't ready for this argument.

"What did I do?" Javier demanded with an arched brow.

"Nothing. Never mind. I'm just really tired," Kiram finished lamely.

Javier gave him a hard look and Kiram knew he wasn't going to let the subject drop.

"If you're just tired then come to my bed." Javier gripped his arm and pulled him closer. Kiram resisted him, but Javier was strong and insistent. "What the hell is wrong with you? A few hours ago you couldn't wait to be with me."

"Well, a few hours ago I hadn't watched some drunk whore suck your cock."

Javier suddenly released his grip, and an expression like pain flickered across Javier's face. Then it was gone. "She was nothing. What she did was nothing."

"It wasn't nothing," Kiram replied. "It was exactly what you and I did. More. You probably had sex with her."

"Of course I did. What else was I supposed to do?" Javier asked. "Decline on the grounds that I'd prefer to bend you? That would have gone over well with the rest of the Hellions and let me assure you Master Ignacio would have been delighted to hear of it as well."

Kiram said nothing, because he knew there was nothing to say. Nothing could have been different. Javier had done exactly what he should have. His position in Cadeleonian society, his very freedom depended on it. This was exactly what Rafie had warned him about and what Kiram had cursed and sworn against on his long walk. It was exactly what he didn't want to think about because he knew where it led.

Some woman—a whore, a mistress, eventually a wife—would always be there between them. She would have to be there to shield them from prosecution. It wasn't Javier's fault but it wasn't something Kiram wanted to accept either.

"Well, tell me," Javier demanded. "Tell me what I should have done differently."

"You should have left me out of it." Kiram had no anger left, only a terrible defeat. Even this argument seemed futile now.

"I tried to send you home." Javier's tone softened a little. "But Atreau and Morisio made that impossible. So you came along and saw what goes on. I'm sorry, but that's the way things are, Kiram. Duke or not, I wouldn't survive if anyone thought I was—" Javier couldn't seem to find the words to define himself and instead pressed on, "And where would that leave you? Your safety at the Sagrada Academy is dependant upon me. If anyone knew what was between us, you know what they'd do to you."

"Yes, I know. This is how things have to be." Kiram couldn't bring himself to look at Javier. "It's the way things will always be, because you're a Cadeleonian and a nobleman. You'll never be able to dance with me or share a house with me or call me your lover."

At first, Javier didn't seem to know how to respond to Kiram's acknowledgement, then confidence flickered over his features and Kiram guessed that he was hoping that he'd made his point and won. Kiram supposed that if he, too, had been a Cadeleonian and had known of no other way for two men to be together he might have accepted the situation. Perhaps he could have been satisfied with what little he could get.

All at once, Kiram understood the longing in Elezar's expression when he had gazed up at Javier. For a Cadeleonian a few stolen hours together would be enough.

But he wasn't Cadeleonian. He'd seen his uncle and Alizadeh dancing in each other's arms. He'd flirted openly and had been courted by charming men who offered their whole lives to him. He could have so much more than the pittance Javier offered him.

"I don't know..." Kiram's heart ached but he went on. "I don't know if this can work between us."

A bewilderment came over Javier. "What? Why? Because of one whore at the Goldenrod?"

"No, it's because it can't just be one. There will be others."

"But you've known about the Goldenrod since early summer," Javier objected.

"I knew," Kiram admitted, but that was so different from being there and realizing that this could be the rest of his life. "But being there tonight made it different. Before it was just some kind of vague joke but now…it's not funny. It's sickening." He could vividly picture the whore's mouth sliding over Javier's erection, her hands clutching his hips. All the while Javier's friends and peers reveled in the same debauchery with unbridled enthusiasm.

Alienation, as much as jealousy, swept through him. He turned from Javier and stared at the embers of the fire. They looked as if they were dying before his eyes.

"I'm sorry. I just can't."

"No!" Javier spun him back around. "You will not just turn your back on me! I'm not some mechanism that you can toy with at your leisure. First you tell me that you find me attractive but you won't let me touch you. Then you give me one night and you say you want to stay with me and now you change your mind again? No! I do not accept it. I know you want me. You fought to stay with me." His hands dug into Kiram's arms.

"I fought to stay in the Sagrada Academy."

"You could give a shit about the academy." Javier pulled Kiram closer to him, his expression both angry and strained. "You wanted to be with me. Admit it!"

"I don't want to be with you now!" Kiram tried to jerk free but Javier wouldn't let him go.

"Yes, you do." Javier leaned so close that Kiram could almost taste the white ruin on his lips. The thick perfumes of the Goldenrod still clung to his skin.

"Release me," Kiram ordered.

Javier's grip tightened, turning painful, and then he shoved Kiram away. Kiram stumbled back.

"Fine," Javier ground the word out. "You want to sleep alone? Then sleep alone. But when you change your mind again you're going to have to get down on your knees and beg to come to my bed."

Javier strode out of the room, slamming the door closed behind him. Kiram dropped limply to the floor. He sat there for a long while, watching the last embers of the fire dim to darkness.

End of Part One

Acknowledgments

First and foremost, huge thanks to Nicole Kimberling and Melissa Miller, I could not have written these books—or any books, honestly—without you.

I'd also like to thank Jemma EveryHope for wielding the Chicago Manual of Style so very tirelessly, and also for making the best tasting yoghurt I have ever eaten in my life.

I'm deeply indebted to Alex, Ian, James, Josh and Sam, all of whom kindly informed and inspired so many of the characters in these books. I could not have hoped for any better examples of men of charm, strength, humor, artistry and honesty. My writing couldn't possibly do you all justice.

And last, but far from least, I have to thank all the readers and authors who have been so kind in their reviews, advice and insights. The fact that there are far too many of you to list on a single page reflects the deep generosity of our literary communities.

Thank you all.

List of Characters and Other Notes

Alizadeh Lif-Moussu: *Bahiim holy man, husband of Kiram's uncle Rafie.*
Atreau Vediya: *Third-year student, Hellion, Nestor's upperclassman.*
Blasio Urracon: *Scholar of mathematics.*
Calixto Tornesal: *Tornesal ancestor who opened the white hell.*
Chebli: *Dauhd's friend and member of Haldiim Civil Guard.*
Chilla Urvano: *Second-year Sagrada student.*
Cocuyo Helio: *Fourth-year Sagrada student.*
Dauhd Kir-Zaki: *Kiram's sister, second daughter of Mother Kir-Zaki.*
Donamillo Urracon: *Scholar of natural law.*
Elezar Grunito: *Third-year student and Hellion.*
Enevir Helio: *Fourth-year student*
Fedeles Quemanor: *Javier's cousin, heir to the dukedom.*
Fiez Lif-Worijd: *Kiram's mother's secretary.*
Genimo Plunado: *Future Count of Verida and third-year student.*
Hashiem Kir-Naham: *Haldiim son of a respected pharmacist.*
Hierro Fueres: *Fourth-year Yillar student, future Duke of Gavado.*
Hikmat Kir-Zaki: *Kiram's mother, a wealthy Haldiim business woman.*
Holy Father Habalan: *Sagrada clergy and history teacher.*
Ignacio Nubaran: *Sagrada master of war arts.*
Javier Tornesal : *Third-year student, Duke of Rauma.*
Kiram Kir-Zaki: *First full-blooded Haldiim admitted to the Sagrada Academy.*
Ladislo Bayezar: *Second-year student.*
Majdi Kir-Zaki: *Kiram's brother, Captain of the* Red Witch.
Morisio Cavada: *Third-year student from a scholarly family, Hellion.*
Musni Rid-Asira: *Haldiim friend of Kiram Kir-Zaki's.*
Nakiesh: *Irabiim Bahiim.*
Liahn: *Irabiim Bahiim.*
Nazario Sagrada: *Historic king, committed atrocities against the Haldiim.*
Nestor Grunito: *Second-year student, Kiram's friend, Elezar's brother.*
Nugalo Sagrada: *Royal bishop and second son of the king.*
Ollivar Falario: *Second-year student, Elezar's underclassman.*
Rafie Kir-Zaki: *Kiram's uncle on his mother's side.*
Riossa Arevillo: *Common Cadeleonian girl, daughter of a judge.*
Sevanyo Sagrada: *Heir to the Cadeleonian throne.*

Shukri Kir-Zaki: *Kiram's inventor father*
Siamak Kir-Zaki: *Kiram's eldest sister*
Timoteo Grunito: *Eldest of the Grunito sons, recently taken clergy vows.*
Vashir: *Haldiim Bahiim, distant cousin of Alizadeh*
Yassin Lif-Harun: *Historic half-Haldiim scholar.*

Places and Peoples
Anacleto: *Costal trade city, home to the oldest and largest Haldiim district of Cadeleon.*
Bahiim: *Ancient Haldiim holy order that traces its history back to the original Jhahiim.*
Cieloalta: *Cadelonian capitol.*
Circle of Red Oaks: *Holy Grove in Haldiim district of Anacleto.*
Circle of the Crooked Pines: *Irabiim Holy Grove.*
Haldiim: *Naturalized minority descended from Jhahiim.*
Irabiim: *Nomadic tribe descended from Jhahiim.*
Jhahiim: *Tribe from which both Haldiim and Irabiin descend.*
Mirogoths: *Cadeleonian name for a vast number of northern tribes, the majority of whom are led by witches and shapeshifters.*
White Tree of the Red Oaks: *The center of the Red Oaks Holy Grove and a symbol of the Bahiim power; oaths and spells are bound by its light.*
Yuan: *An exotic kingdom far across the South Sea.*

Days & Hours
Primiday: *First day of the week.*
Dosiday: *Second day of the week.*
Mediday: *Third day of the week.*
Levaniday: *Fourth day of the week.*
Traviday: *Fifth day of the week.*
Auguiday: *Sixth day of the week.*
Sacreday: *Seventh day of the week.*
Bells: *A system of time keeping by sounding off loud or softer bells, which divide summer days into fourteen brassy day bells and ten wooden night bells. Winter days consist of only ten day bells and fourteen night bells.*

Brief Cadeleonian History

1000: *The Sagrada fortress is built to stand against the first waves of Mirogoths.*

1090-1105: *King Nazario purges Haldiim from all of northern Cadeleon but dies before his forces can break the defenses of Anecleto and other southern cities.*

1150: *Civil war sends the Sagrada King into hiding in Rauma.*

1190: *The Restoration of the Sagrada rulership.*

1200: *Sagrada Academy is founded on the grounds of the old fortress. The school is dedicated to training the brightest nobles. Thirty years later the sons of merchants and scholars are granted admittance.*

1226: The Yillar Academy is founded. Admittance is limited to Cadeleonian nobles and members of the high clergy.

1242: *Second Mirogoth invasion begins in north.*

1250: *Calixto Tornesal opens the white hell and defeats the invading Mirogoth forces at the Sagrada Academy.*

1253: *Bishop Seferino pens his legal rulings on ethics, conduct and conversion.*

1350: *Kiram Kir-Zaki is the first full-blooded Haldiim to attend the Sagrada Academy.*

Excerpt from

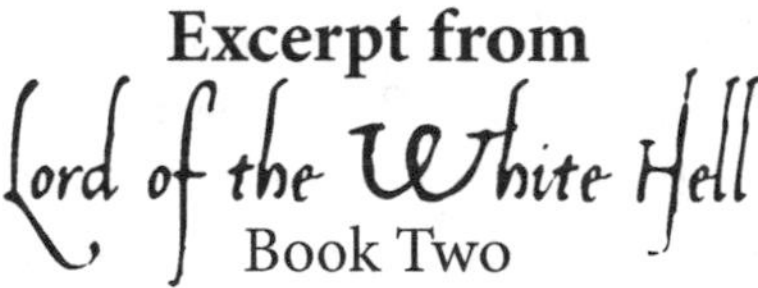

Book Two

Kiram ran hard and the curse rushed after him. He felt its pursuit, like hot breath and sharp teeth snapping at his back. Something sliced through his pant leg and slashed open his calf. The pain flooded him with an animal desperation and his body responded with a rush of speed.

In the back of his mind he knew he should return to the security of the dormitory, but the curse spread between him and the school, so Kiram wasn't going to turn around.

He abandoned the thought of reaching any destination; nowhere could be safe. All that mattered was escape. He had to keep moving. His muscles burned and his lungs ached as he threw himself ahead too fast to even see where he was going.

Flows of snow dragged at him. He fought through them. He tore across the grounds and raced through the orchard. Twilight shadows engulfed him as he crossed the bridge and sprinted between rows of bare apple trees.

Sweat soaked his shirt. His rapid breath pumped out like steam from one of his engines. At some point he lost the orchard path and found himself stumbling through deeper drifts of snow and surrounded by wild, old trees.

He tripped over a fallen branch and crashed into the snow. As he scrambled back to his feet, he caught a glimpse of the roiling black mass rushing through the twilight shadows towards him. He heard whispers like distant screams. Overhanging tree branches splintered apart the instant the shadow curse fell across them–ripped to shreds just as the groom, Victaro, had been.

Raw panic electrified Kiram's trembling muscles. He fought through the snow and raced into the darkness of the dense woods. From overhead came the cry of a bird. A crow. First one then another and another.

"Help me!" Kiram shouted, praying that this once Bahiim mysticism would serve him. *"Please, sisters, help me!"*

He didn't have the strength to waste waiting for a response. He kept moving; then suddenly black wings swept past his head. A crow circled him and then flew between the big pines on Kiram's left. Desperate for any hope, Kiram plunged through the undergrowth after the bird. Other crows swept down from the branches, leading Kiram and calling him, their harsh voices challenging the terrible growls and shrieks of the curse behind him.

Hard cramps bit through Kiram's legs. His lungs felt raw. He staggered blindly after the crows, running between towering trees and snow-covered brambles. Then one of the crows alighted in the bare branches of a huge oak. Kiram fell against the rough trunk of the old tree. His legs buckled beneath him.

The black mass of the curse came up fast, rushing after Kiram. It arched up over the snow like a cresting wave. As its shadow neared Kiram a sick pain punched into his body. Something twisted through his intestines.

It must have blood, Kiram. Alizadeh's voice moved over him like a chill wind.

Then the crows dived from their perches, sweeping down over Kiram and the curse crashed across their backs. Burning feathers and blood spattered the snow and pelted Kiram. Crow carcasses fell, smoking, to the ground. The curse rose like a black steam from the mutilated birds. Kiram pressed himself back against the oak, not wanting even a wisp to touch him. The curse hung like smoke in the air.

Kiram held his breath, afraid on some primal level that the curse might somehow hear him gasp or feel him exhale. He stared intently as the black wisps slowly coalesced into the dark silhouette of a man.

Kiram recognized the long body with its broad shoulders and slim hips. The curse could have been either Javier's or Fedeles' shadow, suspended in the air before his eyes. It took a step closer to Kiram, one hand extending, but then stopped. Suddenly its featureless head turned back as if hearing a call. Its mass dropped to the snow and slithered back across Kiram's tracks. In an instant it was gone.

Kiram dragged in a breath of the frigid air. His entire body shuddered from both cold and shock. The blood streaming down his calf felt alarmingly hot and suddenly he felt aware of the scratches where the crows' bones had grazed his skin. Black feathers matted with blood spattered his arms and face. Pieces of skulls and bodies pitted the snow all around him. His own blood smeared out from his right leg in a rapidly cooling pool.

Impending sobs tightened his throat and tears welled in his eyes. He wanted to curl into a ball and have his mother tell him that everything would be all right. He wanted to be back home and feel his father's strong embrace and know he was safe. Kiram wiped furiously at his face, knowing that he only succeeded in smearing crows' blood across his cheeks.

He couldn't act like a child, damn it.

He watched his breath rise in white clouds and dissipate into the dark. No one was going to come rescue him—certainly not his parents—and if he didn't get back to the academy he was going to freeze to death.

Kiram pushed himself back from the old oak. A pang flared through his calf but the leg still took his weight. He followed his own tracks back towards the academy. Every time he heard a sound or saw a motion in the branches above him he froze in fear. An owl swooped past him. Some small creature shrieked and skittered over a tree limb. Clusters of blue jays watched him in eerie silence.

Snow began to fall in light streams at first, but then it grew heavy. Kiram's old footprints became shallow impressions. He struggled to follow his path back through the forest.

Huge flakes of snow settled in his hair and melted against his skin. Kiram shoved his hands into his coat pockets. At first his feet ached, almost burned from the cold, but now they were numb weights. He couldn't stop shivering.

It couldn't be much further. Kiram thought he could smell oven smoke in the air. Just a little farther, he promised himself, but his steps were unsteady and he wasn't even sure of where he was anymore. Suddenly his boot caught on a buried stump and he tumbled down an incline, slamming into the trunk of a tree.

He struggled up to his feet, but the snow slipped beneath him, and he slid farther down the incline, this time only coming to a stop when his back and shoulder pummeled into the ragged stones of a crumbling wall.

Kiram lay still, too cold to care about his scrapes and bruises. Snow drifted down onto him. He was so tired and this fucking day just wouldn't let up. He tried to roll over but his arm wouldn't move; instead a terrible dislocated feeling shot through his shoulder. His calf seemed dead and he didn't have the strength to force himself up to his feet again.

He had to rest. Just for a few minutes, then he'd go on. Kiram closed his eyes. He imagined how he would brace himself with his left leg and use the wall to support his weight. He'd get up; it wouldn't be all that difficult. If he couldn't climb the slippery incline, then he'd follow the wall. It had to have been part of the academy grounds at one time. Doubtless it would lead him close enough that he could catch a glimpse of the dormitory. He'd probably be back in less than an hour.

With that thought a delirious calm settled over Kiram. He felt a little warmer, almost comfortable, now. Perhaps the snow was letting up. His muscles relaxed and he slept as blankets of snow settled over his body.

The hands that gripped him felt like heated brands. Kiram opened his eyes and for a moment saw nothing but brilliant light, then felt the sensual heat of the white hell.

Javier's black hair and dark eyes came into focus and slowly Kiram made out the rest of his features. He leaned over Kiram. Dark sky spread out behind him. High in the sky a crow circled.

What kind of crow flew when it was so dark? And when had it stopped snowing?

"Kiram." Javier's voice seemed strangely distant and his expression was strained. "Can you hear me?"

Kiram tried to respond but found himself producing only a weak groan. Javier's hand felt blazing hot as it stroked his cheek.

"Just stay awake, Kiram. Stay with me," Javier said. Then he straightened and looked back over his shoulder, shouting, "I found him!"

Kiram was aware of being lifted up against Javier's chest and the sparks from the white hell crackling around him. He thought he heard Nestor's voice and Elezar's as well, but he wasn't sure. Only the heat and light of Javier's presence felt real to him. Slowly the range of his awareness grew. His shoulder and calf hurt. His hands and feet ached. A strange bouncing motion sent pangs through his shoulder. They were riding, he realized. He was on Lunaluz, leaning against Javier, and still high above them the crow circled, calling.

"The curse." Kiram tried to get the words out but his lips felt leaden. "It's in Fedeles. That's where it hides."

"I know." Javier's voice was rough.

Of course Javier knew. Kiram leaned back against Javier's chest.

"Fedeles destroyed my engine." It alarmed him that he couldn't get more than a whisper out and his words sounded slurred. "He didn't want to do it. He was crying the whole time. I think the curse in him drove him to it."

Suddenly Kiram realized what that would mean. The man who controlled the curse must have found out that Scholar Donamillo planned to use Kiram's engine to free Fedeles. How had he found out? Only a few people knew anything about it, aside from himself, Javier, and Scholar Donamillo. Genimo knew apparently and perhaps Morisio had guessed at the truth. One of them must have let some vital detail slip to the man controlling the curse.

"Fedeles tried to tell me about the man who put the curse in him but that's when it came out of him and attacked me." Speaking just a few words felt exhausting. Kiram drew in a deep breath. Javier said nothing, but for a moment he dropped the reins from his right hand and gently touched Kiram's chest.

The shadows of apple trees danced and jumped as he and Javier rode past. Behind them Kiram could hear other riders. He closed his eyes for just a moment and then immediately opened them again when a blaze of white light surged over him.

"Don't sleep, Kiram. Stay with me." Javier gripped him hard and a searing heat flared through Kiram's chest as Javier opened the white hell again...

The adventures continue in:
Lord of The White Hell Book Two
&
Champion of the Scarlet Wolf Book One
Champion of the Scarlet Wolf Book Two

CPSIA information can be obtained
at www.ICGtesting.com
Printed in the USA
FSHW01n1440030818
50939FS